"What do *you* want, Roses?"

It was an easy question to answer. I wanted Wilkie to come back to me, to lie with me, to kiss me again. To make me cry and fly and burn with his beautiful, insistent, stunning touches. And I wanted to pleasure him, too, as he had done to me. I knew there was much more to these touches than what he had so far given me.

I was curious. And I was willing.

My desires surprised me with their vehemence.

"I want *him*," I whispered.

Aye, what I *wanted* was Wilkie Mackenzie. Something I knew I could never have.

**Coming soon from
Juliette Miller
and Harlequin HQN**

Highlander Taken

JULIETTE MILLER

HIGHLANDER
Claimed

HARLEQUIN®
entertain, enrich, inspire™

Recycling programs
for this product may
not exist in your area.

ISBN-13: 978-0-373-77759-4

HIGHLANDER CLAIMED

Copyright © 2013 by Juliette Miller

For M,
the Highlander I claimed for myself.

HIGHLANDER
Claimed

Clan Mackenzie,
Book 1

CHAPTER ONE

THE BRUTE WAS UPON ME.

His clawing hand lashed only inches from the rough fabric of the men's trews I wore. I skittered out of his reach, thankful that I'd chosen the unfashionable training garb this morning, instead of a servant's dress, which would have been far easier to grab.

But Laird Ogilvie was quick for a large, slightly overweight, middle-age lout. Blustery determination reddened his face.

"Your mother escaped me only through death," the laird said callously. "You'll not be so lucky."

Lunging again, his fingers caught the back of my shirt and yanked, causing the tunic to choke me around the neck. He took the opportunity to push me facedown into the plush furs of his expansive bed. I turned my head and gasped for breath, struggling against his hold.

"Why do you insist on wearing the clothing of men, lass? 'Tis most unbecoming. I'll get rid of them for you, shall I?"

I had timed my visit to the laird's chambers poorly. It was my job to tidy up his rooms each morning and return all the cups and bowls from his evening's revelries to the kitchens. And I had carried out my duties faithfully for almost five years, always careful to avoid his presence. Yet today, he had waited for me, keeping himself hidden until he was sure we were alone, and the door was closed. Now it was too late to escape him.

"In this keep, my word is law and you'll not forget it," he spoke gruffly. His hands continued to push the cloth of my tunic higher up my back as he held my wrists with his other hand. "You forget the change in your status. You are no longer the daughter of a landholder, nor entitled to the privileges that accompany such a position. Your mother was equally forgetful. After your father's death, she, too, had difficulty coming to terms with her demotion. She could have continued to live in your farmhouse. But she refused me. Stubborn, she was. Desirable, aye, but mightily stubborn."

I struggled against the pressure of his body, bearing down on mine.

"I stripped her of her land, aye, in the hopes she would submit to me. Still, she fought me." One of the laird's hands held my own in his viselike grasp while the other smoothed along the bare skin of my hip, following the curve of my waist, roaming higher. "It was only when I used *you* as my pawn, not long before her death, that she finally gave up her futile resistance. You should be grateful to her, lass. She would agree to anything to keep me from pursuing you. *Anything.* But now that she is lost to us, there is nothing to stop me. I have been watching you for some time. But you already know that, do you not, Roses?"

Aye, I knew it. My mother had offered me a sad warning as she lay dying. It was one of the reasons I hid myself under loose, men's clothing and avoided the laird at all costs.

"You're a kitchen servant," the laird continued, "but you could be so much more. 'Tis time for you to make yourself useful. A mistress of the laird is afforded special privileges, you realize. Private chambers, lightened duties, fine dresses, time and protection to stroll the gardens freely."

Were these the same words of enticement he'd whispered to my mother?

"Nay."

"Nay?"

"I'll not agree."

He was silent and still for a moment, then I heard his soft chuckle. "I didn't ask for your agreement, lass. I own you, and I intend to take what is mine."

I heard a soft whimper and realized it was I who had uttered it. The sound of it gave clarity to my choice—the choice that was nestled uncomfortably against my front pocket, in a rough leather pouch. A knife. I was allowed to use it for kitchen and garden duties but kept it with me for protection, though this was the first time I needed to use it for that reason. Knowing it was there now, digging into my hip, gave me but small comfort as the laird pulled on the waistband of my trews. His grip on my wrists slackened as he focused on his goal, pushing my shirt up to my neck where it bunched against my hair.

The laird froze. There was a note of shock in his voice when he spoke again. "What is this? This mark?"

I didn't answer. I concentrated on making my movements as inconspicuous as I could as I grasped toward the knife with my left hand.

Ogilvie's fingers brushed across the skin near the middle of my back, drawing a circular pattern. He seemed distracted, almost amazed, before his harsh tone returned.

"Who put this ink to you? Answer me!"

"I know not what you speak of," I gasped.

But it was a lie.

I had spent most of my life attempting to keep the tiny tattoo between my shoulder blades hidden from sight. I bathed carefully when others were around. I wore my hair long. And I covered myself with bulky clothing. Now, I squirmed wildly, equally terrified by the exposure of this small inked mark and the rest of my body. My mind whirled to a shadowy memory that had instilled a lingering fear into the mind of a lost child.

An ancient, superstitious healer had been summoned by my parents when I'd been ill with measles as a very small child. A wizened face. A crooked finger, pointing and accusing. A shrill warning, never forgotten. "A witch's mark! She'll be beaten, flayed, burned at the stake! Keep this hidden! At all costs—keep this hidden."

Laird Ogilvie continued his study, drawing across the ink with his fingertip. "It looks like a seal of some description. A seal of—"

The chambers echoed with a sudden, weighty silence. It was the type of silence Ogilvie and his officers typically employed when a servant interrupted one of their gatherings just as a critical piece of information was about to be revealed.

I didn't know if he was considering my flaying, my burning or something else entirely. Whatever the laird had been contemplating, his renewed enthusiasm for carrying out his task was now making itself felt. He fumbled with the fastenings of his trews.

And it was then that I made my move.

The force of my strike embedded the sharp blade into the side of his abdomen. My many months of discreet sword training with the young clan warriors had left me ill-equipped to aim small. Luckily for the laird, the knife was not a large one. If he'd had a chance to consider it, Laird Ogilvie might have rejoiced at his overindulgent mealtime habits: his extra padding would most probably allow him to live.

I withdrew the knife and was able to use the laird's shock to slide out from under him and step away. He touched his stomach and considered the blood pooling in his hand with confusion, not believing that his own servant would dare react to him as I had just done.

I took advantage of his stunned silence and, with haste, fled the room.

Surprised by my own rebellion, and the calmness with which I had carried it out, I felt a lurch of genuine panic boil in my heart. What had I just condemned myself to? Death, severe and vengeful punishment, at the very least, or the life of a clanless vagabond. I decided on the latter.

My fear gave me wings. I flew down the staircase, following the halls to the kitchen. I paused only for a moment before entering. Realizing I was still holding the bloody knife, I returned it to its pouch, quickly making sure that no blood was visible. Rearranging my clothing, I forced myself to appear as calm as I could manage. After all, the kitchen servants were used to my strange outfits and my rushed execution of tasks. In the kitchen, I hastily grabbed a large bag and stuffed several loaves of bread into it. I took a small wooden bowl. On a whim, I also took the needle and stitching thread, and a lidded cup of the healing paste I'd made for Ismay only the day before.

Ismay stood near one of the tables, organizing her

herbs. My closest friend, my secret mentor in the ways of healing. She looked at me, alert now to my unusual behavior. I gave her a brief hug. It pained me greatly to realize I might not see her again. She returned the hug with some confusion, her brown eyes questioning.

Matilda, the lead cook, paused in her task of doling out instructions to her underlings. She eyed me with her usual disapproval as I passed by her, glancing at the bag I carried.

"The laird requires assistance," I told her as I exited to the out-of-doors, before she could ask me to explain.

I ran to the stables. It was midmorning, so the men of the keep were occupied with training, hunting or tending the fields. I grabbed a bag I had hidden among the stalls, carefully filled over time with items I could use in case the need arose: a fur-lined coat, several lengths of rope, a flint and a small sword. It was this sword I used when I practiced with Ronan and Ritchie, the red-headed brothers of my own age who had found my interest in soldiers' training amusing. They'd spent many an hour teaching me how to fight and how to ride. Skills I was blessed now to possess.

I had known all along that my destiny lay elsewhere. Most of my clan had long forgotten about my mysterious arrival as a child of three or four, accepting me as another daughter of a clanmember, and then as a servant and pair of hands. My unusual looks were occasionally commented on: hair so fair it was almost white, and light green eyes, not at all like the darker hues of my parents and friends. But there was too much work to be done to ponder excessively over the details of my foreignness. With mouths to feed, walls to build and crops to tend, there was little time left over to dwell on the origins of an outcast child.

I had not forgotten. The questions visited me daily. They resided in my dreams. And they made me less willing to accept my fate as the servant of a tyrannical laird whose intentions for me had been written in every glance in my direction since I came of age. But I'd known this was coming. I'd known it all along. I had waited for this day.

And here it was.

At the last moment, I grabbed a war helmet and stuffed it into the remaining space in my bag.

Several horses were grazing near the stables. I slipped a bridle onto a chestnut pony that I had ridden before—and draped a saddle blanket into place. I used a tree stump to mount the horse and climbed on. He could sense my frantic state, and it unsettled him. I was profoundly grateful that the stable hands were used to seeing me ride. They glanced up from their chores but didn't dwell on what I was doing.

My immediate concern was to put as much distance between myself and my crime during this calm before the storm. The laird was, perhaps, weakened by loss of blood. He might be unconscious, not yet able to issue orders to have me followed, caught, beaten, killed. But that wouldn't last long—I felt certain he would recover if a fever didn't set in. I knew firsthand that Ismay was a highly talented healer. After all, she'd relied on me to gather the herbs she needed to make the healing paste, a good strong brew.

I skirted the horse around the loch, gaining speed, at full gallop by the time I reached the open gates of the keep.

I never looked back.

Riding faster than I'd ever ridden before, I pushed my horse until his coat was lathered with white sweat. I was fortunate that the ground was dry and a slight breeze stirred the air; the horse's prints would not be deep, and the wind might erase them before they could be followed. I rode until the sky bled purple, then black.

Still I rode until the horse stumbled, almost spilling me onto the ground. Only then did I let him carry me forward at a slower pace, until we walked almost silently but for his soft-struck footfalls through the star-laden night. We neared a small brook, which cut through the wooded land like a snake of silver, illuminated by the dappled moon and a splash of bright stars.

I dismounted then, to drink and let the horse rest for a time. He found a small patch of grass, which he snatched up in greedy mouthfuls, reminding me of my own hunger. Glad for my stolen meal, I ate most of the bread I'd taken from Matilda's kitchen. I wondered what the scene there would look like now, busy with the scandal of my crime and my desertion.

I lay on the ground for a moment, using my bag as a pillow, and wound the horse's reins around my hand. I slept for a time, waking with a start when my horse pulled on the rope clasped tightly in my fist.

There was no sound, save the light splash of the stream nearby and the soft rhythmic chewing of the horse. No far-off shouts or thundering hoof beats. No sign that the laird's henchmen were on my trail. But my sense of security was hardly robust. Here I was: alone, homeless, an outcast. With blood on my hands and now only one small loaf of bread in my bag. I had no shelter to seek out, no clan to rely on.

Yet I had considered where I might go if I found myself forced to flee. None of the options were entirely appealing, but I had decided I would travel to the Macduff clan, far to the north. Laird Ogilvie's niece, Una, had been married to one of their upper-ranking clansmen, several years before. I could seek her out; she might remember me and allow me to remain with her clan, to work in their kitchens. But it would take several weeks to reach their lands.

I led my horse to a fallen tree and remounted to resume my journey. I was fairly certain I was traveling northeast. I tried to recall the maps that the laird and his men often displayed on the grand table, as they discussed skirmishes, gatherings, marriages and disputes. There had been days when I'd been cleaning the meeting room, polishing the pewter of the candlesticks, and the maps had remained in place, unrolled. The names were familiar enough, from the discussions over the tables I had served. Ogilvie. Machardie. Stuart. Macduff. Mackenzie. Buchanan. Campbell. Macsorley. Morrison. Munro. Macintosh. Macallister. What I was less familiar with was the placement of the clans' territories.

Searching the memory, I tried to picture the map and the configuration of the boundary lines across the landscape in my mind. I'd tried to read the maps, to decipher the shapes of the letters, to match them to the names of the clans I knew. But it had been too difficult. My mother had begun to teach me to read as a child, but there had been little time to practice it, so my knowledge was limited. Instead, my education had consisted of garden work, household chores, cooking and cleaning. Once my father died, the most important skills required of my fallen status were to remain meek, mild and appropriately subservient at all times. I'd never mastered any of those arts, I'd be the first to admit.

It was much easier to recall the stories Laird Ogilvie and his ranks told about the clans and the strengths and weaknesses of their lairds. They'd discussed these things often, and I, pouring their ale, refilling the quickly emptying platters, attending to their requests, artfully dodging the grasp of their hands, had been privy to a wealth of information.

From their stories I knew that the Mackenzie clan lands were due north of Ogilvie's, spreading widely to the east. Laird Ogilvie had said the Mackenzies presided over a large territory—larger than Ogilvie's—of rolling fields, craggy terraces and richly stocked forests. Their lands would be closest to where I found myself now, I guessed.

Mackenzie.

The name made me uneasy.

I recalled one session where Laird Ogilvie and his highest-ranking officers had spoken of the Mackenzie men in particular. The hour had been late and the conversation loose.

"'Twas last year, in the skirmish at Ossian Lochs, over the coveted king's lands," one of Ogilvie's men had said. "Absolutely deadly, that Laird Mackenzie. He watched his father die at the end of an enemy's sword. And in response, he cut a line through Campbell's troops that ran my blood cold. Mad, he is. Wickedly lethal."

"Aye," agreed another. "He's huge, and that wild black hair does nothing to tone down the menace of him."

Laird Ogilvie had agreed. "Knox Mackenzie is dan-

gerous, guarded and altogether sour. It might be true that his clanspeople are gifted in the ways of the land. Their fields and orchards are rich with crops, aye, and their harvests are bountiful enough to feed not only their entire clan but also to trade with other clans for valuable commodities. But he's gruff and entirely lacking in the diplomacy of his father."

"And what's the next brother's name? Wilkie, is it? If you ask me, his swordsmanship skills are overstated."

"But the women surely do fall at his feet. They flock around him like birds. He'd be easy to defeat—he's too distracted." This had inspired laughter.

"Aye, and the youngest brother, Kade—a savage. Always armed to the teeth and eyein' a man up like he'd as soon kill him as pass the time of day."

"The sisters, however," one of the men had slurred, "are quite pleasing to the eye." More familiarly lecherous laughter.

Laird Ogilvie had continued, "I'm sorely tempted to overrun their keep and take a bit o' that food for myself."

"Aye. And I'll grab the sisters while we're at it."

The thought of running into one of the Mackenzie brothers as I passed by their keep was less than appealing. But one key detail stuck fervently in my mind. *Their fields and orchards are rich with crops.*

My empty stomach rumbled at the thought. No matter how intimidating the Mackenzie brothers may have been, the plan that was playing out in my head didn't involve meeting them or in any way alerting them to my presence. But it did involve their bounty. Such was my hunger, I decided I would head in the direction of the Mackenzie keep. If I could pilfer some resources from their crops, I could sustain myself for the coming days and weeks of travel to the north. It was risky, aye, but I had little choice; there was no other food to be found on the windswept Highlands. Now, I sorely regretted not asking Ritchie and Ronan to teach me archery. At least then I could have hunted along the way. As it was, I had no choice but to avail myself to the Mackenzie gardens, if I could find them.

This is what I had become, I reflected bitterly—an aspiring thief, a vagrant, a homeless wretch. All because I couldn't stomach the advances of Laird Ogilvie. Was I completely foolish to choose the fate of a wanderer over the fate of a mistress? Very likely so. I had considered this question many times since I began to suspect the laird's intentions toward me. And I'd unconsciously made the decision: in my bones and my soul, I just couldn't make myself submit.

There was no point wallowing in my predicament. After all, I'd seen it coming. I'd surprised myself at my speedy, well-crafted and—as yet—successful getaway. Neither self-pity nor self-loathing would better my situation. What I needed was to reach the outskirts of the Mackenzie keep, to fashion a ladder or find a tree to climb to scale the walls, and to wait for the cover of night.

Before I could do any of these things, I heard the unmistakable rhythmic beat of galloping horses, coming from the south, the same direction I had traveled.

A group of Ogilvie's men, no doubt, and hot on my trail.

I kicked my horse into a faster pace, through a lane of sparsely dotted pine trees. One side opened out to vast fields of scrubby purple heather. On the left was a sharp incline rising up to rocky cliffs. It was too steep for a horse. But there was no way I could ride across the open fields; I would be easily seen. If I rode straight ahead, I knew I would be overtaken—my pursuers' steeds would be larger and faster. Warriors' horses, not a field horse, like mine.

Without warning, my horse neighed loudly and reared, throwing me to the ground. I landed on the hard, painful edges of my pack. But I jumped up quickly, too frightened to dwell on bumps or bruises.

I heard men's voices getting closer. "Spread out!" one of them shouted.

I reached for the reins of my unsettled horse and slid my saddle blanket off the horse's back. I waved it at him. The horse immediately galloped off, in the direction of the approaching search party. I took the opportunity to run and began to climb the incline of the lower cliffs.

"The horse!" a man yelled, too far into the distance, I hoped, to yet see me.

But there was another pursuer who was closer, galloping straight toward me. And I was not hidden enough. The shrubby trees were too sparse.

It was only seconds before the warrior reached me. I armed myself with my small sword and turned to face him. I knew resistance was futile, once he called out to the rest of the search party. I would be surrounded, beaten, taken back to Ogilvie to be punished.

But the warrior did not reach for his sword. Instead, he removed his helmet, revealing disheveled, very-red hair. "Roses. 'Tis me, Ritchie."

Ritchie. My friend and my trainer. The one who had

taught me how to fight and how to hold a sword correctly, as I was doing now.

"Nice technique." He smiled briefly, a quick flash of mirth. Then his face grew serious. "I'll not reveal you, Roses. But you must be quick. Do whatever you can to escape, and don't come back. I know nothing about what you did to anger Laird Ogilvie, but he's hell-bent on getting you back. He has dispatched search parties in all directions. He wants you found." He turned to look behind him at the approaching soldiers. "Go! Before the others catch up."

"Ritchie," I said, gasping for breath, with relief and gratitude.

"Go!" he said, more forcefully. "Be safe, Roses."

The furtive warning in Ritchie's voice charged me, and I turned from him. I looked back only once to see his horse vanishing into a glade, wishing I could thank him, but he was already gone.

I climbed as fast as I could up the craggy terraced cliffs, farther and higher for what felt like a long time, until I reached a sheltered grassy cove. My lungs and legs burned with my exertions, and I sat for a moment to catch my breath. I could see that I was high above the vast rolling grasslands now. So high that I was afforded a magnificent view, across the heather fields.

My heart skipped a beat as I looked over the rise of a nearby hill to see the grand central stone castle of the Mackenzie keep—Kinloch, if I remembered correctly.

Within the confines of the keep, I could see tiny people milling about. Spaced cozily across the castle's grounds were smaller stone and wooden buildings, and acres of farmland, striped with green and gold crops, artfully decorated with fruit trees, vines and gardens.

The landscape was richly colorful, dotted with the tiny orange, red, green and yellow shapes of the laden orchards and gardens that looked on the verge of harvest. It was far more lush and skillfully tended than the Ogilvie keep. And it looked wildly inviting, especially considering the emptiness of my stomach, which twisted and growled at the sight of such plenty.

The stone wall that circled the central area of the keep's castle and gardens looked as tall as two men, at least. If I used a ladder—which I hoped I might be able to build with some wood and the rope I had brought—I might be able to scale it.

I would use the daylight hours to scout for a place to find a shelter to sleep tonight, after I returned from my raid. To my intense relief, I found one easily. The hillside was steep and gouged with small caves, shielded from the wind by massive boulders and packed tree glades. I found one that was not too cramped, extending deep into the smooth rock. At the back of the cave, a slit extended up to a thin crack of daylight, giving warmth and soft light to the cozy space.

Delighted by my find and feeling hopeful at the prospect of food, I went in search of wood for my ladder. What I found first, farther around the western back of the hillside, was a picturesque waterfall splashing into a clear pool. I took a long drink. I washed my hands and my face before continuing to gather lengths of sturdy, thin branches.

I returned to the cave and wound the lengths of rope I had brought around the rungs of my makeshift ladder, fashioning what I hoped was my portal into the Mackenzie gardens.

The only thing left to do was wait until darkness

veiled then settled thickly around the landscape of my new—and quite comfortable—temporary home. I prepared my bag, checked my ladder once more for weight-bearing consistency.

I strapped my belt, strung with my knife and sword, around my waist. Figuring that a disguise would be the best course of action, I wound my hair into a loose braid, coiled at the back of my neck, then fastened the war helmet onto to my head and set off on my way.

The stone wall of the keep was farther away than I'd estimated. It may have been as much as an hour before I reached it, and by then, my lack of sleep and lack of food was beginning to take its toll. Attempting to ignore both, I positioned my ladder, waiting atop the wall, listening for sounds of stirring in the near vicinity. My eyes had adjusted by then to the spare light offered by a sliver moon and some cloud-veiled stars. I could see no one. I adjusted my weight on the thick surface of the wall and pulled the ladder over, placing it against the inside wall so I could make my escape. I climbed down to the ground and found myself on the far side of a small loch from the looming castle and within sight of the silver-edged silhouettes of garden hedges and gnarled, fruit-heavy trees. I sneaked around the water's edge toward my goal. I fingered the first pear of my harvest, taking several bites before I could continue. Its sweetness was indescribable. I picked as many fruits as I could carry.

As I walked past the edge of the smooth expanse of the loch toward the wall, I was surprised to notice that the yellow hue of morning had just begun to creep above the horizon. I'd taken too much time. Soon, people would begin their day's chores. And I was still inside the wall. Taking quick steps now, I secured my helmet and approached my ladder. Just as I started to climb, a sound drew my attention.

A splash.

I turned to see a man walking out of the loch.

A very big, muscular, naked man. Very naked.

And he was looking right at me.

We were both stunned into frozen silence. But then he tensed and moved in my direction, jolting me into action. I clambered up the ladder as fast as I could, pulling it up behind me and jumping heavily down to the ground on the far side, my bag of fruits and vegetables secured to my back. I left the ladder where it lay and ran for my very life. I didn't look back, but I knew he was coming.

I ran and ran until my legs threatened to buckle under me. My back had gone numb with the weight of my load as I struggled farther and farther up the hill.

I could hear him gaining on me.

"Halt!" he yelled, and his voice reached into my body and grabbed my heart, such was the fear I felt. It wasn't just the strength of the command but the closeness of it.

And I did halt.

On the other side of the sharp jutting rock was my shelter. I dropped my bag and turned to face him. I pulled my sword from its belt.

And he was there, not ten feet from where I stood, fully clothed now and holding his own—much bigger—sword.

As far as I could see, he was alone. Would he have told others about his chase?

The first thing that struck me about him—aside from his size, which I already knew about, in every regard—was his captivating looks. His black hair, still barely wet, hung to his shoulders, and he wore a small braid stitched back from each temple, as was customary for clansmen. Despite the small distance between us, I could see that his eyes were a vivid shade of blue. His face was fierce not only in expression but also in countenance: fierce in beauty. I was dizzied by my fear and by my reaction to his dazzling presence.

"Who are you?" he asked, his broad chest heaving as he breathed heavily from the chase. It was a command, that I supply him this information.

I did not speak. I had no intention of giving up my identity. He might return me to Laird Ogilvie.

He held up his sword and asked the question again, this time more quietly but no less commanding. "I said, to whom am I speaking?"

I held up my own small weapon. It was far less impressive than his own, but I knew how to use it. I'd been training with men for months and had learned how a quick jab could be just as effective as a long swing.

"You want to fight me, aye?" he asked. There was a note of jeering confidence in his question. I allowed him this. My call to arms was clearly foolhardy. I did not want to die here on this hilltop, at the hands of this beautiful warrior, but I had no other option than to fight.

"Show your face," he said.

I did not.

"Please leave me," I said, attempting to deepen my voice.

A slight crease appeared between his eyebrows, as if he was having trouble making sense of the situation and my request. He almost smiled. "I'll not go until you reveal yourself," he said, and his tone sounded patient, if I was placing it correctly.

"I cannot."

"Then we shall have to fight. You've been caught stealing from our lands. 'Tis punishable by death, thievery. If there's a reason for your actions, give it."

"I was hungry," came my falsely stern, muffled reply.

To this he smiled, clear confusion written across his heartbreaking face. "That's a fair reason, then. Reveal yourself and you can keep your bounty. If you agree never to return to thieve from us again. Show your face."

"I cannot."

His mild amusement irked me. "You cannot," he repeated. "Why is this?"

My fear, and something else, was causing my control to weaken, to slide. I willed myself to hold it together. "Leave me! Here, take your food! I'll go, and not bother you again."

His smile faded, and I realized that I'd forgotten to disguise my voice. He said slowly, as though to make sure I understood, "I'm afraid I'll *not* be leaving. Not until I know who I'm dealing with."

We stood, swords raised, at an impasse of sorts.

Would he show me mercy? Would he force me to return to Ogilvie? Or would he kill me?

As if in partial answer, he stepped closer, clearly not intimidated by me. He lifted the tip of his sword to my chin, as though to use it to tip my helmet backward.

I struck his sword with my own.

He was surprised by my hit, and he lashed back with his weapon, so quickly I barely had time to react. And we were close now, so close that his returning strike sliced across my arm, ricocheting pain throughout my body. My sword, as I fell to the ground, slid across the muscle of his side. He growled and struck my weapon with such power that it sent a jolt of fire through my already bloodied arm. My sword went flying, so I could hear the *wo wo wo* of its spinning flight before it landed with a clang far out of my reach.

Stunned, pained, grasping to maintain consciousness, I lay still on the ground as he stood over me. Blood was flowing freely from the wound on his torso. He kneeled and removed my helmet. My hair had loosened and spilled onto the ground as he freed it.

When he saw my face, his jaw dropped. He stared for many moments, surveying me with his eyes. He fingered a lock of my hair, rubbing it gently between two fingers for several seconds, as though fascinated by the feel of it, or the color.

"You're a lass," he finally said.

"Aye."

His expression colored with a strange sort of awe that reached to touch me in places I had never before been touched. Inexplicably, I felt a part of myself open to him, like a flower when it first sees the sun. I craved more of this connection. My senses wanted to touch, to feel, to drink in the scent and the sight of his magnificence. His face was too beautiful, too glorious. I was blinded and dazed. And he, as well, looked momentarily overcome.

A long moment passed before he continued, clear notes of disbelief rasping his words. "You're an angel."

"Nay, not that."

"An angel so lovely she stuns my mind. Wearing the clothing of men."

He sat down next to me, somewhat heavily. The cloth at the front of his tunic was now saturated with blood.

"Why did you strike me?" I asked. "Now I've injured you." In the aftermath of our battle, I felt appalled that it was my own hand, my own sword, that had damaged this unearthly creature.

"I wouldn't have," he countered. "If you'd heeded my command."

My eyelids felt unusually heavy. "Aye," I admitted. "'Tis a weakness of mine. I'm not very good at heeding commands."

His hands were on my arm, where my wound was dripping a crimson puddle onto the dirt. "You're injured, too."

"Not so badly as you, I think."

He would need stitching, that was clear enough. Had I brought the stitching thread and the needle? I couldn't recall. My memory seemed fuzzy at its edges.

"The cave," I said.

He eyed me skeptically, that hint of amusement still lingering in his eyes, despite our circumstance. "Which cave is this, lass?"

I motioned toward the cave, and he moved to help me sit up. The scent and heat of him seemed to swirl all around me and inside me. The heat of his solid thigh burned through the layers of our clothing as he supported me. Feebly, I led him toward the cave, and he, too, for all his size and ferocity, swooned slightly as we walked.

"There," I said, not at all sure I wouldn't black out and crumple helplessly to the ground at a moment's notice.

I crouched onto my hands and knees at the entrance

of the cave and crawled into its interior, sliding onto the welcome warmth of the bed I'd laid. The bloodied warrior crawled in after me, lying down beside me. We held each other's gaze, and the blue of his eyes seemed to pour into me; it fed me a comfort the likes of which I had not known for a very long time, or maybe ever. I was profoundly grateful, if death was upon me, that I could at least die in the glowing presence of this glorious warrior.

"I'm Wilkie Mackenzie," he said.

So *this* was Laird Mackenzie's notorious brother. I could now understand why it was said that women fell at his feet.

Emboldened by his confession, I told him my name. "I'm Roses." I had been an Ogilvie for most of my life, but now, I had severed myself from that clan irrevocably. I was on my own.

"Roses," he said, as though wholly satisfied by my introduction. He did not prod me for more. "An unusual name." His eyes glimmered in the half-light. "The pleasure is mine, Roses."

"You exaggerate, warrior," I whispered. "I've hardly given you pleasure."

"If we live," he said, his eyes drowsy now from his blood loss, "that is something we will have to remedy."

"Aye," I heard myself reply. "It is."

And darkness overcame me.

CHAPTER TWO

When I awoke, it took me several seconds to figure out where I found myself. My body felt trapped under a heavy weight, and my arm throbbed with a dull searing ache.

I blinked, letting my eyes adjust to the dim interior. The cave.

Vivid light seeped through the narrow door opening. Late afternoon light. I had been asleep for several hours.

The warrior lay next to me, so close I could see the stubble on his now-peaceful face, framed by the long strands of his dark hair. I couldn't stop myself from reaching out to touch the thick silk of it, smoothing it back from his strong brow, fingering the braids that knotted back from his temples. His features were bold and striking, hardened by work, war and sun, softened only slightly now in this dark haven. Or tomb. Time would tell.

His arm was slung over me, pinning me against the bulk of his huge heated body. I tried to move, but he grasped me tighter, causing him to grimace and groan even in his unconscious state. I tried again but could not budge him.

Should I attempt to sneak away from him, to take my bag of food and flee northward?

I dismissed the option almost instantly. I was too

weak. I had no idea as to the extent of my injury. Or
his. And I had no intention of leaving him to die. I remembered the look on his face when he'd removed my
helmet. The direct fascination in his eyes, the impact of
his blue gaze. The new, tingling awareness of my own
heat and my own skin, and more than that: my own *life*.

I would take my chances.

"Warrior," I said, trying to rouse him.

No response.

"Wilkie," I attempted. "You must let me go, so I can
tend to your wound, and my own. I'll fetch water for
you to drink."

His eyes opened, blue even in the semidarkness.

"Roses," he mumbled.

"Aye. 'Tis me. Release your grip on me, warrior."

"Kiss me, angel. Before this life leaves me."

His eyes seemed to gain focus, and I thought I detected a brief glimmer in their sapphire depths. I was
wary, mainly because of his size and his obvious
strength, but he was a temptation to me in ways I did
not understand. I wanted to disengage from his grip and
at the same time settle yet closer to him.

"Then will you release me?"

A hint of a smile lingered in his eyes but did not
touch his lips, which parted only slightly. "Aye," he
whispered.

I brushed my lips softly against his mouth. I meant
it to be brief, a means to the critical end of attending
to our injuries. But the feel of his mouth against mine,
the warmth of his breath on my face, held me there. I
let my lips touch to his for a moment longer, savoring
the soft contact. Then he kissed me back, sweetly, his

mouth just open, so I could feel the wetness on his lips. I pulled away, shocked by the feel of it.

"Let me go, warrior."

He obeyed my request, drawing his arm away from me. But the action pained him greatly, and he groaned and closed his eyes as he lay back on our makeshift bed. I could see then that his injury was indeed severe. The front of his shirt was near-saturated with his blood. He faded from consciousness again, although his sleep seemed fitful and agitated.

I jumped up, ignoring the burning ache in my left arm. Using my knife, I cut away Wilkie's tunic, revealing the gaping wound inflicted by my own hand. It was longer but less deep than I had feared, running in a diagonal line below his rib cage along his right side. I was relieved to see that the edges were cleanly sliced, so they would be relatively easy to sew back together. Ismay had allowed me to assist her with wound care and stitching, even though Laird Ogilvie had once forbade it. She saw no harm in it, she'd said, and was only too pleased to have a willing, eager student.

Infinitely grateful that I'd happened to grab the needle and thread and the healing paste in the midst of my hasty departure, I intended to put them to good use now. But first I needed to clean his wound. Looking around the cave for a vessel to carry water, I spied the bowl.

I ran down to the pool and filled it.

Wilkie remained unconscious, and I used his stillness to my advantage. Washing away the blood from his torso took several more trips to the pool. Then I carefully sewed his wound, taking care to pull the edges neatly together before smoothing the area with healing salve. I found the process strangely taxing and was heated and exhausted by the time I'd finished but pleased with my efforts. I cut a clean strip off of his tunic to keep the wound covered, but when I tried to lift him, he wouldn't budge. The man was possibly twice my own weight, and my strength had been decidedly tapped. So I tucked the strip around him for now; I could tie it when he awoke.

I took a moment to admire the graceful lines of his chest, so powerfully built, the muscles curved and sculpted. His chest and arms carried many battle scars, lines of paleness against the brown of his sunned skin. I traced several of them lightly with my finger, imagining the battles he had fought over land, honor, women. I clearly wasn't the first to wield a sword against this seasoned warrior.

It was then that I was reminded of my own battle scar. I had been so immersed in my task of healing the warrior that I'd temporarily forgotten my own injury. But now the pain flared as if in protest. My body felt unusually warm, almost tingly in places.

I went back to the water's edge. Quickly, I removed my tunic. Before I did, I unclasped the glass-jeweled pin that adorned it, a small piece that had belonged to my mother, given to her by my father on their wedding day. It was the only belonging of theirs that remained in my possession, and I wore it each day, as a tribute to their memory. I stopped briefly to look at it, to run my fingers over the smooth rounded surface of its face. A daisy, with curved metallic petals; at its center was an amber-colored glass jewel that gleamed now, in the sun. My mother's name had been Daisy. *The sweetest, prettiest flower,* my father used to say. *My Daisy, my*

Roses. I have my very own flower garden, right here, in our house. My lovely girls.

I placed the pin on a small rock to the side of the pool and scrubbed my tunic to remove the blood, the memory of my parents surrounding me peacefully. Their kindness and generosity. Lost to me now. I hung the tunic on a near branch to dry in the breeze.

I washed the sweat and tears from my face. I cupped my hands and drank. Carefully, I washed my wound, removing the dried blood there and surveying the damage. The burning sting of the raw, exposed flesh made my eyes water. But the sword had sliced across the skin, rather than cutting deep, so the injury would likely not require sewing. I could douse it with healing salve and bandage it, and leave it to heal on its own. And I would forevermore carry the scar inflicted by Wilkie Mackenzie. Like a seal.

A seal.

It looks like a seal of some description.

I pushed the unpleasant memory out of my mind, concentrating instead on drying myself, and quickly. The warrior might wake at any time. Or his clansmen might have found his trail, or mine. They'd have noticed his disappearance by now, for certain. It was hours since he'd spied me at the wall, as he'd emerged from his own pool. I let that memory linger. I had beheld his magnificence, even amid the panic of the moment. I had never seen a man so beautiful and so…naked. And not a shred of modesty. Just confidence.

I wore my thin sleeveless shift—which I had shortened to a length I could accommodate with men's riding clothing—leaving my tunic off, for now. I didn't want to aggravate my wound with the thicker fabric yet, as it was bleeding freely again since I'd removed the layer of dried blood. I carried my tunic and the bowl, now filled with fresh water.

The warrior still slept. This worried me slightly.

I applied healing salve to own wound, which stung frightfully, bringing tears to my eyes. Once the pain had eased, I wrapped a second strip of cloth from the warrior's tunic around it several times to apply pressure. It was the only cloth I had access to, aside from my own clothing, and it was in such a state of disrepair already, it couldn't be salvaged.

After my bandage was in place, I sat next to the warrior and placed my hand on his forehead. No fever, yet.

He needed an experienced healer, one with knowledge, teas and tinctures. Would he wake soon? Would he be able to make the trek back down the mountain? He should drink.

I lifted his head gently into my lap.

"Warrior," I whispered in his ear. "You must drink. Wake now. I have fresh water."

He groaned softly, and his eyes blinked open. I held the bowl to his lips.

"Drink this. 'Tis cold and will quell your thirst."

He gulped it thirstily, drinking most of it. This relieved me. I put the bowl aside and smoothed his hair back from his face. He turned his head to gaze up at me, the expression in his eyes unfathomable. There was fierceness there, and something more. Was he still vengeful? If I healed him and comforted him, he might forgive me my crime. I dared to imagine he'd let me go and trade food for duties I could perform for him, such as sewing or preparing healing paste, or…gardening, even. It was a lofty hope, though, I knew; he'd be unlikely to trust me inside his clan's walls. And what of this warrior and his kinsmen—could *I* trust *them?* I knew of the ways and intentions of tyrannical lairds and their ranks, and I was wary.

The warrior winced briefly at his own movement as he reached to touch the long off-white end strands of my hair. I hadn't yet braided and bound it after it had come loose during our chase and our battle, so it hung down around my shoulders to graze his arm. He wound his fingers through it and held it to his cheek where he rubbed it softly against his skin.

"You left me," he accused, somewhat sulkily.

"Only for a moment," I said. "I went to bathe my wound."

His gaze traveled to my bandaged arm, as though he'd forgotten.

"I cut you."

"Aye, but I'll live. And I cut you. Now I must heal you."

His head turned just slightly, so that his cheek barely touched the pillowy curve of my breast. I blushed at the contact, as the thinness of the cloth of my shift would have, in different circumstances, been fairly scandalous. I had not yet put on my tunic. The warrior's breathing became heavier then, so I could feel the hot strikes of his breath through the very light layer of my clothing. Where his heat warmed me, sensation gathered and pooled, spreading across my skin and deeper, to the lower depths of my stomach. Against my will, my body responded. My nipples, so close to his mouth, budded into tight peaks, almost painfully.

And he noticed. The black pupils of his eyes grew, swallowing all but the outer blue edge of his irises.

This sudden darkening made him appear all the more dangerous.

I was unsettled enough to consider how I could carefully lower his head back to the furs, to remove myself from his hold, but his hand remained coiled around my hair.

"Your hair is so fair," he said. "As wheat. As honey. As gold."

And I didn't want to run from him. His touch was too delicious. I knew it was sinful to gain pleasure from such things, but it was hardly a most pressing concern. Here I was, a traitor and a thief. In the past few days, I'd stabbed two men, stolen as much food as I could carry and now found myself trapped with a fearsome warrior who might just as well kill me as save me. My list of crimes grew longer by the hour. Kissing a handsome stranger was the very least of my wrongdoings. Surprised by my own urges, I leaned ever so slightly forward, allowing his mouth just the tiniest bit closer…

The thoughts evaporated as his mouth closed over my breast. Even through the thin veil of my shift, the pressure was exquisite as he pulled my nipple farther into the hot flame of his mouth, licking his tongue against the underside of the tip, biting gently with his teeth. The scraping, scalding pressure funneled into my body, between my legs, where I grew moist and swollen, tingling with expectation.

A small moan escaped me, and him, too, as he moved to reach for my other breast. He held the full weight with his large hand, rousing sparking pleasure in my body with the pinching, circling pressure of his fingers.

It startled me, my reaction to him, the need he summoned in me. But I offered no protest when he lifted the front of my shift to gain access to my bare breasts. He gasped a savage, deep sound, touching me with the most careful placement of his fingers, rubbing me gently and pulling me to his mouth. With no barriers between my skin and the slippery play of his tongue, the craving that had begun the very first time I'd looked into his eyes grew in its power. The pulsing heavy ache in my nipples as he teased me with his teeth and his mouth swelled and compounded to touch my heart, my core, my soul, overwhelming me entirely. I held his head, stroking his hair, offering myself to him.

"Angel," he said, almost panting. "You're a dream, yet I feel you. I've never felt so much. Do you feel me?"

"I feel you, warrior. I feel all of you. Everywhere."

"How can you be here, like this, burning me so? You can't be real. Who knew death would be so enchanting and so achingly beautiful?"

His words slurred at the end, and it occurred to me then that he might have been somewhat delirious and that his heavy breaths and his moans were double-edged. He needed to be careful not to rip his stitches, and the way his arm had looped itself around my waist was endangering his recovery. I suspected that the severity of his injury was the only reason I was able to extricate myself from his grip, to place his head gently on the furs and lie next to him.

"You must rest, warrior. I'll stay here with you." My fingers smoothed his unruly hair.

"Roses," he murmured, his eyes never leaving my face.

"Aye. I'm here."

"Where have you come from?" he asked. "Why are you alone?"

Only hours ago I had fought against him to avoid a very similar question. But now, softly touching his chest, with his hand cupping my face and his blue eyes vivid and sublime, I wanted to give him whatever he asked of me. I wanted to satisfy his curiosity, and more.

"Clan Ogilvie."

"Ogilvie?" He contemplated me thoughtfully, as though surprised by this information. "You don't look like an Ogilvie."

"I wasn't born an Ogilvie. I was adopted as a child of three or four."

"From where?"

"I don't know, warrior. My origins are a mystery." A wretched mystery that had left me with a small inked tattoo and a restless spirit. "And now I work at the Ogilvie keep as a kitchen servant. Or at least I did. Until yesterday."

His thumb brushed across my bottom lip. He studied my face as I studied his. I could feel his aching beauty down to the pit of my stomach.

"I have many questions to ask you, mysterious angel," he said, "but first I need you to kiss me again. Your lips are too sweet. If I'm to die, let it be with your taste in my mouth. Kiss me, angel. I'll die a happy man."

"You'll not die, warrior." The thought jarred me. I needed to seek out help for him. I felt his forehead. Too warm.

He murmured a husked word that might have been *please*.

I leaned over him, running my fingers along the rough surface of his jaw. His dark-lit blue eyes were dreamlike, his lips beckoning me. I touched my lips to his, as I had once before. His hand reached to grip the nape of my neck with raw strength, even in his weakened state. He held me in place as he returned the kiss. I felt his tongue lick my top lip, then slide gently between them. As soon as my lips parted, his tongue delved farther. He tasted of desire and of sweet hunger. I opened to him, wanting everything about this connection to continue. I had never felt anything like the sensation this warrior delivered with the touch of his tongue to mine.

He seemed to forget himself then, and he moved as if to rise over me, to hold me closer. But the effort clearly speared him with pain. He fell back, releasing his hold.

"Warrior?" I whispered, but he was gone to me.

I could stay here and watch over him and do my best to help him. But I was not an expert healer. Ismay had taught me well in our many stolen moments, and she'd often commented on my natural abilities, but there was much I felt I still didn't know.

I had to seek out his family, and quickly. They would take him home to his comfortable, lush chambers, to their team of healers and their stores of medicines, cooks offering hearty broths and ale, to the best care a man could be given.

I laid my riding blanket over him, up to the middle of his chest. And I adjusted my own clothing, pulling my shift back down into place. I replenished the bowl of water and left it within his reach. Then I found the bag of loot I'd stolen from his clan's gardens. I put an arrangement of fruit next to the bowl of water.

"I must get help for you, warrior. I'll come back to you as soon as I can."

I took a moment to loosely stitch together the gaping rip in my tunic, at the shoulder, where Wilkie had sliced through it, making a small attempt to improve my ragged appearance. Then I eased it over my head and fitted it into place, taking care not to dislodge my bandage. I went to hunt for my sword, which, after some searching, I was able to find. I strapped it to my belt, grabbed three apples for myself, and began walking down the mountain toward the Mackenzie keep.

CHAPTER THREE

As I APPROACHED THE guarded gates of the keep, I could take some comfort from the assumption that they were unlikely to turn me away. Not when I was the one who could lead them to their missing clansman. And not just any clansman: the laird's powerful brother. Once he was returned to them, I hoped they would let me go, peacefully.

When Wilkie Mackenzie recovered—*if* he recovered would he awaken in anger? I thought again of his kiss. Of his mouth on me. The fresh memory of it brought warmth to my body, and it infused me with an unrestful anticipation. But still, *I* was the one responsible for his injury. And if he died, it was possible that the blame would be placed on me. I might be punished or killed in retribution.

There was much activity in the vicinity of the Mackenzie keep. Search parties on horseback were taking leave, it appeared. Wilkie's absence had made itself known.

Two guards watched my approach with puzzled expressions. I stood before them. "I would request to speak with Laird Mackenzie," I said. "I have news of Wilkie Mackenzie's whereabouts."

The two guards looked at each other, skeptical, but they took my words seriously, and they didn't waste time. "Follow me," one of them instructed, and began walking toward the stone castle. Several young boys were playing in the gardens, and the guard called to them. They scampered over, eyeing me, my clothing.

"Run to the yards to see if the laird can be found there. He is needed in the hall urgently. Hurry to it!" he commanded them. The boys ran off, gleeful with their assignment.

I was led at a brisk pace along a wide path to the looming stone castle. I was struck again by the beauty and orderliness of the landscape. Workers paused in their tasks and stared at me as I walked alongside the guard. I envied these workers their teamwork and camaraderie, their clan and sense of belonging. I wished I, too, had a clan I could feel a part of and that I could be allowed to contribute to in a meaningful way. I had felt as if I'd belonged to the Ogilvie clan for a time, until the death of my father and my mother's quickly following decline. Since then, I'd felt less like kin and more like a servant and outsider who didn't quite fit either my role or my surroundings. My spirit had been well and truly stomped upon, my wings insistently clipped. In my heart, I felt my destiny lay elsewhere.

The guard escorted me through the giant wooden doors of the castle, into a grand entrance hall. Tapestries adorned the stone walls, and fine, wooden furniture decorated the room's interior. The details and upkeep of the castle were clearly more refined and prosperous than those found in the Ogilvie keep.

I wondered, as I sat in a chair and waited for the guard to return, whether Wilkie had woken. I knew he would call out to me if he found me gone. I felt an undeniable longing to go back to him, to heal him with my own hands. But it was best this way. The fever was upon him, and his chances of survival were far greater under the care of his clan. And I badly wanted him to live.

Commotion and loud footsteps approached from the interior of the castle. And into the room strode a small crowd of people, led by an enormous man who could only have been Wilkie's brother, Laird Mackenzie. His resemblance to Wilkie was striking, his hair equally as black, but he was even larger, his look more imposing. Rather than a vivid blue, his eyes were a distinct shade of light gray. To his right stood another brother. Kade, if I remembered correctly. This brother was similar in size but slighter, almost lanky, his hair a dark shade of brown, his eyes blue, like Wilkie's, but lighter in hue. The look in his eyes suggested less restraint than his brothers, an innate recklessness that was, at a first impression, somewhat unsettling. This effect was further emphasized by the veritable arsenal he wore: several belts strung with a number of knives and swords, as well as a leather strap across his chest fitted with pouches and pockets where more small knives and other sharp objects were cached.

I stood.

They stared at me as though I had two heads, and I realized I must have looked strange to them. I'd been so distracted with Wilkie's care, and the emotions inspired by his kisses, that I'd forgotten to braid my hair, which hung long and loose down my back. Still dressed in now-ragged men's clothing, which I'd taken care to rid of bloodstains, but hadn't been entirely successful with the task, and with a sword strung in my belt, I must have looked a right savage.

But there was little I could do about it now.

Before my study could wander further, the laird spoke.

"I am Laird Knox Mackenzie and this is my brother Kade Mackenzie. To whom do I speak?"

"My name is Roses."

I was glad he didn't ask me about my clan. There were more pressing questions on his mind. "You have news of Wilkie," he said, with brusque impatience.

"Aye," I said. "He is injured. I know where he lies, up the mountain to the west. I have stitched his wound, but I fear the fever is ailing him."

The laird reacted instantly, barking orders at the assembly. "Fergus, prepare the horses and—"

"He'll need a litter," I said. "He can't walk, and carrying him would injure him further."

The laird's head snapped in my direction, his face registering mild outrage. Kade looked almost amused.

All was briefly silent in the wake of my interruption.

"You and I will have a long talk upon our return," the laird said to me, his glare blazingly direct. "First we find Wilkie." He turned to his brother. "The lass can ride with you."

"I can ride," I offered, but my request was ignored. It seemed I was not to be trusted. Gratitude was not their foremost reaction to my sudden appearance, I reflected with some annoyance.

The group was quick to assemble, and I was led outside and hoisted upon a colossal horse, in front of Kade. "You'll show me the path to Wilkie," he said.

He wrapped massive arms around me and spurred his horse into a full gallop, followed closely by the others. I feared getting poked or speared with one of his many weapons, but I had no choice but to cling to him.

We made quick time of the flatlands and soon were traversing the steep slope of the hillside. It was so steeply inclined in places I feared our horses would flip from the weight of us, but the men were undeterred. I pointed out the path, and we reached the entrance of the cave just as dusk had given way to darkness.

"Here," I said. Kade leaped from his horse, making no move to assist me, and he walked toward the cave with ground-eating strides, followed closely by the laird and several others. Kade's horse was so large I had difficulty jumping down from the great height I found myself at. I swung my leg over and tried to lower myself to the ground but ended up falling into a painful heup. Brushing myself off, I walked over to the entrance of the cave, and crouched just inside, near where the men were circled, kneeling around Wilkie. The dying light cast a subtle glow into the small space.

"Brother," said the laird, touching his hand to Wilkie's forehead. "We're taking you home." Rigid concern lent a stern severity to the laird's bold features as he exchanged looks with Kade. "He's burning."

Kade lifted the blanket I'd placed over Wilkie's chest, pulling it down to reveal the lightly bandaged wound. He peeled this back, and each of them drew a quick intake of breath.

"You sewed this, lass?" the laird asked me.

"Aye."

"Not a bad job of it," Kade commented.

Wilkie stirred, his head rolling from side to side. "Roses," he said, quite clearly, though his eyes were still closed.

"He's delirious," said the laird. "Let's move him to the litter."

"Roses," Wilkie called out, louder this time.

Kade watched his brother, then his gaze slid to me. "What did you say your name was?"

"Roses," I said quietly.

Kade nodded his head toward Wilkie in a curt, commanding gesture: I was being granted permission—or being ordered, perhaps—to go to him. I crawled over to Wilkie. I whispered in his ear, not caring if I was overheard, "I'm here, warrior."

He settled instantly. His eyes opened, and he blinked several times as though struggling to keep them open. He reached up to lace his hand under my hair, around the back of my head. "Ah, lass. Such a beautiful dream, you are. Kiss me again."

The laird looked less than pleased by the exchange, but he was studying his brother's reaction with interest, obviously relieved to find him alive.

"'Tis time for you to go home," I said softly. "Your brothers have come for you."

"Stay with me, Roses," he said drowsily, and it wasn't a question.

I glanced at the laird, whose attention was directed at me. Would he allow it? His eyes followed Wilkie's hand as it stroked through my hair, then fell at his side.

"Aye," said Laird Mackenzie. "You'll come. Let's go."

CHAPTER FOUR

I WAS NOT ONLY ALLOWED but also expected to remain at Wilkie's side, as he was taken to his chambers and treated by the healer.

His chambers were large and, as expected, luxurious. Heavy furs hung at the windows to protect against the night breeze, which was becoming more biting with each passing day. A fire had been laid in a grand stone fireplace and crackled pleasantly, casting orange light. Wilkie's bed was supported by four vertical curved wooden beams that reached to the ceiling and were hung with thick embroidered curtains, pulled back now, so the healer could attend to his injury.

I took my place in a chair by the fire as Wilkie's attendants inspected and cleaned his wound. I was so exhausted, I could have slept in the hard wooden seat. My eyelids felt heavy, and I struggled to keep myself from drifting.

Kade and the laird hung back, watching the healer attend to their brother. In a flurry of commotion, two younger women rushed through the door, frantic with the news of Wilkie's return. His sisters, it was easy to see, with their dark hair and blue eyes.

"Wilkie," one of them gasped, pressing her hand to his brow. "He's fevered," she said.

"He's alive, and home," said the other sister, "and

strong as an ox. He'll be fine." She adjusted his furs with extreme care, fussing over him.

I envied him, his family close around him, wrenching concern etched onto their faces.

The slightly taller sister, whose hair was as black as Wilkie's, addressed the healer. "Effie, how severe are his injuries?"

"Quite severe," replied Effie. "Who stitched this?" she asked the laird.

"'Twas the lass here," the laird said. "Roses." All eyes moved to me, but I was too tired to take much notice of their scrutiny, which soon shifted back to Wilkie.

Effie gave a noise that suggested she was mildly impressed. "It can remain in place. The wound itself has begun to heal. In fact, the quick stitching probably saved his life. 'Tis a nasty wound indeed." She cleaned and bound Wilkie's torso, then she prescribed a drink of cooled willowbark tea, which she scooped from a pot with a wooden goblet.

But when the women tried to hold his head to make him drink, he swiped the goblet away, sending it flying across the room where it struck the stone wall.

"You must take the drink, Wilkie," Effie instructed him in a loud voice, as though he was deaf rather than fevered. But when they tried again, his reaction was even more violent, and his body began to thrash in agitation as he groaned with the pain of his own unrest.

"Roses," the laird said, signaling for me to go to Wilkie. "You try."

Uneasy under the room's collective gaze, I walked to Wilkie's bed. He lay in the middle of the expanse, so I had to climb up to sit next to him. I put my face close to his. "Warrior, you must drink. Let me hold the cup for you. It will cool your throat."

He turned his face toward me but didn't open his eyes. "Ach," he barely whispered, a slow smile touching his mouth. "My angel has come to me."

Effie handed me the goblet. I held Wilkie's head, lifting him until his lips touched the rim. "Here it is. Take your drink, warrior," I crooned. "That's it, and a little more."

He drank until the cup was empty.

"Stay with me," he said drowsily. "Right here, where I can feel you."

"Aye, warrior."

I laid his head back on his pillow, more peaceful now. I made a move to slide off the bed, but Wilkie looped a large, muscular arm around my waist, pulling me against him. I tried to pry his fingers gently loose, attempting to unwrap his arm from around my hips where I lay practically on top of him. But Wilkie immediately began to protest, pulling me back to him and securing his hold around me, even more tightly. Through the haze of his fever, he murmured my name and other words of endearment that brought heat to my face, and elsewhere. The laird and Kade noticed my blush, which only worsened its effect.

I leaned up to Wilkie, whispering assurances close to his ear that I was still here, that I wouldn't leave him. He quieted and loosened his hold, allowing me to sit. But I was still locked decisively in his ironclad grip.

"He requires rest," announced Effie. She contemplated my placement next to Wilkie and the entwined clasp of our fingers. "The lassie looks dead on her feet.

Would you like me to find a bed for her, Laird Mackenzie?"

Wilkie's words were slurred but quite emphatic for
a man infirmed. "She'll sleep here. With me."

At this, Kade chuckled quietly.

But the laird did not appear to be quite as amused.
"She can sleep in the women's chambers, and be brought
to you on the morrow."

This information appeared disagreeable enough to
rouse Wilkie momentarily from his fugue. His eyes
barely opened, and his voice was husked with illness,
but he spoke clearly enough to be understood. "I need
her. She keeps the darkness at bay."

"Wilkie," said the laird, and his voice was firm, as
though he was confident he could talk some sense into
his delusional brother. "Be reasonable. The lass is neither a figment of your imagination nor is she a captive.
In fact we know next to nothing about *who,* indeed, the
lass *is*—a mystery I aim to get to the bottom of as soon
as she is rested. She'll sleep in the extra bed in Christie's chambers and we can all meet and discuss what's
to be done in the morning. Now—"

"Nay!" Wilkie's voice sounded almost panicked, and
his grasp grew stronger as he attempted to rise into a sitting position. "You'll not take her. *She's mine.*" But the
pain in his side speared him, and he flinched, clenching my fingers all the while in a vise-grip, and fell
back onto his pillows. Shocked by the agonized sound
he made, I used my hands to gently hold him in place.

"Please, warrior," I urged him, wiping away a tear
from my cheek. "Sleep now. Don't damage yourself further. The moment I'm allowed to return to you, I will."

The lingering agony was taking its toll; Wilkie's eyes

were directed at me even as he spoke to his brother, and they were heavy-lidded as he slurred from the effects of the strong brew he'd been given. "I'll *die*. The sight of her. Her touch… She heals me like no medicine could. Let her… Roses. *Angel*." His voice faded as he struggled to retain consciousness. His grip on my body loosened as he succumbed to sleep.

"The man's taken total leave of his senses, to be sure," Kade said lightly, but he was watching Wilkie with worry.

One of the sisters spoke then. "Let me get some furs and make up the bed in Wilkie's adjoining chambers. Please, Knox. Roses can sleep in there, in case he awakens and calls to her." We hadn't been formally introduced, but she'd clearly surmised my name during the proceedings. She sounded as if she'd already accepted Wilkie's pleas and would do all she could to accommodate them.

"Aye," said the other sister, eager excitement written into her features at the prospect of scandal. "I'll sleep with her if you like, so she'll be chaperoned. You must agree, Knox. There's no need to agitate Wilkie further by removing Roses completely from his chambers when it's clearly against his wishes. He's obviously taken an attachment to her. And we must do everything we can to speed his recovery."

Laird Mackenzie looked thoroughly irritated by the situation, but perhaps he was concerned enough about his brother's obvious distress to make allowances. He glanced once at Kade, who shrugged and said, "'Tis a reasonable suggestion. We don't want unnecessary agitation to worsen his condition. We can check in on them from time to time."

The laird's glance rested on me for a moment, as though attempting to read my motives. "I suppose we could." With a heavy sigh, he said, "All right, then. Ailie, you make up the beds. Christie, you'll sleep with Roses. Effie, you'll see to the lass—the shoulder of her tunic is stained with fresh blood. She appears to be injured. You'll tend to the lass's wound. Kade, you'll check in at regular intervals during the night."

Once, it might have occurred to me to question or protest this blatantly inappropriate scenario of sleeping in the adjoining chambers of a man, and one I barely knew. In fact, I felt wildly relieved. I wouldn't be cast out. And I could be near him, this warrior whose blood had mingled with my own and whose eyes and mouth and fingers had already provoked a longing in me that I could neither explain nor deny.

Effie began to gather her equipment.

One of Wilkie's sisters went ahead, through the door of the adjoining chambers, and the other helped me extricate myself from Wilkie's grip. She took my arm. "Come, Roses. We'll show you to your bed."

"First," said Kade, "we'll divest you of your weapons."

The abundant weaponry slung across his body, along with his size and slightly wild-eyed look, was wholly daunting as he approached me. I did as he asked. I removed my belt, holding it out, along with my small sword and knife. Kade grabbed the lot.

I remembered Laird Ogilvie's officers' passing descriptions, then, of the Mackenzies. Lethal. Armed to the teeth.

Aye, Kade Mackenzie was armed to the teeth. But his blue eyes appeared more curious than cutting; he

seemed mildly intrigued by this unusual turn of events
and at Wilkie's sudden desire to have me close. "Your
weapons," he said, "will remain in our care."

"I trust your accommodation will be suitable," said
the laird, nodding once in a brief bid good-night. The
gesture was polite, oddly, and somewhat foreign to me;
it was the gesture of a nobleman, and one that might be
delivered to a woman of his own class. Something I was
most definitely not. It occurred to me then that he wasn't
aware of my lowly status. Tomorrow the truth would
be told, but tonight, I would enjoy the plush chambers
of the privileged few.

THE ANTECHAMBER WAS a long, narrow room with a stone-
bound window seat at one end, generously adorned with
fur cushions. At the opposite end of the room was a fireplace, laid with a recently lit fire. Two single beds were
being draped with thick, luxurious coverings. Merely
the sight of a warm fur-piled bed amplified my fatigue.

Now, in the close quarters, I could get a better look
at Wilkie's sisters. I had noticed immediately the strong
family resemblance between the Mackenzie siblings.
His sisters were indeed quite beautiful. Both regarded
me with blatant curiosity.

"I'm Ailie, Roses. And this is Christie."

"Roses," said Christie, the younger sister, whose
manner was open and vivacious. She took my hand.
"'Tis a pleasure to meet you. However do you find yourself in Wilkie's bed? You'll be the envy of legions." She
was exquisitely petite, and her hair was a minky shade
of dark brown, which she wore loose so it waved gently
around her shoulders. Her eyes were an unusual shade
of light blue and sparkled with a hint of mischief. Eager

questions bubbled out of her, as though she couldn't contain them. "You must tell us the story. What has happened? And where did you come from?"

"Stop interrogating her, Christie," scolded Ailie. She was the taller of the two, slim and elegant in the way she held herself. Her more reserved manner suggested she was the elder sister. Her black hair was swept up in a fashionably braided twist. And her eyes were such a deep shade of blue, they might have been described as violet. "We'll talk of all that tomorrow. Roses needs to have her injury treated, and she needs sleep. Here, Roses, lie here on this bed so Effie can look at your wound."

I lay on the bed, so very grateful for its warmth and its softness.

Effie came to me, setting down her tray filled with teas and medicines, bandages and ointments. As she leaned over me, I looked more closely at her face for the first time. She was perhaps twice my age, short and rounded, with a busy bunch of red curls framing her kind, pink face. "Can you sit up, dear? I'll need to remove your tunic. And the oversize trews you wear, whatever for I wouldn't guess at. I daresay you look like you've been through the wars."

I could hear Kade and the laird in Wilkie's adjoining chambers, in quiet discussion. Then the door closed.

Effie helped me remove my outer clothing. I made sure to keep my back hidden, aware of my tattoo, as always, and careful not to reveal it. My hair still hung loose, covering me, and I lay back as Effie attended to me. She treated and bound my wound, chattering gently of its successful healing thus far, despite the blood. She described her methods as she worked, to make me feel at ease, perhaps, as Ailie and Christie watched intermittently, and attended to tidying up the room. And I was grateful for their chipper yet restful presence. Effie gave me some tea and a dose of medicine. She felt my forehead and expressed concern at the warmth, but she hoped that the medicine was administered in time, that it would override the beginnings of any danger. Then she tucked the furs to my neck and patted them.

"'Tis brief, your underclothing," she whispered, putting her face close to mine. "But 'twill hardly be an issue, lassie." She was smiling kindly, with only a hint of chiding curiosity. She seemed to be most entertained by the near-scandal of my presence in Wilkie's antechamber and pleased to be privy to the drama of it. "Ailie and Christie will find clothing for you on the morrow. Something more…suitable."

I wanted to thank her for the offer and assure all of them than it wouldn't be necessary; I would be on my way on the morrow, if I could just get some bread. Some pears, maybe. But I was asleep before I could even get the words out.

"ROSES."

The darkness was too thick, the sleep too deep.

"Roses."

I sat straight up, utterly bewildered. For the briefest, panicked moment, I thought I might be in Ogilvie's dungeon, cast forever into the fetid gloom for my brazen desertion. My mind flashed then to the cave. Was I alone? But I could see now: the pattern of the stone-laid floor near the dying embers of the fire. The shadowy outlines of the bed and the room.

"Angel, where are you?" came the muffled, husky murmur. *"Come back to me."*

My awareness settled into place. I could see that Christie was asleep in her own bed; she didn't stir. I eased myself from the warm cocoon of my furs and went to the door of Wilkie's private chambers. It was unlocked. No one was with him, and his chambers were quiet. I entered and closed the door behind me. Wilkie lay in his bed, his eyes closed, but he was writhing slightly, murmuring. His hair was in disarray and damp from his own sweat.

I went to him and held my hand to his forehead. Still feverish.

At the touch of my hand to his skin, his eyelids fluttered but did not open. He groaned softly in a spoken word. "Roses."

"Here I am, warrior," I whispered to him, leaning close. Wilkie's room was dark save the flickering light of a fire that had been loaded with wood, to keep the room warm for him. But it was too warm, I thought. He was overheated. I pulled the furs down from his chest, draping them back over his bandaged side, to his waist.

I went to Effie's tray, which had been left on a table next to his bed, and I poured a goblet of cooled medicinal tea. When I climbed up next to him to try to revive him enough to drink some of the liquid, I was surprised to see that his eyes were open, blazing in their sudden blueness, still bright and slightly bloodshot from his fever. He drank willingly when I offered him the cup. It was only then that I realized I was clad only in my brief underclothing.

I made a move to leave him, to go and cover myself. His hand clasped my wrist with surprising strength.

"Stay," he said, his voice deep and rasped from lack of use. Not a command, a request. The grasp of his hand loosened almost immediately, his fingers feathering the light downy hairs on my arm.

"Let me go, warrior. I'll dress. Then I'll return to you."

"Stay," he said again. "I'll not look at you." But his eyes were already on me, burning into me.

My thin shift did little to hide my body, but then again this warrior had already seen me, and much more than that. He had, in fact, tasted me, pulling sensuously with his hot mouth, biting with his teeth. The thought sent a hot flush to my cheeks and to my breasts as I remembered the feel of him. I hoped he couldn't detect my heat in the dim light. Or my secret, rising desire for more of his tantalizing touches.

"I might look at you just a little," he amended, watching as my body responded to him, as my nipples grew tighter. A hint of a smile played at the corners of his mouth, and his eyes were light against the dark rims of his eyelashes. *He's breathtaking,* I thought.

"I'm dreaming," he said, as though speaking to himself. "She can't be real."

"I'm real, warrior," I said, drawing my finger across the back of his hand to convince him, so he could feel my touch.

"Are you?" he whispered.

"Aye."

He paused, allowing the reality to settle. "And you're here, in my chambers with me." He laughed softly. "My brothers are truly good to me when I'm ill."

"You fairly insisted on it," I said gently.

His slow smile offered a brief dazzling flash. "Aye.

I remember. I want you as close as you can be. Let me feel you, lass."

His fingertips drew soft lines up my arm, and he reached to stroke the long strands of my hair, smoothing it carefully against my arms and my breasts, as though disbelieving the solidity of me. His touch was possessive and sure, leaving trails of warmth wherever his fingers had lingered.

"My dreams were so vivid," he mused. "You appeared to me, a golden angel. I have never seen a beauty equal to yours. You were the sun, burning me with your golden light. Burning me as I've never burned. When you left me, all was dark. I followed you for days so I could feel again your voice, your warmth and your fair hair, touching me like a feathery wing."

I knew Wilkie's delirium remained; it was clear that he perceived me as a vision, perhaps, or an apparition. I suspected he was associating me with some kind of life force that had led him from the darkness of death and into a healing light. In his weakened state, he was seeing me as his savior.

I didn't know if his desire to keep me close was real, or just a side effect of Wilkie's instinct to survive. What I did know, though, was that I wanted to save him. I wanted his attachment to me to last. I knew that this desire was too intense and too quick. That I should feel such wild affection for him, when we had spent so little time together and knew so little about each other, was, perhaps, inappropriate. Yet it didn't *feel* inappropriate. It felt important. It felt as if I finally had something to lose.

I leaned closer to him. "I'll tend to you again, warrior," I whispered. "Whatever you need."

His lingering smile speared me with intense awareness. His hand stole back to my hair, which he wrapped around his hands, then let fall in fanning designs, as though spellbound by its texture and the play of the light. It was true I didn't know Wilkie Mackenzie beyond a heart-pounding chase, a quick but savage fight and two astonishingly beautiful kisses. His presence, his face and the brush of his hair against my skin now felt familiar to me after brief and close-strung embraces against his bare chest. But his subdued, almost-wakeful energy was new to me and unfathomably intriguing. We were strangers whose mouths had touched intimately, yet the thoughts behind his eyes were wild and unknowable.

"You healed me," he said.

"I sewed up a wound that was inflicted by my own hand," I reminded him softly.

"And what of your wound, inflicted by my own hand?" He helped himself to an inspection of my bandage.

"'Tis nearly healed already," I said.

His hand continued its lazy exploration of my body as his eyes held mine.

"Come closer, Roses," he said. "Breathe on me. Breathe on my mouth. I want to feel your breath on me."

I wanted to comfort him, to do as he asked of me. And I wanted to grant him his wishes. His wishes felt as if they were my own wishes, as if they were one and the same. I leaned over him. My breasts pressed against his bare chest through the thin fabric of my night clothing. I blew softly onto his lips as he parted them to inhale the air of my lungs. He breathed deeply.

"Ahhh," he exhaled. "You heal me well, lass. I intend to take of you all your remedies."

"Which remedies?" I began to sit up. "I can fetch—"

He pulled me back to him, quite forcibly, so I was pressed up against him once more. His body was remarkably hard against my softness. "This remedy," he said, and he fit his hand around the base of my skull, to pull my face to his as he lifted his head. "A kiss, Roses. Kiss me like you kissed me in my dreams."

"Aye, warrior. I'll kiss you. Now be still. You'll overtax yourself."

He obeyed, and his body relaxed. I touched my hands to his shoulders, to relax him further. I ran my fingers along his jaw. I touched his hair and smoothed its thick silk layers. I traced one finger across his lips. His breath was hot against my fingers. I leaned farther over him, breathing his breath, and when my hair brushed against his chest, he made a sound, like a soft sigh. I touched my lips to his mouth. That flavor of him, as I'd tasted twice before, was wickedly alluring. Wanting more of it, I licked his top lip, pushing tiny licks into his mouth, as he'd taught me, sucking gently on his lips and the tip of his tongue as I kissed him, savoring the all-tempting essence of him.

"Warrior?" I whispered.

"Aye."

"Is this kiss remedying you?"

"Nay, lass."

I stopped. "Nay?"

"My fever is far more acute than it ever was."

I touched my hand to his forehead again. He smiled at my confusion.

"My innocent Roses. Stay close to me. My fever burns for you and can only be calmed by your body. And I can soothe you, too, sweet Roses. You must let me."

I wanted to let him. But there was a small reticence in me. "What should I do?" My inexperience was fairly embarrassing at my age. I'd been too preoccupied with work duties to wonder beyond them. Until now. And I was beginning to understand the new fever he spoke of. This warmth, this feeling of heat. Of tingling need. His dark blue eyes were lust-drowsed and hungry for more of my kisses, I could sense this.

"You're getting better, lass."

"Better at what?"

"Better at heeding my commands."

I smiled. "Aye. I get into trouble when I don't heed your commands."

"You and I both. Now you'll do as I tell you."

I was nervous at what he might command me to do, yet in my heart and my very bones, everything about this close company of Wilkie Mackenzie felt right. To look at him, to touch him, to be touched by him: these were the things that felt most important to me at that moment.

"Roses, my sun, my golden light. I must be careful with you. I'll not hurt you, nor take you. Not yet." His words had a strange, thawing effect on me; my skin felt dewy and hypersensitive. "You'll do as I say."

The beauty of his face, artfully shadowed and lit from the fading firelight, it fairly stunned me.

"Aye, warrior," I whispered.

He wrapped his hand around the nape of my neck, pulling my face closer to his. "Kiss me again."

I did, kissing him gently, exploring his lips with my tongue, pushing just inside his mouth. He returned the kiss, fitting his mouth to mine, tasting, delving into me more insistently, feeding me with his taste and his fire, which seemed to ignite my body with a pleasurable flush.

I felt his hand on the back of my thigh, over the light cloth of my underclothing. He pulled me harder against him, so I was slightly straddling his leg, still clad in the rough leather of his trews. He held me with surprising gentleness, introducing a lazy rhythm as he rubbed me against him, still playing my tongue with the luring pulls of his mouth. Shockingly, the rolling clench of his hand on the barely shielded skin of my backside fed a spiky warmth to the sensitive place between my legs. He took his time, ever so slightly increasing the pressure and the pace. His strength gave him total control, and he continued to work my body with his hands, squeezing and caressing in undulating grasps. I didn't know what he was doing. Or *how* he could be doing it. But the building sensation was so needy, so sweet, with its promising, blinding forward momentum, I felt myself rocking ever so slightly against him, melting under his touch. The fever of my body grew in its power until it overwhelmed me, coursing with a compounding swell to surge through my very core, spasming in delightful, nearly unendurable bursts. I coiled and moaned with an almost painful pleasure, unable to quiet myself as the sweet fire pulsed through me.

The waves calmed, and I slumped against him, weakly kissing his lips. My body felt heavy and honey-soaked.

"Warrior."

"Hush now."

He drew the furs over us, and I barely registered the warning footsteps, the click and creak of the door opening. I knew I should have hidden myself or fled. To be caught like this, scantily clad in Wilkie's bed and locked in an inappropriately intimate embrace: the entire scenario should have been mortifying. My reputation—if I even possessed one now would be even more tattered than it already was. But I was too entranced by him, by what he'd just done to my body. I couldn't quite summon the shame or even the energy to remove myself from him, not from within this hazed stupor that radiated from my deepest depths. I was floating as though in a wondrous dream where reputations mattered little and the only consideration was the nearness of my warrior.

"Availing yourself to healing remedies, I see, brother." I recognized Kade Mackenzie's low voice but had no compunction to open my eyes; they felt as heavy and sated as the rest of me. "Just checking to see that you're still alive."

"Aye," Wilkie said, and the sound of his voice, so deep and comforting, as I lay against his chest, as close as I could be. "Still alive."

The footsteps retreated as Kade took his leave. He was clearly not as incensed by the possibility of scandal as Laird Mackenzie had been. He paused at the door and asked, "What's wrong with the lass?" Amusement rang in his words.

"Nothing's wrong with the lass," I heard Wilkie's voice say lazily, his hand still warm and intimately placed. "She's fine."

I thought I heard a note of Kade's soft laughter as the door closed behind him.

I lay with Wilkie for a long time, flitting in and out of a replete half sleep, until I was awakened by his moans and his uneven breaths, from warring dreams or from the pain of his injury I couldn't be sure. I stroked his hair to ease his unquieted sleep. I ran my fingers along the stubble of his days-old beard, savoring the scratchy feel of it, mesmerized by the rugged beauty of his features. His arm wrapped more tightly around my waist, and the strength of him seemed to buffer me from the uncertainty of my predicament, softening my own unease.

I was becoming accustomed to the insistent embraces of Wilkie Mackenzie. Despite the newness of our familiarity, every aspect of his touch consoled me. It may have been foolish to find such a degree of contentment in a connection that might soon be broken. I knew Wilkie Mackenzie was likely to be a brief, temporary fixture in my life. But he was such a magnificent presence, so unexpected and so very, very beautiful. I wanted only to savor the pleasure of him while I could. I knew that when he finally let me go, I would miss the warmth of him. And the anticipation of his lips touching mine just once more.

When Wilkie's breathing evened, and the black of night gave way to a purple-hued dawn, I kissed him once more with the lightest touch of my lips to his. Then I slipped from his bed and returned to the antechamber, where Christie lay undisturbed. I crawled back into my bed.

And in the wake of Wilkie's enlightening caresses, I could not bring myself to fret about the uncertainties that the day would surely introduce. I still felt an echo of a pulse in the core of my body. It was an exquisite feeling, of fruitfulness and warm promise, as though my body had become a quivering vessel. Despite injury, fatigue, soreness, I felt more alive than I had ever been. I slept, thinking only of him.

CHAPTER FIVE

EARLY THE NEXT MORNING, I was summoned by Kade to meet with Laird Mackenzie in the grand hall.

There was a loud knock on the door, which roused both Christie and myself. Christie rose and opened the door to him. He did not enter but stood in the door frame, filling up the space.

He was generous enough to give me several minutes to adjust to my surroundings before he began doling out orders.

"After you dress," he said to me, "I will take you down to the hall to discuss what has happened and what will happen. The laird is expecting us immediately." He made no move to leave, to allow me to rise and dress. He seemed temporarily overcome by curiosity.

"What of Wilkie?" asked Christie.

"He sleeps," he answered, still staring at me.

Whatever leniency I had detected in Kade Mackenzie last night had receded almost entirely; he was as formidable as I had yet seen him. His weapons gleamed brightly in the subdued sunlight that streamed through the small window and brought attention to the glint of the many blades that hung from him, as though they'd been sharpened and polished with care to face the day. I was glad for Christie's presence then, as she rose and pushed him out the door, so she could make a move to close it, taking no notice of his ferocity. "You don't expect her to dress while you're standing there intimidating her with all your swords and knives, now, do you, brother? Wait outside."

"I wasn't intending to intimidate anyone," he said.

"You intimidate everyone, fierce warrior, and you know it. Why else would you carry no less than three swords? Are you expecting to be attacked here in our chambers? You've already stripped Roses of her weapons, and I—" she held out her arms as though to prove it to him "—have nothing on me, I swear it."

Watching the ease of them in each other's presence, I felt a small pang of emptiness that might have been jealousy. With no siblings, nor family at all, to call my own, I felt fascinated by their playful banter, their natural camaraderie. She was so entirely unruffled by his presence, as only a sister could be. To me, he appeared frighteningly intense. Yet she treated him with all the gentleness of a child, ushering him out the door insistently and taking care to avoid any of his sharper edges.

Once Kade had retreated, I rose, putting on my battered tunic and my oversize trews.

"My dear Roses," said Christie, surveying my outfit with a critical eye. "We must do something about your clothing. Ailie, you should know, is a talented seamstress. While you're meeting with Knox and Kade, we'll make it our quest to find you a more flattering outfit. And when you're returned to Wilkie, he'll not believe his eyes." Her eyes glimmered at the thought. So welcoming, she was, and kind. It was clear from her openhearted manner that Christie had already accepted my placement here, perhaps not at Wilkie's side, but at least somewhere near it. She appeared excited by the prospect of planning our day together, primping me for her brother's approval. And as appealing as her intentions sounded, I felt wary of my own secrets: my tattoo and the horrified reaction to it that shadowed my memories. I would have to take every care to make sure it was kept covered.

But I knew there was no guarantee that I would see out the day at Kinloch, nor even the hour.

I wished I could go to Wilkie. I wanted to see him and to touch him before I faced his brothers, in case they cast me out. I felt disconcerted by this separation from him and most of all by the thought that I might not be allowed to see him again, even to bid him farewell.

"What is it, Roses?" Christie asked. "Why do you weep?" She placed a hand on my shoulder.

I wiped the tear away. "'Tis nothing. I'm fine."

"I've never seen him look at anyone the way he looked at you," she said quietly. "I've never heard that kind of longing in his voice, not once." She spoke with an almost reverential tone, as if the connection she'd witnessed with her own eyes carried weight and power. "Don't let Knox and Kade frighten you. They have Wilkie's best interests at heart, always. They will do anything to speed his full recovery. Clearly you will play a part in that recovery. Take heart."

And I did. Her words calmed me. "I thank you for your kindness, Christie," I said.

"And I thank you for having the courage to save Wilkie, and to summon help for him. Now go. They'll not want to be kept waiting."

She opened the door for me, and Kade motioned for me to follow him, which I did. He led me out of Wilkie's antechamber, down a hall lit with candles that sat in grooves carved into the stone walls, down a wide, curving set of wooden stairs, to the grand hallway. Having only a hazy memory of the castle's interior from the night of my arrival, I was agog at the splendor of it. The Mackenzie castle was not, as I'd guessed at my first impression, wildly more prosperous than the Ogilvie manor. Rather, I realized, it was merely much more beautifully maintained. Careful attention had gone into each and every detail of both the land and the manor, administered by a clan who clearly cherished their space and were talented at enhancing all it had to offer. I valued this sentiment and felt even more drawn to this clan by the discovery.

We entered the grand hallway, with its richly colored hanging tapestries, its fine furniture, its highly polished pewter candelabras. I could appreciate that someone had taken special care with these candelabras; I had polished many similar pieces in my time but had never achieved such a rich gleam. Not that I had tried especially diligently, but still. It was admirable.

Laird Mackenzie was pacing in front of the large fireplace. He was the only one in attendance, and the look on his face as we approached him suggested he was tired of waiting, and had other pressing matters to attend to.

He took in, again, my disheveled men's garb and stared at me coldly. "Sit," he commanded, signaling to one of several chairs placed near the fire. I obeyed him, and took my place.

Kade sat in another chair, but the laird continued to stand, and his eyes did not waver in their scrutiny. I felt wildly out of place under the laird's direct gaze. I tried to smooth my long hair, aware that I hadn't brushed it in quite some time.

"I expect you to answer all of my questions truthfully," the laird said. "Are you willing to speak to me?"

I was hungry, and sore. I felt chilled and at the same overheated. I wanted to eat and bathe, to sleep and, most of all, to visit Wilkie. But all those things would have to wait. I knew I owed the laird his explanation. "Aye, Laird Mackenzie. I am at your service." I sat up straight and waited for the inquiry to begin.

"Firstly," the laird said. "I will thank you for summoning us. For not leaving Wilkie to die."

This surprised me. I wasn't used to receiving thanks from anyone, especially a man of Laird Mackenzie's station. But my small satisfaction at the redress was short-lived. I knew that as soon as he learned that I had been the one to injure Wilkie, the laird's gratitude would most certainly give way to anger and hostility.

"I could not have left him to die. Not when it was my fault—"

"We'll get to that in a moment," the laird said. "Tell me first, where do you hail from?"

"Clan Ogilvie."

"Ogilvie? You've traveled far, alone. We can arrange for you to be returned to your clan." He paused. "Once our brother has healed."

"I cannot return to Ogilvie," I said.

The two men exchanged glances.

"What reason do you have for running from your clan?" asked the laird. "'Tis a dangerous course of action, leaving yourself alone and unprotected."

They awaited my response.

"I'm the adopted daughter of an Ogilvie clan landholder, Oliver Ogilvie. I was skilled in horticulture, and was training as an apprentice healer. I was valued as a gatherer, gardener and provider of medicinal herbs. For a time. Upon my parents' deaths, I was relegated to kitchen duties. I carried them out dutifully for the most part. But, more recently—"

"Why were you reassigned?" interrupted Laird Mackenzie. He knew, as I did, that it was unusual for a clanmember to change positions in the household; usually a demotion was the result of misbehavior of one sort or another.

"I—" This was somewhat difficult to answer. "I believe he reassigned me because I refused certain... proposals. See, the laird intended…other duties. Which I wasn't willing to perform. I didn't set out to, but—" I faltered.

It was true that I might have possibly been putting myself at risk admitting the details of my story to these powerful brothers. But I was no longer acting purely in the interest of self-preservation. I wanted to see Wilkie again, soon. And from the little I did know about the Mackenzies, I suspected they valued integrity and honor. And so did I. I had committed crimes, aye, but not out of spite or malice. Only because I had been provoked by a bully who had carried out unspeakable wrongs against my family. I could lie to these brothers or tell them half-truths. But I knew them, so far, to be curious, forceful and very thorough. They also had every power over the decision of my fate and whether or not I would be allowed to return to Wilkie. And that, above all else—to be hereafter denied his presence— terrified me.

"But what?" Kade prodded.

"I—I retaliated."

"Retaliated?" asked Kade, highly interested. "In what way?"

"With a small kitchen knife." I touched my stomach to approximate the area where I'd wounded Laird Ogilvie. "There."

They considered this briefly.

"Laird Ogilvie forced himself upon you while you were under his care and protection," the laird repeated, as though to make sure he understood.

"He attempted to, aye. I wasn't amenable to his suggestions."

The two men continued to stare at me with a mixture of confusion, amusement and disbelief. Kade, especially, seemed entertained by my tale. "So you fled, making your way alone across great distances, to find shelter for yourself in a cave on top of a mountain."

"Aye."

"A courageous undertaking," Kade commented.

"A desperate undertaking," I clarified.

Kade studied me, rubbing his hand along his jaw, as though in concentration. "Aye, it appears you were desperate. Even so, the choices you made took a certain element of courage, I daresay. And to present yourself here, to us, in this way, without knowing what our reaction to you might be—also a daring endeavor."

Laird Mackenzie seemed less interested in my personality traits and more concerned about the details of my backstory that would explain not only what had brought about my arrival at their keep, but also what had led to Wilkie's injuries. There was impatience in his tone and his manner when he said, "And we can be grateful for the lass's audacious nerve. If she wasn't bold enough to present herself, Wilkie may not have survived the night." He returned to his line of questioning. "You say you were adopted by an Ogilvie landholder. Who are your parents, by birth?"

"I have no knowledge of that. An Ogilvie farmer— my father—found me, wandering as a child."

Kade rose, and the noise of his weaponry jangled from his movement. He stood with his legs apart and his hard-muscled arms folded across his chest: a man's stance and one that commanded attention. I met his gaze and detected in the slight narrowing of his light blue eyes and the lifted tilt of his chin that he admired my intrepid retaliation against Laird Ogilvie. I could read in his expression a small but unmistakable hint of respect. This detail not only gave me heart, but it also made me feel less afraid. And I was grateful to him for that.

"Roses, the wanderer," said Kade.

"That was many years ago," I said. "I was but a child of three years."

"And still you wander," he commented.

"I would prefer not to wander. I was given no choice."

The laird drew his hand through his dark hair. At that moment his resemblance to his infirmed brother, whose presence I missed so fervently it felt like a physical ache, was remarkable. It occurred to me then that I'd never looked like anyone I knew in the entirety of my life. "Was it you who injured Wilkie?"

I took a deep breath. I didn't want to anger them, and I knew this information would. But there was no way around it. "I stole some fruit from your orchards, and was taking my leave with it, using a ladder I had made. Wilkie was… Wilkie saw me and chased after me."

"She's not only brave but also industrious," commented Kade.

The laird ignored this, waiting for me to continue.

"He chased me to the cave," I said. "I refused to reveal myself to him. He attempted to remove the helmet I wore, with his sword. I struck at it. He struck back, and I reacted."

"By nearly gutting him," Kade pointed out, not without anger. Despite it all, I found that I *wanted* their respect and their approval. I had a fleeting thought that in different circumstances altogether, I might *like* these brothers. The men continued their quest to intimidate me, seemingly having difficulty believing that the person they stared at now was one and the same as the attacker who'd struck down their mighty warrior of a brother. The same brother who had held me firmly locked in his grasp, for comfort, unfathomably. It occurred to me then that Wilkie, in his unconscious mind, had fought to hold me close until he was possessing of his strength once again and could exact his revenge. But I remembered his eyes, and his mouth on my lips and my body as he kissed me, and I felt reassured that this was not his reason for wanting me near.

After several long seconds, the laird continued his line of questioning, "And Ogilvie has no idea where it is you've fled to?"

"Nay. If he knew where I was, he'd come for me. He'll seek revenge upon me, I'm certain of it."

"So you ask us for protection," the laird interpreted curtly. Here was the incense I'd known to expect. But his words, even if blanketed in anger, surprised me. In fact it hadn't occurred to me to ask them for protection. It had been a long time since I'd relied on anyone other than myself for defense of my person. Ogilvie's gated walls had provided little sense of safety for me in the past. I would admit, as I considered it, that the Mackenzies' walls afforded an entirely different sensibility.

"Even after you caused our brother grievous harm with the small sword you carry," followed Kade, less amused now. "Another courageous undertaking, I daresay, considering the size of you."

"He struck me first."

"I find that highly difficult to believe," Kade retorted. "Wilkie would never strike a woman."

"He believed me to be a man," I explained, fearful of Kade's quietly ferocious tone. "I wore a war helmet. I refused to show my face to him. Until after we were both injured. He removed my helmet."

"How severe is your wound?" asked the laird.

I proceeded to roll up the left sleeve of my tunic, where the new dressing was seeped through with blood. I unwound the bandage.

"Clearly he had no intention of harming you seriously," Kade commented.

It was a slice off the top layer of muscle of my upper arm that pained me more than I was willing to admit. Now that Kade mentioned it, I was certain he was right: if Wilkie had intended to injure me fatally, he very likely would have.

"How long had you been traveling, when Wilkie found you?" the laird asked.

"Two days," I said. "I lost my horse when I was caught by a member of Ogilvie's search party. He allowed me to escape."

"He allowed you to escape, even after Ogilvie had ordered you to be returned?" Laird Mackenzie sounded highly irked by the thought of a soldier disobeying the orders of his laird.

"He is known to me," I explained. "He taught me how to fight."

Kade folded his arms across his chest. "And why, pray tell, would a lass have the inclination to learn swordsmanship?"

"To protect myself."

"From?" the laird prodded.

"From Laird Ogilvie, as I explained. I suspected his intentions some time ago. I was afraid of him. And so I asked Ritchie to teach me some skills. In case I needed them."

"Where were you intending to go?" Kade asked.

"I meant to travel to the Macduff lands," I said. "Una Macduff was first of the Ogilvie clan. It was years ago when she married, but I had hoped, if I went to her, she might show me mercy, and allow me to stay. I passed by your keep, and I saw your fields from afar. I had no food for my journey."

"So you decided to thieve from us," said the laird.

"I'll repay you, Laird Mackenzie. I'm not a thief." I corrected myself. "I wasn't a thief. Until yesterday. I offer you my services," I said. "If you have need of a kitchen servant, or I'm skilled in the gardens. I can assist Effie. Ismay, the Ogilvie healer, continued to teach me in quieter moments. I can sew, as well. I'll work until my debt is done."

Laird Mackenzie paced across the stonework in front of the crackling fire. "You really have no idea about your bloodline?" An almost pitying note clung to his question, as though he felt for me in this regard and considered it a great loss.

His mild empathy touched me. And in the aftermath of this intense interrogation, I appreciated their patience and their acceptance of all I had revealed. I had a sudden and wild longing to *belong* to a family like theirs, and to know the kind of affection they so clearly shared for one another. For a very brief moment, I grappled with a desire to show them my tattoo and to reveal my deepest, darkest secret. I wished this horrible mystery could once and for all be solved, whatever the consequences. I imagined sharing it with them might bring me one step closer to them, that they might see that I trusted them, and they might be more inclined to trust me, in return.

But I couldn't bring myself to do it. Such a revelation would likely see me cast out in due haste and with disgust. I would never see Wilkie again, not even to bid him farewell.

So I decided against it. "Nay," I said, thoroughly drained.

The laird stopped pacing. He spoke softly, yet there was a steely authority to his words. "You will remain here, for now, to comfort my brother. It seems you have a calming effect on him, which may help him to heal more quickly. It will be up to him to decide how you'll be employed."

I fell silent, and he continued.

"You will stay in his antechamber, under chaperone, to serve his requests for your company. Your reputation, at this point, is hardly an issue, but if you wish it, your presence in his chambers will remain secretive, aside from myself, Kade, Effie and our sisters, who will assist you with clothing. You will be fed, and you will be under our protection until our brother is fit enough to decide your fate. Our clanspeople, if they ask, will be told that you are an apprentice healer to Effie, hailing from a distant clan...Macduff, perhaps. And you will assist her as she tends to Wilkie's injury." His light gray eyes were unsettlingly cool. "Do you agree to these terms?"

Did I have a choice in the matter? I could return to the cave, to Ogilvie, or travel for weeks across the windswept Highlands without food in the hopes that a long-ago acquaintance might take pity on me.

"Aye."

"'Tis settled, then," said the laird. "Until Wilkie revives."

Once the meeting had concluded, I·was taken by Christie and Ailie back to Wilkie's antechamber, where a bath was being prepared for me. Wilkie's sisters—now that they had been informed of the ongoing arrangements of my stay—were determined to clean me up.

A large bathing tub, filled and steaming, had been placed next to the fireplace, where flames danced invitingly. An embroidered privacy screen had been placed next to the tub, and several luxurious-looking garments had been laid on one of the beds.

Ailie led me to the bath. "Here, Roses. A hot bath will ease you."

I hoped she was right. I could admit that I still was not feeling myself at all.

The scent of soap perfumed the humid warmth of the room. Ailie and Christie laid out a robe and a drying cloth. I did not yet begin to remove my clothing, although it might have been expected of me. Christie touched my hair, stroking it lightly. "Such unusual hair you have, Roses. 'Tis lovely. So long and so fair." I felt out of place being served and attended to; I had always before been the one doing the serving.

Christie remained welcoming and verbose, buoyed by the intrigue of my arrival and my presence. Ailie was quieter, and I suspected she wondered at my ongoing placement in her brother's chambers and what it might mean to him, to her, to all of us. I guessed from her manner and her curious eyes that she could feel it, and so had I, and strongly: an unusualness to the intensity of my connection to Wilkie, and his to me. She seemed to possess an extraordinary perceptiveness, and I found, rather than feeling wary of her study, I felt drawn to her.

The sisters began to help me undress, and I was hesitant, conscious as ever of revealing my tattoo. But the heavy mass of my long hair covered me and I made a point of moving carefully so as not to displace it. I eased my sore body into to the tub.

The hot water was divine and seemed to wash away many of my aches and my fears for the moment. I washed my body and hair with a scented soap, rinsing several times.

"We brought several dresses for you to choose from, Roses," said Christie, easing me immeasurably with the happy, easy sound of her chatter. "I thought the green, to go with your eyes. Aside from your golden-white hair, it was the first thing I noticed about you. The light green of your eyes. But then Ailie thought the pale yellow, to offset the tones of your hair."

"Either one of them will be perfect," I said.

"Do you have a favorite color, Roses? You know I guessed it to be pink, I don't know why. So we brought a pink one, as well."

"It *is* pink," I told her. Not that I had ever had the opportunity to wear a pink dress, or a green one, or a pale yellow one. Course calico fabrics woven from wool by Ogilvie seamstresses were generally varying shades of beige or brown.

"Ailie orders the fabrics from Edinburgh. Occasionally we even make the trip ourselves, with escorts, of course. Kade came with us last time. And Knox the time before that. 'Tis so sophisticated, Edinburgh. I simply love the activity of the place, and the shops. Have you ever been to Edinburgh, Roses?"

"Nay, never." In fact, before this adventure, I had never been away from the Ogilvie keep before, or at least not that I could remember.

The steam of the bath did odd things to my thoughts, hazing them in subtle incoherence, as if I was not wholly aware of this place. I felt almost alarmingly dazed and distant, and I missed Wilkie. My fingertips yearned to feather themselves over the scar-roughened textures of his skin. My mouth watered at the thought of his taste, the exploration of his tongue.

As though in answer, I heard Wilkie's voice, calling to me from his chambers. My name.

"I should go to him," I heard myself say.

I rose from my bath, feeling wildly unsteady, looking for a drying cloth.

"Nay, Roses," urged Ailie, gently easing me back into the bath. "You cannot possibly go to him like *this*. Finish your bath, then we'll take you to him."

But there was a crashing noise coming from Wilkie's chambers, as if he was up and bumping into things. He was looking for me, calling to me.

"I must," I said, stepping from the bath, barely noticing my nakedness and the drip of the bathwater onto the floor, such was the muddled and needy state of my mind. "He needs me."

More banging noises could be heard from Wilkie's chambers.

"What's he *doing* in there?" asked Christie, to no one in particular. I heard another crash and a groan. My name.

I was becoming frantic, making my way toward Wilkie's door as Ailie acquiesced, wrapping a dressing gown around me, not bothering to dry me first. "Here, then, Roses. Wait. Let me tie it." She pulled the tie tight around my waist just as I was able to open the door.

And Wilkie was there, reaching the door at the same time. When he saw me, his eyes widened. He was flushed, his blue eyes blazing. Behind him, several chairs were overturned, and the furs of his bed were disheveled; some of them had fallen to the floor. He was dressed only in his underclothes. His wound was rebloodied from his exertions, and a small line of dark red had bled through the bandages.

Before I could even react to him, I was surrounded in an all-encompassing clinch against his big, fiery body. He buried his face in the damp strands of my hair, weaving his fingers through it almost painfully, inhaling deeply, holding me close as though trying to pull me into himself. "God in heaven, deliver me," he murmured, clearly overcome by delirium. "I need you, angel."

He was unsteady on his feet and leaned us against the wall, swaying slightly as though he might fall.

"Wilkie!" cried his sisters.

I tried to pull away from him, to lead him back to his

bed. But he wouldn't budge. He was thoroughly unconcerned by my robe, my wetness, the inappropriateness of our coiled embrace, and his own aggravated injury. He held on to me tightly, blindly pressing his face into my neck, breathing heavily of my scent.

"'Tis dark indeed without your sunlight, Roses," he rasped gruffly, quietly, into my ear. "Come back to me."

"I'm here, warrior," I said, unsettled both because I wanted to calm him and also because the worried faces and hands of his two sisters were pulling me away from him. They were leading Wilkie back to his bed and me along with him, as he would not loosen his hold on me. They were wiping at his wound and calling for Effie. I felt disengaged from them, focused only on Wilkie and his clear delirium, and also my own, and his strong refusal to follow any request unless I was within his grasp. I held on to his hand as he was eased back into his bed. All was hazy, as though I was channeling Wilkie's fever, following him into it, deeper and deeper, to lead him once again back into the light.

I was aware only that I was holding his hand. Abstractly, I noticed that Christie was settling me into a cushiony chair next to his bed, draping me with furs, giving me a sip of tea, as Effie arrived and once again attended to Wilkie. My focus was entirely on the hold of his hand, the heat and strength of it, the rough texture of his fingers. As my consciousness drifted from me, I grasped his hand as tightly as he was clutching mine. It took effort, maintaining my grip even as darkness overtook me. If I could just hold on to that hand. I would be strong and safe. Warmed by the sun. Alive. And I would not be alone. If I could just *hold on…*

CHAPTER SIX

AND WHEN I AWOKE, I was locked in Wilkie's embrace, still clutching his hand so tightly that my fingers felt numb and sore. I was lying across his chest, and our legs were entwined under a layer of furs. We were alone, and Wilkie slept.

The curtains had been opened, spilling in full-day sunlight. A basin of water had been filled and was lightly steaming, as though it had been sitting there for some time. Food had been laid on the table by the window, along with the now-familiar pot of cooled willowbark tea. I realized I hadn't eaten since I'd wolfed down the stolen fruit. I remembered the three green apples I'd had as I'd walked down the mountain toward Kinloch. It seemed many days ago, and perhaps it was. Time seemed stringy, and I had no idea how much of it had passed as Wilkie and I had slept, flitting in and out of consciousness.

The peaceful scene made me wonder if we were being allowed our private slumber, if I'd been accepted as a fixture in Wilkie's bed, for now, and one that was easier to leave in place.

I tried to rouse Wilkie. He was drowsy, but when I kissed his lips and whispered to him to let me go, he seemed to hear me, and he released his hold.

Food had never tasted so good. I ate a bowl of cold

meat stew, scooping it with chunks of crusty bread. I drank a cup of broth, then some tea.

I still wore the robe Wilkie's sisters had draped around me, which was cinched at the waist with a belt.

I combed the tangles from my hair. I braided and coiled it neatly around my head, gathering it at the back. I fingered a light yellow velvet gown, but before I could remove my robe to dress, I heard Wilkie's voice behind me.

I hadn't realized he'd awoken.

"Come to me, lass. Let me bask in your glow."

He watched me approach him, his blue eyes clear now, with no traces of his earlier haze.

I felt his forehead, and he was cool to the touch. I couldn't resist letting my hand skim the line of his face and his bristled jaw. The roughness of his texture was so unfathomably fascinating to me. I felt changed by this warrior. That first moment I'd looked into his eyes, something inside me had shifted. As if I could suddenly see color, whereas before him all had been muted and dull. But I was unsure whether his feelings were as intense now as my own, so I tread carefully. "You're feeling better now, warrior."

"Aye," he said, and I was relieved to see that the look in his eyes was one of raw affection and a returned fascination. "Your healing powers are potent indeed."

"I haven't healed you enough," I said. "Let me feed you. Are you hungry?"

"Starved." He sat up slightly and was able to move without causing himself to wince.

I brought him some food, and I fed it to him. He ate well. I held the tea to his lips as he drank. His eyes never left my face.

"Your *face,* Roses. Your lips. The color of your hair. Why is your hair so fair?"

I wasn't sure how to respond to this. "I don't know. The sun, perhaps. I spend much of my time out-of-doors. More than I should."

He reached up to finger the bound braid of my hair. "You've a halo, angel."

I fed him another bite of bread. "Yours is a fierce appetite, warrior. 'Tis a good sign. Your health is returning to you."

"I feel as though I haven't eaten for days. How many days, I wonder. How long has it been?"

"Since...?" I knew what he meant; I was fumbling over which part to refer to.

"Since we fought, and fell," he clarified, entirely unperturbed by the recollection.

Now, the very thought of how close he had come to death—and all because *I* had wounded him—was enough to flood me with an ocean of regret. "I'm sorry I wounded you."

He watched me for a moment, and I could not read his expression. "'Twas my own fault, for letting my guard down. I was unusually distracted. Practically blinded, in fact." His mouth quirked at the memory of his own reaction. "'Tis understandable, under the circumstances. Would you not agree?"

He took another bite of bread and waited for my reply, which I did not give. I wasn't sure what answer he was expecting. Instead, I returned his light smile and offered him some tea, which he drank, watching me all the while.

"So," he began. "Let's start at the beginning, and where we left off in the cave, where I believe you made a promise to me, which you have barely begun to up-hold." Again, I was unsure of his meaning, yet I didn't interrupt him. I was, briefly, mesmerized by the shape of his lips as he sipped his drink, and the memory of the gentle brush of them against my own. "Tell me, then," he said. "Why did you flee your Ogilvie clan?"

There was never any doubt I would be wholly honest with Wilkie. But I stumbled over my words nonetheless. "I had to. I—I struck the laird with a kitchen knife. I would have been killed, I think, or banished to the dungeons. I've never been to the dungeons, but I've heard it said that hell itself is preferable."

"Very likely so," he agreed. "You make a habit of wielding blades at hapless men?" His question was calm yet chiding, and I found myself mildly hurt by it. I hadn't set out to injure Laird Ogilvie, or Wilkie; nor had I wanted to.

"Of course not. 'Twas the first time I'd ever struck out at anyone. I only did what I had to do to escape him."

"I'm sure you had good reason to attack the laird of your keep—certainly a crime punishable by death, or worse. You were wise to run." I wasn't entirely pleased with the direction this conversation had taken. And I couldn't decipher the layers of his emotion. Was there anger there or merely curiosity? He continued, "You knifed him intentionally?"

"Aye," I confirmed quietly.

"Why is that?"

I paused. I didn't want him to think badly of me, but he was entitled to the truth. Every truth. I knew it and he knew it. We were bonded already, in a meaningful way. I didn't understand it, but already it was the surest thing about me. I would answer any and all of his questions. My warrior, I was learning, was protective, possessive and extremely direct.

At my brief silence, his eyes visibly darkened as he watched me. He may have guessed at the answer I hesitated to give.

"He wanted to add me to his collection of mistresses," I finally said, "As is probably clear enough by my desertion. I had long thought about attempting to flee from him. But I had nowhere to go. In the end, I decided exile was preferable to servitude of that kind. Work is one thing, captivity quite another."

Wilkie's fist constricted, and the muscles of his arm grew taut and strained. I wanted to ease his reaction, but I thought at this moment it was better to leave him be. In the end, I didn't touch him, leaving my own hands clasped in my lap.

It was some time before he asked his question.

"Were you able to fight him off?" His fist remained clenched. He looked so quietly furious that I almost feared him at that moment.

"Aye," I assured him, but my whispered affirmation was barely audible.

"You succeeded in escaping before he was able to—"

"*Aye,* warrior. He didn't know I was armed. I surprised him with my attack, and I fled immediately."

He lowered his gaze and considered this for a minute or more. Then he raised his eyes to me and I could see there an anxious, tentative question. "So you *never…* agreed?"

I understood what he was asking. "Nay, warrior. Not once. Not to anyone."

His relief was palpable, and his tender smile was the

most beautiful thing I had ever seen on this earth. It touched my heart and stole my breath. "You…are the only one," I told him, meaning to continue, but stopping once the words were spoken. They summed up everything I needed to say. And even as I said them, I felt the now-familiar honey-sweet ache low in my stomach. His hand reached for mine, enveloping both of my own, clasped tightly in my lap. He loosened my grip and held one hand, stroking his thumb lightly across my palm, as though sensing my shame and attempting to soothe it all away.

"You did what you had to do," he said. "It took courage to do what needed doing. I'm not angry with you, lass. How could I be? You're an angel, after all, 'tis it not so?"

In fact I didn't know what I was, or even *who* I was. Or where I had come from. I had a raging urge to show Wilkie my tattoo, to reveal all the dark mystery of my past, to see if this uncommonly intense and sudden bond was stronger than my fear. But I couldn't do it. I was too afraid he would be repulsed by me, that he would no longer want me, that he would cast me back into the bleak darkness of my former life. "Nay. I'm not an angel."

"You're *my* angel," he said, insistent. His expression was affectionate, and his dark-lit blue eyes searched mine for signs that I might be reassured. "You're never to fear me. All right? I just want to learn you."

"All right."

"So, hungry, exiled and alone, you raided our orchard for food."

"Aye," I said. "I'm sorry about that, too."

"Not I." His half smile touched my secret places,

warming me yet further. "If you hadn't stolen from us, I wouldn't have followed you. I was intrigued, aye. I thought you an easy conquest, or I wouldn't have chased you alone. And when you spoke, with your voice undisguised, I had a feeling you were not what you first appeared to be. You looked so…"

I waited for him to finish, and when he didn't immediately reply, my curiosity got the better of me. "So what?"

"So small. So slender. I wasn't expecting you to be quite so fierce."

"I'm sorry," I said, willing myself not to weep at the thought of my ferocity and its outcome.

"Not I," he repeated. "If you hadn't struck me, I wouldn't have struck you, then I wouldn't have removed your helmet and laid eyes on the most beautiful creature in this life, or any other. At that moment, our fates entwined, Roses. I know not why, but I know it to be true—I am bound to you forevermore. There is nothing to regret."

My heart fairly sang at his words. My warrior wanted me here. I could stay with him, at least for a time. *You will be fed, and you will be under our protection until our brother is fit enough to decide your fate.*

"You *did* surprise me at the loch, aye," he said softly.

I blushed again, remembering when and how I had surprised him. I'd wanted to look away from him, but he was too alluring, in my memory and even more so here and now.

"Would you like me to change your dressing, warrior? And wash you?" The heat that flushed my cheeks only burned even more fervently as I realized what my offer might have suggested.

"I would like you to do anything to me that you would like to do."

"I'll wash your hair for you, if you'd like," I said.

"My hair isn't the only thing that's dirty," he teased, but I was too shy to indulge him.

"I've assisted the Ogilvie healer," I said. "I've tended many wounds." If the pretence was that I was Effie's assistant, then I might as well make myself useful. And there was nothing I would rather have been doing in this moment in time—or any other—than tending to Wilkie Mackenzie's needs.

"You sewed me up like an expert," he said. "Effie said she couldn't have done it better herself. And that's saying something—she doesn't give praise lightly, especially when it comes to the healing skills of others."

I began to peel back his bandage, making sure not to open the wound.

"Did you train to be a healer?" he asked.

I told him some of the details of my history and my family, as I had explained to his brothers. He seemed shocked by my admission that not only I but also my mother had been recruited to be Ogilvie's mistress, and that our status had been lowered because of her refusals.

I looked up at him to find him watching me with an inscrutable expression. "You are surprisingly stoic considering the oppression you've endured," he said. "I'm sure I would be more bitter had my family been treated thusly."

I considered this. "I harbor bitterness toward only one person. And he is not here, nor do I hope to ever meet with him again. I know that my parents would be pleased that I had avenged my mother's plight in a small way, and escaped his clutches. I can make peace with that, and do my best to find a life for myself elsewhere."

Wilkie continued to watch me, and I detected in him, as I had in Kade, a sense that he respected not only my honesty, but also my point of view. It occurred to me that I had surprised these brothers, that they might not have expected me to admit to my bold and traitorous reactions to Ogilvie; I also got the sense that they felt my actions entirely justified. I didn't feel as though I *needed* this assurance, but I was grateful for it nonetheless.

Wilkie followed a line of thought, speaking it aloud. "'Tis true that Ogilvie is well known for his fondness for keeping numerous mistresses. So much so that he's never taken a wife. Not a particularly stout plan for the future of the Ogilvie clan, if he produces no legitimate heirs."

"Nay," I agreed, hoping to change the subject away from the man who had been all but my nemesis for several years. "Your wound is healing well, warrior."

It was. The edges of the cut were already beginning to knit together. I walked over to the basin and filled a bowl with the still-warm water. I used a clean cloth to wash the area around the wound, taking care to be gentle with him.

"Your potent healing paste recipe may have saved my life, according to Effie," Wilkie said. "That, along with your sewing skills."

"I could share the recipe with her if she'd like. I've made it often for Ismay."

"Write it down and she can add it to her book."

"I— Well, I don't know how to write. But I can dictate it to her."

"Is that so?" he asked, and there was astonishment in

his voice, and maybe a thread of pity. "Were you never taught to write, lass?"

"Nay," I said quietly.

"Can you read?"

"My mother started teaching me once, but there was too much other work to be done. We never had enough time for the lessons."

He touched a fingertip to my chin and tipped my face up to him. "Well, that, sweet Roses, is something we could remedy."

I couldn't help smiling at him. "You're going to teach me to read, warrior?"

"Aye," he said smugly, as though he'd found a new mission in life. "That I am."

I felt overjoyed at the thought of Wilkie teaching me, making an effort for me, and spending his time with me in any capacity at all. If his intention was to teach me to read: that would require *time*. My future, at least for the short term, might not be daunting and unknowable; it could be charmed, if Wilkie was near. "I would very much like that."

Once Wilkie's wound was cleaned, I smeared the healing salve across it with the lightest touch so I wouldn't pain him.

"Your touch," he said softly. "'Tis so light, yet so sure." The husk to his voice and the words themselves fed a curious sensation into my lower stomach, not one of lack of food but of longing.

And I was beginning to understand what my body was craving.

"If I bring the basin to this bedside table, can you lean over it?" I said.

"Aye."

With some effort, both with the weight of it and the fullness of it, especially with my still-sore arm, I carried the basin to his bedside. He adjusted his position, so he could lean over the large bowl. I held his head and unwound his braids, then I used a smaller bowl to wet his long hair, savoring the feel of its thick, silky texture. I used some soap to scrub his hair, and I massaged his head gently, which caused him to sigh.

"Your hair is so lovely, warrior. Thick and soft."

"Is it, now? How should I take that? A warrior with lovely hair."

"'Tis so very black. Why is your hair so black?" I teased him, mimicking his earlier question.

"I don't know. The loch, perhaps," he mused, smiling. "'Tis inky black, and I've taken a swim in it almost every morning of my life."

"Isn't it cold?"

"Invigorating," he corrected. "Good for the constitution, according to my father, who may also have had something to do with the color of my hair. His was equally black."

I wanted to ask him about his father, but I knew the former Laird Mackenzie had been killed a year earlier in the ongoing battle between the Campbell clan and the occupiers of Ossian Lochs, the king's expansive Highland estate; this had been discussed regularly by Ogilvie and his men. I didn't want to upset Wilkie or to stir up sad memories. I was touching my warrior, holding his head, running my hands through his hair, and I preferred to relish the moment. There would be time for that discussion—I hoped—another day.

I rinsed, making sure to wash him clean of all the slippery soap. Finding a cloth, I dried his hair and combed it with my fingers, and braided the two small braids at his temples.

"There, that's better," I said.

He lay back on his pillows.

"Would you like me to wash your hands?" I asked him. Ismay always reminded me to wash patients' hands; she insisted it was a necessary step to prevent infection.

"If it would please you," he said, his blue eyes smoldering with heat and teasing encouragement. When I hesitated, he added, "It would very much please *me*."

I squeezed the excess of soapy water from the cloth and gently washed his hands. The look in his eyes as I carefully cleaned his hands—that, along with my own unabashed desire—led me then to wash his sculpted arms, his bare chest and his stomach, where he was ticklish. *I love that he's ticklish,* I thought.

"I am allowed to be here with you, like this?" I said. "Where are your sisters?"

"I assured them I am capable of chaperoning you myself, and asked them to take their leave."

"Is that what you are?" I couldn't help but smile. "My chaperone?"

"Aye. My first task was to ensure that you were warm in the night." His crooked grin tugged at my heart.

"Well, you succeeded very well in that task. I can assure you of that. I may never have passed a warmer, more comfortable night."

"And to keep you safe from would-be intruders. Well-protected."

I let the wet cloth slide over his shoulder and down the hard surface of his brawny arm. "Also a task very well executed. I commend you for that. I felt very safe indeed."

"Next, 'tis my duty to make sure you have been well fed."

"I have not had such a feast since…well, for a very long time," I told him, quite truthfully.

"As your chaperone," he said, "I take my duties very seriously, you must understand. I'll not have a single need of yours overlooked."

"You are very thorough," I agreed, enjoying his game. "All of my needs have been admirably attended to." I had washed all of him above the waist. I laid my cloth down by the basin. I fitted a new dressing into place, and he sat up as I wound the bandage around his torso, allowing my fingers to graze across his skin. Once his bandage was secured in place, I pushed him gently back to lie against his pillows.

"I thank you, m'lady, for your healing touch," he said, bowing his head to me in a gesture of playful formality. "But there is one more detail I believe needs addressing."

"I wish I *could* heal you with my touch," I murmured, drawing my fingers around the edges of his new dressing, registering only then his last statement. "What is this detail you speak of? There is nothing else I need."

"I'm just getting to that," he said. A hint of amusement played across his lips. "Keep touching me. I feel better already."

I let my fingers wander past the confines of his bandage to caress his chest once again with my bare hands, exploring with some fascination the roughness of him, the broadness of his shoulders, the intricate play of muscle and sinew beneath his bronzed skin. Such a masculine creature he was, hard and angular and battle-scarred, so different from my own pale curves.

He continued to watch me with lazy interest as I carried out my investigation. I felt the long strands of his damp hair, which I smoothed back from his neck and his face.

"Your sisters are very kind," I said.

"My sisters shouldn't have kept you away from me for so long. If they hadn't, I wouldn't have had a need to at least attempt to charge into your chambers and carry you back to me."

"You only need to call me and I'll come to you, warrior."

"Come to me now."

I smiled. "I'm already here with you."

"Come closer to me."

I leaned up against the side of him that wasn't injured. I kissed his bristly cheek, reveling in the soft-rough texture against my lips. I kissed along his jawline and up to the corner of his mouth. He turned his face just slightly, so his lips barely brushed against mine. We sat there like that for several moments, playing this lightest of kisses. My fingers continued to trail over his skin.

"You kill me with your sweetness," he whispered.

He licked my lips open, parting them, and his kisses grew in urgency, his tongue becoming more demanding, probing and expressive, as though tasting the nuanced flavors of an exotic fruit he wanted more of. Catching his tongue, I gently sucked it into my mouth. Wilkie made a deep, primal sound, then he pulled back, and his eyes were dark and lit with his fierceness.

My heart leaped in twin beats, in my chest and lower.

His voice was gravel-edged when he spoke. "In my dream, Roses, you offered your breasts to me."

I fell silent. Did he want me to answer him? Did he want me to confirm that I, wholly captivated by him, had indeed committed this wonton, beautiful act, an act that provided me with an inspiration to stay with him, to heal him, to do anything he asked of me from that moment forward?

We remained, for a moment, locked in a connective deep gaze that brought the pulse of my heart to the surface of my skin.

"Reveal yourself to me," he said. His voice was low, roughened with dark, masculine authority.

I paused. But I remembered the feeling of his mouth upon me, in the cave, as I held his head in my lap. The gentle suction, the melting revelation of it. I was so enticed by him, I could think of little else. In my former life of struggle and servitude, of distinct lines between right and wrong that were drawn, then adjusted by the people who made them, I might have wondered at myself, at my own brazen allowances. But here, with Wilkie, those lines felt far away and hollow, as if they belonged to someone else. I wanted to please him. Watching his eyes, I slowly parted the top of my robe, opening the garment, revealing myself to him. I felt his gaze upon my sensitive skin, and the tips, softened by the warmth of his body, peaked into aching buds.

"Your plush, golden beauty is more than I can bear, Roses," he whispered.

My breasts felt full and heavy. I wanted him to touch me.

"Put them to my mouth so I can taste of your sweetness," his husked voice commanded.

I hesitated only for a moment, and his eyes flashed in challenge. I did as he asked, leaning to him, and he took my breasts in his roughcast hands. He caressed them, very gently plumping them together, so my nipples were close to his mouth. He breathed on me, kissing me, tracing around the peak with his tongue, one, then the other. Drawing a nipple into his mouth, he licked softly from within the warm, wet embrace. The pleasure was heavy and hot, liquid in its effect, swirling from the warm fire of his mouth into my body, to the low pit of my stomach, to the soft throbbing in my most secret places. I heard myself moan with the pleasure of it.

"Aye, my Roses," he said huskily. "Moan for me, and only me."

My moans seemed to excite him. His mouth became more insistent, and one of his hands moved to the back of my upper thigh, gliding across the skin there and higher. Immobilized by the mind-numbing effects of his grip, I was powerless to resist him. He roughly pushed the hem of my robe up to my lower back. His hand smoothed lower, holding behind my knee, which he adjusted outward just a little, so my knees were slightly apart. Taking one of my nipples into his mouth, he drew strongly while he explored my skin with his still-wandering hand, traveling higher, between my legs, where his fingers touched gently, so very intimately, along every contour. He felt me tense and responded by tightening his grip and tugging with his mouth in a dueling sustained rhythm so the rolling sensation built without pause. I had no choice but to relax into the compounding pleasure. He found the delicate folds of my entrance, lingering, using the moisture there to silkily caress me. And then he centered his fingers on the nub just in front, rubbing softly with his hand, playing me while he sucked my swollen breasts.

I felt blinded, with only Wilkie's fingers and his mouth as anchors to this world. I gave myself over completely to his power, which drew pleasure out of my body the likes of which I had never imagined. His fingers tugged, circled and dipped only barely into my entrance, teasing miraculous sensation that eased, then rose, then eased back and rose again, each time climbing higher. And higher. The very height of the impending rise seemed impossible, and I squirmed against him, unsure if I could handle any more of this. I didn't know if I could survive the swell that was being promised. But Wilkie held me in place, squeezing more tightly, tugging more strongly, increasing his pace. The pulls of his mouth and his fingers worked together, until I was overcome. The pleasure peaked, and held, searing my senses with such an ecstatic overload that I sobbed with it, saying Wilkie's name to him. Pleading. Digging my fingernails into his skin. The peak fragmented, then, coiling into clenching bursts that gripped on a heart-breaking emptiness. The waves rolled, so enchanting, so very sublime, that I went limp against him, basking in the lingering bloom of feeling.

I could say nothing. I could feel nothing except the softly clenching core of my body and the warmth of Wilkie's chest as his arms wrapped me close to him.

We lay there for some time. I settled in and out of a drowsy, enchanted doze as our hands and our mouths continued to touch and to taste. I felt fluid and slippery, and I thought of Wilkie's own pleasure, of his own burn. Could I do to him what he had done to me—twice? I felt his hardness through the cloth of my robe, which he had pulled back over my legs to cover me. I was inexperienced and shy, but I wanted to try. I let my hand that rested on his stomach slide lower, to barely touch the leather of his trews.

But it was then that I heard the distant sound of people, down the hall, maybe, or on the staircase.

I pulled away from him, panicked at the thought of being found as we were. I had no doubt Laird Mackenzie was well aware that I had, indeed, slept in Wilkie's bed. If he hadn't ordered for me to be left in Wilkie's fevered embrace, he had at least sanctioned the arrangement. Still, if he discovered us here, as we were, it might cause him to second-guess his decision.

"I should go back to the antechamber," I said.

"I'll have you returned to me soon. For now, aye, it might be best if you take your leave. If my brother finds you half naked in my bed, and awake, he might react badly. He doesn't take well to scandal."

"Am I a scandal, warrior?"

"You are much more than a scandal, lass," he said enigmatically, grasping my hand and pulling me back to him, kissing me deeply on the lips, so desiringly, I felt the burning pit inside me flare upward. *I wanted more of him. Much, much more.*

But the commotion was getting louder and closer.

I withdrew from Wilkie, glancing back at him as I took my leave. He looked bereft, his fierceness overlaid with a kind of longing. And I felt as lost as he looked, at the prospect of this small separation from him.

"I'll seek you out as soon as I'm able to," he said.

I nodded, savoring one last glance at him, the swarthy, muscular, brawny shape of his shoulders, his beautifully built chest, tapering down to his taut stomach, his hips, where his loosened trews were slung low.

He smiled at my lingering glance and continued to hold his hand out to me as I slipped from his grasp and ran to the door.

"'Til soon, angel," he said.

I shut the antechamber door behind me just in time. I could hear the commotion burst into Wilkie's room not seconds after.

The antechamber was empty. The fire burned low, and the bathing tub and privacy screen had been removed. I wondered where Christie was. I busied myself with straightening up the beds and deciding which gown I would wear. I touched the fine fabric of the dresses they'd left for me, astounded by the careful workmanship and the quality. A new shift had been laid out, too, exquisite in its soft filmy fabric. I had never worn clothing such as these beautiful garments. They seemed too fine, too luxurious. I worried at being overly conspicuous in one of these gowns. But then I realized that my tattered oversize menswear was far more peculiar than a beautifully made noble's dress. After some deliberation, I chose the light yellow gown. The green one was lovely, too, and the pink. But the crushed yellow velveteen was simply too soft and luxurious to resist.

I heard Kade's voice, quite clearly; he had a distinctive character to his voice, deep and slightly rasped. "He's awake, and looking almost himself. The fever has broken."

"Can you rise, Wilkie?" I was familiar enough now to identify this speaker as Laird Mackenzie. "Storms have been brewing. There's much to discuss."

"What storms?" asked Wilkie.

That I could hear their voices even through the wooden barrier between the two chamber rooms was somewhat distressing. I didn't want to eavesdrop, yet I had little choice. These were big, tough, important men, and they had no compunction to speak in quieted tones. I could distract myself. I took off my robe and slid the new shift Ailie and Christie had left for me over my head. It fit perfectly. I slipped on the yellow gown, and I adjusted it to fit my shape. It fit me almost too snugly in the chest—somewhat more low-cut than I was used to—and slightly more loosely at the waist. But it was a beautiful dress, draping gracefully in generous folds to the floor. I smoothed my hair, reattaching the pins, and I put on my old, worn boots, which I was glad to see were covered by the material of the dress I wore. Despite my attempts to block out the men's conversation, I heard every word of it as I fitted my new outfit into place.

After a lengthy pause, the laird said, "Sit, brother. You're still woozy. We can talk here." I wondered if Wilkie had tried to rise and pained himself. I wished I could return to him, but I knew it was not my place to interrupt them.

"I can't say I've ever seen you quite so content to remain bedridden, brother," commented Kade. "Usually you'd be back at the yards by now, barking orders at everyone within earshot."

Wilkie exhaled a soft chuckle. "Aye. It seems I'm uncommonly comfortable in this particular sickbed."

"Be that as it may," the laird interrupted, as though the topic annoyed him, "the sooner you're on your feet again, the better. Ogilvie's men approached our guards on the day of Roses's arrival, and several different search parties have visited since then, some more than once. Inquiring, as it were, about a lass with distinctive blond hair, and wearing the clothing of men at last sighting. Laird Ogilvie is most interested in having her returned to him, and promptly. His men scour the Highlands for her."

The mention of Ogilvie's name jolted me. I knew he would search for me. But still, to hear it described in Laird Mackenzie's war-hardened voice, it jarred me. In Wilkie's arms, I had felt safe and comforted, protected. But there were no guarantees. Wilkie was not the foremost decision-maker in this keep, after all; Laird Mackenzie was.

Wilkie's reply was stiff and laced with anger. "And what did you tell them?"

When the laird continued, his voice contained traces of forced composure, as though trying to mollify Wilkie's reaction or expression. "I sent them away," the laird said evenly. "I told them we had seen no one by that description. But I would prefer not to be spinning lies. Or to be harboring a fugitive who has inspired a most fervent search by Ogilvie. His guards spoke of his bloodlust. He wants the lass found immediately and has threatened to kill members of his search party if she is not returned to him. 'Tis a potentially volatile situation, as she was seen by a number of people in and around our keep. Word has a way of finding its way to wherever it wants to go."

"Fugitive," Wilkie repeated, as though the word left a bitter taste in his mouth.

Kade relayed the information I had given them earlier. "She's a kitchen servant of Ogilvie's, Wilkie. She stabbed him with a kitchen knife when he—"

"I'm aware of all that," Wilkie said, cutting him off. "She told me of it herself."

"She's a thief and a liability," said Laird Mackenzie. "If we harbor her here, and Ogilvie gets wind of it, he'll stop at nothing to retrieve her. Including storming our keep. His guard so much as confirmed it."

"Then we fight Ogilvie," said Wilkie bluntly. "We defend what's ours. He has no claim on her."

"In fact, he does," said the laird. "She's not *ours,* Wilkie. She's one of his clan."

"Who he's bound by duty, therefore, to protect," Wilkie countered. "If he fails in his honor by attacking her virtue, then he forfeits all rights to her."

There was a brief bout of silence then, as though something was being considered.

"I propose we escort her to Macduff," Kade suggested. "If—"

"She stays with me," Wilkie said, a fierce quiet determination coloring his words.

"Wilkie—" the laird began.

"She's mine," Wilkie interrupted.

"You intend to keep her as a mistress, brother?" asked the laird. "You do realize a contingent of Morrison's five daughters and two nieces arrive in less than a week as our guests, to be presented to you as prospective brides. Laird Morrison is ailing and wants a younger replacement, and he has no sons. He also rules one of the largest landholdings in the Highlands. Adjacent to our own."

"I'm aware of Morrison's credentials, Knox," said Wilkie steadily. "What I'm not certain of, though, is why you feel the need to incessantly list them to me."

"You will be master of your own keep, Wilkie," the

laird continued. "And expand the Mackenzie name and holdings in the process."

"It seems I have four siblings to assist me in that very endeavor," countered Wilkie, and his voice was gentler when he said, "Two years have passed, Knox. 'Tis time for you to remarry. I can honor my duty as a Mackenzie by swearing my allegiance to my brother and defending my clan's keep just as effectively as I can by marrying a Morrison."

"In fact," said the laird, "you can honor your duty as a Mackenzie by securing the alliance of our army with that of a potentially strong neighboring army. Your allegiance to your brother—and your laird—requires you to act with the best interests of your clan in mind. And those interests include marrying a daughter of Laird Morrison."

"You and Kade can feast at the Morrison buffet. I have no interest in any of those heifers." That Wilkie's insolence was even tolerated by the laird made it seem more apparent than ever before that these brothers shared a bond that went deeper than many. Wilkie's disagreement in the face of his brother's clear orders was, for the moment, indulged. But I couldn't help but wonder if Wilkie's refusals would carry much weight. I admit that I felt distressed by this overheard conversation, but I had no expectations beyond my next encounter with Wilkie. I had no plans but to learn to read. I had no hopes but for one more kiss.

"You weren't quite so disparaging of one of those heifers—Maisie, was it?—last time we visited their keep and met at least some of them," Kade mused. "I do recall the two eldest were not in attendance that weekend. Yet the rest of them were."

"Which is why I can emphatically confirm that I am not interested," Wilkie retorted.

"Wilkie," the laird began again. "You are aware that we are in discussions with Laird Morrison regarding your betrothal to Maisie, his third-eldest daughter."

"Why the third-eldest?" asked Kade, with a jauntiness to his question that suggested he already knew the answer. "Has Morrison given up attempting to marry off his eldest daughter?"

"It seems she has decided to join a nunnery," Laird Mackenzie said, sounding less than riveted by the topic.

Kade, as I was now becoming accustomed to, sounded almost amused by a subject that might have been less than amusing to anyone but him. "Aye, I suppose two or three failed attempts at marriage would be enough to convert anyone. But what of the second-eldest, then? Stella, isn't it? Shouldn't *she* be next in line for marriage? You should be so lucky, brother. I've never seen her, but I believe she's the reputed beauty of the group. I've heard her admired upon more than one occasion."

Laird Mackenzie continued, "Maisie has expressed a distinct, insistent preference for Wilkie, and has commissioned her father to allow *her* to be the one to secure the alliance. The one named Stella has agreed to it. Laird Morrison explained in his last letter that Stella is somewhat of an introvert. *Reclusive,* I believe, was the word he used. She is not ambitious enough to override Maisie's requests for Wilkie's hand. Not only that, but I can tell you, Wilkie, that Laird Morrison is somewhat incensed that you stole Maisie's virtue at your last visit and have not yet proposed to her. He's most urgent, upon those grounds more than any other, to have this betrothal secured. He mentioned her concern over… Well, in case an heir has already become part of the equation."

"First of all," Wilkie said, sounding highly irritated, "believe me when I say I was not the first to have touched her virtue."

"Yet you admit you may have left her in a compromised position," the laird said.

"She put herself into any number of positions, despite my attempts to restore her self-respect," Wilkie replied. "In fact, I was attempting to take my leave and told her that several times, and quite emphatically, at that. She was… I won't go into details, but suffice to say it felt more honorable in the moment to oblige her than to refuse her. Yet I made it perfectly clear to her that nothing would come of it. I made no promises. And as for an impending heir 'tis not an issue." He sounded somewhat uncomfortable when he clarified his point. "I made very sure *that* would *not* come to pass."

These details were distressing to me, to be sure. But it was hardly surprising that a man like Wilkie Mackenzie would be highly sought-after, in every regard. To learn that he was in fact on the very verge of being betrothed to another woman sent a cold chill through my bones, but it didn't settle. After all, I was used to being an outsider and to having little value, to having nothing to hope for beyond my limited realm. Wilkie had introduced hope and joy and beauty into my life, and in highly concentrated form. And this tumble of beauty was so new and so fresh that it lingered—insistently—even in the face of this unwelcome information.

"Regardless," the laird said, becoming increasingly agitated. "Her father is most interested in securing an alliance, and soon. If you don't favor Maisie, then choose one of the others. He has no less than seven daughters and nieces to choose from. He made a point of stating that you have the choice of either of the sisters—any, in fact. Stella is less than willing, yet the laird is more interested in securing this alliance than indulging the whims of his daughters."

Kade managed to sound entertained. "*That* would ensure harmonious family relations between the sisters."

"You can take your pick, Wilkie, is what he was implying. But be sure of this—you *will* marry one of the Morrisons, and I'm afraid that's the end of it," the laird proclaimed. "The arrangements have already begun. They arrive next week, and if Laird Morrison insists on it, the marriage will take place during their visit. This is not news to you, brother. You agreed to it some time ago."

"In fact I never agreed to it," Wilkie said. "I agreed to *consider* it. You, of all people, Knox, know that I have had second thoughts about marrying a woman I have no feelings for—"

"You had *feelings* of one sort or another—" interrupted the laird.

But Wilkie countered the laird's interruption with his own. "I did *not* have feelings for her. We shared a brief moment in time. One that has now passed. Let me remind you that marriage may not be the only way to secure an alliance with the Morrison army. I have always taken your point of view to heart, brother, and followed your orders dutifully. But I am having difficulty with this one. I beg you to consider other options."

Wilkie paused, and I got the impression there were layers of emotion at work between the brothers. Wilkie's voice sounded heavier, more grave, when he continued. "I agreed," he repeated, "to consider marriage to a Morrison, out of respect to you, and our father. But I am thinking of our mother when I tell you this—now it seems I have another preference."

This was the first I'd heard any of the Mackenzies mention their mother, and though Wilkie mentioned her with fondness in his voice, I couldn't help but wonder what he meant by this comment.

"Wilkie," the laird continued, now somewhat exasperated but clearly affected by Wilkie's mention of their parents. "You have the choice of any woman of noble blood in all of Scotland. Yours for the taking." His voice was so low I could barely hear his next statement. "I've made allowances to speed your recovery. Take what you need of her. Do what you must. But this lass is not—"

Wilkie cut off the laird's statement before he could finish. "Cupid's arrow has pierced my heart."

"That was Cupid's sword that pierced you," replied Kade dryly, "and you can be thankful that it missed your heart."

The laird had heard enough, apparently. There was the sound of movement. "The decision is final, Wilkie, but if you insist, we'll continue this discussion further when you're fully possessed of your judgment," he said, as though by now thoroughly convinced that his brother was still plagued by the delirium of fever. "Kade and I have a meeting to attend. We'll leave you to your rest. And I suggest you make the most of it. We may have need to fight sooner than we thought."

"What do you mean?" asked Wilkie, rather testily.

"The Campbell rebellion," explained Kade. "'Tis escalating once again, and quickly."

"I'll come with you," Wilkie said.

"Are you sure you're up to it?" Kade asked. "You—"

"Aye," Wilkie replied. "Get me a shirt."

I could hear the sound of rustling clothing as Wilkie dressed, cursing only once from the effort. The laird said nothing further, perhaps still embroiled in his annoyance over Wilkie's stubbornness. Their footsteps retreated as they strode down the hall to the staircase and below.

I COLLAPSED INTO A CHAIR by the dying fire. I had much to think about. For now, I would savor the memory of each and every succulent sensation of him, and look forward to the next stolen moment.

Christie came to me, entering the antechamber quietly, as though wary of being observed. As soon as she saw me, she stopped, agog, staring for several seconds at my new presentation.

"Well, *that's* certainly an improvement," she said, in that kind but honest way she had. "You'll put Wilkie in a state, to be sure, when he sees you." Christie smiled at the thought.

She sat with me, contemplating my somber expression.

"What are you thinking, Roses? You had such a thoughtful look on your face when I interrupted you."

I smiled at her, attempting to dislodge my own worries. "'Tis nothing, Christie."

She leaned back in her chair, watching the flicker of the fire for a moment. I could see she had no intention of letting me off so easily. "That was some commotion the other night, was it not?" she began. "Wilkie calling to you, and very nearly barging into your chambers as a man possessed. I've never seen anything like it in all my life. I've certainly never seen my carefree brother behave in such a way. Not a once."

I paused and decided to indulge her curiosity. I wanted to trust her and had a strong feeling that I could. "Aye," I agreed. "I believe he was overcome by his delirium."

"I *believe*," Christie said, "he has been overcome by *you*, Roses. You should know that Wilkie has never allowed a woman into his own chambers before. He's an intensely private person, for all his social tendencies. He'll visit, aye, and he receives many invitations." She paused, as though considering how to delicately express what she wanted to say. She was treading more carefully than I had yet seen her do. "Yet he is not one to *issue* invitations, if you get my meaning."

I understood what she was implying. And I couldn't help but confess: "I wasn't so much as issued an invitation, I'm sure. It was more of an order, I believe, to help him and assist his recovery." Yet it was far more than that; I knew it, and Christie did, too. In my own mind, Wilkie's request to have me near was much more than an invitation. He wanted me and needed me. In those deathly, fevered, magical moments at the cave and beyond, we had been an inexplicable necessity to one another. Our fight and our blood had bonded us. This was a realization that pleased me but also worried me. I knew how indelible that bond felt to me: permanent and alarmingly all-encompassing. But I wondered if Wilkie felt it as intensely as I did. I already felt owned by him. As if he had issued me with a new tattoo, this one inked to my heart. Could our connection last here in

Wilkie's reality? Or would it be forced aside, as Wilkie's duty took precedent?

Without meaning to, I spoke my question aloud. "I wonder what is to become of me."

"I don't know, Roses," Christie replied. "Only Wilkie—and you—can decide that."

"Perhaps he'll keep me close until he tires of me," I commented, feeling somewhat dejected at the errant thought. Would I become a kitchen servant of the Mackenzie clan, or would I be cast out, escorted perhaps— or perhaps not—to the Macduffs'? Christie couldn't answer me, nor confirm her brother's feelings either way, but it felt somewhat cathartic to voice my very real concerns. "Or perhaps he'll want me as a mistress after he weds one of Morrison's brigade of daughters and nieces. Maybe he'll take me with him to the Morrison keep when he becomes their new laird. Or perhaps he'll choose some other heiress to marry, as is his birthright."

"I wish I could tell you what you want to hear, Roses. But none of these decisions are mine to make, I'm afraid. 'Tis all in the hands of my brothers."

"My future is uncertain indeed," I agreed, appreciating her sympathetic manner, even if her words offered no comfort.

"Would you even be *willing* to become Wilkie's mistress? 'Tis not a particularly glamorous prospect, Roses, and a woman possessing of your beauty might prefer to wait for a husband of her own, rather than to share a man with his wife—and perhaps even other mistresses—waiting for his visit, and meanwhile foregoing a marriage and legitimate children of your own. You do have a choice."

Ah, dear Christie. I loved her already for her candid take on each and every matter, even if the matter being discussed was the man of my heart and the unlikelihood of my ever being allowed to marry him.

But Christie was right. Of course I *did* have choices. I'd been given no choice in the matter of becoming Ogilvie's mistress, yet I had chosen another path, despite the significant difficulties that choice had introduced. I could leave Wilkie, as I'd left Ogilvie, and sneak away and make my way north as I had originally intended.

But the prospect of becoming Wilkie's mistress was, most certainly, a very different one to becoming Ogilvie's.

"What do you *want* to become of you, Roses?" asked Christie.

Her question caught me somewhat off guard, and I took a moment to consider it. What *did* I want? This was a path I rarely chose to wander. My personal wants were not something I reflected on often; they were largely inconsequential in the grand scheme of my life. Work, servitude, survival, the needs of others: these were the only priorities I had ever known. What I *wanted* was a frivolous indulgence I rarely pondered. Yet I did so now. I had nothing else to do, mainly, divulging my innermost thoughts to Christie as I waited here for Wilkie to return.

"What do you want for your life, Roses?" asked Christie, mirroring a question I was asking myself at that very moment.

"I would like my own garden to tend," I told her with utter honesty, and she listened with quiet, eager interest. "A small house, like my father's house, made homely by the loving attentions of my mother, surrounded by the acres he worked." I paused, thinking. "Safety. Belonging. The freedom to work and express my talents for the good and prosperity of my clan and my own."

Christie was quiet, watching me, so I continued.

"I think these are lofty aspirations, indeed, for someone like me," I said. "I'm a servant with no past and no family." I stopped, wondering if I was revealing too much.

"Tell me more, Roses," encouraged Christie. "I won't share your secrets, unless you'd like me to. Wilkie will get them out of you anyway. He's not one to take nay for an answer. And he's most interested in you, 'tis clear enough."

"'Tis not something I've had much need to consider before, Christie. For many years, all day, every day, I've been told what to do and when to do it. To attend to menial, undesirable tasks that no one else wanted to perform. I lived in the crowded servants' quarters, adjacent to the kitchens. And I'll likely be relegated to similarly damp depths at Macduff's, if I make it there, or somewhere yet unknown."

Christie listened, wide-eyed. "Do you *want* to go to Macduff's?" she asked.

"Not really. I had no other choice but to head in that direction, on my journey. I don't have acquaintances beyond clan Ogilvie, except the one. But I've heard nothing very positive about Macduff's keep, except that there are especially good hunting grounds along their northern border, according to Ogilvie's men. They described Macduff as old, crotchety and not particularly welcoming…and his son as a massive bearded ruffian who delights in showing off his impressive strength."

"Aye, I've heard similar things," she commented. "They don't sound particularly appealing."

Nay, it was true. Those details, I could admit, had whispered their warnings once or twice. But that was at a time when I'd had no other reasonable alternative.

Now, it seemed, I might.

"You could stay here, Roses," Christie said, following my thoughts. "You may have no choice in the matter, in fact, if Wilkie gets his way."

Kinloch, with its vast, carefully tended fields bursting with abundance, with its order and its warmth: it was the most inviting place I had ever seen or imagined. Ogilvie's assessment of Laird Mackenzie was less threatening to me, too, now that I'd met him for myself. The laird was gruff, aye, but he seemed fair, and I hadn't detected cruelty in his manner, even if he was as intimidating as any man I had ever met. Kade was not at all as severe as he had been described, although the descriptions of his armory had hardly done it justice. That the Mackenzies had so far shown me tolerance only added to Kinloch's appeal. Wilkie's sisters, to be sure, were some of the kindest, most welcoming people I had ever met. And all these details were only a crown to the most urgent desire I had ever known: Wilkie.

But the decision of whether I would stay or go could ultimately be made by only one person: Laird Mackenzie, who was, for now, indulging his brother's peculiar new obsession. I detected in the laird's manner that he was hopeful that Wilkie's affliction would soon wear off, that Wilkie would keep me in his bed until he tired of me. I had a strong feeling that if he could talk some sense into his delusional brother, Laird Mackenzie would likely order me away at his first opportunity.

"What do *you* want, Roses?" I detected in Christie's repeated question a prod for confirmation, as though she had Wilkie's interests in mind and was concerned about the suddenness and strength of his reactions to me.

And I could assure her in this way without hesitation. It was an easy question to answer. I wanted Wilkie to come back to me, to lie with me, to kiss me again. To make me cry and fly and burn with his beautiful, insistent, stunning touches. And I wanted to pleasure him, too, as he had done to me. I knew there was much more to these touches than what he had so far given me.

I was curious.

And I was willing.

My desires surprised me with their vehemence.

"I want *him*," I whispered.

Aye, what I *wanted* was Wilkie Mackenzie. Something I knew I could never have.

CHAPTER SEVEN

AILIE ARRIVED. SHE WAS dressed in a cream-colored gown of an unusual design, with half sleeves and a fitted section at the waist of a different, light green material, which flattered her slim figure. Ailie's hair had escaped its bindings, and curling wisps of it framed her face, giving her a young, carefree look that was slightly removed from her usual poise and elegance.

She noticed my outfit right away, pulling me gently by the hand so I was standing before her, and she circled me, taking in all the finer details of my outfit, as though responsible for making sure all was exactly as it should be.

"You look beautiful, Roses," she said. "The gown fits you well. Here, though, let me adjust the waist. 'Tis a wee bit looser than I intended." She pulled a needle and thread from a small bag she wore, I would learn, almost always. She began to sew at the mid seam at the back of the dress. With my hair tied up, I was glad I had checked to make sure my tattoo was securely covered by the dress.

"You'll get used to it, Roses," said Christie. "She adjusts people's clothing all the time and is, in fact, sought out by all the ladies of the clan for her flair with tailoring. 'Tis her obsession, though, so we humor her."

"Humor me, indeed, dear sister. Who was it that

woke me at an early hour this morning to seek my advice and my skill when in fact you were assigned as Roses's chaperone and were instructed to check in on her on a regular basis?"

I felt the color rise to my cheeks immediately. I was devoutly grateful that Christie's attentions had been otherwise diverted.

"Aye, well, here I am now, and look, she's fine," said Christie. "Wilkie's up and about and Roses didn't need a chaperone at all, did you, Roses? When I found her, she was confined to the antechamber alone."

"Perhaps Roses needs a *new* chaperone, and one that's not quite so easily distracted," Ailie said. "There," she added, satisfied that the adjustments were suitably executed. "Much better." She smoothed my dress into place and eyed the garment critically. "She won't need a chaperone except at night, soon, anyway. Wilkie will no doubt return to training today or tomorrow, and Roses will be busy with Effie. We've been instructed to take you to the healing quarters now, Roses. Has Knox told you that that's to be your cover, while you're here at Kinloch? To distract rumors. We thought we might say you hail from the Macduff clan, and that you're a healing apprentice, since you do have some skill."

"Aye," said Christie. "Since it's the farthest lands from our own, few of our clanspeople have any association with the Macduffs, so any gossip will likely fade away before it can be confirmed."

I nodded. "The laird informed me," I said. "I'll be honored to be Effie's apprentice, and I hope I can be useful to her."

The sisters led me down the hall, and we descended a back staircase. I couldn't help noticing once again the clean, orderly appearance of every aspect of the Mackenzie manor. The candles that lit the staircase had even been scented, and a citrus and spice flavor lingered in the air. We walked down a dimly lit hallway, where several chambermaids passed us, carrying fresh sheets. They eyed me curiously.

I guessed that we were nearing the healing quarters; I could smell the medicinal herbs and treatments even outside the open door.

The healing quarters were large, astoundingly well stocked and admirably well organized.

I wished I could have shown these quarters to Ismay, they were so very impressive. Ismay's work area included a small corner of the kitchen, where she had only several small tables to prepare her medicines. Here, separate chambers housed several beds where injured or infirmed patients could be attended to, but the Ogilvie healing chambers were cramped and somewhat dismal—not at all a pleasant place to coalesce. And they had been inconveniently located, being several minutes' walk from the kitchen area.

In comparison, these Mackenzie healing quarters were clean, comfortable, spacious and gave the impression that the infirmed were in decidedly good care. The walls were lined with thoroughly crowded shelves, crammed neatly with bottles, jars, books and instruments. Tables in the middle of the room were used for mixing and preparing medicines and tinctures, where several bubbled away on various heating devices. And the far end of the room was arranged with three currently unoccupied beds.

Effie was already there, and she looked up from her recipe book, noticing immediately my new look, and the dress I wore. She spent several seconds surveying my body. "Well, well. The coveted Wilkie Mackenzie has finally met his match," she said enigmatically.

Christie and Ailie took their leave for a time, to oversee the preparations for the visitors who were due to arrive next week. I spent much of the day discussing recipes with Effie, who I found to be patient and exceedingly knowledgeable. I shared with her my healing paste recipe. She was mildly surprised that I was unable to read or write, but not overly so; many servants, after all, were not taught.

"I'd like you to make me a batch of that paste, lass, if you wouldn't mind," she said.

I assured her that I would be more than willing.

"I'm not sure if I have all the fresh ingredients here, however," she said. "I'll have to show you the medicine garden."

She led me down a short corridor to a most exquisite garden the likes of which I had never seen. It was a moderately sized patch full of well-tended medicinal herbs and plants of all descriptions. The most unusual thing about this garden was that it was protected on all sides by a high rock wall. At the far wall, an arched wooden door had been left open; through it, I could see the training yards far in the distance where several soldiers were practicing and discussing their moves. I could see that Wilkie was not among them. Against the west wall was a picturesque bench, as though this garden had been designed not only for the plants it grew but also for contemplation, as all good gardens were.

"Why is the garden gated, Effie?" I asked.

"We have a variety of plants here that are difficult to come by," she explained. "We get them from throughout

Scotland, England, even from as far away as the Continent. We thought it best to keep them guarded from livestock and from wind. And many of them are also quite valuable. Best to keep them walled in."

"What a very good idea." I thought of the Ogilvie medicine garden, which was interspersed throughout the vegetable gardens. It was true that many of the plants did not survive more than one season, due to competition with other plants or from the occasional passing sheep; they often needed to be re-sourced. To separate them out like this would likely have been far more effective in seeing plants through from year to year. This was not the first clever idea I had come across at Kinloch, where industrious invention was clearly valued and encouraged.

We picked the herbs we needed and returned to the healing quarters, where we busied ourselves for much of the day.

I was grateful for Effie's company, which was steady and unobtrusive. For the moment, she seemed less interested in the drama surrounding me than in my knowledge of medicinal herbs, and she asked many questions about Ismay's techniques. I wasn't experienced enough in the methods of healing to answer many of her questions, but she was impressed by my knowledge of herbs and plants.

It was midafternoon when Christie and Ailie returned. They sat on stools, watching as I prepared a fresh pot of willowbark tea for the evening, in case Wilkie's aches were paining him. The sisters relayed their progress in preparing menus and guest chambers.

There was one detail Christie had mentioned earlier

that I couldn't help but ask about. "Does Wilkie train every day?"

"Oh, aye," said Christie.

"He trains every day that his innards aren't threatening to spill," clarified Ailie. "Besides, 'tis not long 'til wars will be fought."

"Which wars?" I asked.

"Ossian Lochs. The situation has not improved, and in fact grows more explosive by the day."

"Clan Stuart's lands?" I asked, recalling Ogilvie's mention of it, and the Mackenzies had mentioned it in passing, as well.

"Aye," said Christie. "King William's lands. The grandest keep in the Highlands. The king's landholders maintain the keep, and it was hoped that his wife Mary would produce an heir. She has had difficulties."

I knew some of the details of the situation, and the sisters seemed willing to discuss the topic freely with me. "So there's no heir to claim it."

"Not by Mary," continued Ailie. "And she is now past childbearing. But the king has a public mistress, and he also, many years ago, had a secret one. The public mistress bore him no children, either. But his secret mistress, whose name is not known, *did* bear him a child. An heir. A product of the king himself. Ossian Lochs will become his, as soon as his whereabouts can be traced. 'Tis his birthright."

"Even if he was born out of wedlock?" I asked.

"In this case, aye. The king has decreed it. 'Tis his only child, and he has dictated that the child will inherit the estate. But the child remains elusive. The king has scouts searching throughout the whole of Scotland, England and across Europe. They've yet to find him."

"Why was the child hidden?"

The sisters indulged my questions patiently and willingly; I could sense that they were intrigued by me and eager to engage me in conversation. "Queen Mary, it seems," said Christie, "was wickedly jealous. She asked her husband to give up his mistresses, and he obliged her—partly. He ended his relationship with Elizabeth. But he continued to see his secret mistress. Mary had spies who revealed that the king continued his relationship with the second, secret mistress. Mary was outraged. She ordered her guards to kill the child and the mistress. The mistress was able to hide the child and was killed soon after. 'Tis a tragic ending. But the child is believed to have escaped."

Ailie said, "But the child's whereabouts remain unknown. Campbell believes that the child is dead, and that rights to Ossian Lochs should be forfeited instead, to him."

"Is it not true?" I asked.

Ailic continued. "There's no proof that the child is dead. The king believes him to be alive, and so does Knox."

"Has anyone ever seen him?"

"I don't know how they would identify him, even if they had," commented Christie. "The king is wary of imposters, so hasn't divulged the child's identifying features. Several people have confronted King William with one lost child or another, claiming to present the son of the king. But he has confirmed each time that those children are not his son."

I tried to recall Ogilvie's discussions but couldn't remember the finer details. "Why is it that Campbell feels entitled to Ossian Lochs?"

"King William's sister married the laird of the Campbell clan many years ago, and bore a son to him. She died in childbirth. Laird Campbell felt that his son was the rightful heir to Ossian Lochs, as the king's nephew. He refused the king's decree that the missing child should claim the lands, since the child is illegitimate issue. In most circumstances, that would mean he has no birthright to claim the land."

"So the Mackenzie army will fight to stop Campbell from claiming Ossian Lochs," I said, making sure I understood.

Ailie nodded. "Our father led the battle to overthrow the rebellion. It was he who killed the elder Laird Campbell, but not before he was fatally wounded in the fight. Our father lost his life in that battle. And now the king's nephew is old enough to renew the rebellion, to attempt to gain the land for himself and to avenge his father's death. Our brothers fight because Ossian Lochs are not the nephew's lands to claim. The king himself decreed it. Our brothers fight for the king of Scotland. And they fight so that our father did not die in vain."

I felt their loss. I understood only too well the devastation the death of a father could introduce; my own father's passing had been the single most pivotal event in my life—at least of those I had any recollection of.

"'Twas a good death, if there can be such a thing," Christie said. "An honorable death. Our warriors will fight for the cause, as he fought. To serve the king and to honor our father's memory."

I worried at the thought of Wilkie going off to battle. But then, he was a warrior, and that was what they trained, day after day, to do. I knew firsthand that his skills and his strength would serve him well.

And although I had little knowledge of the intricacies of Highlands politics, I admit I found it interesting. I had often listened to Laird Ogilvie, his ranks and his guests as they'd discussed boundaries and skirmishes, and I'd overheard enough to remember his take on the Ossian Lochs situation. "The nephew is now the new Laird Campbell?" I asked.

"Aye," confirmed Ailie.

I paused momentarily, remembering something: one of many snippets of information I'd regularly overheard as I'd served at the table of Laird Ogilvie. "Ogilvie sides with Campbell," I said to Ailie and Christie.

The sisters stared at me, alert, understanding the implications of this, as I suddenly did.

"Is that so?" Dark interest burned in Ailie's eyes. "How do you know this?"

"I heard him say it," I said. "He plans to assist Campbell with his rebellion. Campbell has visited the Ogilvie keep, several times. I served him myself."

Ailie was disturbed by this. "Knox is under the impression that Ogilvie sided with the king. As all of our neighboring clans do. Or so we thought." Ailie's thoughts were far away for a moment. "So they amass a wider army than Knox thought," she mumbled, as though speaking to herself. "There may be more clans being approached by them, as well."

Ailie squeezed my hand. Her eyes were bright, determined. "Roses. We must go and tell Knox of this news. *You* must tell them. They're meeting with his officers, as we speak, in Knox's private den. Come, they'll be most interested in what you've shared with us."

A meeting, with Wilkie's brothers and fellow officers? Sharing a table with the laird himself, a man who would like nothing better than to see me banished? And Kade, the stormy-eyed brother whose weaponry was intimidating even to seasoned warriors? The thought sent a bloom of apprehension through me.

Ailie might have read the fear in my expression. She placed her hand on my shoulder. "You don't need to fear our brothers, Roses. They'll be interested in what you have to say. The news you have provided might very well save lives, Wilkie's among them. And we'll be right next to you all the while."

"Aye, Roses," urged Christie. "We'll not let them frighten you."

Their words calmed me somewhat, but my heart seemed to have taken flight in my chest.

Wilkie's sisters led me through a maze of hallways, to a small, narrow passageway. To the private den of the laird himself. Ailie knocked on the door and was rewarded with a deep and irritated call to enter.

Laird Mackenzie, Kade, Wilkie and four other men were already seated at a round table, and a fair feast had been laid upon it. My stomach growled at the scents of roasted duck, freshly baked bread and lamb cooked with sage.

The men appeared entirely shocked by our arrival. As soon as we entered the room, they stood in unison. Every single one of them stared at me. They took in my hair and the dress I wore, I couldn't help noticing, for several long seconds.

Wilkie's jaw dropped slightly in his shock, but his expression then adjusted, to one of quiet agitation. He glanced in turn at the four high-ranking officers at the table, noticing the direction of their gaze. Then his eyes returned to me. Was he angry at our intrusion? Or for some other reason?

"Knox," began Ailie, "You must hear what Roses has told us. She has news of Campbell."

"Campbell?" thundered Laird Mackenzie. "What news of Campbell?"

"You'll definitely want to hear this," said Christie, as though enjoying their suspense.

"In that case, Ailie, Christie, Roses," said the laird, more politely now but no less forcefully, "join us."

Wilkie jumped up, walking over to me. He slung his arm around my shoulders, guiding me to a chair next to his, and pulled it out for me. His expression was no more readable than before, but his hands were sure: if I was to be here, among his family and peers, I would be seated next to him. He poured me a goblet of ale, and he began to fill my plate with a selection of delicacies.

After some adjusting of the seating arrangement, Christie sat on my other side, and Ailie next to her. Their goblets were filled by Kade, and they helped themselves to small portions of food.

I sat, feeling small and wildly out of place, but the men seemed mostly at ease, although their eyes were discomfitingly curious.

"What did you wish to speak to us about?" began the laird, somewhat impatiently.

But I couldn't speak. Their collective gaze was overwhelming me.

Wilkie sensed my extreme unease.

"Take a drink of your ale, Roses," encouraged Wilkie, handing me my goblet. I had never tried ale before, as Laird Ogilvie's stores of it were limited, and he preferred to keep the drink for himself and his guests;

servants were not offered such things. I took a few long sips, feeling thirsty. It had a bitter honeyed flavor I found pleasing. "Slowly," Wilkie said, almost smiling. "'Tis a strong brew."

I set my cup down, aware I was being observed by nine pairs of eyes: the Mackenzies and the laird's officers, who were big, staunch-looking men with watchful eyes and plentiful weapons.

"Tell us what you know of Campbell," Wilkie said, more gently than his brother yet no less urgently.

"I—I can tell you that Campbell was a guest of Ogilvie's not a fortnight ago. Or maybe just." I readjusted, not knowing exactly how long I'd been here. "I served their table. I'm certain that Ogilvie has offered his allegiance to Campbell's rebellion at Ossian Lochs. They discussed it in some detail." I paused, having a passing thought that disturbed me.

"Ogilvie sides with Campbell?" pressed Laird Mackenzie, shock splashing across his words.

"Aye." Something occurred to me then.

Wilkie detected my unease immediately. "What is it, lass?"

"I'm already a traitor to Ogilvie. And I'll give you any information I can. But the others of the Ogilvie clan—they won't be harmed?" I thought of Ismay, and of my friends and acquaintances in the kitchen whom I had worked alongside for almost five years. I even thought of Matilda, who had never approved of me, or my work, but who had very occasionally slipped me extra slices of dried venison, a treat she knew I liked, when she thought I was getting too thin. I thought of Ronan and Ritchie, the fledgling warriors who had taken me under their wing to train me in the arts of sword fighting and horse riding, because I'd been so interested; Ritchie, too, had saved me from unthinkable miseries at the hands of Laird Ogilvie by letting me escape when he'd found me on my wayward journey. And the others of my clan who had shown me kindnesses over the years, even though I'd had the aura of an outsider, and I had been low in status.

It was Kade who first answered my question. "The men who fight in his army are always at risk. That's their fate, as warriors. If they attack Ossian Lochs alongside Campbell, then they ask to be harmed. And if what you say is true, then they act as traitors to King William, and for that they deserve retribution."

The laird continued, and his words were somewhat more reassuring. "The clanspeople who reside and remain at Ogilvie's keep will not be in danger from us. We aim to defend the king's rightful holdings, not to stage aggression unnecessarily across the Highlands."

"Did they say when they plan to hold their rebellion?" asked Wilkie.

I thought carefully. "They didn't say. First they discussed who else they might approach, to join their alliance. If there were any other lairds who were discontent, or who thought their holdings were smaller than they should rightfully be. They mentioned Buchanan."

"Buchanan," said the laird, mulling this over.

"His keep is small," offered Wilkie, "and in a state of some disrepair, though that's likely a result of Buchanan's laziness more than anything else."

"Did they mention others?" asked the laird.

I wished now that I'd paid more attention at the time. I struggled for the names that they'd listed. "Macintosh. Munro." Ailie gasped lightly, and I couldn't help noticing that the brothers took special attention to the name Munro. I had no idea why that might be, and I continued. "Macallister was another name they mentioned. But I'm fairly certain they decided against all three, as they each have shown their loyalty to the king on more than one occasion, or have links to the royal family through blood or marriage."

"Any others?" Kade asked.

"Mackenzie," I said.

The laird stiffened.

"They dismissed you outright, Laird Mackenzie," I continued. "They spoke of your staunch loyalty to the king. They knew you'd never join their rebellion." And it was then that Ogilvie had described the traits of the Mackenzie brothers that had lingered in my mind. I didn't go into those details now.

Wilkie, Kade, Laird Mackenzie and their four officers talked for some time, discussing their plans to gain more information through messengers, to find out if any of the lairds I had mentioned were considering joining—or had already aligned themselves with—the rebellion. Occasionally they asked me more detailed questions, but I had told them all I knew. I was able to eat some of the delicious food. And after a half goblet of ale, I was starting to feel woozy. Without thinking, I stood and began to gather the plates, to clear them away to the kitchen. It had become second nature for me, through my many years of training. I stopped when the room went silent, and I noticed that everyone was staring at me. Wilkie's eyes flashed. "Sit down, lass," he said quietly, but with total authority.

I sat.

"Roses is tired," said Wilkie. "I'll escort her back to her chambers."

But Ailie and Christie stood, summoning me to rise, guiding me away from Wilkie. "We'll take her back to Effie, Wilkie. She's been recruited to assist in the healing quarters, since she's obviously skilled. Effie said she's a wealth of knowledge on healing plants. Come, Roses."

Wilkie considered me and his eager sisters, who beckoned me to follow them.

"Whose idea was this?" asked Wilkie, inflamed. He did not appear to like this idea at all.

"Mine," offered the laird baldly. He curtly dismissed the other officers before continuing. "'Tis a reasonable cover while she's here."

Wilkie rose abruptly from his chair, with minimal outward signs of discomfort; his pain was eased by his renewed ferocity. The warrior in him had returned in no half measure. Even in the tumultuousness of this moment, I was struck again by his sheer size and strength, and by the beauty of the lines of him. His off-white tunic made his skin appear all the more dark and swarthy. His wild black hair and his face, still shadowed by his days-old stubble, made him look like a renegade pirate. And his energy seemed to radiate in waves of allure that made me want to go to him. But he was already here, storming over to me and standing over me, huge and looming.

"You're to return to your chambers and stay there until I come for you," he said.

I took his hand before I remembered the publicness of the scene. But when I loosened my hold, he clasped my hand strongly, not allowing me to disengage.

"Please, warrior," I said. "Let me make myself useful. There's no need for me to remain idle when I can be assisting in the healing quarters. There's no need for me to hide away."

"You're wrong!" he shouted, startling me. "There is *every* reason for you to hide away! Do you realize that swarms of Ogilvie troops scour the near vicinity? For *you?* Are you aware that they will stop at nothing until you're found and returned to Ogilvie?" His volume rose even higher, and his grip became even tighter. "Have you any idea what Ogilvie will *do* with you if he *does* get his hands on you? Have you *considered* this, Roses? *Have* you? I would have thought you might have, after what he—" He broke off, breathing heavily and glaring at me.

I was upset enough by his tirade to flinch back from him, but his grip was beyond secure.

Kade rose from his chair and walked up behind Wilkie to place his hand on his brother's shoulder. I couldn't help but notice that both Kade and Laird Mackenzie looked at Wilkie as though they'd never seen him before, as if his reaction was entirely out of character.

"Wilkie," said Kade. "Steady on, brother. She's well protected here. There's no harm in her employment in the healing quarters, if she desires it. 'Tis as safe as your antechamber. As long as she's not wandering the Highlands alone, there's little threat to her. We'll all negotiate—or fight—alongside you if Ogilvie shows up."

Some semblance of control returned to Wilkie's manner at Kade's words. His voice was even, and his eyes were directed at me, although it was his siblings he was addressing. "I will speak to Roses in private for a moment."

Without waiting for agreement, he pulled me by the hand out into the hallway, shutting the door behind us, and led me around a corner. He faced me with fire in his eyes, and I backed into a small alcove, trapped by him. I placed my hand on his chest, not to push him away but to *feel* him. His heart was racing.

"Roses," he hissed. "There will be *no* healing quarters! You're to return to my chambers and wait for me there. I don't want you attracting unwanted attention, especially in this dress—" He broke off abruptly, his eyes lightly skimming my dress only briefly, then looking away, as if the sight of it burned his eyes.

"You don't like the dress, warrior?"

"*Nay,* Roses. I *don't* like the dress. 'Tis far too... fitted."

I smoothed my hands down my garment, unsure of his meaning. "Fitted? Ailie adjusted it herself—"

"Roses, you're to go back to my chambers and wait for me there," he repeated, as though the topic of my clothing was upsetting to him.

I could see he was unsure whether or not I would heed his command, and this aggravated him further. He waited for an answer I did not give.

"Roses?"

"The time goes very slowly waiting for you in your chambers," I said softly. "Let me work to repay my debt to your clan. For the fruit."

"You never even *ate* the fruit!" he seethed, running his hand through his hair in exasperation. "You have no debt to my clan! You're with me." I wanted to attach a world of meaning to those three final words, but I didn't dare.

"I'm with you, aye," I said. "Whenever you want me.

But I'm not *with* you when you're training and meeting. I'm alone. I feel only despair when you're not with me."

His tone gentled by a single degree. "You have no need to despair, lass. I told you I would return to you, and I will. At my very first opportunity."

I was entirely aware that my words would anger him, but I had the strong feeling that sitting idly in Wilkie's bed, waiting for him in his absence, would very nearly drive me mad. I wanted this man, so much and in such an unrealistic capacity that it made me feel reckless and quietly irate. I had to do *something:* to be busy, to react, to somehow fight for the life of what we were. "You want me to lie patiently in your bed for you, warrior? As your faithful servant awaiting you? Is this what you desire of me? Submission and servitude?"

"Are you deliberately trying to provoke me, Roses? You're not my servant!" he growled.

"Nay?" I said, sulkily. "What am I, then?"

He studied my face, as though reading there the reasons behind my insolence. And he countered my tactics with his own. His manner calmed considerably. He leaned over me, so his hair skimmed across my lips. His hand cupped my face, and he kissed me, his tongue gentle and fierce simultaneously, opening me to him. His mouth succeeded in warming all the coldness out of my body, infusing me once again with his honeyed glow.

"You're my sunlit angel," he said. "And I want you safe."

But I wanted more of him, now. And I was hurt by his plan to keep me sequestered away, like—well, like the fugitive that I was. I didn't want to feel shameful and afraid anymore, hiding, as I had for so long. Wilkie had introduced an energy, an optimism and a sense of self-worth to me that was new and so very life-affirming. I wanted him with me, to feel again the closeness and heat of his body. If I did as he asked, how long would my isolation last? I might wait there for hours, or longer, lying idle in his antechamber, alone, wondering about my fate and my future: it caused what felt remarkably like a small glimmer of panic in my heart. I wanted too much—more than he could give—and I knew it. *I made it perfectly clear to her that nothing would come of it. I made no promises.*

"What's to be my fate, warrior? You intend to keep me as a captive? To hide me away in your chambers and soothe me secretly, at your whim?"

Wilkie contemplated me coolly, as though my words stung him. "We'll discuss this when I return to you." There was a distinct bite to his words.

I felt crazed by lust and longing, and the thought of loneliness crowding around me once again, as it had so insistently before him. The threat of his sudden departure shone light on the precariousness of my future and the juxtaposition of its two very different possible outcomes, upsetting me greatly. "I don't want to discuss this when you return," I dared to say. "I want to discuss it now."

He remained frozen in place, clearly surprised and also enraged by my refusal and maybe by my desperation. He was a man used to being in control, and to giving orders. I had no way of knowing if he was thinking what I was: who was *I* to lay conditions and make demands, on *him?* I was a servant and clanless vagabond; he was the second-highest-ranking nobleman of one of the most prosperous, powerful clans in all of Scotland. He tried again, and his tone was stern and commanding. "I'm not having this out with you now. I'm returning to the meeting. And you're going to my chambers. We'll talk about this later."

But I wanted him too badly not to fight him, and fight for him. "*This? What this?*"

"What do you mean?" His patience was becoming more and more frayed around the edges.

"I mean *this,* as in the impossibility of me staying here with you and giving myself to you wholly, which is my every waking wish? Or *this,* as in you being undecided about what it is you want to do with me?"

He watched me for a moment, fierce and direct. "I'm not undecided about what I want to do with you."

I looked into his eyes, and I could see both sureness and worry in them. Again, it frustrated me that I didn't know the depths of him well enough to read the layers of his emotion. I wanted to discover and learn all the intricacies of him, so I could banish his pain and his fears, to soothe him and comfort him. But my own worries were rising up in equal measure, and they were dark and biting, yet hopeful, too. More hopeful than they had ever been before. Which made the dark doubts seem all the more spiky.

Voices spilled into our tense little bubble, causing Wilkie to step back and look away.

"Wilkie?" It was Wilkie's sisters. "Roses? Oh, there you are."

They were there, sensing the tension and attempting to defuse it. "Are you finished talking?" asked Ailie.

"Nay," said Wilkie abruptly.

"Because Knox has asked that you return to the meeting," said Christie.

Wilkie looked at his sisters, and he said, "Tell Knox

that I must respectfully decline returning to the meeting this evening. Tell Effie that Roses has been detained. And—" to Christie "—Roses will not require a chaperone until I call for one."

And with that I was swept into Wilkie's arms, tight against his big, warm body and carried to his private chambers.

CHAPTER EIGHT

As SOON AS WE ENTERED Wilkie's rooms, he set me down gently on his bed. His temper had been calmed by the walk and the closeness of our bodies as he held me against him.

Wilkie lit the fire, saying nothing. He took his time, feeding the flame with small, then larger, pieces of wood, until his chambers were infused with the dancing yellow glow, which reflected off his hair, his face and his clothing.

I felt a fluttery moth of joy in my heart at the very sight of him, an inexplicable happiness that we were here together and that we had emerged from our small argument as—almost—equals. I'd succeeded in keeping him with me. To be separated now from him would cause me physical pain. I had never felt an attachment to anyone this strongly—not even to my mother, as a child, since I had once known life without her. I couldn't remember even a single recollection of my life before I'd been delivered at the Ogilvie keep, but I had always, perhaps because of my mysterious early years, had a strong sense of independence. So it seemed strange now that I would yearn like this. And burn like this. The sight of Wilkie, with the curves of his muscular shoulders straining against the fabric of his tunic and illuminated by the firelight, it lit a different kind of fire. In me.

"Warrior," I said, and my voice sounded softly husked. "Come here."

He stopped his movement, catching a note in my tone that grabbed his attention. He walked to the bed, his gaze direct and darkened.

"Warrior," I said, reaching for his hand. "Please forgive me. I'll wait here for you, if it pleases you. I will do anything for you, anything. I will heed your every command, as I promised I would. I acted that way only because I wanted so desperately to have you and to give everything of myself to you, now and always. I told you once that I wasn't good at following orders, and 'tis true. I've had every need, in the past, to defy. It was how I protected myself and kept true to myself. Sometimes I forget myself, with you. I forget that I don't need to do that with you. I'll try harder, I promise. I'll devote myself to pleasing you. 'Tis all I want to do. I don't want to defy you, Wilkie. Please forgive me."

He sat next to me on the bed, stretching out his legs over the furs, putting his arm around my shoulders so I could lean against him. "I don't want your blind obedience, lass." He carefully unwound my braids, stroking and smoothing the long strands with his hand. "'Tis me who should be apologizing. I have no idea what's come over me. You drive me daft with your golden beauty. To have you seen and looked at—"

I paused and leaned closer to him. I kissed the corner of his mouth.

"I will allow you to work with Effie," he said. "But you will not venture out-of-doors. At all. Unless I'm with you. I'm being as open-minded as I can, Roses, but 'tis not safe for you to be overly visible. Ogilvie's men are looking for you. For now, we need to keep your presence here quiet. Already there's a risk that you were seen, when you first arrived. It could endanger your safety if word gets to him."

I thought about this. It could endanger many people's safety, if Ogilvie ordered his army to invade Kinloch to get me back. Was his pride so very offended by the small uprising of a servant? I certainly didn't want to aggravate a battle, and in fact, the thought horrified me for many reasons. I wouldn't be allowed out-of-doors, to watch Wilkie train. Or to visit the open gardens.

"I am your willing captive," I said.

I meant it to tease him, almost, and to apologize for my earlier refusals, but his eyes turned stormy at the comment, and I regretted my words. "Don't be angry. I want to be with you, warrior. The thought of you leaving me, while you train, at all, it makes my words unruly."

He frowned. "I'm no better than Ogilvie, keeping you captive, here in my bed. 'Tis a strangely powerful urge I have, to keep you close to me. It clouds all my judgment. It burns in me like I've never burned, Roses." He was troubled by this.

Wanting to ease away his distress, I sat up to face him, thinking about what I could do to distract his frown.

In fact, I felt quite lively, as if the effects of my injury and the stress of past days had lifted almost entirely. I was here with him against all odds, and was invigorated by the discovery that my warrior could pleasure me in confoundingly powerful ways. My energy seemed to hum from within me, as though the spark of the argument had livened me, now that it was over. I felt playful, and it was a feeling I hadn't felt for some time. I climbed onto him, carefully, straddling him. "Warrior.

If I can assure you of one thing, let it be this—you are nothing like Laird Ogilvie." I kissed his lips, but he remained still and impassive, still frowning at me. "I want to be here, with you." I let my fingers glide across his shoulders, down his arms, across his stomach, tickling him. He squirmed a little. "I like your touches. And I want to heed your commands, every one." My fingers traced across his chest. And I leaned closer to him, so my breasts pressed against him. I took care not to hurt him. I licked his lips open, very gently, with my tongue. "Give me a command, warrior. Anything."

He watched me, and there was wariness in his eyes but also hunger. His chest rose and fell with his heavy breath. Straddling his hips as I was, I could feel a hard pressure underneath me, the part of him I was curious about. Still kissing him lightly, licking into his mouth, I moved my body on his, rubbing myself against his hardness ever so slightly. My fingers continued to glide across his skin.

"I want to soothe my warrior," I whispered to him. "To ease away his frown with my kisses. I want to do everything he tells me to do." He was kissing me back now, and I drew his tongue into my mouth and played it, gently suckling.

Wilkie gave a small sound of agonized surrender. Then, in a sudden movement, he adjusted us, and laid me back against the pillows. He might have aggravated his injury again, because a fleeting grimace crossed his face.

"Be careful, warrior. You'll hurt yourself."

"I'm almost healed, lass. All the more quickly from your soothing attentions."

Wilkie sat at my feet. He removed my boots and my

stockings. And he removed his own. Then he clasped his hands around my bare ankles, like manacles. "'Tis my turn to explore with my careful touch."

He inched my legs slowly apart, at the same time pushing my ankles back toward my body, so my knees were bent.

I felt my heartbeat in unusual places.

He leaned down to kiss my toes and the tops of my feet. Then he released his grip and began to draw feathery lines with his fingers on my skin, as I had done to him. His mouth began a wandering path up to my ankles, to my calves, and he was murmuring soft words to me. "Everything of you makes me daft with longing. Your skin, so glowing and golden. Your lips. I feel so *much,* Roses, more than I can bear. I want to see you." His hands, so large and warm, smoothed ever higher, the roughened surface of his fingertips scratching slightly against my skin. The gathered fabric of my gown pushed up to my knees.

My question was barely audible. "Warrior?"

"I want to feast my eyes upon your womanly softness."

I couldn't speak. I felt frozen and bathed in warmth all at once.

Measuredly, so very slowly, so I became aware of the anticipation, the fear, the scandal and the desire all at once, Wilkie lifted the hem of my dress to my waist.

I MOVED MY HAND TO COVER myself. It was too intimate, being exposed to him like that, as vulnerable as I could possibly be.

"Don't cover yourself, lass. I want to kiss you. Let me."

Wilkie gently pried my hands away and placed them

at my sides. Then he began to kiss the insides of my knees, which he eased apart with his hands as his mouth continued its tickling, kissing pathway ever higher.

I wriggled up the bed, farther away from him, overwhelmed by the blossoming sensation and by the thought of what he was doing and what he was going to do. I had never imagined such a thing. He waited until I quieted, sensing my stirred unease. Then he grasped his hands at my hips and slowly dragged me back. Closer to him, in fact, than where I'd been. So close that I could feel the humid strikes of his breath on my most intimate flesh.

"Warrior—" I breathed. I rose slightly, to look at his face.

"Aye," he whispered, his dark eyes challenging me, inviting me.

"Are you going to…?" My question couldn't quite find itself.

"Nay, lass. Not until we're wed. I'm only going to kiss you."

Already overcome with Wilkie's intentions, my mind had trouble grasping the words he had spoken. "*Wed?* What do you mean?"

"I mean I want you. All of you. As mine. How can I let you out of my life if I can't bear to let you out of my bed?" He was kissing me again, on the skin of my inner thigh. "But first, I have to taste you."

"Warrior," I gasped. "You can't wed me. Your brother would never allow it. I'm a kitchen servant."

He was undeterred, and the combined effect of his hot breath and the scrape of his whiskers on the sensitive skin of my inner thigh was almost more than I could bear. "No longer."

I was very distracted by what he was doing with his mouth but shocked enough by his pronouncement that I continued to question him. "But what of the legion of heiresses who vie for your hand?"

"You heard that, did you?" he asked with a light sigh. "I have found none that inspires even a spark of the roaring flame of you, Roses. I might very well die if I don't have you soon."

I might have brought up an obvious point: that Wilkie could, in fact, have me. All of me. Soon. Now. I was more vulnerable—and willing—than I had ever been. I wanted this man more than I'd ever wanted anything in my life. In any capacity he was prepared to give. Everything about his presence fed me a sense of un-bridled hope. But I was quite literally speechless from the wet, adamant exploration of his mouth. His *mouth*. So close—

"*Wilkie*. Are you—"

"Aye, lass. I'm going to kiss you. Now lie back and let me."

Wilkie pushed my thighs farther apart. I was about to protest, to try to escape him once again, when I felt his tongue glide across the closed seam of my entrance. The pleasure delivered by that one wet, sweet fire stroke was so acute that I squirmed and grabbed fistfuls of his hair. I wasn't sure if I was trying to push him away or pull him closer, but his strength and his dominating hold made the uncertainty irrelevant. He breathed on me again, in warm, tangible puffs. Then his tongue licked me in a long, hot sweep that began low and trailed greedily upward, and again, until his mouth closed over the small nub. In an alternating rhythm, his tongue pushed gently into me, then he was sucking again, then pushing into me. The tender suction of his mouth and the rocking undulations of his touch were a revelation. Subtle, soft, cyclical pulls and licks gathered pleasure and warmth where his mouth was centered. His hungry feasting was relentless. The pleasure grew and bloomed to such unbearable heights that I feared I might not survive it, that I might cry or faint or die from the overload. But then, at its ecstatic peak, the searing pleasure fragmented, settling into lush, rippling waves that clenched through my inner muscles so forcefully that I sobbed from the sheer plenitude of feeling, repeating his name, clutching his hair in grasping handfuls.

Wilkie continued to lap at me until the ripples calmed. Then he climbed up to lie next to me and gathered me into his arms, cocooning me in his warmth, tucking my head into the hollow of his neck. He wiped away the tears at the corners of my eyes with his fingers.

"Roses likes my kisses," he said, sounding pleased with himself. "You are mine to protect. You will visit Effie to help her when I allow it. You will wait for me when I ask you to. And you will let me kiss you whenever and wherever it pleases me."

Still recovering from the lingering effects of his miraculous kisses, I couldn't quite manage to whisper my agreement.

"Roses?" he said, with mock sternness, enjoying my stupor, kissing my lips.

"Aye."

Aye. Whenever and wherever it pleases him. That was one command I could most certainly agree to.

CHAPTER NINE

THE NEXT MORNING PASSED quickly in Wilkie's absence, as I was enthusiastically ensconced in the lively attentions of Effie, Ailie and Christie, who were no longer content with the minimal information they had so far been given about me. It was now quite clear that Wilkie was up and about, restored to almost full health, no longer delusional or delirious. And I was still residing in his chambers. And not just his antechamber, but his bed—after several dramatic displays in which he would not take nay for an answer. That we had shared several private moments—at Wilkie's insistence—was known and seemingly accepted by his family. There was no comment about our sleeping arrangements, or any of the delicate questions that might surround that particular topic, which made me profoundly grateful. They appeared to have accepted me as a fixture in Wilkie's rooms, for now.

Effie, Ailie and Christie were highly amused that they had been given strict orders by Wilkie to attend to me. I was to be offered clothing, my wound was to be checked to ensure it was healing properly, and I was to be fed in a particular room as chosen by Wilkie, where he and Kade would meet us for the noontime meal.

All activities, to be sure, that were pleasing enough. I could not help considering, however, my tattoo and my eternal quest to keep it from being discovered. I would need to be careful.

I was content to listen to Effie's free-flowing commentary on life in general within the Mackenzie keep and to answer her questions, and those of Wilkie's sisters. By now I found the three women's presence entirely comforting, and even enjoyed the spark of their chiding interest in Wilkie's unusual—and sudden—attachment to me.

I put on my new shift and selected a light blue short-sleeved dress, for the specific reason that its neckline at the back was high enough to keep my secret hidden. I slipped the dress over my head and emerged from the small secluded area cordoned off by the privacy screen. I was summoned to a chair, where I was attended to by all three of them.

"If you don't mind me saying, lassie," Effie mused, "the man's taken total leave of his senses. You know, he stormed into the healer's quarters this morning, demanding that I immediately attend to you personally. I told him I had several patients to check on—and luckily, none of them have particularly dire afflictions and can easily be looked after by Fiona and Thora. And it's a good thing, too, because I don't think he would've taken nay for an answer. 'Tis most unusual—wouldn't you say, Ailie?"

"Aye," Ailie agreed. She was brushing out my hair as Effie spread a final treatment of healing salve on my wound, declaring it as well as healed. "I've never seen Wilkie take an interest in anything beyond fighting, eating, swimming and hunting."

And if Effie was a wealth of information about the wider workings of the clan, it was Christie who I found to provide the most personal—and informative—details on Wilkie and his family. She seemed incapable of filtering her thoughts, as though she'd never had need to do so; her youthful naïveté was endearing, and I felt a strange sense of protectiveness toward her. I wasn't sure why that was and wondered at it. She was likely my age, or not much younger. And I felt close to her, after confessing to her the extent of my desire for Wilkie during our intense and connective private conversation in the antechamber. "That's not entirely true, you two, and you know it," Christie said. "Wilkie's highly interested in women. He just chooses to visit their beds, rather than bringing them to his own."

That Christie didn't feel the need to shield me from this information was a small relief to me. I appreciated her honesty. My importance in Wilkie's life was yet unknown, to them, and even to me, even after his brash declaration earlier that morning. I had strong doubts that Laird Mackenzie would entertain Wilkie's intentions for me, if they were sincere, and Christie was merely stating the truth of the matter. The far-off vision of marriage to Wilkie seemed too otherworldly, too lofty, to even be seriously entertained. And it didn't hurt me, to hear of his other women. I had no claims on him as such, and I could hardly blame other women for conquesting the likes of Wilkie Mackenzie. But what I did feel at that moment was a thin, bright tightness in my chest. A low ache that, after some reflection, I could identify: I *missed* him. I knew he was training with his brothers and the other warriors of their clan, preparing for battle, as they had need to do. I wished I could see him. I wanted his warmth and his insistence to wrap itself around me, as I'd become used to. I wondered when he would return to me.

"Well, he's certainly got every woman in the Highlands swooning after him, isn't that the truth," Effie continued. "He's caused many a lass to tantrum over his lack of engagement. He seems to tire of them quickly. And shows no interest in their ongoing maintenance. And then *you* come along, Roses," she said, studying me subtly, as though attempting to find the answer written in my hair or on my skin. "And he'll not let you out of his bed nor willingly out of his sight."

"You only have to look at her, Effie," said Christie. "I daresay Wilkie has never seen anything quite like her. Have you ever seen hair this color?" She smoothed her hand along the locks of my hair, running her fingers through it as though mesmerized.

"Let me braid it, Christie," Ailie scolded her. "Wilkie said he'll be back at noontime, to make sure she's being well entertained."

Christie laughed at this. "We best do it properly, then."

I heard it in Christie's laugh as I felt it in my own mind: this frivolous attention to my well-being was overblown, wholly out of the ordinary and not far from ridiculous. "I'm sorry you have to be bothered with this," I said, feeling self-conscious. "I'm fine to finish dressing myself, and if you give me some tasks to help with, I'd be grateful. At least I could make myself useful."

Effie found this even more amusing. "Good gracious, nay, lass. Wilkie would be outraged. We've been given strict instructions, see, and we'd not hear the end of it if we were remiss in our duties."

Once the dress was fitted and my hair had been braided, I was told I'd be given a limited tour of the Mackenzie manor.

"Wilkie's worried that you'll be seen," explained Ailie. "Messengers come and go regularly."

"And, apparently, Ogilvie has heard that you've been spotted in these parts. He's near-crazed with bloodlust," Christie informed me.

While I already knew that Ogilvie was after me, I was deeply disturbed that he had narrowed his search to Kinloch. Would he attack? I knew Ogilvie's warriors were well-trained, or at least they seemed as such from my inexpert viewpoint; I'd watched them often.

Christie was less concerned, seemingly highly entertained by the unending scandal surrounding me. "I overheard Knox saying that Ogilvie's messengers have called on him several times since you've arrived. Laird Ogilvie is most insistent that you are returned to him."

"He knows I'm here?" I whispered, standing, feeling more and more desperate to see Wilkie.

Several pairs of hands gently returned me to my seat, then continued to groom me.

"Knox has told them you are not with us. But Ogilvie is unconvinced. One of his messengers thought he recognized you, upon his first visit."

"Whatever did you *do,* Roses?" asked Ailie quietly. "And why did you flee?"

I had no doubt that the sisters were privy to at least some of the information I'd shared with Laird Mackenzie and Kade about my background and my reasons for being here, and the details of Wilkie's injury and my own. That they hadn't asked these questions immediately seemed to confirm that I had been discussed by all of Wilkie's siblings at some point while he and I had shared our fevered slumber. And everything I knew about this family so far—their closeness, their concern for Wilkie, and their curiosity in regards to our connection—made it reasonable to assume that the sisters were informed.

But they wanted to hear it from me, it seemed.

Seeing no point in hiding anything from these women, who had shown me only kindness, I told them how I had defended myself, and why. I told them of my journey, my thievery, my encounter with Wilkie. I told them of our small but vicious battle. I told them everything. Actually, not *everything*. And they were curious about the details I left out, I could read this on their faces. But even Christie refrained from asking those particular questions.

"Oh, Roses," said Ailie, aghast. "How did you dare to run like that? Alone and defenseless? You must have been terrified."

"Aye. I was. I had read the laird's intentions, though, so I think I knew I would act when the time came. I was relieved to be free of him. I was most frightened when Wilkie ran after me, after he saw me. I think I would rather he killed me than return me to Ogilvie."

Effie made a small sound, as though she was either impressed by my bravery or amused by my foolishness, I couldn't quite tell.

"There," Ailie finally said. I was given a small hand mirror so I could inspect myself. My hair had been artfully braided and wrapped in a fashionable twist at the back. And it gleamed from the careful washing and brushing. The neckline of my ice-blue dress was high at the back but, again, lower than I was used to in the front, accentuating the curve of my breasts in a flattering manner. Fashioned like the dresses worn in Paris, Christie had claimed as she'd laced its bodice, wistfully vocalizing her wish to travel to the Continent one day.

As I took in my own reflection, I was mildly shocked at my own transformation. It was certainly a dramatic change from the wild-eyed, bloodied savage who'd shown up on the Mackenzie doorstep only a short time ago. This new reflection was beautiful, I had to admit, but didn't seem entirely like *me*. I smoothed my hand along the silky fabric of my dress, remembering for the first time since my arrival: my mother's daisy pin. Had I left it pinned to my tunic? I would have to check. I vaguely remembered taking it off, at the pool by the cave, and placing it on a rock there. I felt almost certain that I'd left it there. I'd have to tell Wilkie that I needed to retrieve it. It was the only possession I had that had once belonged to my parents. My one keepsake of their memories.

But I wouldn't have time to worry about it now.

I was escorted from Wilkie's antechamber and down the stairs. I was excited, both to be up and about and also by the news that Wilkie would visit me at noontime. It wouldn't be long until I could see him again. My stomach felt fluttery at the prospect. And, shamelessly, my secret places piqued and tingled at the promise of his nearness.

Effie excused herself, and I was led to a drawing room by Christie and Ailie, where a light meal brunch had been laid, by an open window. I felt wildly refreshed by the sunlight that streamed into the room, and the light breeze that carried with it the scents of autumn, of crops on the brink of harvest, of ripe fruit and earthly bounty.

I sighed as I stood near the window, taking a deep breath of the healing fresh air, appreciating the view and my good fortune at that moment.

Ailie watched me, registering my fascination with the garden and my obvious comfort in the breeze and in the softly settling rays of sunlight, which touched my face and my hair. "Perhaps Wilkie will allow us to escort you on a stroll through the orchards, Roses. I'll ask him."

I couldn't help smiling at her. "I would love to, Ailie. Very much."

"You mustn't get overly sunned, Roses," said Christie, serving me a cup of tea, and noticing how I was basking in the sun's warmth.

"Just for a moment, Christie," said Ailie. "She's been cooped up for weeks." Had it been that long?

At first I wondered at Christie's concern. Then I realized; of course: it was unfashionable for a woman to be overly sunned. It was true that I'd never much considered protecting my skin from the sun; I enjoyed the feel of it far too much to hide away from it. And since my work had called for me to spend most of my time indoors, the little time I had been able to enjoy out-of-doors pursuits had been spent helping in the gardens, or covertly practicing my sword fighting or horse riding skills. So I had little cause to worry about such matters. And I'd never before had the luxury to consider the fashion of paleness, nor any other fashion, for that matter. Servants' dresses were coarse and cumbersome. Men's riding trews were frowned upon on a woman but had allowed me to move more freely, and to hide my body from Ogilvie's wandering eyes. So I'd worn them at every opportunity. My looks in general, and the paleness of my skin in particular, had never been something I'd paused to consider.

And my skin was not creamy and pink-cheeked, like these sisters, but rather golden in hue, so I rarely burned from the sun, even if I did happen to spend hours out-of-doors. And now, the pooling warmth simply felt too good for me to move away from the rays' light caress.

It was at that moment that Wilkie and Kade strode into the room, talking animatedly, in good spirits. "I've never seen you so savage in training, brother," Kade was saying. "I feared for Crispen's life. It seems you're not only fully recovered but possessing of a new vigor."

"Aye, it would seem so." Wilkie laughed, and then he stopped in his tracks when he saw me standing by the window.

Just the sight of him there, roughened and energized from his morning of sparring, it weakened my knees. His masculinity clung to him along with the sunlight. His black hair was windblown and wild, and his eyes darkened the moment he looked at me. The combined effect made him look dangerous and achingly, mind-numbingly beautiful.

He walked over to me, dreamily, and he was there with me, staring down at me with an intensity that brought a flush to my cheeks. His eyes looked almost disbelieving. "Angel," he said.

His voice seemed to touch me in my most intimate places; those same places that were already tingling and over-sensitive from the very thought of him now swelled and moistened at his closeness. I wanted him to touch me and kiss me, and bear me down to the floor to do unspeakable things to my body. I craved him, the taste of him on my tongue and the feel of his skin under my fingertips.

Instead, mindful of the very intrigued and watchful eyes of Kade, Christie and Ailie, I somehow managed to return his soft greeting. "Warrior."

We stood like that for a moment, drinking in the sight of each other, thinking thoughts—at least on my part—that were wholly improper and wickedly alluring. I felt, after a minute or more of this quiet torture, that feeling again: that if Wilkie had touched me then, very lightly, on my most intimate flesh, I would have erupted into those exquisite quivering spasms he so easily seemed able to inspire within me.

When he reached for my hand, I almost drew back, afraid of what his touch might do to me. But he grasped both my hands firmly in his own. He leaned closer, so his mouth was close to my ear. "You are the sun," he whispered.

Then he leaned in as though to give me a kiss on the cheek. Nothing untoward, just a public greeting under the collective gaze of his siblings. But then, instead of kissing my cheek, Wilkie moved to touch his mouth lower, to the side of my throat, in an open-mouthed brush that made me gasp.

Ailie and Christie exchanged a meaningful glance, then returned their gaze to me, to the spectacle of us.

Embarrassed by my own obvious weakness to him, and feeling the burn of it across my cheeks and elsewhere, I tried to smile at him, at Ailie and Christie, at Kade, whose measured stare was taking in his brother's unusual behavior.

"How…how did your training go?" I asked, hoping my voice didn't give away the extent of my longing.

"I hope you didn't aggravate your injury, Wilkie, by overdoing it," said Ailie, and I was grateful to her, for breaking the observant silence among the three of them. "Effie said to go easy this day, and for several days."

"'Tis a good thing Effie wasn't there, then," said Kade. "Wilkie did not go easy and, in fact, very nearly skewered several of our clansmen."

I felt the urge to lift Wilkie's shirt, to check his bandage for fresh blood, but it was all I could do to remain standing and presentable, as Wilkie's clasping hand was now sliding gently up my arm. The rough surface of his fingertips were barely scratchy on the inner skin of my upper arm, where he grasped me so that the outer edge of his fingers touched ever so slightly, and very briefly, against the curve of my breast. His hand roamed up to my neck, where he curled his hand around my nape, holding it there. That he felt completely at ease touching me this way in front of his family was unsettling to me, mainly because it was inspiring heat in me that I was struggling to control.

"What of Ogilvie's messengers, Wilkie?" Christie asked, with her usual eager clarity. "Have they discovered that Roses is here?"

I was almost thankful to Christie. That one comment succeeded in cooling me, a degree if not more, and Wilkie, too, froze in place. In a slow movement, he looked over at her.

"They have discovered nothing," he said. "Nor will they."

Christie's next question was directed at Kade, perhaps in the hope of gaining more information than

Wilkie might be willing to give. "Knox said they'd returned, more than once, and that one of the messengers spotted Roses. Is it true?"

Kade replied, "We think that Ogilvie believes it to be true."

Seeing the look on Ailie's face shocked me into my own brazen realization. Her face, so lovely in its colors: the paleness of her skin framed by curling tendrils of her inky-dark hair, and the striking violet shine of her worried eyes. I couldn't let Ogilvie attack Kinloch. It was my fault that Ogilvie's men buzzed around the area like agitated bees, seeking me out for their laird's revenge. What if Ailie or Christie was hurt? What if Wilkie was struck down by an Ogilvie warrior?

I couldn't let that happen.

I had no plan, but I knew I must leave them to protect them.

Leaving Kinloch was, to be sure, the very last thing I wanted to do. This place had been nothing but a magical sanctuary for me, as though a figment of a wondrous dream. I didn't want to be its downfall. I couldn't bear the thought of this peaceful, beautiful place being overrun and sullied by Ogilvie and his men. I envisioned Ogilvie warriors on horseback, storming into the keep, cutting down workers, trampling the gardens, bloodying this family. I couldn't abide the thought of the people of this clan—Christie, Ailie, Effie, even Kade and the gruffly protective laird himself—being put in harm's way because of my own willful desertion. That my own warrior might be placed in danger was a thought I simply could not tolerate. Not when there was something I could do to prevent it from happening.

Triggering an attack by Ogilvie forces would be far

more catastrophic than simply removing myself, for a time. I could return to the cave, to remain hidden. Maybe, after some time had passed, Ogilvie's ire would fizzle out; maybe he'd forget about me as he concentrated on the Ossian Lochs rebellion and the conquest of other, newer potential mistresses. And maybe then, I might be allowed to return to the Mackenzies.

To remove myself from Wilkie: the thought sent actual shards of pain through my heart. But a temporary separation would be better than death. To lose him through battle—a battle caused by *me*—would be unbearable, especially when I could so easily defuse the situation by simply disappearing.

"I must go," I said, pulling away from Wilkie's grip. "I'll not have Ogilvie attacking you, when it's me he wants. 'Tis not right for me to put you in danger as I've done."

Wilkie grabbed my arm. He looked at me warily. Kade, too, looked thoughtful, as though I'd surprised him.

"What's your meaning, lass?" Wilkie asked, almost impatiently.

"I mean I must go! Away from here! If they come looking for me and storm your keep, you might be hurt. Any of you. Ogilvie has a strong army. I know, I've watched them and walked among them. Ogilvie can be a cruel and devious man. If I go, then they'll leave you in peace." I tried to pry his fingers from my arm, and I was ashamed to feel the hot prick of tears welling in my eyes. "I must go, warrior. Give me back my weapons. Release your grip on me."

Wilkie's clasp on my arm did not release; instead,

it grew tighter, so tight that it pained the injury he had inflicted on me with his sword only weeks ago.

"Please, Wilkie," I said, and the tears were streaming freely now. I felt frantic with fear and despair at the thought of leaving him, of putting behind the beauty of him and all that surrounded him, to resume my exile, alone, and through the long days and cold nights across the windswept Highlands. But it was the only thing I could do to keep them safe.

"Don't be daft, lass," Wilkie said, pulling me back to him. It riled me that he seemed to be entirely dismissive of my resolve. In fact, he appeared almost annoyed.

I struggled against his hold, but he held me with both hands now, and I couldn't dislodge his grip. "If I go now," I said, "and if Ogilvie's troops arrive, you can tell them that I was here, but that I've fled you. That you didn't know which direction I'd taken. They'll come after me, and they'll not bother you over this again." My tears still flowed, and they shamed me. I should be stronger than this. I turned to Wilkie's stormy-eyed brother, who contemplated me with an expression I hadn't seen in him before. He looked almost…sympathetic. But my own voice sounded soulless, distant. "Kade, can you retrieve my weapons?"

Kade eyed me, then he looked at Wilkie. I couldn't see the expression in Wilkie's eyes as he returned his brother's gaze. "Nay, lass," Kade said.

The thought of making the trek alone, pursued, and without my sword was unthinkable. But then it occurred to me that I'd left my knife at the cave. And my blanket and bowl. The fruit. And my mother's pin. I would start there, camp the night, then make my way toward Macduff's at first light.

"You make things more difficult for me," I informed him, "but if that's to be the way of it, then so be it." I tried again to pry Wilkie's fingers loose from my arms.

"Warrior," I said, with as much authority as I could summon. "Unhand me."

"Nay, Roses," he said, his voice low and calming, as though he was speaking to a spooked horse that was threatening to bolt. "You are not leaving this keep. Ogilvie's men are of little threat to us. Our army is far superior to his, and our walls are sound. We have guards in place and our weapons are at the ready. Our keep is well protected. And so are you."

It was then that I lost myself. I put my hands over my face, and Wilkie allowed this, loosening his embrace slightly. I sobbed with the shame of bringing this upon them, with the fear I felt for them, and for myself, for all that was lost to me: my family—twice—my sense of worth, my distance from ever feeling a real sense of belonging, my constant, tiring vigilance against a predator who had watched me for many years. I lost myself then because Wilkie, my warrior, had managed to unfurl all of those feelings of injustice and inadequacy. With his grip and his words, with his touch and his promises, he'd given me everything I'd long craved and everything I'd ever wanted, if I had ever been so bold as to imagine such things. Now, my whole heart and my whole soul desired nothing else but to stay with him and to believe him.

Wilkie held me against his chest and let me cry. My tears wet his tunic. He wrapped his strong arms around me. And Christie and Ailie were there, too, comforting me.

"Roses," said Ailie, her eyes wide. "We'll not let you

wander alone. You'll stay with us. We'll hide you and take care of you."

"You'd be killed for certain, Roses," added Christie. "And who knows what else might happen if Ogilvie's men caught you? It doesn't bear thinking about."

Even Kade said, "We would not be honorable men if we cast you out, lass, knowing full well you were in grave danger. Let us do what we are trained to do—defend our keep and all who reside within it."

"You're mine now, Roses," said Wilkie. "My clan and my family will protect what's mine. 'Tis their honor and their duty."

I thought of Wilkie's own duty, to his brother and laird. "Laird Mackenzie wishes me to go. He sees the trouble I bring, the disruption and the danger."

It was Kade, surprisingly, who reassured me. "Our brother's thoughts are embroiled in military alliances and the continued fortification of our army, at all times. 'Tis true he is somewhat more reluctant to recognize what we all can clearly see—that Wilkie has become not only smitten but thoroughly obsessed with you. We should all be so fortunate to find such a powerful connection." Kade sounded almost wistful at the thought. Upon first meeting him, I would not have picked him for a romantic, but he was decidedly less threatening as these unexpected layers of his personality revealed themselves.

I wiped my eyes, having some difficulty absorbing the kindness of them. It was potent and life-affirming. And it had been a very long time since I'd felt real affection of this kind. My parents had given it, wholeheartedly. Ismay, as well. And now the Mackenzies, even those I had never expected it from.

"I'm sorry I've brought this upon you," I said.

"What you've brought upon us," said Kade, "is a brother who is crazed by you to such an extent that he could very well cut down Ogilvie's entire army single-handedly. I'd not worry overmuch about the caliber of our forces if I were you."

Wilkie continued, choosing not to acknowledge Kade's remark. "Ogilvie knows he has little chance of overpowering our men and storming our keep. My guess is that they're bluffing. Knox is of a mind to invite Ogilvie, alone, and discuss it in a civilized manner. 'Tis likely that we can offer him a trade of some description. Bribes have a way of smoothing grievances."

I hoped he was right.

Wilkie wiped a stray tear from my cheek. "All right, then? No more daft talk of running off?" He gave me a look of gentle sternness. "You know I'd come after you, so it's safer for all of us if you stay right where you are."

"Are you certain? I couldn't bear it if anyone here was harmed because of me."

"And I," Kade retorted, "couldn't bear if Ogilvie, the lout, were to better a single man of ours. I'd consider our leadership decidedly faulty."

"'Tis settled, then, lass," said Wilkie, as though impatient to be done with the entire discussion. "Agreed?"

I nodded. And I admit, I felt a euphoric sense of relief, that I wouldn't have to leave him and wander alone across the hills, with men on my trail and but a single knife in my possession. And that my sleeping quarters tonight would not be in a lonely cave but in the plush and occupied bed of Wilkie Mackenzie.

"Good. Let's eat," said Wilkie. "I'm half starved."

"WE WANT TO TAKE ROSES on a stroll through the orchards," Christie informed her brother. "She's been cooped up for days and the fresh air would help restore her to full health."

We were seated in the same room where I'd taken tea with Christie and Ailie, by the open window. Other warriors and workers often took their noonday meal in the great hall, I was told. Laird Mackenzie believed that mealtimes should be shared and should offer plentiful, hearty nutrition, not only to fortify the hard-working clanspeople but also to invite camaraderie. It was a good opportunity to discuss tactics, or crop irrigation, or techniques by which to build the most durable walls. And we could hear their loud banter and laughter from where we sat, behind closed doors. But Wilkie was not willing to let me partake in the wider clan's activities. He thought it still too dangerous that word would get to Ogilvie that I had indeed taken up residence at Kinloch. Until discussions could be organized between Laird Ogilvie and Laird Mackenzie, it was best to remain quiet and hidden.

And I guessed, for that same reason, that he wouldn't want me to wander the gardens, even under the careful escort of his sisters. But he surprised me, maybe when he noticed my eager anticipation at the question. I waited for his answer and took in, behind him and in the distance, the softly swaying grasses and the heavy-fruited trees.

"She's already visited the medicine garden, with Effie," Christie offered. "It'll be fine."

"We'll stay away from the gardeners," persisted Ailie. "We'll be very cautious, Wilkie. And Roses can wear a hat, to cover her hair. So she won't be noticed. Look at her, she's dying to go."

Wilkie did look at me, and his fierceness softened. He thought about this for a minute or more, watching my face all the while. "All right," he finally said.

He'd said aye! I would be allowed to walk in those glorious gardens, to bask in the sun and the air, with the feel of the grass on my feet. I could eat a piece of sun-warmed fruit, and maybe I'd even have a small opportunity to study the design and the horticultural techniques. Silently, I clapped my hands together.

Wilkie smiled at my expression. "Roses often talks of the gardens."

I hoped I might find a pear to eat.

"That's a very real possibility," commented Kade, jarring me slightly. I hadn't realized I'd spoken aloud. To Wilkie, he said, "They'll be wondering what's keeping us, Wilkie. Let's go."

Wilkie's smile had faded. "You're to stay at this end of the orchard, only," he instructed his sisters. "And in the birch grove. Nowhere else."

"Aye, Wilkie," Christie assured him. "Don't worry yourself. We'll not go far."

Wilkie pulled his chair close to mine and stared into my eyes. He looked mildly panicked. He brushed his lips against mine, very briefly, then withdrew.

Kade was exasperated. "For God's sake, brother. The inner orchards and gardens are within the walls. Let the lass take some sun. You'll see her at dusk."

"She'll taste of pears by then," said Christie. It seemed a strange comment, but when we all looked at her, she stared at Wilkie innocently. "What?"

Wilkie stood, and it seemed too sudden, too abrupt.

He walked from the room followed by Kade, without so much as a backward glance. And I felt lost and desolate at his hasty departure.

But Christie and Ailie swept me up in their quest to entertain me and to take me out-of-doors, and I couldn't help but feel uplifted by their exuberance and by my own anticipation.

Christie left to retrieve a hat for me to wear, and then I was escorted through the side door to the airy glittery day.

Had I ever felt so alive? Nay, that wide-open world had never felt so reassuring nor so kind. There was a new solace in its contained beauty, here inside the walls of this keep. I was shielded from foes and predators. The day was sunny, the plants positively bursting with rich promise, and I was in good company. My new sisters, one on each arm, chatted happily. And I took wild comfort from the knowledge that Wilkie was nearby and that we would reunite as soon as day gave way to night.

If we saw people in the distance, we took care to skirt their vicinity, although it felt strange to be so sly and secretive. In my past life, people had taken little notice of me; now, to have to keep myself hidden and disguised, in my elevated mood, it felt almost laughable.

"No one would take notice of me." I tried to reassure Ailie and Christie. "I'm sure of it."

"Actually—" Christie smirked cagily, as if she was letting loose secret information "—there is a rumor that Wilkie is keeping a lass in his private chambers. I overheard several of the cooks discussing it. Trust me, Roses, they'll take plenty of notice if word gets out that you're here and you're real, and you're currently strolling the gardens. Wilkie is popular, not just among our clan, but far afield."

I found myself wishing Christie didn't provide quite so much information on that topic. But, then, I knew of this already. And I supposed it would make for interesting news, that the laird's handsome, sought-after brother had a secret of this kind.

We walked among a young birch grove, and the leaves dappled the sunlight on its soft grassy floor. "Let's take off our boots," I suggested, wanting to feel the coolness of the grass and the earth. I sat and began to unlace my shoes, registering momentarily the old, worn state of them. I felt shamed by this, that Ailie and Christie might notice and would be reminded once again of who I was and where I came from. But it could hardly be helped.

The sisters hesitated, as though removing their boots would never have occurred to them. "I haven't walked barefoot since I was a child," said Ailie.

"Oh, you must do it now, then," I encouraged. "'Tis a wondrous feeling. So free."

They followed my lead, and we walked, reveling in the softness of it, and before long we were running and playing like children through the grove and farther, to the edge of the pear orchard.

We sat under a gnarled, laden tree and ate several of the pears, letting the juice run down our chins and commenting on the delightful ripeness.

"See?" Christie laughed. "Roses *will* taste of pears tonight."

"Christie," scolded Ailie. "Don't be childish."

I couldn't help smiling, feeling utterly comfortable with these sisters. Never having had siblings, sharing this time with them, listening to their playful bickering, I found them fascinating. And at Christie's comment, I lay back on the grass. I closed my eyes and thought of Wilkie kissing me, tasting the sweetness on my lips. The thought brought warmth to my body, and I could feel the light throb begin again between my legs, where he'd touched me and inspired such sweet sensation. I wanted him to do it again, here, now.

We heard the crack of a twig nearby, as though snapped by a footstep. I opened my eyes and saw that both the sisters had become alert.

"We should go back now," Ailie said in hushed tones. "Wilkie said not to stay out for too long. Come." She began to rise, and Christie and I moved to follow her.

I saw a dark shape emerge from behind a nearby tree. And another.

Ailie made a small sound of distress at the exact moment I, too, noticed that these were not Mackenzie gardeners.

They were Ogilvie warriors.

CHAPTER TEN

MY MIND WHIRRED WITH PANIC. Where did they come from? How did they get inside the walls? Hadn't Wilkie said that the keep was well guarded? Had they found a hole in the defense?

There were four of them, and they surrounded us. They wore hoods, but I recognized their faces, although I knew none of them by name.

Christie, Ailie and I huddled together in the middle of their shrinking circle, and when one of them reached to grab Christie's arm, she let out a high-pitched scream. I was glad she did, too, as it might alert others to our plight.

The Ogilvie warrior was caught off guard by the noise she made and let go of her momentarily. And Christie screamed again, calling Wilkie's name, twice. But then the Ogilvie warrior grabbed her again, and he sneered at her. "We might have found ourselves more than one prize, men."

Christie screamed again, and the warrior pulled her up against him and covered her mouth with his hand. She struggled, and her screams were muted to near silence. Ailie was grabbed by another warrior, and the look on her face brought all the pain of my earlier realization home to me: they were not safe. And it was my fault they had been put in this dire and horrific situation.

Before a third warrior could grab me, I reached down to pick up a thick stick that lay on the ground near my feet.

I took off my hat.

"Unhand them. 'Tis me, Roses. I'm the one you want. Leave them."

One of the warriors chuckled. "A clever disguise, lass. No one would have guessed you were, in fact, a kitchen servant." He stepped closer, but I held up my stick like a sword. It would barely sting him if I swung it, but it briefly kept him at bay.

"I'll come with you willingly," I said. "There's no need to manhandle me. Or them. You should take me now, and let these two go immediately. Mackenzie warriors will have heard the screams—they're not far. They'll be on their way as we speak. Let them go."

"Let's take all three," said the warrior holding Christie.

"Nay!" barked the warrior closest to me, the biggest, and the apparent leader of the raid. "Leave them! We take this one. Now!"

With some regret apparent on his face, the warrior released Christie, and the second released Ailie. The sisters backed away, clutching each other's hands, but they didn't run. They were watching me, their eyes terrified and helpless. They could do nothing to save me.

"Run!" I yelled at them. There was a question in Ailie's eyes, but she heeded my warning, and she pulled Christie along with her. I felt overwhelmingly relieved when they were out of sight, so much so that it overshadowed my own fear for several seconds.

I dropped my stick, and I followed the lead warrior, flanked closely by Ogilvie's men.

Only then did the sickly weight of my terror begin to make itself known.

Could I try to fight them off? Unlikely, as there were four of them, each about twice the weight of me. And they were armed. I barely acknowledged the thought of my own weapons, hidden from me, so far from my reach they may as well not have existed at all.

Something occurred to me then, as we quickly approached the wall of the keep. Could I somehow take one of their weapons? I knew how to use a sword, and they wouldn't expect that I would possess such a skill. If I could get my hands on one of theirs, they would be caught unawares. I could take small comfort in the fact that they were unlikely to kill me; there was little doubt in my mind that Ogilvie had ordered me to be delivered very much alive.

It was a risky plan. But I eyed their belts, where their swords and knives hung, and I began to consider how I might take possession of one of them.

The lead warrior threw a rope over the wall. Within less than a minute, the rope was pulled tight. Which led me to believe that there were more Ogilvie warriors waiting there, on the outer side of the wall. Why hadn't they been seen? I supposed it was the boldness of their raid that might have been unexpected. And the stealth of it, and silence. A handful of men, sneakily penetrating the keep in broad daylight: this tactic might not have been anticipated. The Mackenzies had expected an army. Or a bluff. Not this.

One of the warriors climbed the rope and disappeared over the wall.

I was hoisted onto the back of a second warrior, the one who had held Christie. I was ordered to hold on.

The warrior's hair was long and bunched into knotted strands that hung down his back. Holding on to him as I was, I could tell that he hadn't bathed in some time. His high, feral odor, combined with my own fear, rolled my stomach, and I thought for a moment that I might be sick. But I turned my face to the side and took a deep breath of the floating breeze. I may have imagined it, but, briefly, I could smell the fruity scent of ripe pears. That sweet, happy perfume stirred something in me, and my fear gave way to anger. Now that Ailie and Christie were safe, I didn't have to go with these men meekly. I could fight.

And I was in a perfect position to reach for the warrior's knife.

He climbed up the wall, holding the rope, pulling us up, fist over fist.

I knew my chances of escape, or even survival, if I chose to fight, would be far greater inside the Mackenzie keep than out on the open plains. Or, at worst, back inside the confines of the Ogilvie manor. If I could stall for time, Wilkie might come for me. He might reach me.

"Hurry, man!" gruffed one of the warriors on the ground. The warrior I clung to climbed faster. And he was nearly to the top of the wall. So I took my opportunity. I grabbed the knife that hung from his belt. Before I could question my own outlandish plan, I plunged the knife deep into the warrior's back, gouging just above his waist on the right side.

I'd surprised him, and he screamed a yell. He let go of the rope with one hand, and I released my hold on him, falling heavily to the ground. Realizing he'd dropped his cargo, he jumped down after me. I was glad he hadn't landed on top of me, but still, it was a good fifteen-foot drop, and I was winded.

The injured warrior touched his hand to his wound and, seeing the blood on his hand, grew furious.

"You feisty wee bitch!" he yelled, and he slapped me across the face so forcefully, I fell back. I fought against the blackness that lurked around the edges of my vision and the small white stars that inflected the scene before me.

I tried to back away from them, still lying on the ground, but the lead warrior grabbed me roughly, pulled me up and spun me around. He looped a cord around my wrists, too tightly, painfully, and he threw me over his shoulder.

"Tie her onto me! I can hear them coming!"

Something was strung around my waist and my shoulders, pinning me tightly to the warrior. My ribs and my stomach pained me where it was slung over the warrior's shoulder, and my head was down, dizzying me. I heard myself groan slightly. My hair, now loosened from my struggles, covered my face. With me strapped to his back, the lead warrior began to climb.

I was losing my battle against the rising tide of unconsciousness, as the pain of my position and the bruised right side of my face settled in. I thought I imagined Wilkie's voice in the distance, calling to me. I knew I was dreaming him. I wished I could see him one last time, before I was lost to him for good.

There was commotion now, and I wondered if we'd reached the top of the wall, if the soldiers on the outer side of the wall were yelling and jumping. I opened my eyes to see a blurred figure climbing the rope behind us, grabbing the leg of the Ogilvie warrior, slicing it with

a knife. The red of the blood that spilled seemed surreal, almost theatrical in its abundance. And then we
were falling again, and the hard, jolting collision with
the ground stunned me anew. I couldn't breathe, and
my hair was in my face. I was sandwiched between two
men, one of them limp and lifeless, one furious. There
was so much commotion. And blood.

And then I could hear him.

Wilkie.

"Roses" was all he said. He cut me free of the dead
Ogilvie warrior and carried me to sit me under a tree.
He took a very brief moment to push the hair from my
face, to study me with fierce concentration. And once
he saw that I was alive and conscious, he ran back to
rejoin the fight, his sword already raised. I could see
that Kade was there and others. A crowd was gathering in the distance.

Wilkie was dueling with the warrior I had injured
with my knife. I could only watch in amazement at the
skill of him, the grace of his attack. It seemed a strange
thing to appreciate, but his movements were so clean,
so articulate, and so very confident, I could only have
described it as such: beautiful. Like everything else
about him.

What was not quite as beautiful, however, was the
sight of his sword slicing neatly through the neck of the
Ogilvie warrior, separating his head from his body, both
of which thumped heavily to the ground.

Almost simultaneously, Kade thrust his own sword
into the chest of the last Ogilvie invader, who fell to his
knees, propped up only by the force of the metal that
skewered his heart. He was looking at me, as the life
seeped from him along with his blood. "He'll continue

to hunt you," he said. Then he crumpled and was still. His statement disturbed me greatly.

And Wilkie, too, it appeared. He grasped the head of the decapitated Ogilvie warrior by its long matted hair and threw it over the wall. "Take that to your laird," he muttered, thrusting his sword back into its scabbard.

As foul and underhanded as those particular Ogilvie warriors might have been, I regretted their deaths. And I regretted that the Mackenzies were now as deep into this battle, if not more so, than I was.

But I could not regret that I was still here, inside the Mackenzie walls, with Wilkie with me, now kneeling beside me, touching me carefully.

"Roses? Are you all right?" He was feeling my arms for broken bones, then my legs. "Did they remove your shoes?" he asked gruffly, noticing my bare feet.

It pained me slightly to speak. My throat was sore, and my jaw bruised. "I removed them. In the birch grove." I read his train of thought, and I reassured him. "They didn't hurt me, warrior."

His eyes burned with anger. The aftermath of conflict clung to him and shone out of his eyes. He looked big and mean and severely powerful, his muscles dusted and flexed from the fury of battle. I could feel the brutality of him lurking behind his grip as he fingered my body gently, checking for bruises and sources of blood, which there was much of. I didn't believe any of it was mine. I'd been spooked, that's all. And my face was sore, as well as my ribs, but they were minor bruises, I thought.

Kade stood behind Wilkie, looking equally ferocious. His light blue eyes were wild with a barely calming aggression. "There's more to this than a prick with a kitchen knife," he said. "There must be. He's asking for war."

I returned his turbulent gaze and thought about his statement. That Laird Ogilvie was taking extreme measures to get me back into his clutches was now clear enough. And I agreed with Kade: the lengths Ogilvie was taking to seek me out seemed overblown compared to my small crime with the knife, which had surprised him more than injured him. I had no way of deciphering his motives, nor his actions, but I wondered if his devotion to carrying out his revenge, and on me in particular, might have stemmed from a quarrel with my parents. Perhaps he harbored a residing anger over some wrong my father had committed. Or a lingering resentment over the vehement refusals of my heartbroken mother. I knew of nothing else. Fleetingly, I thought of his muttered words as he'd attempted his violent act upon me. His fingers on the skin of my shoulder blade. The amazement in his voice and another note, too. Greed, perhaps. *It looks like a seal of some description.*

I had no solution to offer. I had purposely avoided contemplating the significance of my inked mark. Ogilvie's quiet fascination had offered no clues to the residual mystery of its—and my—origins. But something about that faded memory of Ogilvie's reaction to it, combined now with the very real danger I had brought upon the Mackenzie clan, shone a light on the connection. If showing the mark to Wilkie and his family could somehow provide information that might protect them, then that, rather than my own self-interest, seemed more crucial at that moment. I decided then and there to reveal my secret, once and for all.

"I want to show you—" I began, struggling to move.

"Nay, Roses," Wilkie insisted, interrupting me and putting his hand on mine. "Lay still for a minute. You're hurt. Your cheek is bruised, and you may have other injuries."

Ailie and Christie returned, wide-eyed, and they knelt beside me, alongside Wilkie.

"Roses made the men release us, Wilkie," Christie said. "They were going to take us, as well."

Wilkie's eyes flashed. I was stunned by the fierceness of him, and the gloriousness of his face. I wanted only to look at him and watch him. I wished I could hold him and shield him from war, and calm away his ire. I vowed to show him the mark, later. But my precarious courage on that one hidden point faded, overshadowed once again by my fear; I wanted so badly to keep him.

"I'm going to lift you, very carefully," he said. "And take you to Effie."

Such was the strength of him that the movement barely jostled me, and he carried me through the gathering throng of curious onlookers, not caring if I was seen. Word would surely be out soon, if not already, of the fight and what caused it. And there was no hiding the three dead Ogilvie soldiers who lay on the ground.

The crowd parted for us, but I took little notice of them. My attention shone in one all-focused direction: my warrior, who'd saved me in so very many ways. I placed my hand against Wilkie's chest, to feel his heartbeat.

"Warrior," I murmured, having nothing else to say, just wanting to speak to him. And he seemed to instantly understand this.

"Aye, lass. I'm with you."

He was with me. And I with him. And that was everything and the only thing I wanted or needed in this great wide world.

"WILL THE LASS REMAIN here for her rest, Wilkie?" Effie inquired. "She is fatigued."

I was tucked up in my bed in Wilkie's antechamber, carried here by Wilkie, who refused to leave my side, and fussed over by Effie, who would administer one more round of medicines before we slept. Christie was due to come to me soon. Wilkie and I had been tended to in the healing quarters, fed and questioned. I had light bruises along one side of my face, which was mildly swollen. And my ribs were purpled but not broken. Wilkie had opened his wound, which Effie had restitched a portion of and rebound.

"Aye. I will watch over her until Christie arrives," he directed her, in a tone that was almost bored; it was the tone of a man who was used to being obeyed and had never known any other way of it.

But as soon as Effie made her leave, Wilkie very gently lifted me, still wrapped in furs, and carried me to his bed. "What about Christie?" I asked him.

"She will return to you in the morning, when you are safely back in your bed. Until then, I will be your chaperone." There was no humor in his pronunciation this time, just tenderness and resolve.

Laird Mackenzie was irate over the attack and had ordered his men to double their efforts in safeguarding the keep. A party would be sent to carry a message to Laird Ogilvie, to meet and to negotiate, before more blood was spilled. I silently prayed that the negotiations would be successful. I tried to suppress thoughts of what might happen if they weren't.

I had worried that Laird Mackenzie would be angry at me, for introducing this conflict into his peaceful world. I'd apologized to him for this very reason. And in his typically abrupt manner, he'd informed me that his world was far from peaceful, that peace was hard-won, this day and every day. Instead of anger, what he showed me was curt concern, promised protection and surprisingly humble gratitude over the well-being of his sisters, who had relayed their tale to him. Ogilvie, I decided, had wildly misread Laird Mackenzie; Mackenzie's sternness stemmed from a single-minded drive to maintain the safety and success of his family and clan. Under the admittedly thick top layer of his brusque manner, he was, in fact, brimming with kindness. And I found this a heartening discovery, one that drew me deeper into my emotional attachment to the Mackenzie clan.

It had been a day full of emotion, to be sure. But I felt surprisingly removed from the heart-pounding events of the afternoon. My focus now was entirely on these chambers, on Wilkie and on soothing away the stresses that showed clearly on his face.

My weapons had been returned to me, and they sat propped against the stone wall in the antechamber. Their presence there brought me no comfort, nor Wilkie, I detected, from his stormy demeanor.

He crouched by the hearth, adding logs to the fire, and his thoughts seemed far away. Then he came to me and sat in a chair near the bed.

He was still upset and stormy.

I lay quietly, warm under the layers of furs. I closed

my eyes for a moment. I was still too modest and naive
to entice him in a knowing way. But I wanted to please
him tonight, to calm him and give him pleasure, as he
had done to me. I wasn't at all sure what to do, but I
wanted to try.

After a time, I heard him undressing, the clunk of
his boots, his belt, the sound of fabric dropping to the
floor. And I felt the heat of his body next to mine as
he lay down beside me, pulling the furs to his midriff,
below where the fresh bandage was wrapped.

We lay quietly for some time, allowing the events of
the day to dissipate.

Absentmindedly, he let his fingers sift through the
end strands of my hair. I sat up slightly and leaned
closer to him. He watched me as I carefully fixed a
twist in his bandage and smoothed a stray lock of hair
from his forehead.

"I aim to soothe you tonight, my warrior," I said,
and my voice sounded breathless and nervous with my
twilit intentions. "You know I would do anything for
you. You saved me."

He opened his mouth as though to speak, but I put
my finger gently across his lips to silence him, and
I traced the plump of his lower lip with my fingertip. I kissed him then, and I used all the skills I had
learned from him, carefully exploring his mouth with
my tongue, tasting him, playing him. I was hungry for
closeness to him. I crawled farther across his chest so
I was almost on top of him, and I could feel the hardness of him against my leg.

I kissed his face, the bristle of his cheek. I softly bit
the lobe of his ear, working my kisses down his neck,
to his chest. I took one of his nipples between my teeth,

and he squirmed and chuckled. The sound of that small laugh encouraged me; my efforts to ease his tension were working.

"You are a temptress, lass. You undermine my control." His eyes were so very dark, compelling and fierce. Inviting me to tempt him further.

I was curious about the rise of him, under the covers. I remembered the beauty of his body, a brief flash of recollection, that first time I had seen him emerging from the loch. I eased my body to the side, and I dared to drag my fingers lower, across his bandage, and lower still, to the bulging swell. Over the furs, I rubbed my palm on the mounded surface, feeling his heat through the thick layer of his covering.

He let me touch him in this way. I could see that he liked my careful caresses. I fingered his length through the bulk of the covers, fascinated by the hardness of him.

After several minutes, and as I became more adept at reading his reactions, Wilkie let out an uneven sigh. His blue eyes were fiery with his burn. "My Roses. Your touch is a miracle. So soft, yet so very potent. I can't get enough of it, lass."

Shyly, I reached for the edge of the blanket. I pulled the covers down, to reveal him to me.

I gasped. The size of him was astonishing. The change in him! The image as I remembered him, at the loch, did not at all match the discovery I found here.

"Warrior," I whispered. The sight of him both fascinated and alarmed me. My education on these matters was decidedly limited, but I knew the very basics, and I wondered at the mechanics of it, of *us*.

"Touch me, lass. Don't be frightened by me."

I did as he wanted, touching him, tentatively at first, running my fingertips over him, marveling at the silkiness and the heat. He was hot to the touch. I let one hand explore lower, to the soft, looser skin below, as my other hand gripped his shaft more tightly, rubbing along the length of him to the tip, where a slick of wetness had gathered. Shamelessly, I wanted to touch my mouth to him, to taste him. He groaned deeply as I swirled my finger across the broad end.

As though reading my thoughts, he murmured his request in a dark voice, rasped from his passion, "Put your soft mouth on me, Roses."

Leaning over him, I gripped his engorged shaft with both hands and lifted it away from his stomach. I touched my tongue to him, tasting salt, lightly licking at his essence. I placed my lips around him, taking more, struggling to fit my mouth around his thickness. I took as much of him as I could, squeezing my hands gently around the base, working him slowly, getting a feel for his response. My long hair fell to brush across his skin.

"Ah, God," Wilkie growled, and I'd never heard him use our Lord's name in vain before, but he repeated it more than once.

I was too inexperienced to know how to please him. His body was tensed and arched, his fists grabbing handfuls of the furs at his sides, as though he was laid out on a torture rack. It took me some time to find a rhythm. I sucked on him as tenderly as I could, drawing him farther and farther into my mouth, using my tongue to stroke him.

Wilkie let out an agonized groan, and I was mildly startled when his shaft jerked and hot liquid jetted into my throat, flooding my mouth with his milky seed. It was difficult to accommodate all of it. Wanting to keep him and soothe him and drink him into my body, I swallowed more than once and suckled gently on his softening shaft until I had taken all of his essence.

Wilkie lay still as I continued to tenderly kiss his body, loving the feel of him and enjoying a small sense of jubilation, that I had been able to please him in this way. I liked learning him and learning how I could pleasure him best. I could sense that he was floating now, as I had floated after he'd kissed my intimate places.

"Come to me, lass," he said huskily, and I climbed up and lay into the crook of his arm as he held me against him. "Your touch is the most profound thing on this earth. I have never felt anything like you."

"Nor I, you."

"Never leave me," he said, watching my eyes, searching for compliance.

"Nay, warrior. I'll stay with you and soothe you, each day and each night. Close your eyes."

He did. I reached to touch his hair and kiss his face. I smoothed my fingers in feather touches across his skin and his hair, as my mother used to do to me when I was a child, to calm me when I couldn't sleep, to make me feel drowsy and loved with her gentle attention and her nearness.

His breathing became deeper and relaxed, and even then, I continued to savor the feel of him and the taste of him.

"I love you, warrior," I whispered to him in his sleep, kissing his lips once more. I settled in against his warmth, laying as close to him as I could be in the fire-lit darkness, considering my fate and his.

But I could not sleep.

I rose, wrapping a fur around myself like a cape. I went to sit on the stone-bound window seat of Wilkie's chambers, which had been draped with cushions and furs. Outside the window, the stars hung low in the clear night, and the harvest moon glowed yellow, casting a golden glow to the orchards and fields below.

Sometime later, I heard Wilkie stir and reach for me, patting the space where I had been. He sat up.

Seeing me at the window, he came to me, wrapping a fur around his waist. Then he sat with me, holding me against his chest. Together, we watched the night.

"What are you thinking of, lass?"

After a moment, I told him. "I have a memory, or perhaps it's only a hazy dream, of my very earliest life. It comes to me now and then."

"Tell it to me," he said quietly.

"There's a fair-haired woman. She's very young. She's crying. There are shiny tears in her green eyes. And she's walking away."

The silence that followed was soft and comforting and contemplative.

Wilkie's deep, velvet voice had all the effect of a tonic, a cure, a remedy to every sadness. "It makes sense that whoever gave birth to you would have had fair hair and green eyes, love. I'm sure she was very beautiful, like you, although 'tis difficult to imagine anyone matching your loveliness."

"Why do you think she would give me away?" I asked, knowing already that it was a question that would likely never find an answer.

"I imagine she must have been in danger of one sort or another," he said. "'Tis the only explanation. Or not able to feed you, or care for you."

I wished I could learn the truth.

"Tell me of your parents that raised you," Wilkie said.

"They loved me as their own. My father's name was Oliver. He had strong hands and a tireless work ethic. His whistling tunes run through many of my memories, though they became less and less frequent as his dislike for Laird Ogilvie began to take hold and grow."

He was stroking my hair. "Why was that?"

"I think maybe he saw the future, just like I did."

"Laird Ogilvie's pursuit of you, you mean?" he asked.

"Aye, and my mother, too. She was so very kind, so very in love. Her face lit up whenever my father walked into our cabin. It was tiny but lovingly cared for, always neat and clean. It was a treasured childhood, mine. Until its decline."

Except for that one long-reaching moment, involving a wizened old woman and a never-forgotten warning.

But I didn't speak of that now.

I thought of the one possession of my parents', now lost to me: my mother's pin. I wished I could retrieve it.

"Retrieve what?"

I hadn't realized I'd voiced my wish aloud. A fleeting thread of alarm quirked through me now as I wondered if I'd spoken the previous recollection aloud, as well. But then: I thought not. That was a secret too guarded, too buried. "A pin," I said, "given to my mother by my father on their wedding day. 'Tis all I have left of them. I had it by the small pool at the cave. I think I may have left it there. One day I'll have to go back, to see if I can find it."

"I'll have it retrieved for you," he said, his fingers weaving themselves through my hair. "It will not be you who ventures to the pool, lass. Not for a while. 'Tis too dangerous. You know that."

I turned to him, leaning my head into the crook of his neck, and his arms closed more tightly around me. I did not feel confined by him, only grateful of his protection, only thankful of his nearness and all that he was. I could still taste him and feel the warmth and fullness of his essence inside me. "Tell me of your parents, warrior. What were they like?" I asked him shyly; the question felt wildly personal, and I knew these were details he kept close to his heart and rarely spoke of. I wondered if he would willingly talk about them. I was surprised when he answered my question openly, and with genuine emotion coloring his words.

"My mother died when I was ten years old," he said. "She had difficulties when Christie was born. She died several days later. I remember her well. She was gentle like Ailie, and she had Christie's exuberance but was somewhat quieter. She had dark hair—not quite black—and pale gray eyes, like Knox's. She was often praised for her vibrant beauty." He paused, remembering, his voice softened by affection. "She once called me her fiercest warrior son, when I won a swordsman ship contest when we were small children. Kade didn't appreciate that comment and decided to arm himself to the teeth, making a point of equipping himself more heavily than either Knox or I. Our mother noticed this, and soon after she called *him* her fiercest warrior son. Kade was immensely pleased by this, and to this day he still makes sure to wear more weapons than we do." He laughed softly at the memory.

"What about Knox?" I asked. "Did he not get jealous?"

"Nay, he never had the need to. He was laird-in-waiting and my father always treated him as such. The two of them were very similar in temperament and in looks."

I pictured Wilkie as a small, proud boy. And Kade, vying for the attentions of his elegant mother. And I imagined young Knox, perhaps a miniature of his noble, striking father.

"I'm sure she would have been very proud of the men you have all become."

"I hope she would. The very last thing she said to us before she died was this—'Promise me this: always follow your heart.'"

This silence was laced with sadness but also somehow charged, almost sparkling with it. I almost didn't dare ask it, but then I said softly, "And are you?"

"Aye, lass. I am," he said, his eyes deeply, darkly blue. "I am following my heart, to you." He kissed my lips for a tender, lingering moment.

Then he settled me against him and looked out again at the low-hanging moon.

His next comment was murmured, like a private thought spoken aloud. "I am following my heart, but I am not following my brother the laird's direct orders. Therein lies the problem."

And so I understood his conflict a little bit more clearly, and how difficult a problem I had introduced for him. He could justify and allow his desire for me in part because he imagined he was living the last words his mother had spoken to him, by keeping me close; yet this desire warred with his duty to his brother and his clan, their outreaching prosperity and the strengthening of crucial military alliances.

I was disturbed by his dilemma. And I was also comforted by his confession. *I am following my heart, to you.* Hope ballooned in my chest. Maybe, just maybe, there could be an alternate solution to Wilkie's betrothal to one of the Morrison women, another way of securing the alliance between clans and armies. Maybe, if Knox was reminded of his mother's dying words and if he knew of Wilkie's claim on me, maybe he would somehow allow us to be together.

My eyes felt heavy, but my mind continued to churn.

"Come on, lass," Wilkie said. "Time for bed."

He carried me back to his bed and lay facing me, securing the furs tightly around us. His hand on my hip relaxed, and his breathing slowed as he fell asleep. I noticed this about him: he was a good sleeper, drifting easily into his dreams.

My drowsing thoughts were fluid and disturbed. I wondered if Knox was unrelenting in his orders and Wilkie wed another, would I be able to share him or to leave him when the time came? I thought not. I was too deeply invested in this man to ever be separated from him now and survive it. His presence in my life was too strong, too all-encompassingly fundamental to go without, now that I had experienced his magnificence. His blood had mingled with mine, and I had taken his seed into my body. He was in me, and I could feel him. I was overwhelmed by all that he was. As Wilkie described me, I considered: *you are the sun.* I, too, felt his light and his essence inside myself and all around me, like a newfound life force. Before those moments when I'd seen and touched him for the first time, by the loch and in the cave, every memory seemed faded and dull. When Wilkie had stormed his way into my life, darkness had become light.

I realized with some distress that I was no longer willing to live without him.

CHAPTER ELEVEN

I WAS DREAMING A BEAUTIFUL dream. I lay in my cave, warmed by a stoked fire that heated me to such an extent that a dewy sweat covered my skin. I kicked off my furs. My dark warrior came to me and lay with me in our quiet haven. He lifted my shift, cooling my skin deliciously. He eased my legs apart so he could kneel between them. His mouth was kissing the skin of my stomach. He lifted my shift farther, over the swell of my breasts, which he kissed and nuzzled until they were aching and heavy. He placed his hot mouth over the tip of one breast, and the vibrant pulls sent quickening channels to the core of my body, which grew slick and honeyed and wanting. I arched to him, and he took my other nipple, using the wetness of his mouth on the first to swirl sensation, teasing in pinching tugs. I was writhing and moaning, wanting more. I was pleading with him. I needed him to ease the scorching emptiness, to stroke my rising tide. I felt him touch my entrance with his heavy shaft, gliding its very tip against me. This lightest touch was the fulfillment of every desire I had ever known. With its subtle persuasion, this touch fed a spiraling burn throughout my being, igniting my body into a thousand suns, blinding me with sensation as it raged lusciously through my clenching core.

But then the touch was withdrawn, and I was left

floundering and irate from the removal of such intense ecstasy. My anger awoke me, and I opened my eyes.

We weren't in our cave but in Wilkie's chambers. He was not a dream lover, but a real one. I reached for him, and my hands found the thick silk of his hair. His hands were forcing my legs wider. And his mouth was on me, caressing my lingering rapture, releasing it anew with his greedy attentions. The rippling waves were not as intense this time, but long and lush and brimming with molten, starry pleasure.

I lay on my back as he continued his tender kisses, and his fingers were everywhere, lightly learning my every curve and contour.

I pulled, ever so slightly, on his hair. He looked up at me. His eyes glimmered with mischief, a sight which relieved me greatly. Gone was his angst and his turmoil, for now.

"My Roses wakes," he said.

He crawled up my body and lay on top of me, holding his weight, but still lying heavily against me. I was very aware of his bold, immense hardness, pressing along my near-naked body.

"You pleasure me, warrior."

His dark eyes were smug and simmering with his own heat. "You are the sweetest fruit."

"And what of your own pleasure?"

"You are my pleasure."

But I wasn't convinced. The dream touch of his body barely *inside* me ignited me with a new awareness. I wanted more. "You're holding back," I said, and I was surprised to feel that I was mildly incensed by this.

He smiled at my light anger. "For now."

I suppose I knew why he would not take me fully, as

I knew by now exactly what it was that I wanted him to do. It was an activity, after all, for a marriage bed. But our own circumstances, it seemed to me, were unusual. What we had *already done* were activities, too, that were reserved for a marriage bed. And every one of them the most sublime experiences of my life, in equal measure. I didn't know if Wilkie would marry me—he had mentioned his intention to do so, but fleetingly, and had never repeated it—or if he would even be allowed to, if he wished it. His duty might steer him, by necessity, to one of the heiresses who fought for his hand. Those were rivers yet to cross.

Here and now, I knew what *I* wanted.

I had already resolved not to live without him. It mattered not whether he owned me now, or later. In my heart, I was his already.

I wanted to give myself to him. I wanted him to take me and fill me. I wanted to feel him inside me, deeply. The thought, to be sure, was intimidating. The *size* of him. I wasn't sure how we would fit together. But I knew enough about the pleasure he was able to unrelentingly give, and I wanted more of it. I wanted more of *him*.

I began to move a little, inching my way higher, as I lay underneath him. I arched my hips toward him, until I could feel his hardness pressing against the skin of my thigh. The promise of him there, so close, was stunningly alluring. My burn was so fierce for him I thought I might spasm again from the mere possibility.

"Roses." His deep voice sounded stern, questioning.

I moved farther, seeking, positioning. But Wilkie, as though reading my thoughts, flinched away from me, rolling off of me so suddenly and violently, he half fell from the bed. He grabbed a fur and wrapped it around his waist. Then he walked over to the fireplace. He gripped the wooden edge of the hearth with his fingers. The sight of those fingers and their brutal strength aroused me beyond belief, and his body, lit by the fire, was hard and sculpted.

His chest heaved slightly, and his breathing was uneven.

I worried that I had hurt him or angered him. He tugged at his hair with one hand, and I sat up, concerned by his rash behavior.

"I'll not use you," he said, staring into the fire. "I worship you."

"Worship me now. However it pleases you. I am yours."

His head flicked moodily in my direction. He didn't answer me.

"Come back to me," I said.

He remained frozen in place.

"I won't touch you," I promised. "I'll heed your every command."

Our heavy gaze connected. I was still secretly rippling from his touch.

"I want you to, warrior," I whispered. "Please."

"I cannot, lass. Not yet."

"You cannot." I remembered our first meeting, by the cave, and I mimicked his words now. "Why is this?"

"You're too pure."

His high-handedness irked me. I felt my brow furrow. "I'm not too pure."

"You are. You're exquisite. And innocent. I'll not use you, Roses." His voice was low when he continued, and I could hear there the note that I feared: the slightest hint of pain. And uncertainty. "I want to take you as my wife. Only then."

I stared at him, and I could see him read the questions in my eyes. Was it true? Could it happen as he described it? And if we *were* to be wed, what was the point in waiting for a wedding night? And why, then, was his voice inflected with hesitation?

A thousand questions swirled around us. But there was one utter certainty that outshone any of the buzzing difficulties: even if I was never to marry Wilkie, it didn't change how I felt. I wanted him regardless. I wanted anything of him he would give. The blaze of that insight was almost more unsettling to me than any other.

I turned away from him, lying on my back and staring at the ceiling, frustrated and upset.

He returned to the bed and lay next to me. He grasped my jaw with his hand and faced me to him. "I *will* marry you, Roses. You're too beautiful to escape me. My heart can't bear a single moment apart from you. Your body is sacred to me now, and I'll worship you fully only when we are joined by wedlock." He leaned closer, brushing his lips to mine in a slow, succulent sweep. "Until then, I will adore you every minute of the day. I will please you and soothe you every hour of the night. Will you marry me, Roses? Will you become my wife?"

It still seemed unfathomable that he was within my grasp, that I could keep my warrior as my own. I had a strong feeling it wouldn't be as easy as he seemed to believe it might be. But now that I'd detected the less intimidating layers of Laird Mackenzie's personality, I dared to hope it could one day be a possibility.

And I didn't want to sulk or waste precious moments

of his loving. If Wilkie continued to give me the kind of pleasure he had so far given me for a thousand days and nights, and nothing more, it would be enough.

I returned his light kiss, holding my lips to his very softly. "Aye, warrior. I'll marry you. And I'll hold you every minute of the day and night, from this day, and every day."

He smiled against my lips. "Roses said aye to me. My beloved is my betrothed."

"I've never said anything but aye to you."

He laughed softly and stared deeply into my eyes. "My body burns for you, lass. And my heart breaks for you. When I thought you'd been taken from me—" His eyes blazed with such fury, I touched his lips.

"I wasn't taken. I'm here with you."

He absorbed this, and his eyes slowly calmed. He was silent for a long moment, contemplating me, then he said, "Tell me. What would you choose to do?"

I didn't hesitate. "Stay with you."

"Aye. I mean, after that. You'll stay here with me. And you'll marry me. And I'll keep you as close to me as I can, when I train and when I work. But what else would you choose to do, with your time? You grow restless when I'm not here to give you all my careful attentions." The corner of his mouth quirked.

"Oh. I would choose to…" I watched his reaction, wondering if he would allow such a thing. "I would continue to assist Effie, if she wanted me to. But most of all…I would choose to help tend the gardens. The medicine garden. The vegetable gardens. The orchards."

Wilkie looked at me as though he'd just discovered a new and fascinating treasure: my thrumming excitement. And it was true; I hadn't explained to him the extent of my wish, to tend plants and trees and herbs and vines, to spend my days feeling the soil and the grass, and watching the fruits of my labor grow. "If you want to tend the gardens, lass, then the gardens it is. When you choose to. If you choose to."

I lay still for a time. Maybe I hadn't woken up, after all. Maybe all of this, and all of him, was still a hazy beautiful production of my subconscious, hopeful mind.

I held him close to me, not moving, barely breathing. I didn't want to upset this perfection. I didn't want to wake up, or to unbalance with a word or a movement the beauty of this moment. The fledgling seed of hope and optimism that Wilkie had introduced into my life at our very first encounter took hold in me then, shifting, digging in, imparting a shred of itself into my psyche. Changing me, as though my very spirit was coiling itself around his, daring to bloom and flower from the sustenance he provided.

CHAPTER TWELVE

THE NEXT DAY, I WAS assigned a bodyguard.

He was a massive, unruly-looking warrior named Fergus, and he seemed less than pleased by his new assignment.

He was called into Wilkie's chambers and introduced to me. He nodded once to me, where I sat in a chair by the fire. Then he hastily returned to his post, closing the door behind him.

Wilkie had woken early and had disappeared for a time, and I had set about tidying his chambers, getting dressed and brushing my hair until it was smooth and gleaming. I awaited Wilkie's instructions obediently and did not consider leaving his chambers, as yet.

And so I still sat with my brush in my hand, my dress on but my feet bare, warmed by the fire.

"Fergus will remain outside this door, Roses. He's one of Knox's most trusted men. The walls and gates have been fortified with soldiers, both inside and outside the walls. There will be no more surprise raids. We were surprised by Ogilvie's determination, but we are not intimidated by, nor tolerant of Ogilvie's tactics. Messengers have been sent to deliver an invitation to negotiate. So it will be business as usual." Except for the one enormous warrior who was now relegated to ensuring my safety. "Fergus will guard you until I can return to you."

I thought this unnecessary, but I didn't argue with him. The storm of Wilkie's fury over my near-abduction lurked in his eyes once again. And I was wary, as well, after yesterday's events. I would be more careful.

"When will I see you again?" I asked quietly, my heart already heavy at the thought of his departure.

"I'll see you tonight."

Many, many hours. My expression must have shown the despair I felt at being separated from him for so long.

"If I can, I'll come to you sooner," he said. "Once you finish preparing yourself, Fergus will escort you to Effie's healing quarters, where you may spend the day with her." I knew this arrangement was difficult for him to concede to, much less to offer; it was meant to appease me, so I wouldn't argue with him or subtly accuse him of keeping me captive. "If you want to," he added. "Or you may prefer to rest."

I rose and walked over to him. I reached up and touched my fingers to the braided hair at his temple, drawn to his fierceness and wishing at the same time to calm it. The warrior in him was in full force this morning, as he prepared himself for his day of training, hunting, planning battle tactics and leading men—manly duties befitting his station as the brother of the laird.

"You are very accommodating, warrior. What I want to do is come with you, wherever it is that you go. But I will do whatever pleases you and keeps you from worrying." I stood on my toes, but even then I couldn't reach his lips to kiss him. "I feel very small, barefoot in front of you, with you in your boots and your belt with your sword and your knives." He looked down at me, but he didn't lean closer. I gently wound his hair around my finger, pulling his face to me until I could brush my open lips against his.

He kissed me, almost reverentially, but then he pulled back. "Where did you come from?" he whispered, smoothing my hair back from my face.

"I—"

"Nay. I mean, how did I find you? You are more than anything I could have dreamed up. I'm ruined forever, you realize."

"Why—"

"You know what I'm going to do, lass?" he asked, his dazzling face lit with his idea. "I'm going to bring you with me. Many of the men are away today, on a hunt. Guards are manning the keep in numbers. I'm meeting Kade to take stock of what we might need, if Campbell's rebellion is imminent. And I want you armed, too, lass. I'm going to give you back your sword."

I was overcome with his offer and my own excitement. That he wanted me with him, even as he worked, felt heavily significant.

"Will you teach me?"

"Teach you what?"

"How to fight, with a sword."

"You already know how to fight with a sword," he said. "Do you not? If you get any more proficient with your small sword," he mused, "I could be in grave danger."

I frowned at the reminder that I had hurt him.

He lifted me into his arms, holding me against him, so my bare feet were suspended off the floor. He was happy, I could read it in his eyes. "Nay, lass. I don't want my Roses frowning at me. Smile at me. You defended yourself well, as you have had the need to do. Now we fight on the same side. And you have me to protect you. I'll teach you technique, if that's what you want. And tonight, we'll read."

I couldn't help smiling back at him then, wrapping my arms around his neck, kissing him and kissing him again. The strong stripes of his eyebrows, his closed eyes, his face, his lips. "I have long wished I could read, and write."

"Soon you'll be able to. I think you'll be a quick learner. Nay, lass. No more kisses. I'm late, and 'tis the least of my crimes, all because I can't get enough of my sweet, blonde, sunny lass. God, you're sweet. Nay, stop. I can no longer plead dire injury nor fevered delirium. Only lust and obsession, which my brothers are somewhat less tolerant of. Come, now. One more kiss. But only one."

I could feel the lust and taste the obsession he spoke of as he returned the kiss, like milk and honey on my tongue. I wanted to wrap my legs around him or, oddly, to lie down in front of him. But I pulled away from him, not wanting to be the further cause of disruption to his schedule and his duties. "Are you certain you want me to stay with you?"

"Aye. I've never been more certain of anything in my life."

FERGUS APPEARED ALMOST comically relieved to be freed from his new assignment so soon. And Wilkie led me, his hand tightly around mine, through the manor and out-of-doors. The day was bright and clear, with only a few high wispy clouds to soften the light.

Some distance from the rear of the manor was a series of rectangular stone buildings and a large open area where use had cleared the grassy field to a dry and somewhat dusty training area. In the far distance a small group of boys listened as a trainer instructed them, and a few soldiers sparred farther afield. There was an archery stand with six targets set up but no one currently using them. As Wilkie had mentioned, most of the men were otherwise engaged today, and the training yards were sparsely populated.

We approached the nearest outbuilding to find Kade sitting on a cut log, under the roof of a lean-to constructed against the side of a stone building. He was sharpening a sword with a large circular fine-textured stone that spun when a foot pedal was used. Little sparks flew as he worked.

Next to him, there was a rack where ten or more swords of various sizes hung. It was clear by the bright shine of several of the swords which ones Kade had already sharpened.

Kade looked up when he saw us, and his eyebrows rose at the unexpected sight of me walking alongside his brother, my hand firmly in Wilkie's grip.

"Wilkie," Kade said in a casual greeting. "Roses." He removed his foot from the pedal and turned to face us.

"Roses and I are going to spar," Wilkie said. "She's asked me to give her some pointers."

Kade appeared entertained by the thought. He stood and leaned against the stone wall, folding his bare, muscled arms to watch us.

Wilkie grabbed the smallest sword—still much larger than any sword I had ever trained with—from the rack and handed it to me.

"Maybe the lass should be the one to give *you* some pointers," Kade commented. "Would you like me to fetch you some armor, brother? Some chainmail? At least use a shield. We don't want you confined to your chambers again. Or is that your sly intention?"

"I'll confine you to your chambers if you don't clapper your face."

"I'd like to see you try. I'll let Roses have the first go at you, and if she can't finish you, I'll step in."

"Go and sharpen some swords," grumbled Wilkie, but from the easy tone of their companionable bickering, it was clear that they in fact were enjoying each other's company.

Wilkie raised his sword to me, taking his stance, smiling smugly at me and narrowing his eyes as though in a mock threat.

"Terrifying," commented Kade.

The scene brought an uneasy memory to mind of our fight, of Wilkie's spilled blood and my own. I did not raise my heavy sword to him, feeling now that practicing with Wilkie wasn't something I really wanted to do after all. The memory of his near-death was too close to the surface. And I was distracted, too, by the intense beauty of him. The sun shone in gold-lit shards on his black-on-black hair. His white teeth flashed. His face was sun-bronzed and jeweled by the tiny shimmery glint of his day-old stubble and his laughing blue eyes.

"Hold it steady," Wilkie instructed me.

Warily, I lifted my sword an inch higher. Even holding the handle with both hands, it was heavy enough to feel and to act unwieldy, as though it had a mind of its own. I didn't feel confident enough to use it. Not like this. Not against Wilkie.

I lowered the sword. "Let's not, warrior. I'll watch you instead."

"Come on, lass," he urged me. "Hit me. Move your hands higher up the handle. All the way to the hilt. You'll have a steadier grip. Give it a good swing."

Given our history with swords, Wilkie might have expected me to be more practiced than I was, or stronger, or more confident. In fact, I'd had only occasional, light training, and my recent bouts with bloodshed had left me decidedly queasy. In fact, standing here like this, face-to-face with him, weapons in hand, it was wildly clear to me that Wilkie outmatched me to such an extent in every aspect of swordsmanship that even playful sparring with him was surprisingly daunting. Kade had once commented that if Wilkie had intended to kill me that day we'd met at the cave, he would have, and I was sure he was right about that now. I knew Wilkie wouldn't hurt me intentionally, but the size and strength of him, his height, his easy hold on the gargantuan weapon: the whole spectacle was making me regret my request.

And his eyes spangled with the challenge, the thrill, as though the feel of a sword in his hands kicked up a spirited natural tendency in him to compete and to win.

"Is this where you exact your revenge on me, warrior?" I said, maybe in response to my own sudden urge to be careful. He was too big and too lethal to play with in this way. The last time we'd faced off, we'd almost killed each other. My survival instincts were recalling that memory and shining a light on it now.

"Don't be daft, Roses," he said, but he held his sword higher. "Hold it up, that's it."

I did as Wilkie told me to. And I swayed the blade

back slightly, to get a feel for its weight and its power. Wilkie touched his sword lightly to mine.

"The gown lends an entirely different sensibility to the lass—especially with sword in hand—than the men's clothing did," Kade said blithely.

"Aye, it does," agreed Wilkie.

"And what sensibility is that?" I asked.

Wilkie gave me a roguish smile. "She's not nearly as meek and mild as she looks." His smile widened when I blushed at his insinuation.

Kade chuckled. "I guessed that to be true the very first time she strode into the Kinloch hall, in fact. Very determined, she was."

"Indeed she is," Wilkie replied to his brother, then, to me: "Whenever you're ready, lass. Show me what you've got. Give it a good swing."

I did, egged on by his teasing. But when I swung it back in the direction of Wilkie's sword, the sheer size and density of it gave it a much fuller, faster momentum than I had anticipated. My huge, unruly sword clashed with Wilkie's unflinching blade with such force—steel against fast-held steel—that the impact jolted up my arms, into my shoulders, up my neck, ricocheting through my body in a ferocious bolt. I felt as though I'd been struck by lightning. The sound of it thrummed in my ears. I was so shocked by the unexpected force of it that I dropped the sword and stumbled.

Wilkie caught me before I fell, and his sword was some distance away now; he'd flung it as soon as he'd felt my reaction. His face registered confusion, as though he thought me invincible and couldn't quite fathom my weaknesses.

I was suddenly and fully encompassed in his total

embrace. His hands held my face, his eyes searching for signs of pain.

And there *was* pain. A physical ache in my chest at the sight of him and his heartbreakingly compassionate reaction to me. He acted as if *he* was the one who'd been hit—as though my shock had physically manifested itself in *him* as much as in *me*. That he absorbed so much of my emotion touched me deeply. He cared for me, I knew that. But this vehemence of his dire, clenching concern was proof again that we were deeply, uncommonly bound.

It had been a long time since anyone had shown any kind of care for me at all, beyond critiquing the end result of my cooking or cleaning duties, or asking why I was late, or disciplining me on a not-yet-completed task. The extent of Wilkie's protectiveness lavished my starved soul with the sheer miracle of all he had to give, like a flood where before there had been a small and single raindrop.

"What's happened, lass?"

"I'm all right, warrior," I said, gasping. "I wasn't expecting the force of it."

He set me on my feet and brushed me off.

Kade, I couldn't help noticing, was watching Wilkie with an intense gaze, as though his brother's behavior was somewhat fascinating to him. "That sword's too big for her," he commented. Aye, it was; that had been well and truly established.

Once Wilkie was satisfied that I was stable enough to stand and walk, he led me over to where Kade stood and sat me onto the log seat.

"What's this?" asked Kade, feigning mild shock. "No blood? You're losing your touch, Roses." He referred, of course, to the growing list of knife attacks I had recently carried out. All in self-defense, I wanted to remind him. But I detected an edge to his playful chiding.

"Where's Roses's small sword?" Wilkie asked Kade, ignoring Kade's comment.

"Inside," Kade said, indicating the nearest building. "Either hanging on a hook by the furnace, or on one of the workbenches."

"I'll get it," Wilkie said, and walked off, disappearing around the corner of the building.

Once Wilkie was out of sight, Kade turned to me. His eyes studied me for a moment, coolly noticing my dress and the way my hair was bound. His arms were still folded across his chest, and he wore only two weapon belts today: fewer than usual. I thought of the story Wilkie had told me, of their mother's praise, of Kade as a young boy and his desire to impress her. As I pictured the image, I felt my perpetual unease in Kade's company give way, just slightly.

"If Wilkie ordered you to be escorted to Macduff's," he said evenly, "would you leave willingly?"

His words might have renewed my reserve, but they were spoken with quiet, sincere curiosity.

I was surprised by his question, at the directness of it. But not, as it sank in, by the topic itself. Wilkie had told me himself that he was making waves in his own diplomacy and obedience by keeping me so close to him, especially as plans for his marriage were already well underway. I knew the story. I knew the laird's intentions and the reasons behind them. And I knew how closely Wilkie held his duty to his heart. Kade's question, to be sure, caused my own heart to skip a beat, but I didn't hesitate. "Aye," I said, and I worked hard to keep my voice steady. "Of course."

Kade seemed equally surprised by my quick, decisive answer. His eyes watched my eyes and contemplated my face for a minute or more. "You've surprised us all, with your bold escape from Ogilvie and the way you strode into our keep to alert us to Wilkie's whereabouts when he was injured. It was a courageous act and one that probably saved Wilkie's life. We are indebted to you. But we are also trying to figure out how to handle a complex situation. 'Tis a decision that will need to be made soon."

I didn't need to ask him the details surrounding the decision he spoke of, and he didn't offer them. "I'll do whatever Wilkie asks of me," I said. "I love him."

Kade's concentration of my face deepened and his light blue eyes rounded just slightly. Then his expression softened, and a hint of a smile played at the corner of his lips. And in this brief respite from his total fierceness, he looked kinder and more handsome than I had yet seen him, as though a cloud had moved away from the sun and deeper layers of Kade's humanness had finally been allowed to shine through. "You won't be sent away. Not now. Not yet. Knox would prefer that you *were* sent away, as your presence here is compromising Wilkie's resolve in certain directions, as you may already know. But Wilkie would seek you out and follow you, possibly putting his own life in danger to do it."

"I would never want him to put himself at risk for me."

"When it comes to you, lass, it seems that Wilkie will not be reasoned with, and it is more than obvious that if you are put in danger, Wilkie will come to your assistance at whatever cost. And I can't say that I blame him." Kade's last statement caught me off guard in its subtle but clear lightness. If I didn't know better, I might have thought that Kade was complimenting me.

But then his smile faded completely, and his manner became serious. "I will ask you this, Roses—are your intentions true?"

I couldn't be sure: I didn't know much about Kade at all, beyond his dedication to his profession and his closeness to his own family, but I suspected he was weighing up a decision. And I had a distinct feeling that whatever answer I gave him now would play a part in that decision. This searching earnestness in him and his obvious concern for his brother made me feel inclined to choose my words carefully and give him every honesty. "I—I have no intentions, Kade, beyond being with him, and doing whatever he asks of me. My love for him has become the truest part of me."

Kade absorbed my answer thoughtfully and said nothing more.

Wilkie returned to us then, and he noticed the edgy and lingering intensity of whatever had taken place. "What's this?" Wilkie asked, looking at me, then at Kade, then back at me. Wilkie's question was left unanswered, and he was distracted enough by his task of strapping my belt around my waist. It felt strange to see it again: a tool belt for a different time and place altogether. Even stranger was its worn contrast against the gown I wore. But Wilkie stood back to admire it, as though he found the weapons and the finery a good match.

Kade watched Wilkie step forward to tuck a loose strand of my hair back into place with the gentlest touch, then glide his thumb absentmindedly over the wing of my eyebrow.

And with a slight squint of Kade's eyes and the sudden set of his expression, I watched whatever decision he was contemplating click into place.

"I'll leave you two to your sparring," he said, walking away into a dust-flicked distance.

WILKIE KEPT ME WITH him all day. I was given a much more cautious lesson, using my smaller sword, until Kade, disgusted, declared Wilkie's instruction all but useless. I was allowed to watch them as they sharpened, discussed and organized the swords, spears and many other weapons housed in one of several armories. And I watched him, never tiring of his voice, the span of his broad shoulders, the easy, rugged grace of him.

I knew, and Wilkie knew, each time he caught my eye, that our connection had fired and set like the steely, permanent solidity of the swords he worked. Yet he was honor-bound to follow the path that would be chosen for him. Kade's quiet conversation had not given me peace. Quite the opposite. Time was running out. I knew not what decisions the coming days would bring, but I knew those decisions would very likely break me. For now, though, I let the nearness of him cling to me and shield me, steeping me in a small window of true happiness. And I was, in that draining moment, content.

IN THE EVENING, WILKIE took me to a wondrous place. The library. Nestled away in the back of the manor, it was a large chamber with tall windows and the old, musty scent of knowledge and history. The walls were lined with shelves that displayed not only books but exotic trinkets and artifacts, the likes of which I had never seen.

I touched my finger to a patterned gold coin. I had never imagined such intricate metalwork, gleaming as it did with shiny golden opulence.

"Pick it up, if you like," Wilkie said. "My uncle brought it back from Rome when he traveled there many years ago."

"Rome," I repeated, fingering the coin, enjoying its solidity. I had never heard of such a place. I liked the sound of its name.

"'Tis a most fascinating city," he said.

"Have you been to Rome, warrior?"

"Aye. My uncle took my brothers and I on a trek through Europe when I was sixteen. My father considered it important for us to see the world beyond Scotland. We traveled for almost three years."

I had barely contemplated the world beyond Edinburgh, a place I had never been and didn't expect to see in my lifetime. I knew only vaguely of the place names of the lower British Isles, from maps of Laird Ogilvie's. I had heard of York and, of course, London, which I thought must be the largest city in the world. But these were not destinations I would ever see. I had little need to consider their cultures or people, when they were so far beyond my scope.

Wilkie laid a sheet of parchment on the table and retrieved a small box from a shelf, which he placed next to the parchment.

"Are you ready?" he asked. He lit several oil lanterns and a number of candles. The oily reek of the lamps and the honeyed scent of the beeswax mingled in the soft-lit night. His blue eyes were light tonight. He pulled out one of two high-backed chairs at the table for me to sit on.

I sat, and Wilkie sat in the other chair, pulling his chair close so his warm thigh was resting against mine.

"Where did your mother's lessons leave off?" he asked. "Did you learn the letters of the alphabet?" Wilkie uncorked the small glass inkpot, dipping the pointed end of the feather quill into it, swirling lightly.

I thought about this as I watched him prepare his quill. I remembered some of the letters. "I remember *A, B* and *C*. And *R*. And *O*."

"'Tis a good start," he said. "There are twenty-six letters. And each one has two forms: big and small."

"Why two?"

"Big ones are for the first letter of names, and when you begin a sentence."

"What's a sentence?" I realized I had a lot to learn, but Wilkie was patient, watching my face as he explained. I tried hard to concentrate, but it was difficult with his face so close to mine, an unruly strand of his soft hair skimming my cheek.

"A sentence is an idea. It begins with a capital letter and it ends like this." He drew his quill from the inkpot, sliding it gently against the lip to remove the excess. Then he touched the tip to the parchment to make a tiny dot.

"A dot," I said.

"Aye. You need to learn each letter and what it sounds like, and I'll teach you that soon, but first, let me show you what the letters are used for."

"Tell me a sentence," I said. I wasn't sure what he meant by this.

He thought for a moment, then smiled. "'One day, I went for a swim in the loch.'"

"Is that a sentence?"

"Aye. And it looks like this." He wrote some letters, and I could see that the first one was bigger than the others, and that, at the end, he drew a dot.

"Tell me another one."

His smile lingered. He wrote more letters. The ink made curled shapes on the parchment in a pleasing, lengthening design. "'I saw a small thief.'"

"The first sentence is longer than the second one."

"Aye. A sentence can be long or short. It all depends on what you want it to say."

"What's the next sentence?"

"Hmm," he said, narrowing his eyes as though in deep concentration. "'I chased the small thief up a very steep hill.'"

"'Warrior,'" I said softly. "Are you really going to write *this* story?"

"Aye. I like this one." He continued to write the sentence and finished with the dot.

"Is that an *I*?" I asked, pointing. I thought I remembered that one, too.

"Aye, it is."

"I don't want to hear the sentence that comes next. I don't like to think about it."

"Which one?"

"The one where we fight."

"All right," he said. "We'll skip that one. Let's go to my favorite part."

"Which part?"

He wrote down another sentence.

"What does it say?"

"What does it start with?" he said. "You can read the first letter."

I smiled at him. I could. "You're a good teacher, warrior. It says *I*."

"It does, lass. You're a natural."

I smiled at him, excited, and he laughed.

"What does the rest of the sentence say?" I asked.

"Wait," he said. "I'm not finished yet." He continued to write, then finished with another dot.

"Please tell me. What does it say?"

"Patience, lass. It says 'I took off the small thief's helmet and beheld the most enchanting angel with hair like ripened wheat on a late summer's day.'"

Amazed by him in every possible way, I said, "You're a very good writer, warrior."

"Thank you." He continued writing and reading. "'The sight of her touched my very heart'—Nay," he said, drawing a line through some of the letters. "'The sight of her *inflamed* my very heart. Her beauty astounded me, pouring into my soul and my body, and changing me forevermore. I wanted only to surrender myself entirely to her healing caresses.'"

I touched his sleeve, waiting and wanting to hear more.

He dipped his quill into the inkpot and continued to scratch the black, scrawling ink onto the dry parchment. I could see the tiny fibers absorbing the black liquid as he wrote. "And now I can think of nothing else but her green eyes and her sweet smile.'"

"Warrior," I whispered, so touched by him, so very in love with him. My heartbeat felt as if it filled my chest and warmed me from the inside out. I let my hand stroke his large muscular arm through the fabric of his tunic.

I liked the way his hand held the quill and dipped so carefully into the ink. I loved how his big brawny body was, here and now, calm and focused. My warrior was not only a soldier, but a learned, knowledgeable nobleman, and I saw new aspects to his character, too. He was a skilled and patient teacher, and he was talented with words. I could picture his description as though he was painting a picture in my mind. I knew this story, aye, but I delighted in hearing his interpretation of it.

I tucked his hair behind his ear so I could see his strong, refined profile more clearly.

"'And I knew,'" he read, "'that from that moment forward I would not be able to bear being parted from such immaculate, plush, golden beauty, not even for a single second.'"

I watched his mouth as he spoke, his perfect lips. I watched the sweep of his dark eyelashes as he blinked, his eyes cast down to the parchment.

"'And then,'" he said, "'when I tasted—'"

"You can't write *that*," I whispered. "What if someone reads—?"

"Shh, I'm writing. '…when I tasted my Roses—'"

"Aye, I can see my name—"

"Let me finish," he said, smiling. "'When I *tasted* my Roses, she was sweeter than honey, softer than the softest petals of a rose, more succulent than the most delicious food, and I was instantly addicted to her nectar and her scent and her face and her pink lips. She guided me out of the darkness with her soft light. The darkness beckoned me, pulling me into murky, directionless corners. But Roses was there. She was the light. And I followed. I wanted only to follow her and see her and bask in the glow of her sun-drenched beauty. She became my hope and my life.'"

I felt the warm line of a tear on my cheek. I was crying from happiness, that I had found him and that I might have provided him with hope or with anything at all. Everything of me, then and now, was dedicated entirely to giving more of myself to him, in any and every way I could. My heart and soul and body wanted only to please him and comfort him and nourish him. Now and always. This was what I had willingly, joyfully become. His.

"'I knew that if I could get my Roses to kiss me with those *lips,* that I would not die, but live. I *knew.* And so I begged her to give to me, to touch them to my mouth. And she did. And I was healed. Those lips on mine were the most intense, life-giving touch I had ever felt. And then, when she opened her lips just enough for me to slide my tongue—'"

"*Wilkie.* What kind of story are you writing?"

"The best kind." He paused and looked over at me. "Say my name again. I like the way it sounds when you say it."

"Wilkie."

His mouth curved in a bemused half smile as he returned to his work. "Now, where was I? Ah, aye, here…'just enough for me to slide my tongue into her delectable mouth…'"

He stopped, smiling at me encouragingly as he wrote another single letter.

"'I,'" I read.

"Excellent," he said. "'I was alive again, and death and darkness were banished by the light and the sweetness Roses gave to me, offering herself to me, feeding me. And, oh, how I love the soft moans she makes when I touch her and drink the sweet spirit of her from her body…'"

The sound of that word, spoken in Wilkie's hushed voice, melted me to my very bones. *Love.*

"'…and if I don't somehow get her to wed me soon so I can make love to her I may very well go mad.'"

As he continued to write, I sensed a sudden heaviness in his heart and my own at the word *wed* and all the issues surrounding that topic and its uncertainties, that I wanted to soothe and lighten.

I took the quill from his grasp and held it, our fingers entwining around it. "Did you really write all that?"

"Aye," he said, and I was happy to see that my touch had eased him; a hint of mischievousness sparked in him as our eyes met. "Well, I was writing it until you took my quill."

"You're supposed to be teaching me," I teased him gently, but I was somewhat breathless from his sentences. "I've hardly learned anything."

He smiled. "Not true. You've learned to read 'I.'"

"I think I already knew that."

He turned to me, straddling my knees between his own, holding my face in his large hands. "You learned that I find this mouth the most irresistible, pink, delectable—"

"I think I already knew that, as well."

His mouth was very close to mine.

Quietly he said, "And you learned that I love you. Deeply. Madly. Insatiably. Did you know that already, too, Roses?"

He kissed me. And again, longer, deeper, warmer. He kissed me tenderly, endlessly. And that was the end of my lesson, for now.

CHAPTER THIRTEEN

On the eve of the clan gathering, Wilkie escorted me to his antechambers, where my bath was waiting for me.

"When you are ready, Fergus will escort you to the hall, where the women are preparing for the arrival of Laird Morrison." He seemed slightly miffed at the mention of the guest's name. Or maybe it was just me, reading my own emotion into his words. "You'd prefer Ailie's and Christie's company than to remain here throughout the day?" he asked, knowing full well I wouldn't want to be cooped up alone in his antechamber for hours on end. And I wouldn't be allowed to accompany him today. The entire clan, Wilkie included, was readying the keep for guests.

"Oh, aye."

"My sisters will keep you well entertained," he assured me. This was true, and I was thankful I'd have their company, and could work, and help, and keep busy.

"There is a spare bed being fitted for you in my sisters' chambers," Wilkie said, "'Tis a front, while the guests are about."

"A front," I repeated, getting his meaning.

He didn't respond but continued staring at me evenly.

"Ah," I said. "To keep my reputation intact." Again I detected a nudging sense of unease in him. I began tentatively. "Will I—"

"You'll sleep with me," he said curtly. He was annoyed and surly on the subject, so I didn't prod him. I suppose I should have been grateful that my reputation was being so thoughtfully considered.

"And now I will give you one small kiss," he said. "Since anything more than that would cause me to be remiss in my duties, such is the temptation of you. But I will return to you this evening." His voice was low when he continued. "And I will kiss you much more than once, and I will taste of your honeyed pleasure on my tongue."

He touched me only with his mouth, the kiss erotic in its lightness, then he left me to my bath and to my day.

In the short time I had been at Kinloch, I'd been cleaner than ever before in my life, I reflected. Still not accustomed to such luxuries, I decided to appreciate my good fortune. I used the rose-scented soaps that had been laid out by women that were not Effie, nor Wilkie's sisters. Having spent years in the gossipy kitchens and servants' quarters of the Ogilvie manor, I knew that the news of my presence and my mysterious arrival would travel like wildfire. My accommodations, whether I was in Wilkie's chambers or not, would be discussed. My rescue would be recounted. My placement and origins enquired about. I cared little. My reputation—as Laird Mackenzie had so generously pointed out—was hardly an issue. And, I couldn't help wondering, if Ailie's and Christie's chambers were to be used as a front, then why was my bath being brought in here? It almost seemed as though Wilkie *wanted* to encourage rumors on the subject.

If I was never to marry Wilkie, if I was never to join with him as I wanted, if I was forever spoiled for another man regardless of any of these details, or in spite of them: I refused to allow myself to fret. That I had much to worry about was obvious enough. I could not predict what the future would hold, and in fact I didn't care to. I wanted to ride the anticipation of seeing Wilkie tonight. He had promised he would teach me another letter. And I felt excited about my day, as well, being included in clan activities and the company of Wilkie's lovely, welcoming sisters. Beyond that, I preferred not to let my worries tread.

One growing prickling worry that refused to be squelched, though, was the issue of the guests that the Mackenzie clan were readying themselves to host. An elderly, ailing laird and his bevy of daughters and nieces, all heiresses in their own right, competing for a husband who would be gifted his own lairdship. And not just any husband. Every single one of them had their eyes on one particular conquest. *My* warrior.

The Morrisons.

ONCE I HAD BATHED, I checked my face in the small hand mirror and saw that a small reddish bruise remained, but otherwise my face was not damaged from my attack by the Ogilvie raiders. My ribs were still sore, and a purplish mark remained from where I'd been slung over the Ogilvie warrior's shoulder, but it didn't restrict my movement much.

I dressed and braided and bound my hair. And I was escorted by Fergus, who said nothing but looked at me once or twice with a slightly confounded expression as he led me down the stairs and into the excitable activity of the hall. More than a dozen women were talking and working. Ailie and Christie saw me and immediately rushed over to ask on my health, as they hadn't seen me since the attempted abduction, and I assured them I was well and ready to assist them in any way they required.

Ailie was particularly invigorated today, and I wondered over her excitement. I inquired, carefully, hoping I wasn't overstepping my boundaries.

"You enjoy the Morrisons' company?" I asked her.

Christie, as usual, was to provide possibly more information than she should have. "The Morrisons will not be the only guests. The Munros will also be in attendance. Ailie is particularly partial to the company of one Magnus Munro, the laird's eldest son. Isn't that so, Ailie?"

Ailie wasn't one to give quite so much away. "No more than any of the other Munros, my dear sister," she said. But her eyes sparked with a quiet animation that all but confirmed Christie's comment.

I was introduced to Beatrice, the head of the kitchen crew, simply by my first name. Several others came to me, too, curious and eager to learn more of my mysterious arrival. That I was a Macduff apprentice healer was a story that was quietly distributed; it was all too likely that someone might disprove it if it was advertised too strenuously. From the looks I was getting and the hushed whispers, it was clear that rumors were already flitting around the manor like glittering moths. "This is Roses," repeated Christie. And I was glad for the simplicity of it. *Roses, the wanderer,* Kade had called me. And it was an accurate description. I was as rootless, as adrift, as a cloud in the sky. Nay, I reminded myself. No longer. In my heart, I was bound to Wilkie inexorably.

I distracted myself by following the lead of Ailie and Christie, helping arrange and set the tables. Ailie, in particular, directed the kitchen staff, ordered the fires to be lit, led the inspection of cleaning tasks, and managed the many other jobs that needed to be done before the guests' arrival in the late afternoon. She carried out her leadership duties with quiet confidence, as though well accustomed to her role. She was the eldest woman of the laird's immediately family, therefore giving her the highest status of any woman of the clan. I knew she wouldn't hold the title of Lady Mackenzie; that was reserved for the laird's wife, and I wondered at Laird Mackenzie and his obvious lack of one. I remembered a vague recollection of Wilkie commenting on it once, when I'd still been hazed by fever. *Two years have passed, Knox,* Wilkie had said. *'Tis time for you to remarry.* So he had been married once. I wondered at his story and his loss.

I felt unusually subdued and acknowledged my growing unease at the arrival of the Morrison women. Again, I recalled the murky memory of the brothers' conversation on the subject. Wilkie had spoken of "the Morrison buffet," and it was Kade who had mentioned a sister called Maisie, in particular.

This detail disturbed me greatly, that Wilkie had spent time with at least one of the Morrison sisters. Had he pleasured her as he'd pleasured me? Or even more? Had he given her all of himself, as he refused me? I wondered at the truth of his insistence that he had no interest in Maisie or Stella, the reputed beauty of the group. I felt almost ill at the thought and wished for a moment I could retreat to Wilkie's chambers and be alone. I knew Wilkie had had his share of women; I could expect no less of a man possessing both outstanding beauty and such an enviable status. What worried me was that one of them, or more, would be here in this room and in his company, in a matter of hours.

"What has you upset, Roses?" asked Ailie quietly.

But of course she already knew. I'm sure it was obvious to all who suspected it: my absolute love for Wilkie would not necessarily be allowed beyond even the next few days, or even hours. Here in the cold light of reality, my hopes over the past evenings, when I'd been held in Wilkie's arms under the light of a harvest moon and patiently read to, seemed bleak and unlikely. And I could see, written in the sympathy of Ailie's expression, that the likelihood of Wilkie's promises to me were most likely empty ones. He'd been inspired by lust in the warm fire-lit enclosure of his chambers. He was passionate and overcome. But it was entirely likely that his words would stay contained in our private embraces, to go no further.

Here, in the busy activity of his clan's people, as they readied themselves for their noble visitors, the reality of my situation settled in.

Wilkie would marry one of his own kind. If I was to remain in his life, it would likely be as a lowly mistress, to be called upon when his wife was tired or ill or bearing his legitimate heirs. Could I share him in this way and take the occasional offerings left to me after he attended to his family?

Nay. I knew it in my heart: if I couldn't have him, and all of him, I would leave the idyllic haven of the Mackenzie clan.

I reached for Ailie's hand. "I'm fine, Ailie. Tell me what else I can do to help."

"'Tis nearly done, I think," she said. "We'll take a

rest in my chambers, Roses, and decide what to wear for the evening festivities."

"I'm not certain if I'll attend the gathering. I'll be content to wait for Wilkie."

Ailie gave me a stern look. "I've been given strict instructions, Roses. Wilkie wants you there. He asked me to help you prepare, then to meet him in the hall when they return for the meal."

I had attended Ogilvie clan parties many years ago as a child and under the wing of my parents. Since then, the only gatherings I'd attended were those that I had served. I felt nervous that I wouldn't know how to act, that it would be obvious to all that I was different and unsophisticated and out of place. But then, if accompanying Ailie to the great hall was the quickest way to see Wilkie again, I would do it. I felt starved for his nearness.

After a time, and once the final preparations had been attended to, I went with Ailie and Christie to Ailie's private chambers, escorted silently by Fergus, who took guard outside the door. Ailie's chambers were equally lavish to Wilkie's but much cozier. Where Wilkie's chambers contained his large bed, a small table, a few chairs and a scattering of his weapons, Ailie's was cluttered with an array of her neatly hung clothing, a large table on which she kept sewing instruments and fabrics and several pleasantly laid out sitting areas. Two cushioned chairs sat welcoming by the lit fire, and a pretty table had been laid by the window seat. I realized then, from the look of the fabrics and the dresses themselves that it was Ailie who had made them.

"You make these beautiful dresses," I said, in awe.

"Aye," said Christie. "Ailie designs them, too, and

many of her ideas come from the fashion books from Edinburgh, London and even from Paris. She's wonderfully talented, don't you think so, Roses?"

"Oh, aye." I fingered the soft fabric of a dress that lay on her work table, of a pale pink velvet material. I'd never seen such a beautiful garment.

"Roses should wear that one tonight, don't you think so, Christie? I like you in the pastel colors, Roses. They set off your eyes, and your hair."

Christie nodded her agreement. "Put it on, Roses."

"I can take it in a little, if need be," Ailie commented, already lifting the dress to hold it against me.

Aghast from the very thought of wearing such finery, I murmured, "I could never wear this. 'Tis yours. 'Tis too fine."

Ailie dismissed this instantly. "Nonsense, Roses. I have many."

"As you should for the amount of time you spend sewing them," Christie said to her sister. To me, she said, "And Ailie's dresses are sought out by other clans, too. No doubt the Morrisons will want to see some of these creations."

"'Tis doubtful they would fit any of the Morrisons," Ailie said, and I detected a note of disdain in her tone.

"Don't be too disparaging of one of your prospective sisters-in-law, Ailie." Christie laughed. But she immediately caught herself when she looked at me, and her laugh was cut short. "Maybe Kade will be the one to get lucky," she said, placing a comforting hand on my shoulder.

"It wouldn't surprise me, in fact. He's mentioned one of the Morrison sisters several times in passing— have you noticed? Now I can't recall which one it was."

"Stella, of course, my dear sister. All the men speak of her. I heard Shamus and Robb discussing her the other day. *Ravishing* was the word they used, if I remember correctly." Christie rambled happily; I could see her vivacious manner was even more piqued this evening by anticipation of the party. "Especially compared to her more comely sisters, I'm sorry to say it. Even if they are voluptuous, which the men react to, of course. Come, Roses. Put this on. You'll outshine every other lass at the gathering."

"Take everything off," instructed Ailie. "You can't wear a shift under this one. It would ruin the line."

I froze.

She'll be beaten, flayed, burned at the stake! Keep this hidden!

"Come on, Roses," coaxed Ailie gently. "You don't need to be so shy with us."

I did as she instructed, glad my hair was down and that I faced them. I could only hope that my secret would not be revealed. And on some grasping level, I almost wanted them to discover it. I wanted them to forgive me for this very darkest of my imperfections, as they had forgiven me for all the others.

They gathered around me.

And so it was, before Ailie was able to slip the dress over my head and with Christie smoothing my hair to the side in an affectionate, curious gesture, that my secret was revealed.

Christie went still.

My fear poured into the empty moment of silence, enveloping me.

"What's this, Roses?" Christie asked, in mild shock. "You've an inked tattoo."

"Aye," I whispered, moving away, my heart racing.

I waited for her reaction as I stood before them, naked and shamed.

Ailie approached me and walked around me to take a look for herself, curious. I thought to run away, to hide. But I was so *tired* of hiding. Instead I allowed her to move my hair to the side and examine it for herself. Christie joined her.

"'Tis an unusual design," Ailie commented, and her voice—to my intense relief—sounded neither repulsed nor frightened. "What does it mean, Roses?"

My voice was barely audible. "I don't know. It was already inked to me when I was found as a child."

"Your parents never researched its meaning?" asked Christie.

The sisters continued to study the mark, outlining it and examining its lines.

I had never thought that there might be someone to consult on such matters. "I— Nay. How would one go about doing that?" I had no access to information of that kind. Laird Ogilvie would certainly be the last person I would have thought to consult on that—or any other—matter.

Could it be possible that the old woman had been wrong about the tattoo's meaning? I had, in fact, never *felt* like a witch. The young, fair-haired woman from my dream-memory certainly didn't *look* like a witch. But then, who was I to know what witches even looked like?

"There are books on the subject," Christie said.

"I was once told—" I began quietly, dreading the sound of the word I was about to admit.

But Christie was halfway through a thought and determined to finish it. "I've seen Knox reading one, just lately."

Ailie continued before I could force out the dreadful revelation. "All the lairds, I believe, like to be informed about the ritualistic tattoos, the clan tattoos, those of clandestine movements and alliances, royalty ink designs, religious marks and so on."

"Aye," Christie agreed. "There are prisoners' marks, too. And marks for military valor."

I took a deep breath to steady myself. "I'm quite certain I wasn't inked for military valor," I said.

"Does Wilkie know of it?" asked Christie. Then, smiling but with eyes cast down, she said, "Of course he does—"

"Nay," I said. "He doesn't."

Both sisters contemplated me, and I couldn't guess at their thoughts.

"I'm afraid," I said, my voice sounding shaky and hesitant, "I don't know what it means." And I could admit: "And I'm frightened by what it *could* mean. I've purposely hid it from him. I thought…that it might be the mark of…something sinister, something Wilkie would be horrified by. I was afraid Wilkie would no longer want me." I was ashamed to feel tears stinging my eyes.

"Surely that wouldn't happen, Roses," said Christie, but I knew, as she likely did, that only Wilkie could verify that for sure.

"We won't tell him," said Ailie, and her expression was uncharacteristically clouded and urgent. "But you *must* tell him, Roses. You *must*. Knox ensures that all his officers are familiar with the inked marks of the Highlands and those that might be seen throughout

Scotland. Wilkie will know what it's about, I'm sure of it. He's always taken a special interest in clan markings and those further afield. 'Tis best if you ask him, and find out what it is. It might give you a clue to your heritage."

And that was exactly what I was afraid of. But I said, truthfully: "I was going to show him, and I will. I was just waiting for the right time."

"So many mysteries to our Roses," commented Christie lightly, as Ailie slipped the dress over my head, fitting it with a critical eye to my body. I felt better immediately once my tattoo was once again covered.

My hair was pulled out to drape over the fabric.

"You'll show him, then, Roses?" Ailie asked me as she continued to adjust my outfit. There was an assertive edge to her question that was unusual, and I could sense that she thought it most important that Wilkie know of this, and soon.

"Aye, Ailie. I will. I promise to."

Ailie nodded, squeezing my hand and looking at my eyes. I could see concern in her expression and a thread of uneasiness. And I understood. At least I could be thankful that *this* was her reaction and not one of pointing fingers and shrieked, horrified warnings.

As though the matter had now been resolved, Christie changed the subject, commenting, "'Tis a bit tight up top." She was standing back with her arms folded across her chest to study me. "Her breasts are fairly toppling out of it."

"They're not 'toppling out of it.' That's the fashion in Paris. Your dress has the same cut. And so does mine. And so will the Morrisons', no doubt," she added, with some emphasis. I had to feel grateful at that last comment. I felt the sisters' quiet support for me and my unstated cause. I loved them for it. And for everything else.

"Aye," Christie continued. "Well, neither you nor I has quite as much to topple out, it must be said."

"Nay. But the Morrisons do."

We exchanged glances.

"'Tis perfect, then," pronounced Christie.

Ailie agreed. "I'll just adjust the waist, here." She was tugging the laces at the back of the dress, drawing it tighter. "Christie, pour the tea. We must get dressed ourselves." Her voice had the slightest flutter at the edges when she said, "It won't be long until the guests begin to arrive."

Christie's dress was a light sea-green, setting off her pale, creamy skin tone. And Ailie put on a flattering dark blue dress, which emphasized the sapphire color of her eyes. Christie brushed her own hair, leaving it down. She fashioned Ailie's hair in an uptwist, leaving curled strands to delicately frame Ailie's face. Then she turned her attention to my hair, of which she braided only small select strands, coiling them around my hairline, leaving much of my hair long, and brushing it carefully. "I daresay you'll get noticed tonight."

THE MORRISONS WERE the first to arrive, just as darkness was beginning its gauzy descent. Seven slightly plump and very lively young women swamped the hall in a flurry of tittering laughter, bright-colored fabric, almost-identical curled brown hair and—as Ailie had suggested—abundant cleavage.

I recalled the conversation of Wilkie's brothers, regarding the second-eldest daughter, Stella.

I spotted her immediately. She stood out from her sisters in several ways: she was slightly taller with longer, darker hair and a distinctive shimmery beauty. And while her sisters bustled into the manor, excited and boisterous, Stella's eyes were cast down, and she did not appear to be at all pleased to be here.

The women were followed by a rather tired-looking but upright older man with a furrowed brow and a determined expression, who looked eager at the prospect of the company of Laird Mackenzie and his brothers, none of whom—I was painfully aware—had yet to make an appearance.

The group was greeted by Ailie, Christie and other upstanding members of the clan, including cousins and other Mackenzie relatives, and welcomed with ale and food. I had met several of this extended Mackenzie family, although I did notice that Wilkie's sisters seemed somewhat protective of me and stayed by my side much of the time. As before, when I was introduced, it was pleasant yet perfunctory, with little information offered.

And it wasn't long until the Munro party arrived, which was comprised of the two sons, two nephews and a daughter of Laird Munro. The Munros had varying shades of strawberry blond hair, ranging from the daughter's almost-blond to the gold-lit copper of the sons. The eldest, Magnus, was a tall and ruggedly handsome man, and I could see that Ailie's eyes only left him when he happened to look in her direction, at which time her cheeks flushed with bright splashes of pink.

"She refuses to speak to him," Christie whispered, handing me a goblet of ale. "'Tis quite amusing to watch. My confident, poised sister turns into a spineless, quivering wallflower."

Christie insisted on topping up my goblet, and after several sips, I began to feel its relaxing, bubbling effects. She chattered about the crowd, giving me fascinating backstories, one by one, as she pointed out the guests. One or two of them looked vaguely familiar to me, and I guessed that I might have served their table at the Ogilvie keep. I doubted that they would recognize me.

Clementine Morrison, the eldest sister, was the first subject. "She's had a run of bad luck at the altar, poor thing," Christie said, in low tones that were almost a whisper. "Her first attempt was a Macallister who decided he was in love with someone else, only days before they were due to be married. Can you imagine? The second was Eoin Buchanan, nephew of the laird, who ended up scandalously running off with his own brother's wife. And it appears that Clementine has had enough. Last I heard, she's due to retreat to a convent in the spring. She's become most devout—look at her dress, after all—'tis much more demure than those of her sisters. She's decided she's had enough of men altogether and will dedicate herself to the church. One can hardly blame her, I daresay.

"So Stella is next in line to secure a new laird for the Morrison clan. And look at her. She's stunning, yet painfully shy." It was true that Stella Morrison was a rare beauty. She had long, dark brown hair that was inflected with blond highlights. The long strands curled at the ends and glowed like glimmer-edged spirals. She was taller than her sisters, and slimmer, and she projected an entirely different aura than the rest of her family. She seemed somber and disengaged from the gathering surrounding her. "I heard from Ainsley

Munro—the lass is a wealth of information, mainly because her brothers and cousins travel the Highlands and attend all the gatherings—that Stella's in love with a lower-ranking stable boy or some such, but that her father has banished him from the keep. And only days ago. So she's heartbroken and has refused marriage to another."

"That must be why she looks so sad," I said.

"Aye, I would say so. That, and the fact that her father will likely hear none of it. If he arranges a marriage for her despite her protests, there's little she can do about it. She's not in a position to refuse his dictates, whether it's the exile of her beloved, or the forced marriage to a man of his choosing."

A man of his choosing. The words lingered in a most unwelcome echo. I knew, as we all did, which man Laird Morrison had in mind. Wilkie had professed to his brothers that he favored none of the Morrison women, but now that I had seen Stella for myself, I wondered if *she* might present a more welcome possibility to Wilkie than the one called Maisie. And Christie continued, as though reading my thoughts.

"*That* one is Maisie," Christie said. "It was she that issued an invitation to Wilkie, with Laird Morrison's approval, last month. She is famously precocious and wishes it to be *her* husband who will inherit the lairdship."

Maisie Morrison was not at all comely like Christie had described; she was in fact quite beautiful, it had to be said. She was not tall and big-boned like her sister Clementine, nor tall and slim like Stella, but rather petite with a rounded, curvy shape that might have even been described as plump. But her shape suited her. She filled out the curves of her dress voluptuously. Her wavy brown hair shone in the candlelight, and her pink cheeks and vibrant eyes suggested an almost wonton frivolity. She giggled and whispered with her younger sisters, clear excitement written on her face.

"Maisie has designs..." Christie hesitated, looking at me, her light blue eyes luminous with light and youthful earnestness. "Well, she has designs to marry a Mackenzie. And since Stella is not ambitious in that way, Laird Morrison agreed to it. Yet I do wonder if that will change, now that Stella's stable boy has been sent away. Perhaps Stella will now be forced into marriage because of her unsuitable yearnings," she said, speaking her unsettling thoughts aloud. Christie squeezed my hand briefly. "I'm glad you're wearing that dress tonight, Roses. You outshine everyone in the room."

"You are kind, Christie. So very kind." In fact I felt almost tearful with it; I wasn't sure I deserved Christie and Ailie's steadfast support, but they genuinely seemed to be encouraging of my presence in Wilkie's life. I couldn't begin to guess at why this might be. And as though in answer to my unspoken question, Christie said softly, "We Mackenzies are all romantics, you should know." She paused, contemplating me quite earnestly, then she said, "Our mother died in childbirth when I was born, Roses. Our father pined for her and continued to worship her memory until his dying day. He never remarried. And I can tell you that all my siblings, myself included, aspire to that kind of devoted love. And we made a pact—if we were ever to find it, we would recognize it for what it was, and not deny it. Knox found it, but his wife was lost to him, also dying in childbirth, and their baby boy along with her. It was a traumatic event for all of us, and one I believe that has changed Knox's outlook. He's harder than he used to be, less indulgent of his own feelings or anyone else's. I suppose that may have something to do with his laird-ship as much as anything else, I don't know. What I do know is that he *has* changed, at least on the surface. He's forced himself to change. But the rest of us continue to believe. I think Wilkie's been overcome by you in this way, Roses. We can all see it. We've certainly never seen Wilkie behave as he does with you. He's truly in a state. He's half mad over you. I must admit it's a new look for him, and I'm finding it quite entertaining—oh, look, here he comes."

At that moment, Laird Mackenzie, Wilkie and Kade walked into the room, and I caught my breath. The three of them together were a spectacle in itself, for their size and masculinity alone. They looked a force to be reckoned with, with their dark hair and flashing eyes, and dressed in their clan-colored kilts, as were the other men. Their presence filled up the room and caught the crowd's attention.

But I only had eyes for one of them.

Wilkie had a wild look, whether from his day of sparring and hunting, or from something else entirely, it was difficult to tell. His gaze immediately found me in the noisy bustle of the crowded space. His eyes wandered my face, my dress—and all it revealed—and my hair. His expression darkened. Fury and fire reflected in his direct stare and brought a rush of heat to my skin. Was he angry? I wondered briefly if Ailie had misunderstood her instructions; maybe Wilkie had wanted me to remain in his chambers and wait for him. I wouldn't have minded, but in fact, now that I was here, I didn't feel quite as out of place as I thought I might. Christie was at my side, content it seemed, to be my companion and guardian. I'd also had half a goblet of the ale she'd offered me, which infused me with a warm ease, and the feeling that I could almost handle the evening. And it further heightened the heat Wilkie's gaze inspired. My dress was fitted and soft. And I wore nothing underneath. He couldn't have known this, but his expression burned me in intimate places, exciting the light swell that ached for his touch.

He walked toward me, and my stomach felt fluttery as he drew closer. There was a definite volatility to his expression; I didn't understand what it meant or what caused it, but it stirred me.

Before Wilkie reached me, his attention was diverted by Magnus Munro, who greeted him and slapped him on the back as if they were old friends. Wilkie was popular, as his sisters had pointed out. This was clear by the unending cluster that sought him out. I watched him as he spoke and laughed with his noble friends and acquaintances. It seemed he was attempting to make his way in my direction, but there were more people who wanted to greet him. Very occasionally, I caught his eye.

Several of the Morrison women, including Maisie, were next in line. Maisie adjusted her dress scandalously low, in an obvious bid to entice him. She was clearly determined to get his attention and unconcerned about the possibility of tarnishing her reputation to do it. She was fairly spilling out of her gown with her eagerness. Stella, I noticed, was nowhere in sight, a detail I was momentarily grateful for.

The Morrison women surrounded Wilkie, blocking any potential attempts of his to evade them. They laughed and fawned over him, lightly touching him with their fingers at every opportunity. Maisie's attentions, in particular, were possessive in nature. She slung her arm through the crook of his, as though he were her escort. He, after a time, subtly removed it as his drink was refilled.

Wilkie watched me for a moment from this short distance, his expression inscrutable. And the sight of him there, surrounded by his adoring heiresses, almost upset my control. What could I do? I could hardly storm over to him and remove their hands from his arms and push them away. I could huff away to his chambers, but I didn't want to voluntarily remove myself from his presence; it seemed wasteful.

He noticed my ire, and he met it with his own. His eyes were predatory, as though he was struggling to maintain his self-control. But his loose-limbed stance appeared, by contrast, relaxed. I could not read his behavior, and this upset me even more. I wished I could touch him, to *feel* his indifference, if that's what this was. I wasn't adept yet at reading him from afar, but his touch gave everything away.

Was the company of his own peers enough to oust me from his favor?

Well, I could be aloof as well, I thought indignantly.

My emotions were raging within me, yet my outermost layer felt calm. After all, I'd already made up my mind: I wanted all of him, with no quarter given.

He was still being circled by the women, and I wondered what he was thinking. I didn't care anymore if I was seen and stared at or whispered about. I didn't care if the Morrison women blocked my way or even if

Wilkie was savoring their explicit attentions. I would go to him.

But I stopped before I began. Maisie Morrison had cupped her hand to Wilkie's jaw and turned his face to hers. She was saying something to him, which he leaned closer to hear. And as he did, she caught my eye in a challenging glare, and her hand was reaching farther to caress his face lightly and to touch his hair.

That glance provided unwanted information. Maisie Morrison not only wanted Wilkie, *she thought she already had him*. It was a glare of ownership, as one might deliver to a thief.

My soul grew cold, and I wondered if Wilkie's dismissal of the Morrison alliance, through his marriage to one of them, had been overturned. I wondered if Laird Mackenzie had agreed to Laird Morrison's proposal at the instigation of his third daughter, who still held me in her watchful glare.

Before I could thaw or react, two large men approached Christie and me, blocking out the sight of Maisie and Wilkie, as though to provide temporary distraction from my anxiety. Their red-cast hair identified them immediately as Munros. And I was glad of the diversion they provided. It gave me a minute to steady myself.

"Are you Magnus's brother?" asked Christie of the one who stood next to me, and quite closely.

"Aye, Christie. We met once when you were still quite young. I'm Angus. Third in line." He smirked, as though the subject of his inheritance was highly entertaining to him. "This is Tosh Munro, my cousin."

Angus Munro had memorable hair: red on the bottom layers giving way to strawberry blond on the top; it

gave him a sunny quality that seemed to match his personality. His presence was energetic and bright, throwing a small amount of warmth into my stunned silence.

"And who might you be?" he said, lifting my hand
to kiss the back of my knuckles. Not once, but several
times.

"This is Roses," Christie offered before I could
speak.

"Why haven't I seen Roses before?" asked Angus.
"Are you new to the Mackenzie clan?"

Christie deftly changed the subject. As far away as
the Macduff clan was, these men were warriors who
traveled regularly between clan territories, to meet and
discuss politics on a regular basis. It was risky to spin
lies. I felt, and Christie appeared to feel the same way,
that it was a topic better avoided if possible. "Not so
new. More ale?"

She poured the drinks.

I felt adrift and loose. And utterly alone, despite the
crowd.

Christie seemed to be enjoying the conversation of
Angus and Tosh. Tosh in particular, whose laughter
she seemed to find infectious. And Angus, feeling shut
out of their burgeoning connection, maybe, homed his
focus in on me.

I really might have had too much ale, I feared. My
vision seemed slightly off-kilter. I enjoyed the light hues
of Angus's hair, I did admit to him. They caught the
candlelight. I tried to excuse myself, to make my way
toward Wilkie, to ask him and forgive him, but Angus
blocked my way.

The room was swirled at the edges, darker now, full
of people, and the noise of it was almost comfortingly

raucous, as though the gathering had found its harmony, even if I had not. Music played. People were well immersed now in their evening.

"You didn't tell me where you're from," Angus persisted, leaning in closer. So close, in fact, that a drop from his drink spilled from his goblet, wetting the pillowy curves of my exposed upper breasts. Angus, noticing this, touched his finger very gently to the droplet of warm liquid, tracing a line. The touch unsettled me greatly. I flinched back from him, but I was already pressed up against the wall. Perhaps noticing my unease, he withdrew his lingering touch. Then, watching my eyes, he licked his finger.

Angus's hand was grabbed by a larger hand, surprising him.

A looming dark figure was at my side. I recognized his scent and the energy of him before I even saw who he was; it infused me with comfort and lit me from within. Wilkie dropped Angus's hand, which Angus then fondled with his other hand, as though it was paining him.

Wilkie looped his muscular arm around me protectively, drawing me close to his body. "Angus," Wilkie said. "I trust you're enjoying yourself. You must help yourself to more food and drink at the table." His words had a suggestive thrust to them, as though behind the kind invitation there was an unyielding order.

"Wilkie," Angus greeted him. His tone was tinged with his lingering surprise, respect, a hint of disappointment at the interruption. He took his leave, fully registering Wilkie's unspoken dismissal.

Truly, I had never felt so relieved and elated. I couldn't find my earlier anger or jealousy. My warrior was here with me. And my inhibitions, as a result of the cup of ale I had imbibed, were fairly nonexistent. I was glad for his closeness now for that reason as much as any other; I wasn't sure of what I might do.

Wilkie looked big and half-crazed in the dim lighting of the now-rowdy crowd. His eyes were not on me but on Angus for a time, and they were dark and smoldering, dangerous in intent. He held me tightly against him, perhaps forgetting himself in the very-public circumstance.

And I, too, in my loosened state forgot all restraints. My body was pushed up roughly against him, my breasts barely contained in the soft pink fabric of my dress. His thigh was pressed up against my own, delivering heat. And his mouth, parted for his heavy breath, was only inches from mine.

I only just stopped myself from pressing my mouth to his, instead standing on my tiptoes to whisper into his ear. "I missed you, warrior."

He didn't respond to me or even look at me, continuing his furious silence, as though attempting to contain himself and having difficulty with it.

It might have been the ale that emboldened me; I felt quietly reckless. I leaned to him again, whispering, "I want to kiss you."

He yanked me closer to him and looked down at me fiercely. *"Roses."*

I stared back at him, alarmed by his reaction.

"I'm a blithering idiot as it is, with desire for you," he rasped at me. "Show me some mercy."

"For me?" I asked him skeptically.

"Aye," he said, and there was clear anger in his voice. "For you."

I glanced over at Maisie. Her glare promised death, upsetting me. "What of the Morrisons?"

"Don't talk of them," he growled. Then, as though able to take no more, he whisked me out of the dark fringes of the hall and into the darker hallway without a backward glance. I had a feeling Laird Mackenzie would be less than pleased with Wilkie's departure. But then, his other three siblings were doing their utmost to make a potential match this night; I'd witnessed at least two of them for myself.

It might have been a full moon, I wondered, since everyone was acting slightly mad, myself in particular. I was still clasped against Wilkie's chest. As soon as we reached the staircase, he lifted me into his arms and carried me to his chambers.

And once he'd kicked the door closed behind us, slamming it, he gently set me down, next to the dying fire. He didn't touch me. Instead, he walked over to the table, where several empty cups and bowls sat, and he upturned the entire table in one violent heave, smashing it against the wall, where several of the vessels clattered loudly against the stones and bounced to the floor. One of them shattered.

Shocked, I took a step back.

But I wasn't afraid of him. If anything, his temper fired my desire for him even more. I trusted him, and I knew he wouldn't hurt me. Or at least I hoped it. What he might do to me with his anger, though, set my blood to a simmering boil.

He went to the bed and sat, taking off his boots and tossing them aside. Then he looked at me.

I had never seen his eyes so menacing and sparked. He crooked a finger, beckoning me. "Come here."

Tentatively, I went to him. I stood before him.

He put his hands on my hips and pulled me between his thighs, hugging me to him and resting his head against me. There was a note of desperation in his embrace.

I ran my fingers along the strands of his thick hair, claiming him and reclaiming him. "'Tis all right," I whispered, feeling the need to comfort him.

"I cannot take this," he murmured.

"Take what?"

"You. Them."

I didn't understand his meaning, but I let the silence linger, hoping he would continue.

"I want to be the only one to look at you," he finally said, raising his eyes to me. "Forgive me, Roses. I want to immerse myself in you and keep your light all to myself. I try to maintain control, yet you make it so very difficult, with your hair and your breasts and your lips for all to see."

My hands could not get enough of the feel of his thick hair and his sun-dark skin. "My lips are yours," I said, kissing his face, his closed eyes, his lips. "My breasts are yours. All of me. Yours."

I continued to kiss him and offer myself to him, every word of it the truest truth. I was his. And he was mine, even if this truth wasn't fully confirmed or allowed. He was here with me, and that was truth enough.

I could sense that his fury was mellowing, transforming into heat. When his temper had cooled, he pulled back. Carefully, so as not to ignite him, I unfastened the pin that held his kilt securely in place. I unwrapped the sash of his kilt. I gently pulled up his shirt, easing it over his head. I traced my fingers over the masculine lines of his shoulders.

He lifted me and placed me on the bed. He lay next to me. Neither of us spoke for a minute or more, simply reveling in each other's nearness. I felt it, and I sensed he could, too; we were where we belonged: together.

I began slowly. "Warrior?" I said.

He lifted an eyebrow, waiting for my question.

"You haven't married every woman you've shared a bed with."

He paused before answering. "Nay, not a single one."

"Have you shared a bed with very many women?"

He contemplated me lazily, and a subtle grin played at the corners of his mouth, as though he was mildly satisfied by my inquisition. His beauty, as his arrogance and the innate authority of him played across his handsome face, was stunning. Here was a man who women fought over. They swooned when he walked into a room. They very nearly fainted when he flicked them a glance. I had heard it discussed over the table of Laird Ogilvie, and now I'd seen it for myself. The attentions of Wilkie Mackenzie were a conquest, an aspiration, a dream. The fresh memory of all those women, batting their eyelashes coquettishly, it boiled in my veins. One in particular. And Wilkie looked almost amused, now that his own jealousy had eased. "Are you jealous, my love?"

The image of Maisie Morrison resurfaced, infuriating me. I was beyond jealous.

He smiled widely, flashing white teeth. He laughed at my expression, and the sound of his laughter sparked my desire and also my relief; I felt his laughter in my intimate places, and I went wet and achy for his touch.

"Your face, Roses. You're quite adorable when you're jealous. Those women don't exist for me now. There's only one woman I want in my bed, and she's here, frowning at me."

I sat stonelike, but my heart thumped heavily with desperate, jaded love. "They existed for you tonight," I commented quietly, remembering their hands touching his arms and his hair, and his unruffled allowance of it.

"I was being polite to our guests and nothing more. I've encouraged Kade to keep them well entertained, and he seemed more than up to the task. The rest of them were circling him like hungry wolves. I, on the other hand, took little pleasure in the conversation, especially as Angus Munro was leaning ever closer to you, drooling on you, and fairly fondling you." This last line was delivered like a quiet swipe, as though I'd invited Angus Munro—nay, begged him—to do what he had done.

"If you had been close to me, he wouldn't have touched me." I was surprised at the petulance in my voice. I felt close to tears at my own need and at the extreme heaviness of my love for him. I didn't want to invite an argument with him, but I couldn't stop myself.

His irritation was detectable. "If I'd been closer to you, I'd have had a difficult time of not ravaging you right there in the corner. Your dress is too revealing."

"You prefer Maisie Morrison's dress?" I asked him, wishing I hadn't. Yet I continued. "Are you spoken for, warrior?"

"What do you mean?"

"I mean, does Maisie believe you to be something more than an acquaintance? Is she your betrothed or not?"

He paused as though considering whether to tell me the truth of it. "Nay, Roses. She is *not* my betrothed. Maisie Morrison and I shared a fleeting moment. She means nothing to me. Knox strongly wishes me to consider her for marriage, to secure the much-needed military alliance with the Morrison clan. I have not agreed. I urged him to negotiate for the alliance to be secured through some other means. I told him that I would prefer that my acquaintance with Maisie remain entirely in the past. And I told him my preference."

I steeled myself for his answer as I asked him, "And what was his response?"

"We're still discussing the matter."

Which very probably meant that the laird had refused to allow him to marry me. The sorrow and jealousy that washed through me gave a bite to my words. "If you prefer the Morrisons' dresses and the company of their beds, then you should go to them. As you have before."

Wilkie was still for a moment. His voice softened a degree. "Don't be daft, lass. You're the only one who has touched my heart. Come here to me. Let me soothe away your jealousy with my kisses."

I remained indignant. I did not move to him. I was picturing another woman in his bed, two of them, kissing him, touching his hair. The thought scalded my emotions, upsetting me greatly.

"Roses," he said with hard authority. His voice was darker when he continued. "You didn't heed my command. I said, come to me." He might have been teasing me, but he was also testing me. He touched his finger to my lips.

I bit at his finger, just missing it as he jerked it away,

and his eyes turned stormy. He grabbed me with his hard-muscled arms and pulled me to him.

"I give myself to you, warrior," I said.

"You'll not—"

"Whether you marry me or not," I said, interrupting him. I didn't want to hear about my purity, not in the heat of this moment. I had a confounding and whole-souled desire for him to dirty my purity with his blood, his sweat and more.

He frowned. "What's your meaning, Roses? You've already said aye to me. I'll not take nay for an answer now."

"I said I'd marry you," I said, and my voice sounded out of sorts. "I'm yours already. But why must you wed me before you'll—" I faltered, too innocent and ashamed and desperate to explain what I wanted from him. I wanted all of him. I wanted him inside me, to take me and make me his, fully. To burn together, with him, now. A wedding seemed a far-off dream, months of planning, hours of separation to make acquaintances and carry out arrangements. And here I was letting my hopes and dreams get the better of me, even considering details like planning and arrangements. A wedding, if it was even a remote possibility, felt a million miles away from this moment.

And the question lurked loudly in my mind: Why would he bed other women and give them his loving when he refused me?

I felt the sting of tears moisten my eyes.

Wilkie saw my tears, and his expression was pained, stricken. "Roses?" He looked into my eyes with total concentration, as if he might see the reason for my anguish written in their depths. "What's the matter? Why do you weep?"

I could barely speak. My words came out muffled and sodden. "You don't want me like you wanted them."

He held my shoulders, and the look on his face was one of disbelief, then slow understanding.

"You want to give yourself to me... You think I don't *want* you? Is *that* why you weep?"

I was still frowning at him, but I nodded just a little.

Wilkie exhaled a small, incredulous laugh. He kissed my face, little tickling kisses at the corner of my mouth, my cheek. He kissed my eyelids softly, once, and again, so my tears wet his lips. My tears seemed to have struck something in him, some animal desire or protective allowance. There was a new edge to his kisses that thrilled me and scared me, as well. Something in him had turned, and there was a new desperation and a heightened ferocity in his manner that made my heart beat faster.

His hand brushed across my breasts, easing the soft fabric down to frame them from below and plump them slightly upward, exposing them to him. He swirled each nipple between his fingers and thumbs, gently tugging and kneading. His touches grew in their strength until they were very nearly painful, scalding me with prickling, deepening heat. "I can't have my Roses weeping like this, when I can soothe away her tears so very easily, if this is what she wants me to do." He sucked my nipples carelessly, one, then the other, only briefly tasting, almost manic in his lightness.

"I want you," I whispered. I had never uttered a truer statement.

He kissed my cheeks and then my lips, and I could

taste the salt of my own tears. He rid himself of his un-bound clothing. His hands fumbled roughly with the ties of my dress, which he loosened. Then he bunched the folds of material up to my waist and attempted to remove my dress. "Take this off or I'll rip it off."

Not wanting him to ruin Ailie's carefully made cre-ation, I peeled the dress over my head. Seeing that I wore nothing underneath, Wilkie fairly purred with the discovery. I was naked with only my hair covering me. But I was facing him, and I no longer cared if Wilkie discovered my tattoo. I wanted him to. I would make a point of showing him. I began to turn my body, but he held me and laid me back onto the bed, insistently, kiss-ing my breasts but not lingering, kissing a line down my stomach and lower. "You want me to *prove* to you that I want you more than I've ever wanted anything in my life, Roses. Is that true, aye? Because I just can't take this anymore."

I gasped as he licked into my sensitive flesh, wetting me with his soft strokes, speaking soft words against my skin. "If you insist on doubting me, Roses, if you absolutely insist on breaking down every defense that I have with your tears and your plush, wet, ripe beauty, then that's what I'll have to do, lass. Is *that* what you want from me? Proof?"

I could only sigh a soft response, already falling, burning, wanting too much.

"And you're ready for me to prove my love for you as I take you fully, completely, entirely as my own?" As though to emphasize his question, he licked deeper into me, using his fingers to gently open me to his in-sistent, exploring tongue until I cried out his name in a whispered moan.

He climbed up my body, rubbing himself against me, supporting his weight above me, positioning himself.

"You want me to take you like *this,* Roses?" I could feel his immense shaft pushing gently against my entrance. His size and his strength gave him total control, and my body, too willing, throbbed with desire as he held himself just touching me. I was afraid and drowning in desire for him, and the combined effect brought a fresh wave of tears, which still spilled to wet my hair. He reached with his hands to roughly spread my legs wider.

"I've waited with you, sweet lass, because once I'm inside you, you must understand, I'll have no choice but to spill my seed. We'll be forever joined."

I tipped my hips up to him ever so slightly, easing him closer, until he was pressed strongly against me.

He began to rub the head of his shaft along my intimate folds, then deeper, only barely inside me, finding a subtle rhythm in the controlled movement. My inner muscles clenched on the emptiness. I thought I might die from raw need.

"I've never once spilled my seed inside a woman," he said, and his voice was low, almost crooning, as he continued to rub me with his body. "I didn't want to be bound to them in that way and beyond that moment." My body was responding to him, and his caresses became silky and honeyed from the wetness he inspired. "With you, Roses, I won't want to separate myself from you. I'll want to possess you completely, and you to possess me. I want to burn with you, to feel you pulse around me as I fill you with everything I have to give. Is that what you want from me?"

I ran my fingers over the coiled muscles of his back,

clinging to him, scratching into his skin to pull him closer.

"You're too sacred," he continued, and his voice was husked with emotion. "You're the one. My sunlit angel. My Roses. Mine."

He pushed himself a fraction deeper, still exploring his lazy rhythm. I could feel his thickness beginning to stretch me. The sensation was dizzying, and my vision blurred at the edges.

"Is this what my Roses wants from me?" he whispered in my ear, biting the soft flesh of my lobe between his teeth. "Say it to me."

"Aye, warrior," I gasped.

"You want me, and all of me? Once I begin, see, there's no going back. And it will hurt you, Roses. There's naught I can do to stop from hurting you, at first. But then everything I do will give you pleasure. I promise you that. As much pleasure as you can take. Is this what you want me to do?"

I sobbed from the wrought strung-out need of my body. *"Please, Wilkie."*

He drove deeper inside me then, and there was a sharp pain as he broke through the fragile barrier of my virginity with one quick thrust. I cried out, and he caught my cry with his kiss, opening my mouth with his, licking into me with gentle, soothing pressure. He held himself still, kissing me tenderly, until my tension began to ease.

"That's the only pain, love," he said, smoothing my hair back from my face. "It will ease into pleasure."

He pushed farther into me, and I felt my body resisting him. He was too much; my unyielding body could not accommodate him.

"Are you—" I started to whimper, then he pushed farther, and I gasped at the burn of it, at the hot stretching demand.

"Not quite, lass. About halfway."

"Half?"

"Relax for me, Roses. 'Tis me, Wilkie. Your warrior. Let me in."

He lifted slightly, taking my breast in his hand, plumping it to his mouth. He lapped at my nipple with his tongue, circling around the tightening nub. Then he bit me, so very gently, scraping the edges of his teeth against my skin, kissing, biting and nuzzling his face against me. He did the same to my other breast, until I could feel my inner muscles relaxing, loosening around him, spanning his heavy invasion bit by bit. He pushed farther, more strongly now, easing himself out, then back in, deeper, and deeper still.

"Almost there, love." He leaned his body over mine more heavily. He kissed me with expert, careful bites and licks, pushing himself more aggressively into my body.

I struggled for breath and thrashed slightly, trying to free myself from the feeling I was being split open. I wasn't certain I could take any more of him. *"You're too big,* warrior," I said, and there was desperation in my voice. "You won't fit me."

"I'll fit you, lass. I'll fit you perfectly." He pushed my legs even wider, adjusting himself, settling deeper with a forceful thrust. Wilkie's soft-edged groan hummed with a note of satisfaction, of finality, and I knew he was fully inside me now. It was uncomfortable, this extreme fullness of him deep inside my body, with the pain of his initial drive still lingering. I wriggled and clasped my hands to his backside, trying to find the pleasure. Tilting my hips back just slightly, I could ease the sensation of being too full, too possessed. I eased forward and back, just barely, feeling my own moisture begin to soften the tightness.

Wilkie pushed his face into my neck. He made a low sound, like a muffled growl. He sounded as if he was in quiet agony.

"Warrior?"

He didn't answer immediately.

"Wilkie," I whispered into his ear.

"Aye," he said, a small exhale. His body was stunningly tense and hard.

"Is it all right?"

Silence.

"Wilkie?" I whispered again.

"Be still, Roses. Don't move."

I obeyed him for a moment. I lay still, letting my body relax around him. The muscles of his back were strained and rock-hard. I ran my fingers over them, scratching slightly, teasing his skin with little pinching caresses, as he liked to do to me. I let my body adjust to him. I tilted my hips back again, easing the pressure, then up to him. And again.

"Roses," he said sternly. "Hold yourself still."

"Why?"

"You reduce my control to that of an untried lad," he said, and there was a rough rasp to his voice. "You're so very tightly around me." He lifted his head up to look into my eyes, and we lay like that for a moment, still and quiet. "I'm inside my Roses," he said, a smile touching his lips.

"Aye. My warrior's inside me. Giving me everything he has to give."

He kissed me then, and his mouth was hungry and possessive, his tongue thrusting into my mouth as he began to move himself within me in a conjoined rhythm.

"I want to feel you pulse around me, lass," he growled. "I want your pleasure to release me."

"We'll burn together."

"Aye," he said. "We'll die together."

And it was then that the discomfort began to turn. The rubbing, burning friction of his extreme fullness inside me seemed to sprout little wings that softened the pain into something else altogether. All sense and all feeling concentrated in the core of my body, now stretched to accommodate his deeply nudging strokes. Sparking tufts of beauty lurked around the edges of my body's tight-sprung tension, funneling ever so slightly, from the inside out.

Wilkie heard the tone of my soft exhale, reading there the response I was beginning to find as he nudged faster, finding the perfect balance of flesh and feeling. He kept his pace steady, controlled, rooting out twinges of ecstasy, only to have it retreat again, just out of reach.

"Let go, Roses. Surrender to me."

He lifted one of my arms over my head, then the other, locking both my wrists easily in one of his powerful hands. My legs were fully bent, my knees clasping against his hips.

I was pinned under him, held down by him, impaled by him. His mouth took mine. I could only submit to him. He was all I could feel or remember. And as I soon as I embraced this total submission, a streaming current began to fill my body and my mind, as a subtle, energetic hum from within. It began in my soul, it seemed, coiling both into and out of the center of me. Wilkie's deep strokes enticed it and forced it higher and ever higher, melting me utterly until there was nothing of me except this overloading devastating pleasure. This escalating tide consumed me in a white-lit explosion of bliss, which held and glided in an expanding spell. And as it did, I felt his own soul inside me. As though to capture Wilkie within me, my body clenched tightly around him in welcoming bursts, pulling at the length of him in rhythmic tugs, inviting all he had to give. Wilkie sighed in a spoken breath, mindless. And I had never felt such an all-consuming joy as then, when his essence pooled hotly into me, flooding me and killing me with vibrant sensation, extending my pleasure into long lush brimming shudders that rolled and waved and met no resistance.

It was a long time before either of us could move or speak. We were dazed and entwined, so completely connected in every way it was possible to be.

I RESURFACED SOME time later to find he had repositioned us so we lay face-to-face on our sides, my leg hitched over his hip and held by his hand. His eyes were open, watching me as I dozed. The masculine features of his face, so dark and shadowed by low light and primal intentions, were heartbreaking. My throat and my inner chest felt fluttery and reckless at the sight of him, aching with desperation, such was his beauty to me.

"Angel," he whispered, staring deeply into my eyes, his own desperation there in equal measure. It was too much and not enough, as though we might die if we were ever to draw apart.

"Beautiful warrior, you are my heart."

And with barely any movement at all, Wilkie gave a hint of a slow nudge where our bodies met. That barely there pressure was enough, stoking sweet rapture, which coursed through my body, holding on, as though I was riding Wilkie's energy. Sensation spun from my center outward in a continuously flowing wave that caressed him peacefully from within and brought him a slow, resounding release that filled me with warmth and love and life.

CHAPTER FOURTEEN

"You must be prepared to be watched and talked about today, Roses," Wilkie said softly. "I will keep you with me as much as I can, but there will times when I will be required to train, to discuss matters of our alliance with the Morrison and Munro armies, and to host our visitors. Fergus will guard you at all times. If you'd like to spend some time assisting Effie, it would give credence to your alibi, and my sisters will do their best to give you as much company as they can."

"I don't need them to keep me company. I'm fine to entertain myself, and I can help them, and Effie, in any way they require."

His hold on me remained equally as tight as when he'd held me during his fevered fugue, yet this hold was more complete, with his heavy limbs wrapped around me and his body tucked against mine. During the night, I'd awoken more than once in the darkness to the intimate caresses of his mouth, his strong hands, his insistent hardness. He spilled his seed into me many times, each release spurred by the rippling responses of my body to his bliss-inducing possession. The night seemed as one long ride of beautiful sensation. The ecstasy never faded, just rolled and undulated through wakefulness and sleep.

"I could have been more subtle about our departure

from the gathering last night," he said, rueful. "Such is my desire for you, sweet. It blinds me to everyone and everything but you. You will most likely be questioned and engaged on the subject. 'Tis best to keep them guessing, for now. My discussions with my brother are not yet resolved. But they will be, soon enough."

"Whatever you ask, warrior. I will keep them guessing, then."

"Now I'm going to pull myself from your body and wash you. Then you'll dress in the adjoining chambers and come downstairs at your leisure. I will see you in a few hours."

"All right." I didn't want him to pull himself from me or leave me. But I felt supremely peaceful. I was subdued with rapture, my body and mind so satiated I might have never known a care in the world.

He didn't move immediately. Still on top of me, he kissed the tip of my nose. "You've a light sprinkling of freckles here, across your nose and your cheeks." He made a point of kissing each one. "And here, across the tops of your beautiful breasts, as though you've been sun-kissed and dusted with gold." He continued his mapped exploration. "Your blond hair catches all the light in the room." He swirled a strand of my hair around his finger, then he traced the feathery line of my eyebrow with his thumb. "The glory of you, Roses. I have never known anything like it. I want to immerse myself in you forevermore. To follow you and feel the sun and the heat and the beauty of you. You're more than my heart can bear."

"I will be waiting for you to return to me, always. I want to lie here, like this, with you, every day and night until the end of time. You are my life." And if

I'd been capable of it at that moment, I might have felt disconcerted at the blunt and far-reaching truth of my own words.

He kissed me once more, then he pulled away from me, and I felt saddened already by the separation. Then again—although I hadn't realized it until now—I was quite painfully sore.

Wilkie went to a side table, where a porcelain pitcher of water and a bowl sat. He poured some of the water into the bowl and brought it to the bed, along with a small cloth. He proceeded to wash me carefully with the cool water, wiping me clean of his seed and my own blood. Then he washed himself.

"You belong to me now," he said. The statement infused me with an undiluted happiness.

"And you to me," I replied, marveling at the lingering liquid warmth of his seed within me. And only me. I thought of the possibility of a child, but it wasn't my most pressing thought. A child, whether legitimate or illegitimate, whether already begun or not to be, seemed a far-off concern. More importantly now was the stunning knowledge that Wilkie's essence had now truly mixed with my own. The very core of not only my body but also my spirit felt joyful at the significance of this. I felt, as Wilkie described, like the sun—or that a glowing, vibrant orb of beauty was within me, where our spirits had mingled and continued to dance even now.

"I believe Ailie and Christie are taking the women on a walk through the gardens this morning, after they have eaten the morning meal. You might accompany them if you choose to." The suggestion was tinged by only the slightest lurk of anxiety, at the memory of my last walk through the gardens. But Wilkie added,

"The guards are doubled and readied, and patrol the outside walls, the grounds and the gate. There will be no more surprise raids, I can assure you. And Fergus will be with you."

I sat up, excited. I'd explored the gardens only twice in all the days and weeks I'd been at Kinloch. I couldn't count the duration of it, of our healing, erotic confinement; the span of time had a surreal, dreamlike quality to it that felt difficult to quantify.

But, now, I couldn't wait to feel the sun on my face once again and to smell the scent of the harvest on the breeze. I smiled widely and clapped my hands together.

Wilkie seemed amused by my animation.

He kissed me playfully, and, as I tried to pull away from him to dress, he held my hand as though he wouldn't let it go. I tugged on it, questioning his intent with my smile. "Let me dress, warrior."

My back was to him, my hair hung long. I thought of Ailie's urgent request. I had been careful to keep my back away from Wilkie, and to use my hair as a shield when I was naked before him here in this daylight. But it was true that I had let my guard down just slightly. Still, I was glad that he had not yet noticed it.

You must tell him, Roses. You must.

I would. I would. But fear once again speared me at the thought. Would he still love me if the old woman's accusation had been true? Could he forgive me for my murky, sinister origins?

But I knew Ailie was right. I must show him.

I *would* show him.

Tonight.

I would allow myself to savor the thoroughness of Wilkie's loving for the day, before I undermined it altogether by unveiling to him my horrible revelation. It was selfish of me, to be sure: to want him so desperately, even as I knew he would likely cast me out as soon as he discovered my secret. No man this privileged, this beautiful, would want to forever align himself in body and mind with a… With the truth of what I was. I wondered if Wilkie himself would watch me burn.

Aye, I would allow myself one more day, and only one more day, to *live*. It was a difficult thing to relinquish, love and beauty of this magnitude, but I would do it. For him. In effect I would be releasing him to follow his destiny and fulfill his duty as the nobleman that he was. I had already claimed the ultimate prize: absolute connection to the man of my heart. I felt undeniably complete in the aftermath of Wilkie's lovemaking. It was a feeling and a memory I could take with me to my pyre.

After a moment, he released my hand, and I held his gaze as he watched me back away from him, retreating to his antechamber; the movement alerted me to my fading bruises and also my newly acquired soreness. Wilkie's eyes were curiously dark, almost dangerous in intent, as though he would leap up and pursue me at any moment.

In the adjoining chambers, I surveyed my choices. Ailie and Christie had been generous. There were several new outfits to choose from.

I chose a light green velvet with white satin trim. It felt too grand for walking in the gardens, but they were the only choices available to me. As I had before, I fingered the velvet material. Could a person ever get used to such finery? I slipped the dress over my head, luxuriating in its refined softness. It could have been made for me; the fit was comfortably snug and flattering, cinching in a fitted bodice, flowing gracefully in straight gathered lines to the floor. I touched the white satin trim, reveling in its silky texture.

I brushed my hair, untangling the long strands and brushing carefully. I braided several plaits and wound each one around my head, pinning the extra length at the back, so it was neatly bound. I put on my shoes.

When I returned to Wilkie, he was up, sitting on the edge of his bed, tying his trews but still shirtless. The bandage was still bound around his middle, but the sight of it didn't spear me as much as it had in earlier days. I knew he was healing well, despite aggravating his wound during his fight with the Ogilvie warrior. What did spear me, but in an entirely different way, was the way his broad, muscular chest rippled and bunched with his movement.

He watched me approach him. His eyes trailed over my dress, my hair, my face. Then he closed his eyes, his dark lashes curving in a gentle sweep against his cheeks.

I moved to stand between his thighs, placing my hands on his browned, bare shoulders. I kissed his closed eyes. "Why do you close your eyes?"

His eyes opened, and he pulled me closer. "You hurt my heart with your loveliness. This dress matches the color of your eyes, and the silk matches your hair. I don't want to share you."

I laughed lightly at his daftness, running my fingers across the swarthy features of his face, enjoying the rough texture of the stubble along his jaw. "There's no need to share me. I'm yours, all of me."

"'Tis strange," he mused, thoughtful, "seeing you

mingling with my family and clan and acquaintances. Still I wonder if I've dreamed you, yet here you are. 'Tis true, I've never felt so possessive of anything in my life." He stopped himself, and he appeared both upset by the thought and by his own reaction.

"You have no need for worrying, warrior. I'll be thinking only of you. And besides, I'm very good at going unnoticed." I thought of all my years at the Ogilvie keep, of being scorned and avoided for my unusualness, of spending days barely being acknowledged aside from the waited-for completion of my unending tasks.

"No longer, lass. You were the talk of the gathering last night, and now, after I swept you away in a dramatic abduction, only to not return for the night...you've no chance of going unnoticed today."

"Well, then, I'll do my best to keep them guessing."

"And now I must go, before my brothers arrive to drag me from my chambers. Wait some time before you make your appearance downstairs. And I will see you later. I'll come find you in the gardens."

I helped Wilkie put on his tunic, taking any opportunity to touch him and savor the feel and the nearness of him. He strapped on his belt and fitted his sword and knife into place.

He kissed me once, and it was a kiss both savage and tender, full of all the depth of our new status: lovers, joined as one.

Then he left me, and I waited for a time, as he'd asked. I tidied up his chambers, straightening the furs of his bed. From my many years of cleaning the Ogilvie manor, I knew the unwritten code of chambermaids: a smoothly made bed was a sign that a room had been attended to. The sheets, I feared, would be noticed, the bloodstain revealing all that had taken place. But I had none to replace them with. If I made the bed and cleaned his chambers, then no one would be the wiser, and I could ask Wilkie to replace them tonight. I could clean them myself tomorrow.

When I felt enough time had passed, I opened the door to find Fergus waiting. I greeted him, and he nodded once, then followed me as I made my way to the activity of the great hall, where all of the female guests were breaking their fast. I tried my best to be inconspicuous, but all eyes turned to me, and the busy conversation paused, the sudden silence deafening.

One pair of eyes bored into me with unrestrained hostility. And Maisie Morrison's sisters, on either side of her, comforted her and whispered to her. Ailie jumped up and laced her arm through mine, leading me to an empty chair between hers and Christie's. It appeared they had saved it for me, and the realization touched me greatly.

"Roses," said Ailie, "come, join us. You must eat, and 'tis a perfect day for a stroll through the gardens."

"I fear I overslept this morning," I murmured, feeling the need to apologize, and wildly self-conscious under the table's collective interest.

The sisters ignored my comment, as though my excuse was entirely unnecessary.

"Hopefully it will be less eventful than our last stroll," added Christie, and I couldn't quite tell if there was a note of dry wit to her comment, or merely the pure candor I was now used to. It occurred to me then that, for the first time, Christie's voice had taken on a fractionally more worldly edge. I looked at her, assessing the difference. Her lips looked sensuously puffy and pneumatic, and her eyes were bright. She'd been kissed well, I guessed, and perhaps for the first time. Tosh Munro? I thought it likely. Full moon, indeed. I took her hand and gave it a gentle squeeze, and she responded by smiling.

She was assessing me with the same gauging inquisitiveness, as though detecting a difference. But before she could speak of it—and I was almost glad at the interruption—Maisie Morrison's pointed voice broke through the stilted tension that my presence had introduced. "We know so little of your visitor, Ailie. You must introduce us properly and tell us more about her. 'Tis not every day we meet such an exotic-looking acquaintance."

"You met Roses last night, did you not, Maisie?"

"Aye, but you didn't mention where she hails from. Or why she's here."

Clementine, whose bitterness may have stemmed from her appalling luck with men, I couldn't help but reflect and sympathize with, said, "She hardly looks like a Highlander, with hair that color. Tell us your story, Roses."

I began to spin the story I had been instructed to give. "I hail from the Macduff clan," I said, adding, in an attempt to change the subject, "I do so look forward to a stroll through the gardens. I've never seen such plenty in all my life."

"Nay," agreed Clementine dismissively. "Macduffs are hardly known for their agriculture." Neither were Morrisons, if I remembered correctly.

But Maisie had no intention of letting the subject lie. "And for what reason do you visit the Mackenzies, Roses? And where are your escorts?"

I wished I made a more convincing liar. I did my best to sound true. "I was escorted here by several Macduff warriors, who left me in the good care of the Mackenzie clan. I was assigned as an apprentice to Effie, the Mackenzie healer, to learn from her expertise."

"Why, we've visited the Macduff keep," said Maisie, "several months ago, for a gathering. It was the celebration of Hamish and Una Macduff's second child. A boy."

I was pleased to hear good news of Una.

Maisie continued, "In fact we had need of a healer during our visit, did we not? It was you, Stella. You came down with an illness, and needed treatment and several days of bed rest. Do you remember seeing Roses? I surely don't."

Stella looked uncomfortable with her sister's interrogation. Her eyes were an unusual light amber color that matched the golden highlights of her dark hair, which hung in long strands that curled at the very tips. She was noticeably more fine-boned than her sisters, and her skin was as smooth and pale as milk. Her beauty disconcerted me, as I thought of Laird Mackenzie's mission to marry Wilkie to one of these sisters. Stella, I thought, would be a much more palatable choice than Maisie for any man, to be sure, with her gentle nature and her unquestionable loveliness.

"I may recall seeing her, Maisie," Stella said, somewhat impatiently. "I was ill. I wasn't taking much notice of anything at all."

"Well, *I* was. And I don't recall seeing a blonde healer, not once. What about you, Clementine? Do you remember seeing Roses among the healers?"

"Nay, I'm sure I would have remembered Roses."

There was a bottomless pause. I tried to think of a lie, an excuse, a fantastically convincing tale that might explain away my nothingness. But I couldn't summon a single one. Ailie and Christie, too, looked blanched and strained with a similar affliction. I decided it mattered not what these uppity heiresses thought, Maisie and Clementine in particular. They had everything to offer yet very little appeal, and I could understand why men had so far skirted them, even with a lairdship and vast wealth in the offering. I hoped more than ever before that Wilkie would not be forced to marry Maisie; she seemed a poor match for him.

Grasping, I said the first thing that came to mind. "I was a kitchen servant for a time, before I was reassigned to the healing quarters."

The Morrison women looked stunned and mutely agog.

Wilkie knew of my low status; he loved me anyway, and that was all that mattered to me. Could others, too, possibly find value in me for *who* I was, rather than only condemning me for *what* I was?

"A *kitchen servant?*" Maisie finally managed, her voice croaked from incredulity.

"Aye," I confirmed, already regretting my impulse to be honest with her.

Maisie's voice was shrill when she continued, her face flushed with outrage. "A kitchen servant and a whore? And this is what he prefers?" She seemed to be asking her question to no one in particular.

I may have been foolish, with so very much still to lose, but I couldn't help myself. That same stubborn streak in me that had refused Laird Ogilvie reared its ugly head now. I attempted to silence myself, and earnestly, but my reply simply tumbled out.

"If I'm a whore, then surely you could be labeled the same," I stated softly, although softness, I admit, was possibly pointless; I may as well have shouted it. And if I thought it had been silent before my pronouncement, it was nothing to the total speechlessness of the hall now. I thought I detected an echo of my comment reverberating throughout the space, but I may have imagined it. What I didn't imagine though, was a grin on the face of Fergus, who stood diligently at his post by the door. I'm not sure why, but I took heart from this.

"How dare you!" Maisie shrieked, rising to her feet, red-faced. Her sisters immediately gathered around her and attempted to comfort her, shooting me with daggered glares.

My defiance shrunk into itself then, and I regretted the scene I'd willfully created in Ailie's and Christie's civilized presence. I felt ashamed, only because I didn't want to disappoint them, after all the kindheartedness they'd shown me. And what would Wilkie think? Would he be disappointed that I had shown such disrespect and revealed my lowly status after he'd been seen with me so publicly? And after he'd asked me to keep them guessing?

Ailie seemed anything but disappointed. Mildly shocked, aye. But unfailingly in control. "Maisie, please. You must admit you were the first to call the insults. I'm sure none of it's of any consequence. Let's finish our tea, then we'll take to the fresh air. I think we'll all benefit."

The Morrisons, all on their feet now anyway and with plates entirely emptied of their contents, seemed

to agree. Ailie, Christie and I—along with the slightly
wide-eyed Munro sister, whose name I'd learned last
night was Ainsley—stood. With clear friction sparking the air between myself and Maisie, we retreated to
the out-of-doors. And I was wildly pleased to do so. We
began our tour, soothed somewhat by the warm sun.

I caught Ailie, briefly. "Forgive me, Ailie," I said.
"My behavior is inexcusable."

"Don't be silly, Roses. They asked for a response."
She squeezed my hand sincerely. "Your past matters
not to me. You are what Wilkie wants, we can all see
that." Her words gave me some comfort, but still I felt
remorseful. I also felt distinctly separate from the group.
I knew I didn't belong among their noble company,
and now they knew it, too. I regretted my impetuous
outburst.

Maisie shot me fiery glances, until I wandered off
slightly from the gathering, wishing for solitude and a
moment to drink in the air and the bright light and the
refreshing scent of the fruitful earth. I wanted some
distance to collect myself.

So I set off along a different path, farther into the
orchard.

I knew exactly where I was going. I remembered the
sweetness of the pears and where to find them. Fergus
didn't question me but continued to follow me from a
slight distance, like a silent giant. The few times I'd
attempted to engage him in brief conversation, he'd
grunted an abrupt answer. So I respected his apparent
desire to concentrate on his vigilance, or whatever it
was he was doing, in peace. His brief grin at my earlier
outburst, though, had lightened the mood between us,

and I sensed we both found an element of camaraderie in our forced companionship.

The beauty of the garden struck me anew. I thought of my first trek through it, under the edgy gleam of darkness. That silver-lined night seemed a thousand lifetimes ago. And I could fully appreciate the golden splendor of the garden now, in the glow of the early-autumn sun. I thought of all that had transpired in the weeks since that dark night. If I'd attempted to dream such an outcome, I could not have come close to the magnificence of my new reality. Even my brief catfight with Maisie couldn't dampen the real spirit of my happiness as I thought of Wilkie. Of the long, languorous beauty of our night together.

The fruit trees were stooped with age and character, dotted together like old men discussing days long past. Fat fruit hung from their branches as jewelry might hang from a queen: colorful, plentiful and richly desired.

I picked the largest pear I could find and took a bite. I ate all of it, then ate two more.

I moved to the next tree and was surprised to hear a voice.

"Who is this who harvests my prize tree, and early?"

I turned to see a man standing there. His expression was friendly, and his gleaming reddish-brown hair caught the sunlight. He was a handsome, upright, earthy-looking man. I glanced at Fergus, who stood with his arms folded across his chest nearby, taking little notice of the stranger; it was obvious the man was a Mackenzie and therefore offered no threat to me.

"My name is Roses," I began, still startled by his presence, which caused me to fumble slightly with my words. "I'm a guest here. I've been told I could have a pear or two, if it's no trouble."

"No trouble at all, lass. Take three, if you like." He paused, as though sensing my unease. "The name's Fyfe. I'm the orchardist. I tend these trees and work these gardens."

I felt my eyebrows lift. "You tend these trees?"

"Aye."

"You're greatly talented," I said. "I've been admiring your work. These are the best pears I've ever tasted."

"I thank you for that."

"And how do you get your beans to fruit so high up the vine? I've never been able to do that." It occurred to me, only after I'd blurted out my question, that I shouldn't have known about his beans. I'd stolen them in the dark of night. But he didn't appear fazed by my question.

"Ah," he said. "A fellow gardener. I've found a kindred spirit, I see. Come, I'll show you."

He chatted easily as we walked, glancing once at Fergus but not ruffled by the appearance of a guard; after all, there were many about.

I found Fyfe's conversation riveting. It was clear that his thoughts, for a lifetime, had been focused heavily on intricately planned designs, experiments, inventions, schedules, and all on the subject of horticulture. It had been many years since I'd had a conversation like that.

"You see this bean plant here," he said, holding the stringy stem between two fingers. He picked a bean and handed it to me.

I put it in my mouth, savoring the taste as I chewed. The just-under-ripe fruit pod was perfect. Crispy, and the little peas burst on the tongue. "Oh, Fyfe, this is exactly what I was trying to do when I grew them myself. But they always tasted slightly bitter."

"The stem must be secured much more tightly than you might think. And the peas must be picked earlier than you might expect. I've made that mistake myself— leaving them too long on the vine. Here, have another."

He held out the bean, placing it close to my mouth, so I had to bite from his hand. But when I bit, he didn't immediately let go of it. He looked at me intently, and he was close enough that I could see that his eyes were a very dark brown, like the earth he tended. "Your hair catches the sunlight in a most extraordinary way," he said. Then he released the bean.

"Yours does, too," I commented. "'Tis the color of copper."

"How long will your visit extend, Roses, if I may?"

"You may. My visit…will extend indefinitely."

"Then you must come and see my house. 'Tis here, in the orchard. I am fortunate to live among the plants, so I can tend them at all hours of the day and night. Since you're a kindred spirit, I can tell you a secret— the beans like to be picked at night, did you know?"

"I've never heard of such a thing."

"It makes a surprising difference to their taste," he said. "You must come by one evening, to test my theory. And I've been propagating a whole range of hybrids you might be interested in seeing."

I thought that sounded wonderful: living among the pear trees, walking out the door in the moonlight to eat fresh-picked peas or pears if you so chose to, tending seedlings inside the warmth of your house before you released them to the ground. "I'd like that very much."

I was startled when he reached out to touch my face.

He ran his finger in a line down my cheek to my chin, drawing his touch slowly away. "Your dress complements your eyes."

My face felt flushed under his attentions, and I knew it was time to take my leave. Before I could excuse myself, a noisy, energetic, hulking form burst, unannounced, through the foliage.

Wilkie.

He stopped in his tracks, his face registering me, my flushed cheeks and the man standing close to me, whose hand was just disengaging from its contact. Wilkie's gaze traveled from my face to Fyfe's hand and back to me again. His eyes flashed. In a sudden movement, he punched his fist to a near tree trunk, which must have pained him terribly, although he did it once more before growling in frustration, shaking out his hand.

"Wilkie!" I cried, going to him, taking his bloodied hand in my own. I wiped his blood with my fingers.

But Wilkie's attention was aimed at Fyfe.

His voice was cold and extremely direct. "You're a friend of mine, Fyfe, a longstanding member of this clan and of great value to your clansmen. I don't blame you for wanting to walk with her and speak to her. But if you ever so much as touch this lass again, I'll see to you with my own bare hands. And I have little restraint when it comes to Roses. Do I make myself clear enough?"

Fyfe was flustered. "Aye, Wilkie. Aye."

"Good," said Wilkie. He slung his massive arm around my shoulders and held me against his body as he led me, at a decisive pace, away. Over his shoulder, he dismissed Fergus.

He wasn't breathing well. We walked for some time

before he spoke, and by the time he did, we were far from the orchard, in a thicker glade of trees, alone.

He released me and stood to face me.

"If I'm to live with you and your clan," I began, hoping I was addressing the issue at hand: his jealousy and not anger over my earlier outburst at the ladies' table. "I will need to speak to some of them upon occasion."

He shocked me by falling to his knees before me.

I dropped to my knees beside him, taking his bloodied fist in my hands. I kissed his bruised, cut skin.

"'Tis too much," he said.

"What's too much?"

"My love for you. I can't survive it."

He looked so big, so strong, yet so defeated, kneeling there in front of me. I wanted only to comfort him, to soothe his angst. I touched my mouth to his lips. "If I can survive it, warrior, you can. Feel me here, with you. Feel my mouth on you. Taste my love for you. I'm here. Let me heal you."

I sucked on his upper lip, touching my tongue to his tongue. He was unfastening his trews as I kissed him. "Roses?" he whispered, so softly I could barely hear him.

"Aye."

He was laying me back on the ground, his seeking hands pushing my dress up to my waist. "I need you now, here, on this earth. My earth. I am wild for you. I can think of nothing else."

"I'm yours, warrior. You know I'm yours."

"Mine."

"Only yours."

His strength was aggressive as he pushed my knees up, so my legs were bent, and I was revealed to him fully. He licked his tongue deep into my body. I thought briefly of our location, out-of-doors, where we could be seen if someone happened to walk by. But the thought faded as Wilkie's mouth did miraculous things to my receiving flesh, causing me to swell and moisten and throb with need for all he had to give. The stubble of his face scratched against my sensitive folds, and his hair brushed against the soft skin of my inner thighs. I could feel the wave begin, deep within me, being drawn from my body by the unrelenting ministrations of his mouth.

Then his touch was gone, but before I could protest, I felt the weight of him on me and the forceful assault of his heavy shaft plunge deeply into me. I ached for him, and he had wet me with his artful marauding, but still my newly tried flesh resisted him, so his repeating thrusts became more powerful, assertive in their demand. His first drives sparked pain, the soreness lingering from the night before. But the pain, as his thickness sunk deeper and farther, gave way to a thrilling adjustment. The friction of his forward, insistent momentum rubbed at the most intimate pleasures he had begun with his mouth. These pleasures grew, blooming in a tidal flush that rose and rose inexorably, forced higher by the aggression of Wilkie's need. Then, in a long gasping moment, the pleasure peaked, erupting through my body in an explosive, all-encompassing rush. I heard myself cry out from the force of my release. The cascading spasms were simply too much. Too intense in their potency. Excruciating in the sheer height of the ecstasy they enforced. My inner muscles clenched strongly around him, milking at the length of him until I could feel the violent beat of his own release and the warmth of his seed pulsing rhythmically into my body. He pressed his savage groan into my neck.

We lay still for many moments, our bodies still clasping intimately, locked in a secret, fluttering dance. Our gazes met in a soul-touching link.

"I'll never have enough of you," he whispered. "Not in this lifetime. Not in a thousand lifetimes. I love you, Roses. I love you with a ferocity that threatens my very sanity."

I pulled him closer, whispering love words into his ear. I loved him. I loved him. He was my beautiful savior. He was my heart and my life.

I kissed Wilkie's hair and smoothed it with my fingers. I never wanted this closeness to end. I wanted to hold him inside me, bound to him in flesh and spirit, until the end of time.

The haze of my rapture began to lift, and I noticed again our surroundings. "I hope no one has seen us."

"If someone has, it'll give them plenty to discuss." He eased himself from my body and helped me sit up, adjusting my dress and fastening his own clothing. Then he stood and held his hand out to me. "I believe it's time to announce our engagement."

CHAPTER FIFTEEN

THE FESTIVITIES ON THE second evening of the Morrisons' visit were even more lively than those of the first. The music was louder, and the ale seemed to flow more easily. On the first night, there had been a flush of reserve in the crowd, as friends and families got reacquainted or, in some cases, met for the first time. But the reserve had now been well and truly laid to rest, as the Mackenzies and their guests ate, drank, discussed, argued and flirted. Making matches and alliances was, in fact, the point of the gathering, and the young people, in particular, appeared suitably dedicated to the task.

Ailie, I noticed, had broken through her shy avoidance of Magnus Munro and was seated next to him, blushing from his attentions. He really was a striking-looking man. Tall and red-haired, he had the air of a hard-edged romantic. And Ailie, with all her cream-skinned, dark-eyed beauty, seemed to have entranced him. I hoped, for her sake, the match would come to pass and make her happy.

Christie was again talking with Tosh and Angus Munro. Angus made no move to speak to me this evening, and I could hardly blame him; Wilkie watched him with a hawk-eyed alertness. Angus, it appeared, had instead decided to vie for the attentions of Christie. It was clear that Tosh was somewhat miffed by his cousin's intrusion, and I hoped Christie was treading lightly. Her open, naive manner might make her more vulnerable than most, and I felt, again, a wave of protectiveness for her.

I also wondered if Angus or Tosh would make a good match for her. If Ailie eventually married Magnus Munro, would Christie be required to marry a nobleman of a different clan? Laird Mackenzie's goal seemed to be to expand his family's holdings as far afield as possible; maybe he would forbid his sisters from marrying brothers.

And so my thoughts treaded across the crowd as I watched the matchmaking in action, somewhat nervously. Would Wilkie choose to make his announcement tonight? And if he did, what would be the reaction?

Wilkie was fairly crawling out of his skin. If he'd been wild-eyed last night, tonight was something else altogether. He remained at my side, attempting, I thought, to keep his hands from touching me too obviously. The rumor mill had had its say, and by now I was certain every soul in the hall knew of my confession: of who I was and what I was, as much as it could be known. No one said anything outright, but I could tell by the look in their eyes.

They were wise to hold their tongues. Wilkie, I'd overheard, was not only renowned for his reckless nature but also his fighting skills; I'd heard it said that he was one of the best swordsmen in the Highlands and highly respected for it. That, along with his unpredictability, kept the open remarks to a minimum.

I wasn't sure if Wilkie sensed this change or knew of it; I wasn't sure if he was aware that my secret was out. Maybe that's what lit his blue eyes with a crazed animation that kept the Morrison women almost at bay.

But there was a change, too, in Maisie's approach. She knew now that she clearly outclassed me, that the reality of my situation gave her a very definite social advantage in our shared quest to keep Wilkie Mackenzie as our own. And we weren't alone. Aside from Stella, whose eyes remained cast down or gazing at some far-off point out the window, Maisie's own sisters ogle-eyed him covetously, and her cousins, too, to be sure.

He kept me close to him, even holding my wrist on occasion. Once he absentmindedly touched my hair. And between us, a fizzling current burned and held like a quiet agony. To be so close to him and not touch him was torturous. To feel his breath on my face and not be allowed to lean closer, to taste him and feel the heat of his skin, it made me ache and fluster and count the minutes.

Wilkie's face registered the same passion, his blue eyes harsh in their intensity. The revelations, the bliss and the absolute connectivity of the past twenty-four hours radiated between us and drew us to each other like an intangible magnetic force. And at the same time, the uncertainty of our future together, the whispers in the room and the ever-present insistence of Maisie Morrison—all pink lips and fleshy cleavage—sparked into the space between us, which may as well have been the vastest ocean.

I needed air.

Or at least a drink of water. Abruptly, I left Wilkie's side to wander across the room, finding a pitcher and a cup. I drank one cup and filled it again. I carried it with me as I made my way back to Wilkie, wondering if it might be a better idea to depart instead to his chambers to wait for him there. Before I could make the decision, I was intercepted by a man wearing a Munro tartan. The other cousin, I suspected, who I'd not yet met.

"Tadgh Munro. You must be Roses." He held up his hand to take mine for a light kiss, a gesture I was not used to but was learning. I gave him my hand, and he touched his lips gently to the back of my knuckles, releasing me almost instantly, which I was fiercely glad of. I had a feeling it wouldn't do to challenge Wilkie's control tonight; his unruliness was too close to the surface. When I glanced once in his direction, he was distracted, predictably flocked by his admirers once again.

"Once you're finished serving Wilkie, you're more than welcome at the Munro keep," he said. "I'll escort you myself."

At first I wasn't sure of his meaning, but his brown eyes glimmered with wicked intent and something more.

"I—" I stuttered, "I must go."

Tadgh's finger traced a departing invitation along the skin of my lower arm as I hastily made my leave and left a blazing, humiliating impression.

And as I drew closer to Wilkie, he immediately sensed my distress. He brushed off the hands of the women impatiently and rushed to my side. "What has happened?" he asked, reading the stricken look on my face.

I attempted a smile, and I cupped his readied fist between my hands. "'Tis, nothing, warrior. I'm fine."

In fact I wasn't fine. My foolish outburst had revealed the terrible reality of who I was. I was being laughed at and looked down upon. I could feel it, I could see it. I wasn't good enough for Wilkie, and it devastated me. I was an embarrassment to my upstanding warrior, who must feel a deep humiliation of his own. To be seen with me and to have to contend with the disdain of his peers: no wonder he looked tight-sprung and ready to burst into flames at a moment's notice. I felt deeply ashamed that I had caused him such disgrace.

And there was more to my sorrow, too. I knew the time was drawing nigh when I would reveal my mark to him. The thought of Wilkie's love shifting, possibly violently, to revulsion or anger was almost more than I could endure. But it must be done, and sooner rather than later. I hated myself for what I was and, even more so, for hiding my true identify from him. I knew why I had done it, to experience the astounding beauty that Wilkie was able to unrelentingly provide, just once, just for a while.

Wilkie's long fingers reached to frame my jaw. His expression, rather than outraged or at all shamed, was anguished. And his dark beauty pierced me anew. "Whatever it is that you're thinking, lass, don't. I can't bear it."

And then, as if all the forces of the universe converged into one forward, gentle pull, it happened. The crowd faded away, and all I could see or feel was his face and his magnetic draw. His lips were slightly parted, so close to my own. Those lips that had done unspeakable, transcendent things to my body. I craved him with every fiber of my being. And Wilkie, as though in response, touched his mouth to mine in a sweet, brief, very forbidden kiss.

The crowd murmured and buzzed. Someone whistled. A lewd comment was offhandedly tossed. And

Maisie Morrison was there, stepping in and claiming some kind of jurisdiction over what had just transpired. She smiled sweetly, her hand lightly placed on Wilkie's muscular forearm, but her words were hissed more than spoken. "Wilkie, you *mustn't*."

I don't believe it was her words that set him off or even the clasp of her fingers on his arm. He reacted only when she placed her hand on my shoulder, as though she might push me away.

"Take your hand off Roses," Wilkie said, and his voice was colored with steely hostility.

She did, slowly, and with an expression of mild hurt, as if she couldn't understand his coldness.

It was then that Wilkie leaped up on a chair. He stood tall and surveyed the crowd with confidence, wholly assured and comfortable in his own skin. He spoke evenly, with his voice only slightly raised, he already had the room's undivided attention.

"Honored guests, friends and fellow clansmen," he said, "I have an announcement I'd like to make."

I almost called out to him, to stop him. *Wait. There's something I need to show you first, warrior,* I thought. *Now.*

"Wilkie."

It was the laird who spoke, not loudly but with broiling authority. I suspected it wasn't Laird Mackenzie's style to yell and force his will at his brother's impulsive behavior, especially in this very public arena. I had no doubt he knew exactly what Wilkie intended to announce. He looked on the verge of erupting. The laird, as far as I could tell, was a patient, thoughtful and highly honorable man, and one who carried the weight of his entire clan quite clearly upon his shoulders. Occasionally, though, I detected a glimpse of a fiery inner turbulence in him, as though under his diplomatic exterior was a strictly tamed wildness—not unlike his younger brother's—that shone out of his flashing light gray eyes. The sheer size of him made his anger a terrifying prospect. He rose from the table, making his request with a forced calmness. "We'll discuss your announcement in my private chambers before we share your news with our guests."

But Wilkie was too far gone.

"I mean to share it now, brother," he said, to which several of the partygoers cheered.

"Wilkie!" roared the laird, and it was a forceful enough command to silence Wilkie, for now. "Come with me," Laird Mackenzie added in a tone that left no room for argument. "We will meet in private to discuss this matter further." He walked from the room in quiet outrage.

Wilkie grabbed my hand and pulled me along behind him.

Maisie watched us go with wide eyes, and the frightened look on her face indicated she was almost having second thoughts about chaining herself to a man who might in fact be half lunatic.

Wilkie led me down the narrow hallway and into his brother's private den, the same room where I'd dined with the Mackenzies and the laird's officers once before. The fire and a number of candles were already lit, and a pitcher of ale with its matching cups waited at the center of the round table, as though this room was kept at the ready for impromptu meetings, like this one, at all times.

Laird Mackenzie was already seated at the table, and he was pouring three cups of ale. "Sit," he said.

We sat, and Wilkie's manner remained one of confidence. This comforted me and allowed me to cling to my last thread of hope.

"This has gone far enough," said the laird brusquely.

"I quite agree, brother," Wilkie replied. "I intended to settle the matter once and for all."

The laird continued, and his voice was blazingly direct. "I am not a man who hungers for power, Wilkie, nor one who abuses it. I have always taken my brothers' and my officers' opinions to heart, and most of all yours. Today, however, is a day in which I must exercise my right to lead. Your judgment has clearly been impaired by your…feelings. But the decision has been made. You will marry Stella Morrison. It has been somewhat clear to us all that you do not favor Maisie. Taking that fact into account and also due to recent events regarding his daughters, Laird Morrison has decided that Stella will be the one to secure the new laird, as she likely should have been all along. She's second in line, after all, and the eldest sister will leave for the nunnery, I'm told, as soon as the wedding has taken place. The arrangements have already been made. Laird Morrison and I have discussed it in detail, just hours ago. I sought you out to discuss this with you, brother, but you were nowhere to be found. The decision is final. The wedding will take place on the morrow."

Hearing the words delivered in that authoritative, resolute timbre, I felt a numbness envelop me, as a thin gauzy film settled over me, stifling me and closing me down.

"Stella?" Wilkie said, in more of a statement than a

question. I couldn't quite tell if the ruling was disagreeable to him or beguiling, and the uncertainty only amplified my despair.

But then, Wilkie stood, balling his fists. His movements were lithe and powerful as he paced, his countenance dark and menacing. To me, he was glorious, even in his hotheaded state. Maybe even *especially* in his hotheaded state. I knew now, intimately, about the sensations his impetuousness could inspire. I grew secretly damp at the mere thought of it, even now, when I knew he was no longer mine. In my mind I was losing him, but my body was not yet willing to give up or give in.

"I'll not marry Stella," Wilkie growled, and his next phrase was spoken in deliberately emphasized single words. "I will marry Roses."

He might have acted on his tempest, but the laird spoke his name in a calming and entirely forceful command.

"Wilkie. The Morrison keep—Glenlochie—as you know, is a prosperous one, with rich lands, strong walls, a large and picturesque manor, a growing, industrious clan. You wish to pass all that up? You prefer to remain here, as second-in-command, when you could be laird of your own jurisdiction, to guide and build and foster through your own learned, earned leadership?"

Wilkie's heavy sigh was laden with layered frustration, the sound of it filling me with a small but insistent sense of dread. "I am willing to forego leadership of Glenlochie, aye," Wilkie said. "Am I not a useful soldier to you, Knox? A contributing counselor and supportive second-in-command?"

"Of course you are, Wilkie. I cannot imagine a better officer. But that is not the point—"

"Knox," Wilkie said, cutting off the laird. "I am secure in my contribution to my clan and family *here,* as your brother, and as your first officer, and I would prefer to remain in this role if it means I can remain true to myself—and to our mother's last wishes."

Laird Mackenzie contemplated his brother intensely, remembering, perhaps.

"Wilkie." The laird paused, running his hand through his hair as though attempting to control his emotions and his temper, which radiated in all directions. When he continued, his rage was no less pronounced, but his voice was even. "I am laird of this keep. You are my brother and one of the most respected men I know. But it is your duty to help this family grow and prosper. For all intents and purposes, you will double the size of our lands when you marry the daughter of Laird Morrison, who has chosen you personally to take over his lairdship. She is a pleasing lass, by any man's standards. And 'tis a plentiful, easily accessible keep with a strong army." His focus, at Wilkie, was unequivocal, his emphasis clear. "A strong *army* that will assist us in our quest to defeat Campbell and to avenge the death of our father. Gaining control of the Morrison troops may be the only way we'll become strong enough to ensure that Campbell and his recruits do not gain control of Ossian Lochs, which is a pivotal military position."

It was this last point that hammered home its impact. Wilkie might be willing to forego his own lairdship, and this in itself was no small matter to overlook. But he would not be willing to pass up an opportunity to strengthen the collective army that would avenge his father's death. I knew the warrior in him—all of him— rose at this opportunity, which he may not have considered fully before this moment. To lead his own army, aside his brother's, and challenge the rebellion that had killed their own father: it was the ultimate score. And one that he could not, and would not, refuse.

"I understand love, brother," said Laird Mackenzie quietly, and it was the first time I'd detected a crack in the armor of the powerful laird, as he addressed his brother. His voice had a rigid edge that was flecked with emotion. "'Tis not always the easiest path. Nor the best one. You can learn to love, and you will decide how the situation between the three of you will play out. Whatever is decided in that regard, your marriage to Stella will take place tomorrow at midday. Laird Morrison wants the deal finalized. Roses, you may remain here at Kinloch, for now, or we will escort you to Macduff's if you prefer that option. Or, if Wilkie chooses to take you with him to his new home, that may be another choice available to you. I would guess that he will likely want you close to him, although his new wife will likely have some say in the arrangement. But Wilkie's fate has already been determined. 'Tis the only reasonable outcome. And it will be the final outcome."

It may have been the layered emotion that clung to Laird Mackenzie's direct and impassioned words that silenced the argument once and for all. I didn't know the finer details of the laird's tragic love story, but Wilkie did. And that, along with his duty as a brother, a son and a warrior, was enough to quiet his personal rebellion.

Wilkie walked over to sit on a small bench near the open door, and no one spoke for several seconds.

A cold chill settled into my bones, seeping with all the stealth of a deadly poison. My drifting hope that I would ever be considered as a bride for the coveted

Wilkie Mackenzie had been entirely unfounded. I could see that now. Maisie was right: I wasn't worthy of him. I was a servant, a wanderer, a thief. A whore. A witch. My secret mark hardly mattered now, in light of this new arrangement.

Wilkie said nothing. He did not protest, nor argue, nor did he move at all.

And that was the only sign I needed. I stood. "I would request to return to my chambers, Laird Mackenzie. You will have much to discuss. With your permission, I will take my leave."

Wilkie did not look at me, locked in his own sifting dilemma, as I stood.

And as I was leaving the room, Kade entered it. I almost bumped into him but caught myself, skirting him, saying nothing. If he registered my sorrow, he did not address it; he nodded a curt greeting, preoccupied with his own agenda, and I left him to it.

Not far behind Kade, Laird Morrison followed, flanked on either side by two of his daughters: none other than Maisie and Stella. Both women had red-rimmed eyes and clearly looked upset about whatever discussion had prompted their appearance here at the doorway of Laird Mackenzie's private den. Laird Morrison barely noticed me, so intent was he to meet with his ally about the sticky matter of securing a husband for one of his daughters. The topic was one that had been fraught, even I knew, with many thwarted plans and false hopes. And Laird Morrison's face reflected each and every one of those disappointments. The deal would be made, here and now. Determination brought a rise of color to Laird Morrison's features as he ushered his daughters along with him. "Enough is enough," he was murmuring angrily. "There will be no more plotting, scheming nor negotiating. This alliance will be sealed once and for all."

I tried to sneak past them through the shadows without being noticed, but Maisie's eyes caught mine and held. Her dark eyes gleamed with disappointment, and, as soon as she saw me, fury. I guessed that she had heard the news: Wilkie would not marry her, after all her attempts to lure him and to persuade her father that *she* should be next in line. Her expression was shattered enough to recognized that she was aware that Stella, instead, was destined to secure the new laird. After all, it was Stella's birthright, as second oldest, if Clementine had opted to live out her days in a convent. And if Maisie wasn't alluring enough to capture Wilkie Mackenzie, then Stella would be offered in her place; Stella, with her unmatched splendor, would succeed where Maisie had failed.

Maisie's stare promised death as I hastily brushed past her. Hatred and a burning jealousy. I could read the blame in her eyes. It was *I* who had upset her careful plans. She'd been so close to claiming Wilkie as her own, but *I,* some outcast servant, some unknown *whore,* had stolen him and undermined his resolve. He'd indulged her and agreed to consider her as his wife—until I came along. Because of me, his lingering doubts had alerted the lairds to the precariousness of the important alliance.

"You'll never have him again," she seethed, so low I could scarcely hear her words. "Never. I'll make sure of it, even if he's not mine." Her words deepened my agony. If *she* was to suffer, then so would I.

I was reminded of the story Wilkie had told me, of

the king's vengeful wife and her quest to see her husband's mistress and child killed. Maisie would have similar resources. I envisioned my own end as Wilkie's offcast lover, hiding my illegitimate baby from Maisie's henchmen, once again hunted. It was no way to raise a child, and I hoped with that part of my heart that Wilkie had not already planted his baby inside me.

And then I saw Stella's face, painted by the light of a quivering flame, heartbreakingly beautiful. Instead of anger, I could see fear and sadness. Pining, perhaps, for her stable boy, if Christie's information was correct.

All the relevant parties were in attendance, to discuss the family matter at hand and to lay all questions to rest.

There was no place for me here. I was an outsider, once again.

I took my leave of them, traversing along the narrow dim hallway, blindly.

The heartache! It fairly stunned me. My body felt leaden and stiff. My heart suffered its lazy beat fretfully as though it was truly broken.

I took little notice of my surroundings, feeling strangely numb and senseless. I reached Wilkie's chambers and closed the door behind me. I removed my dress and laid it carefully on the bed, allowing myself one last touch of its fine fabric. I retrieved my old trews and tunic from the antechamber, and my weapons, which I had placed in a folded pile on a small forlorn chair, where they had sat for some time now, unnoticed. I had thought once or twice of throwing them away, thinking hopefully that I no longer had need of bulky men's clothing to hide behind, or of weapons, to protect myself. Then, I'd been reborn, reveling in the feeling of being wanted instead of hunted.

But it was not meant to be. I could not fight against the laird's orders. And I didn't want to. Wilkie was duty-bound but also entitled and driven. I didn't want to undermine his purpose. Helping his family and clan prosper, and avenging the death of his father: these were certainly far more honorable pursuits than keeping a whispered promise to a lost and lonely servant, whose secrets, once revealed, would no doubt bring a decisive end to a brief love affair. He would build a life with Stella and find happiness with her eventually, when she bore him a son, perhaps, or even sooner. She would be a good match for him. She was as beautiful as he was and would bear him handsome children. She would charm him with the loveliness of her face, her multi-hued hair, her amber eyes. He would forget me and live his life as it was intended: as a laird, a leader, husband to a noblewoman. His happiness would be encouraged by the knowledge that he was living his destiny as it was meant to be, and that he was doing the right thing for his family and his clan. I hoped he would recognize that and make peace with it.

My own destiny was equally clear.

I took one last look around the room, remembering the details of my many days and nights spent within its protective walls: the most beautiful and defining days and nights of my life. And they would remain as such.

Taking care to remain as inconspicuous as I could, I made my way back down the stairs, through hallways, finding a side door to the manor that I knew about from my days spent with Ailie and Christie. I would miss getting to know them, rejoicing in their blossoming friendship and marveling at the prospect of one day counting them as sisters of my own.

Silently, I closed the door behind me.

I was out-of-doors. Always before I had reveled in the first rush of fresh air, the coolness and the freedom. No longer. This air felt cold rather than cool, and alarming in its frank abandon. This air would not provide me with freedom, but with exile.

I allowed myself a small detour as I walked toward the gates of the keep. I approached a small pear tree, which stood somewhat separated from the others. Much of its fruit had been harvested, but there were still a number of scattered pears to choose from. I picked two. I wouldn't need food where I was going. I continued to walk. And I almost couldn't bring myself to eat them. The taste of them brought tears to my eyes. Too delicious and bittersweet: the taste of all I was not and all I would never be. I ate all of them, as a small reward and also a punishment, even swallowing the seeds, in a perverse tribute. And by the time I had finished, I'd reached the gates, which were closed and guarded.

My tears might have made my request more authentic. "Laird Mackenzie has ordered me gone this night. Please allow me to pass."

The guards looked at me skeptically, and I could read their thoughts. Wasn't this the lass they'd been ordered to protect? The one who'd been nearly abducted, and was the very reason the walls had been fortified and doubly manned?

"I am no longer under the laird's protection," I continued. "Trust me when I say he would like nothing better than to see me outside these walls, and as soon as possible."

They surveyed my outfit and my weapons. Then the head guard barked, "Open the gates."

And there I was, back outside the Mackenzie keep, alone under a star-studded sky. The clanging clash of the gates as they shut me out echoed in my ears even after the sound had long ceased.

I headed back to my cave.

CHAPTER SIXTEEN

THE HIKE UP THE MOUNTAIN took much of the night. My legs seemed less agile than usual, and my weight heavier. I made my ascent through woods scented with dirt and freshly dug earth, as though death and decay was rising. Abstractly, I noticed the hue of the light was changing. Night into day.

It was then I found my cave. I entered it, and the sight of the bloodied blanket, left there upon Wilkie's rescue, speared me anew.

I wrapped myself in the dirty cloth. It was all I had left of him.

I searched the cave for my knife, finally locating it in a dim corner. I walked down to the pool and paused to appreciate the pink-stained sunrise, falsely promising a perfect day.

Dropping the blanket to the ground, I unfastened my sword, laying it down. I removed all of my clothing from the waist down, but I kept the long tunic on. And I unbound my hair, letting it hang loose, as he once said he liked it best.

Clutching my knife in one hand, I lowered myself into the cool waters of the pool.

The water, as I remembered it, was inviting and divine. Cool but not cold, as though warmed by the earth, or from a secret underground hot spring.

I didn't hurry. I felt trepidation, naturally. But not fear. This quiet end was far less frightening to me than a lifetime of endless separation and vast emptiness. Of knowing he was forever lost to me.

My heart simply couldn't bear it.

Spying a glint of sunlit reflection at the edge of the pool, I saw my mother's glass-jeweled pin, sitting on the nearby rock, exactly where I'd placed it several weeks ago. But it was of no consequence now. I had no need of possessions.

I ran the knife's blade lightly across my inner wrist, getting a feel for it, studying the existential power of its touch and its promise. Did I want to die? Nay. I wanted to *live*. I'd only just tasted what truly being *alive* actually felt like. Did I want to live the life that was my fate: of Ogilvie's wrath or Macduff's pity? Nay. I would rather die, now that I understood the extent of the difference between surviving and living. The only life I wanted to lead was that of a Mackenzie, and more: as *Wilkie's* Mackenzie. But that path was lost to me. Even living as a Mackenzie meant nothing to me if I couldn't have Wilkie as my own.

But I wasn't ready. And I wept at my choices. I wished there were others.

The rising day was unusually warm, and the heated sunlight on my face and my shoulders provided a small relief in the midst of my sorrow; it felt so comforting that I closed my eyes and laid my head back on the grass bank of the pool.

I thought of Wilkie. Of his hands and his mouth. His black hair and his dark, beautiful presence tightly around me and in me. I may have dozed off for a time, lost in my only reverie.

I couldn't tell how long I had slept, but I awoke with a start to the crashing, thundering sound of horses' hoofbeats just over the lip of the hill, so close that before I could react they were there in the clearing, huge and looming and armed, pulling to a dramatic and sweat-flicked stop.

Was I still dreaming? Was it him, coming to find me and claim me as his own?

Nay. This was neither heaven, nor was I waking to a heavenly new reality. I could recognize that I was fully, starkly awake. I was so immersed in the depths of my longing for Wilkie, *willing* it to be him with all my heart, that for a moment I thought it was him.

His broad shoulders, his wild hair.

He's come for me.

But the hair was not black enough.

The movements were not as graceful

The man that approached me—one of six, I could see that now—was most definitely *not* Wilkie.

He was an Ogilvie warrior. I recognized the face, if not the name.

"Aye," he was saying to the other men. "'Tis her. Surround her. Make sure she has no escape. This time we bring her home."

He was striding toward me quickly, and a few of the other riders were now dismounting.

I was ambushed.

CHAPTER SEVENTEEN

THE SPLIT SECOND BEFORE the Ogilvie warrior reached me, I thought of my knife. But I had dropped it somewhere. I used my feet to feel around on the floor of the pool, but I couldn't locate it.

And then he was here, grabbing me by the arm and pulling me out of the pool in one forceful heave that pained my arm dreadfully and caused me to cry out.

I tried to reach for my sword, which lay only feet from where I stood, but the soldier read my intention and kicked it away, so it, too, was swallowed into the depths of the pool, out of reach to me.

"Don't fight me, lass. You'll only hurt yourself. You can come willingly, or we can beat you and bind your hands and feet. Up to you. But make no mistake about it—you're coming with us to be delivered alive to Laird Ogilvie." He pulled me against his body in a forceful hug, and I was infinitely grateful now that I'd chosen to keep my tunic on, even if I wore nothing underneath it; its wet fabric clung to me and covered me only to the middle of my thighs, but it was better than nothing at all.

The Ogilvie guard held me in a vise-grip against him and began to pull me toward the horses. My struggles made no impact whatsoever and only succeeded in angering him, so his hold became rougher, painfully so.

This pain, I knew, was nothing compared to what was in store for me. I could already picture Ogilvie's face, his glee, his satisfaction. He would have no qualms about making his punishment as brutal and demeaning as possible, I had no doubt. I had refused him, struck him, humiliated him, and his revenge would be thoughtfully and thoroughly carried out. This I knew.

I fought back against the soldier, squirming and biting into his arm, which was strung around my neck. He released me at the same time he struck me, and his blow was so forceful that I fell to the ground. I sat there for a moment, holding my hand against my throbbing jaw, sobbing with fear and grief until my vision blurred. I felt thoroughly defeated.

I was so distraught, it took me a few moments to register a new commotion: the approach of more horses. It would be the remainder of the search party, I guessed, wiping at my eyes to see if I recognized any of them. It occurred to me that if Ritchie was among them, he might be able to help me escape. Again.

But it wasn't Ritchie who rode up.

It was Kade. And Wilkie.

For a moment I thought I was imagining them, that they were the figments of my desperate, grasping mind. *Wilkie.*

And at the same time the relief and hunger and absolute joy at the sight of him swelled in my heart, my terror overpowered every other emotion. Wilkie was in grave danger, as I was. He had followed me here, into the viper's pit of my Ogilvie ambush where we might both—all, Kade included—lose our lives.

Our fates entwined, Roses. I know not why, but I know it to be true: I am bound to you forevermore.

Wilkie leaped off his horse before it even came to a stop, walking toward me as though he didn't notice the Ogilvie warriors.

And it seemed that the Ogilvie warriors were surprisingly tolerant of Wilkie's approach. I guessed that the uneven ratio of Ogilvie warriors to Mackenzies gave the Ogilvie men a sense of jaunty confidence over their advantage. Wilkie did not appear at all intimidated or mindful of his own safety, which almost worried me. Was he so distracted by me and my dire predicament that he had let his guard down? Or was he simply so self-assured as a trained, armed and assisted warrior that he felt less threatened than he appeared?

But when the Ogilvie soldier grabbed my arm and yanked me back into his tight embrace, Wilkie stopped in his tracks. The soldier's massive arm was wrapped around my chest, his sword held to my neck.

Wilkie was only a few feet from where I stood, and the sight of him, real and so close, was enough to weaken my knees. I would have fallen to the ground if the soldier hadn't held me so forcefully. I had thought I would never lay eyes on Wilkie again. And here he was, more beautiful than he had ever been. The hotheadedness of his temperament, in the heat of conflict, was evened and steely. There was none of the turbulence of him that was often so pronounced. Just an utter focus. Fighting filled his days and was his purpose, and it was clear from his seasoned confidence that he was good at his job. Here, however, was a new situation: me. Held by an enemy with a razor-sharp blade to my throat. Wilkie seemed mildly disarmed by this scenario.

He pulled his sword from its scabbard and held it out in front of him. "Unhand the lass," he commanded.

"Drop your sword, Mackenzie," the soldier who held me barked impatiently, and I suppose his impatience was warranted; there was no chance he would unhand me, we all knew that. "Step aside. You're free to go, and do it now. 'Tis the lass we're after. If you attack us, we'll kill you and your brother and take the lass anyway. She belongs to Ogilvie, and she'll be returned to Ogilvie."

Kade had dismounted and was holding his sword in one hand and a circular knife in the other. He appeared almost otherworldly as his many weapons caught the sunlight and reflected it in an iridescent glimmer.

"She belongs to me, as my betrothed," Wilkie said. Maybe he said this as a ruse, in an attempt to convince the Ogilvie soldiers to release me. I *wasn't* his betrothed, after all. Today was his wedding day, aye, but his wife-to-be waited for him at Kinloch, wondering, quite possibly, what was keeping him. He may have come for me out of duty, to secure my safety before he recited his vows and sealed his fate. At that moment, it hardly mattered. Just to see him there, in all his wild splendor, caused my heart to swell with pure happiness, despite the circumstance.

A second, black-bearded warrior laughed. "Your betrothed?" I knew this warrior: a high-ranking officer of Ogilvie's whose name was Dougal. I had served his table frequently enough, I knew him to be loud and excessively outspoken; in fact it was this very man's often overeager conversation with Laird Ogilvie that had provided much of the political and military information I possessed. "I'm afraid Ogilvie intends to take her for himself. He will wed her as soon as she is returned to him."

"Wed her? Not while I live," said Wilkie, defiant.

Dougal chuckled again, dismounting from his horse and walking closer to Wilkie. "I can arrange to have that taken care of. You're outnumbered six to two, soldier. Now step aside or die."

Wilkie remained frozen in place, his eyes darker than I had ever seen them. And he was speaking to me, his voice softened just for my ears, despite our attentive and menacing audience. He spoke as though he didn't care if these enemy soldiers heard his words, as though he was afraid he might not get another chance to say what he wanted me to know. If we were to die—which was a distinct possibility—there were things that must first be said. "Roses, why did you flee? It wasn't finished yet, lass. Your departure was too hasty. I'll not marry Stella Morrison. Kade will be the one to secure the alliance."

With effort, in the consuming distress of the moment, I recalled her face. Her milky skin and her downcast, amber eyes. Stella. The beautiful sister. The one promised to Wilkie.

I looked at Kade, whose eyes glimmered along with the rest of him. "I have asked for Stella's hand, and her father has agreed to it," he confirmed.

"Preparations are already underway," Wilkie said. "Laird Morrison is pleased with the match, and Knox has accepted that it's a reasonable alternative. He's sanctioned our marriage, Roses." He paused, and his voice lowered further. "With the alliance secure, he will allow me to indulge our mother's final wish. We'll be wed tonight, lass."

Everything but Wilkie momentarily dissolved from my immediate awareness. Even in the face of death, it was a moment of true awakening. If I was to live, I could *live*. That my warrior would dedicate himself

to me in this way left me not only with a sense of relief but of billowing awe. He wanted *me* over his own
lairdship and army. He had chosen me, a servant, over
every and any woman of noble blood throughout Scotland. My heart could not contain all the love I felt for
him in that moment; its beat felt heated and up-tempo
from the rush, infusing my body and my world with a
worshipful serenity. A bird chattered. A cloud gleamed
white. Kade sparkled like the savior that he was. I only
hoped we would live long enough to be able to thank
him and to appreciate the importance and outcome of
his sacrifice.

And Wilkie. His very black hair reflected shards of
blue and white from the rays of the day. His eyes, in the
brightness of the morning, matched the color of the autumn sky and shone with vigor and devotion.

I am following my heart, to you.

But we were surrounded on all sides and held at
knifepoint. Oh, how I wished Kade had made his appearance in Laird Mackenzie's den just minutes earlier
than he had! I wished I had waited in Wilkie's chambers
for him. I wished the guards had stopped my desertion.
I wished Wilkie and Kade had reached me before the
Ogilvie party had discovered my whereabouts. But it
was too late for regrets. Before we could live, we would
need to fight.

And I, almost forgetting myself, had a sacrifice of
my own to make. There would be no more hiding, no
more secrets. "Warrior," I said. "I need to tell you—"

"Enough!" Dougal barked at me, cutting me off. He
turned to Wilkie. "As touching as this all is, I'm afraid
your plans are out of the question. We need to be on
our way. We have a captive to deliver. Ogilvie has us

out hunting night and day for this very lass, using valuable men to scour the Highlands, climbing walls and staging raids. 'Tis all becoming fairly tedious, I can assure you of that. Not a mere kitchen servant, after all, is she." Mimicking a melodic noble accent, as though impersonating Laird Ogilvie, he said, "'The king's issue. Bring her to me immediately, or die.'" He chuckled, the sound sinister and unnerving.

Wilkie glowered, but his brain appeared to be working on a number of levels. He addressed Dougal. "What did you say?" This was followed immediately and aggressively with, "What's your meaning, soldier? *'The king's issue'?*"

Dougal laughed uproariously at Wilkie's question. "I'm surprised you didn't discover it for yourself, if you're as smitten as you claim to be. You must be losing your touch, Mackenzie."

Obviously highly secure in his estimations of his soldiers' abilities and apparently amused by Wilkie's ignorance, Dougal said to my aggressor, whose name I didn't know: "Show him the mark. Between her shoulder blades, Ogilvie said."

"Don't be daft, Dougal," growled the man whose sword was still held to my throat. "Shut your mouth, you fool."

But Dougal was enjoying his advantage and wanted to revel in it further. "There's no harm in it, Gregor. There's six of us and two of them. 'Tis no contest. Let him realize what's just slipped through his lucky Mackenzie fingers." An ominous chuckle rumbled in his chest at the thought. "Apparently, Mackenzie, your luck has run out."

The man who held me—Gregor—reluctantly

obeyed. He turned me, removing his sword's touch from my throat yet keeping it firmly in range to strike easily, and roughly yanked the cloth of my tunic down my shoulder to reveal my tattoo.

Wilkie lowered his sword and stepped closer and was permitted by Ogilvie's men to inspect the inked mark for himself. I gasped when his fingertips touched my skin.

He whispered, disbelieving, "It can't be."

"Oh, but it *is*," Dougal confirmed cheerfully. "She will ensure great wealth for Laird Ogilvie—*and* his highest-ranking officers."

What Ogilvie's men were insinuating seemed too wildly preposterous to comprehend. The possibility refused to even settle. My elation at Wilkie and Kade's arrival was being overwhelmed by panic. I had heard Dougal's statement, but the meaning of his words stayed buried beneath the years of careful secrecy, of hiding, always, my hated inked mark. And now it was revealed for all to see. The sunlight seemed to burn me where my skin was bared.

Even if there was a small chance that we could fight these Ogilvie warriors off and escape to the safety of Kinloch, there was no way Wilkie would want me now. I knew what I was: a witch. It was a reality I had privately lived with for most of my life, and I could not believe otherwise, not yet. The weight of my secret had been held for too long and was too ingrained to lightly dismiss. I closed my eyes, hanging my head in shame, and waited for Wilkie's reaction.

But instead of repulsion in his voice, I heard amazement. Where there should have been fearful disgust, there was wonder and a hint of questioning respect.

"How have I never noticed this?" Wilkie's hand reached to cup my jaw, tilting my face up to him. And his eyes were as vibrant as the sky above him. "Roses? Did you know of this mark?"

I couldn't speak, but I nodded with only the slightest movement.

"*Why?* Why did you never show this to me?" he asked.

My voice was barely above a whisper. "I—I was afraid to."

"You didn't think I might want to know you have the seal of King William inked to your shoulder?" he asked, incredulous.

My mind was whirling, struggling with lies and truths and all that had happened and all that *was happening*. "What?"

"Do you know what this *means,* Roses?"

Understanding was, in fact, beginning to edge into my consciousness, overriding the fear, the shame, the loss.

Gregor was getting impatient. Apparently, he was ready to claim his reward for my deliverance, and sooner rather than later. "It *means* that the lass is the lost child of King William. The one he searches for. The key to the king's estate at Ossian Lochs."

"We were told that the king's lost child was a lad," Kade said.

"Nay," Wilkie mumbled, still aghast. "'Twas never confirmed either way."

"Aye," agreed Dougal gleefully. "The king was wary of imposters, so he never described the child's identifying features. Who knew that we would find the king's lost child in our own kitchens? That our very own servant is in fact heir to Ossian Lochs, the most coveted estate in all the Highlands? And that she knew not of her own identity?" He chuckled again, apparently highly amused by the mysteries of life, those same mysteries that had steeped many years of my life in turmoil and dread.

A cool and not entirely unpleasant sensation swirled throughout my body now, as their words sunk in. I didn't believe it could be true. Yet the story, and my past, I had to admit, it matched. Delivered to a childless couple of a distant clan, to be safely and quietly absorbed into a far-away family, out of reach of the king's vengeful wife? Could it be true that the maniacal ravings of a superstitious old woman were unfounded and uninformed?

Once the ramifications of all that was realized settled into place, the mood of our tense gathering changed, as though a sudden breeze had renewed a vigorous animosity. The unlikely conversation that had sprung up from a shocking revelation vanished, then, in the blink of an eye, transforming the scene back into the escalating conflict it was destined to be.

Out of the corner of my eye, I saw Wilkie grip his sword a little tighter and Kade raise his circular weapon subtly, incrementally higher.

"Now step aside, Mackenzies," said Dougal, "and let us be on our way. The lass belongs to Ogilvie."

The soldier Dougal was foolish indeed, if he believed Wilkie Mackenzie to be so accommodating. "We will not step aside," said Wilkie evenly. "The lass comes with us."

At Dougal's covert command, one of the Ogilvie soldiers made a sudden move as though to attack Wilkie.

But before the man even got close, there was a blinding flash of light, and the attacking Ogilvie soldier slumped heavily to the ground. Kade's circular blade was embedded deep into his forehead.

With that, the battle was very suddenly on. Kade was now being quickly approached by the raised sword of an Ogilvie warrior whose name I knew to be Hayes; he had the reputation of a vicious and highly skilled fighter. They would be well matched, and I prayed silently for Kade's success.

Dougal, enraged now by the death of one of his men, hissed an order at another soldier. The man raised his sword at Wilkie, but before he could even gain a secure grip, Wilkie struck. The lightning-quick jab speared cleanly and deeply into the small hollow at the base of the man's throat. In and out, before I—or the man himself—could quite make sense of what had happened. The dying soldier looked entirely surprised and made a slight gurgling noise as black-red blood spurted from the fatal wound in his neck. His eyes rolled back in his head, and his body slumped to the ground.

The remaining guards watched the fallen man for several seconds, as though waiting for him to get back up again. He did not.

Dougal roared a single word, "Attack!"

And the Ogilvie soldiers obeyed in unison. Hayes engaged Kade, and the two others—Dougal and another—circled closer to Wilkie, striking as one. The deafening clang of clashing swords echoed sharply as the men attacked and Wilkie deftly fought them off. Panic lurched in my veins. I struggled in vain against Gregor's strong hold on me. Oh, how I wanted to step in and help him and keep him and distance him from the

wrath and the danger! To see my warrior, threatened
and surrounded: the seething terror in my gut turned
to anger. "Don't harm him!" I screamed at them. *How
dare you attack him!* "Don't touch him, he's mine!"

Despite my terror, I could take some small comfort
in the sheer authority of him. I could only watch in
amazement at Wilkie's skillful finesse. As terrifying
as the sight was, his grace and flair had me momentarily spellbound. He was a warrior to his bones, and
a gifted one.

Either one of the Ogilvie men would have been entirely outmatched by him. The two of them, however,
were a trained and cooperative team. They seemed to
work in well-rehearsed moves that each of them understood. And they were dangerously close to overpowering him. Dougal lunged, slicing across Wilkie's bare
upper arm. Wilkie barely flinched, and I could see that
the wound was not a catastrophic one but deep enough
to possibly impair the movement of his stronger right
arm. The sight of his blood horrified me. I would rather
give myself up to Ogilvie a thousand times than see
Wilkie cut down by his men.

And I could not see Kade, although I could hear the
metallic clash of his fight somewhere in the near distance.

Gregor pulled me farther toward the horses and
Wilkie's attention was momentarily diverted to the
commotion, as I struggled against Gregor's strength.
But I could see what Wilkie could not.

"Wilkie!" I screamed. "Behind you!"

Wilkie twirled, his sword at the ready. An almighty
clash jolted my senses as his sword connected with
Dougal's. Wilkie's sword seemed to have a life of its

own, translating and delivering his energetic power. It seemed the second soldier who had engaged Wilkie had now joined Hayes's fight with Kade, after a pained yell that I could only hope came from the soldier Hayes.

Wilkie and Dougal exchanged several more blows until it was clear that Wilkie was winning. Dougal stumbled, but before Wilkie could strike his final, deadly hit, Gregor, who had apparently decided he did not at all like the way this battle was going, yelled loudly and close to my ear, "Halt your attack, Mackenzie! Both of you! I'll kill her! I'll do it now!"

Wilkie stopped, holding his sword pointed at Dougal but turning his head slightly in my direction. His chest heaved from his exertions, but otherwise he remained motionless. He stared at Gregor with a measured hatred that promised death. I'd never seen him look more fierce, nor more striking. But he clearly knew that the soldier's words were an empty threat. If it was true that the mark inked to my back meant I was the king's child, or if there was even the remotest possibility of it, I knew Ogilvie would kill any man who harmed me. I was the key to obtaining the grand and unsurpassed Ossian Lochs, a holding that Laird Ogilvie—and many men—coveted above all others. These Ogilvie warriors knew it. And so did Wilkie. Gregor amended his statement, a taunting lilt well-pronounced in his words. "Or I'll think of something else to do with her. Half-naked and tempting as she is. Now drop your weapon."

This threat was possibly not as empty, especially clad as I was, barefoot and bare-legged, with a still-wet and clinging tunic that barely reached the middle of my thighs. And nothing under it. The soldier's huge body was not only wrapped around me but also pressed up against me. Cold horror surged through me at the warning, and a spark of alarm flashed briefly across the rage that featured far more prominently in Wilkie's flashing eyes.

Dougal was back on his feet, his sword raised.

Gregor's grip tightened even further. I could feel the coarse hair of his beard brush against my face as he spoke, sickening me. He smelled of sweat and doom. "You should know we'll go to any lengths to get this lass back to the Ogilvie keep," he said loudly to Wilkie, "or I'll die trying. A rich reward has been offered to the man—or men—who delivers her. A *very* rich reward. And I'm eager to collect it. If you delay us any longer, and further bore me with your futile rebellion, I'll first give myself a reward of a different description, right here and right now. So drop your weapon or I'll take this lass while you and Dougal finish your fight, Mackenzie. And then I'll kill her, just to spite you." The soldier's hand, slung tightly around my chest, moved slightly, so his thumb brushed over the tip of my breast. I heard a small, terrified sound and realized it was my own response. "What's it to be, Mackenzie?"

Wilkie did not hesitate. He tossed his heavy sword to the ground, where it landed with a humming clang. He held his hands out, palms up, in a quietly insolent gesture.

Dougal stepped forward to hold the edge of his sword to Wilkie's neck, so it rested just under his jawline. Wilkie stared at him with a look of utter contempt as the blade waited. "'Tis the only way you could best me," Wilkie said to him. "I, unarmed. You, without honor."

Dougal glowered at Wilkie, knowing full well Wilkie's statement was true. The blade of the sword pressed deeper against the vulnerable pulse of Wilkie's neck, and the sight of it there unraveled something in me.

"Please!" I begged. "I'll go with you! Lower your sword and leave him. I'll not fight you. I'll come willingly."

"Tie him up, Dougal," snarled Gregor, whose grasp was becoming more and more insistent, hurting me and frightening me. "We'll bring him with us."

Dougal removed the knife that hung from Wilkie's belt and tossed it out of reach. "I'll kill him," Dougal said.

"Nay," barked Gregor. "The lass will obey any demand of ours—or Ogilvie's—if we use his life as a bargaining tool. Bind his hands behind his back. And for God's sake, do it securely."

Somehow, I could see now, Kade had felled the second of his attackers. He and Hayes stood some distance away, their swords still raised to each other's, circling.

"Ride, Kade!" Wilkie yelled.

Kade, in a lightning-quick movement, grasped a knife from a holster strapped to his boot and flung it at Hayes, where it embedded into Hayes's thigh, causing him to hop and curse loudly. Kade took his split-second opportunity and mounted his horse, heaving himself into the seat in one fluid motion. His horse reared and whirled, lunging into a hell-bent run.

"Ride him down!" yelled Dougal, and Hayes, pulling the knife out of his thigh with a growl and tucking it into his own belt, leaped into action. But Kade was gone, galloping in the race of his life to reach Kinloch, alert Knox and summon the Mackenzie army.

CHAPTER EIGHTEEN

WE RODE AT A PUNISHING PACE. I, in front of Gregor, the Ogilvie warrior whose reward would be granted, in one way or another, by keeping me close. Wilkie rode the horse of one of the fallen men, his wrists bound behind him, and the wound on his upper arm still bleeding. His legs must have ached with the effort of gripping the horse as we galloped south through daylight and darkness and daylight once again. I caught brief glimpses of sleep, slumped against the warrior whose hold on me did not tire. We stopped twice, to drink from small streams we passed. We were not given food. And Wilkie said not a word, barely looking in my direction. Dougal rode his horse next to Wilkie's and just behind, occasionally bumping his horse against Wilkie's in a gratuitous attempt to dislodge him.

And if the question raged in my head, I could only imagine what was going through Wilkie's mind: Kade. Had he reached Kinloch, to notify Knox of our predicament and to deploy the Mackenzie troops? Or had Hayes cut him down?

The landscape and the cut of the hills in the distance began to look familiar, and such was the grueling pace we kept, by the second nightfall we reached the Ogilvie keep. There was no sign of anyone following us. No army.

And then we were entering the gates of the Ogilvie keep.

Aye, there was a settling limitless remorse as we slowed and rode through the gates amid crowds and vaguely familiar faces. How had I lived almost two decades among these people and felt not a single welcoming sentiment? I saw curiosity, recognition, even glee, but I was not a prodigal daughter returning home. I was a disenfranchised foreigner-turned-servant who'd gone virtually unnoticed until the scandalized day of my departure. Word had obviously spread since then of my crime, my desertion and, finally, my unlikely heritage. The final detail giving me, at last, a value.

And I could see it in their faces now, as they swallowed up our party. They touched my bare legs, patting me and attempting to remember an hour, along the path of our half-connected lives, in which we might have shared a work detail, or a laugh, or a sunset. I felt very little. My only awareness was of Wilkie and how close his horse was to mine, and I was thankful that we were kept together until we reached the entrance of the manor. The thought of being separated from him now caused a cold chill to chase up my spine.

Our weary horses came to a stop.

The warrior who held me dismounted, then he grabbed me with his dirty hands and slid me back into his unwelcome, coarse embrace. Wilkie swung one leg over his horse and jumped to the ground, staggering but not falling. And Dougal followed him, liking his small power over a bound and rugged Mackenzie: clearly a position he was enjoying and making the most of. He was almost a head shorter than Wilkie, but he pushed Wilkie forward, toward the large and opening door of the Ogilvie manor. Wilkie seemed to hardly notice him, acknowledging him only as one might acknowledge a small and annoying bug that buzzes around until it can be squashed.

In fact Wilkie seemed almost eerily disengaged. Either that, or so focused that his attention appeared muted, or disguised. Our gaze met only once or twice, and I could read there that the possibility of being forced to watch me be taken by one of these men was threatening some hidden barrier within him. I had no doubt that if his hands could only somehow be freed, he'd have the strength and compunction to cut a very quick and decisive path through Ogilvie's army. A raw and ragged fury clung to him like a shimmering aura.

We were led into the great hall of the Ogilvie manor, surrounded by much commotion. Only vaguely aware of the details of the presentation of us, I could nevertheless tell that there were other visitors being greeted. They were warriors, and the tartan of their clothing identified them—I was almost certain—as Campbell clan.

And it was confirmed as soon as the crowds allowed for us to be received and presented to Laird Ogilvie and his guests: Laird Campbell and ten or more of his highest-ranking officers. They were all seated around the grand table and rose as soon as our party entered the room.

"What is this?" Laird Ogilvie roared, confused and obviously displeased to be interrupted in the middle of what was quite clearly a tactical meeting. I had no doubt they were planning their attack on Ossian Lochs here and now; the tension and anger in their faces as well as their full military dress made me guess that the time for their rebellion was drawing near.

The men rose to their feet as our party approached their table to stand before them.

Ogilvie's eyes bored into me, then Wilkie, a mixture of emotions playing across his face. Greed and triumph, certainly; a stunned temporary surprise at my sudden arrival; and also a fierce unease—which he accompanied by glancing once at Campbell—as though wishing that this presentation could take place elsewhere and not where Campbell could witness it. After all, Campbell wanted to claim Ossian Lochs and all its resources even more fervently than Ogilvie did. Campbell most likely knew nothing of my tattoo, and Ogilvie, to be sure, would want to keep it that way. Alliance or no alliance, these were underhanded men, both of them. And as Ogilvie glanced at Campbell once more, it seemed more than clear that he was reading there a certainty: if Campbell learned of my tattoo, he would have no reservations about claiming me for his own if given half a chance to do so.

And I didn't like the way both men—and many more—were staring at me. I wished feverishly I could cover myself, half bared to them as I was. The tunic I wore had dried in the wind but had ridden up to the tops of my thighs under my captor's jostling and very insistent hold.

Ogilvie's familiar hunger lurked close to the surface of his expression, and I contemplated the look of him after so many weeks away. He was a big man, as tall as Wilkie yet much less defined. He preferred to exercise his leadership at the table, rather than in the yards. This, and his fondness for food and ale, had softened him. His hair was an even brown, kept shiny by the mistresses whose attentions he insisted on nightly, and more than one at a time; it was these ranks I'd been called to join but had refused. Although he was possibly in his late thirties, Ogilvie had not yet taken a wife, too absorbed in the pleasurable variety his title allowed him. His eyes matched his hair and sparked with the lively heat of his many and varied conquests.

To see him again now, after all that had passed in my absence, was somewhat jarring, and I felt an unfamiliar sentiment seep through me which I finally was able to identify: hatred. Here was the man who had stolen much happiness from my life in recent years. He'd purposefully punished me, I could now see clearly in retrospect, in an attempt to break down my resistance. And I had suffered greatly for it. Only since my escape had I fully grasped the extent of my past unhappiness, bestowed almost exclusively by the man I faced now. I could feel my own loathing color my expression as his eyes met mine, but this did not appear to faze Ogilvie. Maybe he was used to being looked at in this way.

"Gregor. Dougal," he greeted his men. "You have returned my wayward servant to me. Well done. I shall meet with you later this evening to give you your rewards." His gaze landed on Wilkie. "And what am I to make of this? Mackenzie? Have you killed more of my men? Is this why my officers bind your wrists and present you as a prisoner?"

"He claims she is his betrothed," Dougal replied.

"Is that so?" Ogilvie surveyed Wilkie once again with a measuring study; he may have been wondering if Wilkie knew of my inked mark, and if he, too, wanted me for that reason. "What of it, Mackenzie? You're trying to claim my servant as your own?"

"She's mine now, Ogilvie. Let us go and your life will be spared."

Ogilvie looked at Campbell, and they both laughed. It was a laughter that stoked the horror of our situation several degrees higher: a laughter of dark intention, bitterness, revenge.

Campbell's hatred was clear in his voice, and it was only then that I remembered fully the truth of this show-down: Wilkie's and Campbell's fathers had taken each other's lives. The bad blood of the past was clearly festering and raw, and right here in this very room. "Trust a Mackenzie to lay a claim on something that isn't his, to take interest in affairs that are not of his concern and to offer threats he cannot enforce."

"Aye," agreed Ogilvie, but his smile faded when Dougal continued his report.

"He and his brother cut down no less than three of our men—James, Hugh and Gannon."

Ogilvie frowned. "And Hayes?" he asked.

"Chasing down the Mackenzie brother before he reaches Kinloch to dispatch their army in our direction, laird," Gregor replied.

Laird Ogilvie looked most displeased and somewhat more rushed. He stepped forward, walking toward me. "Unhand her," he said to Gregor, who—finally—released his hold on me, taking a step back. Ogilvie circled me, his eyes on my body, but it was Wilkie he spoke to. "She is most definitely *not* yours, Mackenzie. She is entirely *mine*. And I intend to wed her immediately."

"Wed her?" asked Campbell, amused. "Bed her, aye, and share her around. Hospitable host that you are, Ogilvie."

Ogilvie ignored the comment. To Gregor, he said, "Fetch the minister and order him to meet me in my private chambers. Immediately." To Dougal: "Have Mackenzie taken to the cells. I'll figure out what to do with him later." And to Campbell, he said, "'Tis some urgent business I must attend to, Campbell. Eat and drink at your leisure, and I'll return to you shortly. I have a ceremony to participate in and a marriage to consummate."

The noise in the room ballooned in a curious swell, the warriors at the table guffawing and murmuring. Campbell, it had to be said, looked mildly intrigued by the urgency in Ogilvie's manner, but he let it lie; maybe he thought Ogilvie's haste was inspired by his desire to exact revenge on Wilkie, a sentiment Campbell would undoubtedly well relate to.

I gasped for breath, panic seeping into my lungs and my heart, darkening my world as though a cloud had passed over an invisible sun. I looked at Wilkie, but his eyes were locked on Ogilvie.

And Ogilvie met his glare, as he sidled up behind me. "She's mine," he repeated to Wilkie triumphantly. As though to illustrate his point, he placed two fingers softly between my legs, to my most vulnerable place, which was bare under my tunic.

I jumped and fled from him—now that I was newly unrestrained—and ran to Wilkie. It was a desperate attempt, surrounded as we were, but I went to his bound wrists, now bloodied from the tight, rubbing constriction, and I attempted to untie the hard leather cord.

But before I could even begin to unbind Wilkie's wrists, I was grabbed from behind and constrained in a punishing embrace. By Ogilvie himself, and I could feel the hardness of him pressed up against the rising fabric of my tunic. I struggled and I sobbed with fear and frustration.

And Wilkie reacted.

He growled, enraged, and rammed his shoulder into Ogilvie, who was so jarred by the force of impact that he released his grasp on me. But I was barely released before my arms were imprisoned again, this time by two guards who had closed in on the escalating conflict. Wilkie had felled Ogilvie and managed to kick him once in the ribs with his arms still bound behind him, before he was attacked on all sides by no less than seven guards. They wrestled him to the cold stone floor, beating him with their fists and their clubs. They'd kill him.

I screamed, losing all sense of myself. "Don't hurt him! *Please!* I'll do it. I'll do anything. *Please stop hurting him!*" The cries rose from my throat, racking my body with the force of my anguish. "I'll do it. Leave him! Take me to the chambers."

Ogilvie was dragged up by a number of guards until he was back on his feet. He was agitated and irate. The guards held Wilkie securely and looked at their laird, as though waiting for his response to my desperate pleas. Laird Ogilvie—and in fact most in the large room—were contemplating me, as though taken aback by the force of my obvious devotion to Wilkie's well-being. This detail appeared to anger Ogilvie even further. "Bring him with us," he ordered savagely. "Cut off his shirt. And have Mumford accompany us."

The hairs on the back of my neck rose in prickling, dire alarm. I knew who Mumford was; I'd heard him discussed, in passing, several times during my years serving Ogilvie's table. A trusted man. Loyal. Fierce.

A skilled weapon maker. And uncannily well versed in the ways and methods of torture.

Wilkie's shirt was shredded by the guards' knives and thrown in scraps to the floor. There was blood on his face, and his hair was wild. He looked dazed and unsteady, but when he saw me his eyes slowly regained their focus.

The agony! The sight of him, bloodied and beaten, still so very captivating even in our shared defeat. His chest and arms were strained and muscled, slick with blood and sweat, his stomach tight and coiled where my fingers had lightly soothed him, once upon a time.

I couldn't soothe him now. But I would do anything I could to save him. Would Ogilvie let Wilkie go if I gave myself willingly?

"Roses." My beautiful bloodied warrior was speaking to me, and the sound of his roughened voice reached between us, reconnecting all that was sacred to me, calming me and strengthening a final resolve. It was difficult to hear him amid the confusion and the commotion of the room, as we were clinched, surrounded and being moved toward a far door. "You must *not* consent to it, lass. No matter what happens. Promise me this."

I wanted to promise him anything he asked of me. But I could not consent to his torture or his death. I could not watch them kill him while I stood aside and let it happen.

We were taken to Laird Ogilvie's private chambers, a room I remembered well. The minister was already in his place. And, chillingly, three hooded guards stood along one wall. The largest, middle guard held a long sinister-looking black whip. Mumford.

Wilkie was led to a wooden stool that had been placed in front of Mumford. Wilkie was ordered to sit and they bound his ankles and tied them to the legs of the stool, fumbling slightly with the ties, which seemed like an odd detail here in this darkest hour.

"Begin," Ogilvie said gruffly to the minister. The minister, a small, white-bearded man, looked highly uncomfortable with the scenario, and his eyes kept darting to Mumford, then back to his open Bible, which he clutched as though the salvation it promised had never been so urgently desired as here and now.

"Our Holy Father, we ask—" began the minister.

"Get straight to the vows, Minister," Ogilvie interrupted, with forced patience.

The wide-eyed minister began again. "Of course." He cleared his throat, not once but several times. "Do you, Laird Errol Ogilvie, take this lass to be your lawfully wedded wife, in—"

"I do."

The minister looked uneasily at Mumford, at Wilkie, then at me. He cleared his throat, then continued. "Do you— What's the lass's name? I must have her full name to make the union official."

"Roses Stuart," Ogilvie said.

This startled us all, even me, who'd never contemplated it: King William was of the Stuart clan. And therefore, it now appeared, so was I.

"Stuart?" asked the minister, his curiosity momentarily overcoming his anxiety.

Ogilvie held one of my shoulders, turning me to present my tattoo. He moved my hair aside and lowered the cloth of the tunic over my shoulder, so my inked mark could be viewed by the minister. "She is the king's issue. She is the child he searches for."

The minister's disapproval was hardly concealed. "Has the king been notified of her whereabouts?" He was obviously becoming more and more distressed by the events surrounding this highly unusual marriage ceremony. As were we all.

"The king will be notified of her whereabouts," said Ogilvie, "as soon as this marriage is official. Now, please continue."

Ogilvie adjusted the tunic back in place, his hand lightly fingering and stroking my hair. In response, Wilkie growled from his chair, a sound of total agony, as though doom and torment mingled with his rage and led him beyond his breaking point.

Ogilvie signaled to Mumford, who lashed the whip fiercely across Wilkie's bare back. Wilkie's teeth clenched, and he braced and grimaced. And he silenced himself.

The hooded guard to the right of Mumford raised his sword slightly, almost in a reflex reaction to Wilkie's beating.

"Continue," barked Ogilvie.

The minister's wide eyes looked into mine. "Roses S-Stuart," he stammered. "Do you take Laird Errol Ogilvie to be your lawfully wedded husband?"

"Nay," Wilkie said softly. Again the whip found its mark, swishing once, then cracking through the cold air before its sound turned abrupt: the sickening, slicing sound of opening flesh.

I could feel the hopeless pleading in my eyes as the minister rushed on, falsely assuming an end to this ceremony would mean an end to the violence. "Give me your consent, lass," he urged. "You must give your consent before the marriage can be blessed by our Heavenly Father."

"Roses, nay," growled Wilkie, his words dipped in pain.

"Give it!" yelled Ogilvie, his face fairly purpled from his ire. Then, to Mumford: "Again!"

The whip lashed into Wilkie's raw skin, the sound cutting into me, breaking my heart and bloodying my soul. Oddly, the other of the hooded guards who flanked Mumford gasped and fumbled slightly. I wondered if they were newly appointed; they seemed to be having trouble stomaching the torture.

"Don't do it, Roses," Wilkie groaned. "*Do not do it. I can take a thousand more lashes.*"

In answer, Mumford thrashed him again. The hiss of the whip as it cut him echoed throughout the room.

Wilkie made no sound. He just closed his eyes as his strung-out body tensed and bled.

It was too much.

Without being aware of my own actions, my body hunched. My fists balled, and I drew them to my face to block out the light and the scene. I wailed quietly and fell to my knees.

I felt Ogilvie's hand grasp my arm and pull strongly. "Get up and give your consent!" he spat. "Or I'll kill him now."

He pulled me to my feet, and I composed myself enough to look Ogilvie in the eyes. The eyes of the man who had prowled around me for many years, infusing my life with fear and dread and worthlessness. As I had once before, under the hungry, almost triumphant gloat of him, I made a decision. And the decision gave me strength even as I knew it doomed me in this life, and Wilkie, too.

"I will *never* give my consent to you," I said. "Kill him and I'll die along with him, but not before I take your life with my own. You will not win. I will be Wilkie Mackenzie's wife, or no one's."

A ripple of disbelief fluttered crossed Ogilvie's expression, quickly followed by all-out rage. *"Bitch!"* he seethed, and he slapped me hard across the face. It pained me and stunned me, but I did not fall. I lifted my head to glare at him, and a few white stars flitted across my vision. I hated him with a ferocity that astonished me, even before he confessed a shocking truth. "You deserve a life of suffering and servitude," he said. "Your father fought me, aye, threatening me with death if I ever pursued you, the insolent fool. It was *my* sword that cut him down on the battlefield. Your mother called to him, even in death, as I took her as my own. Know *that* before you die." His head turned to the executioner. "Lash him until his life bleeds away."

The minister was murmuring frantic, quiet prayers.

For a very brief moment, my eyes met Wilkie's, and I would remember the color of them and the sureness of their love as long as my short life would allow.

I would have lunged at Ogilvie then, as useless as my attack may have been, attempting to find his knife, or to pain him or maim him in any way I could. But the two hooded guards who flanked the torturer in that moment revealed their faces.

Ritchie. And Ronan.

My friends, who had taught me to fight, who'd given me men's clothing to wear, to hide myself from the leering watch of Laird Ogilvie. And Ritchie, who'd allowed me to escape from the advancing search party.

They seemed taller than I remembered them and more imposing.

It was Ronan who thrust his sword into the chest of Mumford, felling him instantly, while Ritchie spoke. "This has all been most informative, Laird Ogilvie. I do believe our allegiance has flipped. Our apologies, Mumford," he said to the executioner, who was now on his knees, clutching at the sword that stuck out of his chest. Ritchie looked at me. "Roses, daughter of King William. Mackenzie. Our apologies to you, as well. We were resolute in our loyalty to Ogilvie, but enough is enough. I regret we did not stop this before the first blow was struck. Ogilvie promised us land and wealth, but 'tis not worth it."

"Ritchie," I gasped, my shock giving way to hope. "Ronan."

Ritchie continued, "Treason is punishable by death, of course, and we have now most certainly condemned ourselves. I hope we can redeem ourselves by offering to secure your freedom. And if you find yourselves in need of two more warriors in your ranks at Ossian Lochs, I fear we are most definitely in search of a new appointment."

And Ronan was cutting the ties of Wilkie's bound wrists and ankles with a knife.

Ogilvie's outrage had transformed into fear—and determination. He held my arm. I tried to shrug him off, but he clutched it more tightly, dragging me along with him as he attempted a getaway.

But Wilkie was free.

And he was upon Ogilvie before the beast could even

draw his sword. Wilkie seemed to have forgotten about his injuries. He had but one thing on his mind: using the only weapons left to him—his bare hands—to kill Laird Ogilvie.

CHAPTER NINETEEN

A FAIRLY POWERFUL MAN in his own right, Laird Ogilvie made several attempts to fight back, to roll Wilkie off of him, and finally to shield himself from the onslaught. But Wilkie was a wild thing. He had been pushed past his limits and was mindless with bloodlust. Damage accumulated. Ogilvie's struggles weakened until it was clear he was having difficulty maintaining consciousness. And Wilkie was tiring, too. The combined effect of his own injuries were making themselves felt, and his fists were now bloodied along with the rest of him.

Ritchie finally stepped in. "Mackenzie."

It took Wilkie a moment to respond; he was still hellbent on destruction. His actions slowed, and he turned to see Ritchie holding out his sword. "Save yourself some trouble, man."

Wilkie paused, then took the sword. He held it to Laird Ogilvie's throat. Ogilvie's swollen eyes could not hide his terror in his final moment. And without a word, Wilkie, with a single thrust, ended his life.

I turned my head to block out the sight of it. The minister stood next to me, and he was rocking slightly and mumbling a soft and endless prayer.

Wilkie stepped away from Ogilvie's body, returning the sword to Ritchie. Then he walked over to me. I wanted to touch him, but the sight of his battered body stopped me from reaching out to him; I didn't want to hurt him. In the end, he quietly held my hand with the barest, gentlest grasp.

One of his eyes was ringed with a blue-black bruise, his lip was cut and still bleeding, his hair in disarray. The colors of him appeared extraordinarily intense: the red, blue and black of him, drawing all my undivided attention. Even in this ravaged, relieved moment, all I could comprehend was his aching, mind-numbing beauty.

Transfixed, we were, in this moment. Together. And alive.

And there, in the aftermath of many tragic, violent hours that had very nearly finished us, Wilkie kissed me. The soft touch of his lips to mine fed me a violent rush of joy that bloomed in my heart and leaked out my eyes. He deepened the kiss, and I could taste his blood on my tongue, sharp and metallic, and I drank of it willingly, wanting to entwine every part of his being with mine, and again, always.

But Wilkie's soft groan reminded me of the severity of his wounds. He'd been sliced once again with a sword, beaten by no less than seven brutish guards, and lashed repeatedly by one of the most renowned executioners in the land. And he hadn't slept for at least two nights. Even the night before that, I recalled, our sleep had been regularly interrupted by more sensual pursuits.

And we were still in grave danger. We'd just killed the laird of the keep. And Ogilvie's men were now, and had been for some time, in conversation with Laird Campbell, a greedy, savage rebel.

I could read in Wilkie's eyes that he was having similar thoughts. We needed to flee, and now. Wilkie turned to Ritchie and Ronan and said, "Men, I thank you for your assistance. It will not be forgotten, and I owe you more than I can repay. You are welcome to avail yourself of the protection and hospitality of the Mackenzie clan. I will be honored to count you among our ranks. And I must ask you now to accompany us, to equip us with horses and lead us to the nearest exit."

"Aye," Ritchie replied. "'Tis only a matter of time before Dougal announces Roses's secret to anyone within earshot, and if Campbell learns that Roses is King William's daughter, he'll stop at nothing to take her for himself. It would ensure his ownership of Ossian Lochs once and for all."

"We can escape through the kitchens," Ronan said. "This way."

Wilkie looked at the diminutive minister, who continued to sway slightly in the aftermath of all that had taken place. His fathomless internal chatter calmed. "Minister," Wilkie said. "Can a marriage be officially consummated *prior* to a wedding ceremony?"

The minister looked thoroughly agog at the question and highly in need of a strong brew of ale. He paused, as though never having considered this particular question before. "I—I don't believe so, nay."

"In that case, I'm afraid I'll have to insist that you accompany us. I'd prefer Roses to marry me in a somewhat more romantic setting than this, and as far away from Ogilvie's dead body as possible. But if we have need to marry on the run, we'll want you on hand."

The minister's watery gray eyes contemplated us both for a brief moment. "On the run?" he asked.

"Aye. We will take our leave immediately, to return to Kinloch."

The minister decided not to argue with the big, aggressive warrior who stood before him. "Lass?" he said to me. "Is *this* a marriage you would consent to?"

I looked at my warrior and uttered the truest word I had ever spoken. "Aye."

With that assurance, the minister allowed himself to be swept along with our getaway party, led by Ritchie. I knew the way. Ritchie, Ronan, Wilkie, myself and the minister fled down a narrow back staircase which led to the small back corner of the kitchen that housed the healing quarters.

And there, sitting at her table, stirring in a steaming medicinal tincture, was Ismay. She was so surprised by our sudden appearance that she dropped the wooden spoon she was holding. It seemed infinitely strange to see her again, here, now. She was entirely aghast at my return and also by the shirtless, bloodied warrior who, despite being huge, rugged and outrageously masculine, clung to my hand as though it were the only thing that kept him from collapsing.

Ismay rushed over to me, sweeping me into a warm embrace. "Roses, I worried so. I feared for your life. 'Tis so wonderful to see you alive..." It was only then that she glanced at my muddied, very brief outfit, her eyes widening. "...and well."

"Come, Roses," said Ritchie, "We must hurry. We must escape and ride for safety. *Now*."

But Ismay's eyes were carrying out a quick survey of Wilkie's many dirtied bruises and cuts. Then she circled him, and she gasped when she saw the deep lashes cut into his back.

"Ismay, this is Wilkie Mackenzie," I said.

He nodded a curt greeting, too immersed in his own aches, fatigue and escape plans for niceties.

Always the healer, Ismay was too overcome by Wilkie's injuries to take much notice of either his identity or his brusqueness. She touched the skin of his back. "Roses, we must treat these immediately. They're deep and dirty. They need to be disinfected, or they're likely to go septic." Her eyes met Wilkie's, then mine. "However did you—?"

"Ismay," said Ritchie, becoming more and more impatient. "If you want to treat those wounds, do it on the way. We need to get outside the gates of the keep before the guards and soldiers are alerted to Ogilvie's death."

Ismay's eyes grew wide. "Ogilvie is dead?"

I happened to know that Ismay had been called upon by Laird Ogilvie, as many of his staff were, to visit his mistresses' chambers, upon more than one occasion, and unwillingly. She had acquiesced only because she felt it more important to keep her job as healer, one Ogilvie knew she valued.

"Well, hallelujah," she said, to which the minister frowned.

Without further ado, Ismay grabbed a bag and began throwing jars of salves, bandages and other supplies into it, including a large bottle of whiskey, which I knew to be a potent disinfectant. "I'm coming with you," she said.

I grabbed her arm. "Nay, Ismay. Our lives are at risk. Ogilvie and Mumford are dead, and *we* are responsible. We're on the run, and I won't have you put in danger."

But Ismay wasn't deterred. "I've been wanting to escape this keep for some time, Roses. I've no family left here, and it hasn't been the same since you fled. And the laird's nephew—heir apparent for the lairdship—is as shady as his uncle. Take me with you. Please. This man's injuries are severe. I can keep him alive."

We didn't have time for me to stand there and talk her out of a life-threatening situation. She was already putting on her cloak and fastening her medicine bag. And secretly, I was glad she would be on hand to treat Wilkie. I had no medicines, and Kinloch—if we even made it that far—was a two-day ride.

And so our growing party of six exited through the back door of the kitchens. There were people about, and curious ones at that, but we did not engage stares nor questions and fled directly to the stables.

"Luckily for us," said Ritchie, "most of the men are engaged with entertaining Campbell and his officers, and attempting to learn more about the commotion surrounding Roses's return. But there's little time to spare."

Wilkie agreed. "'Tis only a matter of minutes before they'll discover Ogilvie's fate."

And we weren't to get away unnoticed. Three men were tending to three horses—horses we would need to steal, and now.

I noticed that two of the men were already armed. And one, seeing Wilkie, narrowed his eyes in an angry glare. He looked at me, then continued his hostile study of Wilkie. "'Tis true, then," he said. "Wilkie Mackenzie is here, attempting to claim one of our servants as his own."

A second man sounded equally riled. "Ritchie, Ronan, why have you not taken this man into custody? Was he not to be taken to the dungeons?"

Ritchie, who would once again prove himself to be

invaluable to our cause, addressed the men who stood between us and a precarious freedom. And while Ritchie was attempting to reason with them, Wilkie was already taking the reins of one of the horses, cinching up the saddle and beckoning me and Ismay with a hurried finger.

"Men," said Ritchie, "I have been ordered by Ogilvie to escort these people to Kinloch. We'll need to borrow your horses."

It was an unlikely story and one which we could all see was faulty, the Ogilvie guards included. But Ritchie pressed on, and I could hear one of the guards asking, "What do they need your escort for? And why do you take the healer and the minister?"

"Ismay," Wilkie was saying in low tones. "You'll ride with Ritchie. You'll need to hold on tight. All right?" Ismay nodded with wide eyes. "Luckily there's not much to either of you, or to the minister for that matter. Our horses will be heavily weighed, but there's naught to do about it.

"Roses, you're riding with me. Come on, up you go." He lifted me up onto a much taller horse than I was used to, but I was glad of its size: it would mean its stride was longer and hopefully swift enough to outrun whoever might pursue us.

Ronan had mounted another of the horses and Wilkie assisted the minister, who was thrust up behind Ronan and who looked as though he might dissolve into a dead faint at any moment; he still clutched his Bible with a white-knuckled grasp.

"We'll need some sort of clearance before you can depart for Kinloch, Ritchie," one of the guards was protesting. But Ritchie was already seated behind Ismay, taking control of the reins, and Wilkie was seated behind me, spurring our horses toward the gate with a swift kick.

"Wait!" shouted a guard.

"Halt! You're not—"

"Stop them!" The confused guards were now pulling more horses out of the stables, saddling them up, understanding that our mission was in fact a getaway.

And Campbell and his men had emerged from the manor with swords raised, running toward the stables to procure their own horses. *"Seize them!"* howled Laird Campbell, with a face as red as a prized beet. *"She's the king's lost child! I want her!"*

More aggravated shouts spiked through the air as we neared the gate.

"Laird Ogilvie is dead!"

"Chase them down!"

"Retrieve that lass at any cost!"

But the two guards who manned the gate never stood a chance. Wilkie, who had somehow gained possession of a dagger—I guessed it was one of Ritchie's or Ronan's—cut down with a vicious swipe a guard who attempted to grab the reins of our horse. The second man, struggling to pull the heavy gates of the keep closed, was knocked and stepped on by Ritchie's horse.

And we were outside the walls of the Ogilvie keep, on our way, at full gallop. Pursued by an assembling number of vengeful Ogilvie warriors—although in fact I wondered if their numbers would be all that daunting—and the hell-bent posse of Laird Campbell and his twelve officers.

I only hoped our horses were up to the task of outrunning equally large animals, and those that carried only one man.

Wilkie's arms were wrapped around me securely, and he pushed our horse harder and faster. I could take comfort from his closeness as I leaned against him, holding my hand to his thigh.

I could see that Ronan's and Ritchie's horses were close behind us.

And far in the rear distance, when I peeked around Wilkie's body, I could see the figures of at least twenty ridden horses, creating a dusty cloud behind them.

Gaining on us.

"Faster," I whispered, but Wilkie needed no reminder. Our horses were at full speed, already slowing slightly from the weight of us and the speed at which they were being pushed to hold.

We were outnumbered vastly. I had a sinking feeling there would be no escape this time if we were caught. In hindsight, bringing along the minister might not have been the best plan of action; it meant that Campbell could force me to marry him without delay. And Campbell would know, too, that there was one sure way to get me to agree to anything. Anything.

Saving him, my warrior.

Wilkie was wild, flailing our horse with the only riding crop he had on hand: the dagger's wide edge. The horse was responding to it, too, but it could only hold such a wicked pace for so long.

And they were gaining on us.

Very quickly now.

I could hear their shouts as they spurred each other forward.

"Get me that lass!"

We were approaching the rise of a hill, traveling at such speed that I hoped there weren't cliffs or rocks or unseen holes on the far side of it. But we couldn't slow. We would have to risk pitfalls in the interest of saving our own lives. And I could hear a loud, thundering noise, very close and all around us. Dust seemed to be rising from all sides, oddly, and the noise was deafening. Shouts circled in the air, as though the wind had picked up the noisy approach of our pursuers and amplified it, swirling it in all directions.

I heard Ismay scream and turned to see what I could. I caught only a brief glimpse of Ritchie answering the jab of a Campbell officer with his own sword, fighting him off but only just barely, as the soldier rode now at his horse's flank.

Wilkie pushed on, and we were nearly to the top of the hill.

And when we reached the top, we were afforded a most alarming, beautiful, astounding view: the Mackenzie army, approaching from the north, riding straight toward us in numbers of several hundred men.

CHAPTER TWENTY

WE RAN STRAIGHT INTO them, among them, swallowed up by Wilkie's clansmen, absorbed, amazingly, into a sudden sea of safety.

And I could see that Campbell's men were in such close pursuit and were caught so off guard by this sudden materialization of an enemy army that several of them rode right into the Mackenzie masses. As Wilkie turned our horse, I caught sight of two Campbell officers being cut down, impaled by the swords of a number of Mackenzie warriors, who may have attacked out of sheer surprise more than anything else.

Campbell was livid and appeared almost crazed with his many frustrations, yelling, "Pull back, men! Pull back! The Mackenzies are too many!" He swore loudly at the sight of two of his men being slain, then he repeated his orders in a high-pitched shrill. *"Pull back!"*

The remaining soldiers of the combined Campbell and Ogilvie forces followed their leader's order, retreating and forming a row that faced the front line of the now-halting Mackenzie troops. In the center of the Mackenzie front line were Laird Mackenzie, Kade and Fergus flanked on either side by two Munros, the distinctive bright red color of their Munro tartan standing out among the mass of blue and green of the Mackenzies.

For several seconds, no one spoke, and only the sound of the horses' stomping feet and puffing snorts could be heard.

But then Laird Mackenzie's gruff, loud voice rang out.

"Campbell! You are outnumbered by at least ten to one. You cannot win this. I would take great pleasure in killing you here and now. Unlike you, however, I value honor, and I will give you one chance and one chance only to make your way peacefully back to your keep, and stay there. You have no rights nor jurisdiction over either this lass or Ossian Lochs, nor will you."

Campbell's retort was inflected with bile; he was not only a sworn enemy of Laird Mackenzie, but he was clearly highly miffed at the unexpected turn of events. Disappointment featured heavily in his body language. "I would take as much pleasure in avenging my own father's death as you would, Mackenzie."

"Aye," said Laird Mackenzie. "Which is why our best course of action might be to let their war die with them. And your rebellion along with it. The lass is the rightful heir to Ossian Lochs. We have already summoned the king to have him officially confirm the identity of his lost child, Roses Stuart."

The king! The thought of meeting him was but a drop in the ocean of overflowing emotions I felt in this moment.

As the lairds addressed each other, Wilkie had walked our horse back up to the front line, stopping to stand between the horses of his two brothers. I caught Kade's eye. I might have imagined it, half blinded by the glint of his shield, sword and all the other shiny paraphernalia strapped to him, but it almost looked as if he winked at me.

Wilkie addressed Campbell. "Any unwelcome notions you might have entertained, Campbell, to take her as your own in your bid to obtain rights to Ossian Lochs should now be decisively laid to rest."

Laird Mackenzie continued, "If there's a bone of honor in you, Campbell, you'll recognize that this matter is now settled, and we can all endeavor to maintain peace. You are not the rightful heir to Ossian Lochs. Accept it and return to your own lairdship—a plentiful, well-appointed keep, at that. Use your energies to prosper among your kin. And let us do the same."

I couldn't determine whether Campbell had been convinced or not by the Mackenzies' suggestions. Either way, it was clear that he and his remaining ten guards, along with a pathetically small turnout by the Ogilvie army, were not in any position to dispute Laird Mackenzie's proposal. At least not today.

Laird Mackenzie added, "We will therefore be allied not only with the Munro army and the Stuarts, but also with the Morrison army. You have no chance of defeating our combined forces, now or at any point in the future. Go home and stay home."

Regardless of whatever his future plans were, Campbell's rebellion, for now, would not bear fruit. This was as obvious to him as it was to the rest of us. But his parting words were ominous indeed. "This is not the last you will see of me, Mackenzie. Watch your back. This is not finished. The lass, even if she is the daughter of the king, is illegitimate issue. She is not entitled to anything, least of all the king's Highland estate."

"That is a matter," said Laird Mackenzie, "for the king to decide."

"We will take our leave of you," Campbell said, somewhat loftily, as though he was in fact doing us a favor. "Men, we ride."

And with that, the Campbell warriors and their Ogilvie conscriptions turned their horses and galloped into a fading distance. We all watched them for many minutes, until they were but tiny dots on a faraway horizon.

And so, this battle was over.

Relief rushed through me as an almost physical surge, and Wilkie, too, seemed almost overcome with it; his big, intense, hard-muscled body fairly slumped over me.

Laird Mackenzie contemplated me and his brother.

"Roses. Wilkie," he said, more quietly as his army began to disassemble, laughing and loudly discussing the easy victory.

We were in our own conversation now: Laird Mackenzie, me, Wilkie and Kade. And Laird Mackenzie shocked me greatly with his next words and the slight bow of his head as he spoke, "Daughter of King William, I will ask for your forgiveness. I did not believe you worthy of my brother, and I was mistaken. I hope you will accept my humble apology."

I would have stopped him sooner, but I was almost too stunned to reply. "I— Nay. There's nothing to forgive, Laird Mackenzie. You were acting in the best interests of your family. I have every respect for your motives."

"Please," the laird said, "call me Knox, if you will. You are family now."

I was speechless and could only nod, wide-eyed, at

this massive, fearsome, highest-ranking nobleman who was now humble and apologetic before me, and soon to be my brother.

The laird continued, rueful. "If only you'd shared with us your mark…"

"Aye," countered Kade, "but she did not know of its meaning. Wilkie has good instincts, it seems."

Wilkie, whose pain, exhaustion and relief may have combined to make him as surly as he'd ever been, said, "My instincts were all about Roses's spirit and nothing to do with her royalty."

Laird Mackenzie contemplated Wilkie, and he almost smiled—the very first time I had ever seen him do so. "Mackenzies," said the laird. "We return now to Kinloch to prepare for the arrival of the king, and to arrange two weddings. I assume you would still like your marriage to take place at Kinloch?" He may have noticed the inclusion of the minister among our getaway party.

"Aye," I confirmed. As much as I wanted to marry Wilkie, and as soon as possible, I knew he was in fact too weary for riding his horse a pace farther, let alone participating in a marriage ceremony. I also liked, now that it was an option, the idea of marrying Wilkie in a chapel, surrounded by his family, as a wedding was meant to be.

"Laird Mackenzie," I said. "I beg you to reconsider and to camp here tonight. Wilkie needs rest. And his wounds need to be tended to. If they're left too long, they might get infected. We've brought the Ogilvie healer with us—Ismay—and she's highly skilled and prepared with medicines. His injuries are severe, and he hasn't slept in several nights."

The laird looked at Wilkie, seeing perhaps only now the damaged, exhausted state of his brother. He glanced once in the direction of the Campbell troop departure and seemed to decide that my request was reasonable and safe enough. I hadn't noticed it before, either, but the daylight was beginning its wane; the sun hung low in the hazy sky.

"So be it," the laird said. "Summon your healer. I'll notify the men."

Laird Mackenzie gave me one more respectful nod, then he and Kade dismounted, speaking to their troops about the night's arrangements.

And I spotted Ismay, still astride Ritchie's horse with Ritchie's arms wrapped around her. At Laird Mackenzie's lead, Ritchie dismounted and made a move to help Ismay.

It didn't take long before we were all assembled together, laying out sleeping furs, with fires being built and food and drink being passed around. A messenger party consisting of twenty men was sent back to Kinloch to give news of the outcome of our escape and our victory. Laird Mackenzie wanted the remainder of the army to camp the night, as a defensive measure. And I was glad of it. We would leave at first light.

"Now," Ismay said, taking a brief survey of Wilkie's lashes, bruises and cuts. "These wounds will need to be cleaned, and well. Take him down to the river while I prepare the medicines. You can assist him with cleaning, Roses. Once that's been attended to, then we'll wash the wounds with alcohol—which will likely cause him quite a bit of pain. But it must be done. Perhaps we'll summon some assistance—he might need to be held down."

Wilkie eyed Ismay. "That won't be necessary."

Ismay ignored this, having treated many equally severe wounds and also witnessing the reactions to certain methods of treatment. "His brothers might be called for. Then I'll treat and wrap the wounds. And we can administer several tinctures that will help prevent the fever."

She poured a cup of whiskey, handing it to Wilkie. "Drink this," she said.

"All of it?" I asked.

"Aye," confirmed Ismay. "It will dull his pain when I treat his wounds."

Wilkie tipped back the drink.

"Here is some medicinal soap," Ismay said, handing me a small brown cake. "It shouldn't sting too much. That will come later."

I was concerned by the weariness in him, but when I felt his forehead, he didn't seem overly warm. "Come with me, warrior. I'll help you bathe."

We walked down a slight embankment, where a path descended to a small pebbly beach. We could hear the conversation of the nearby camp, but we were far enough removed by distance and the cover of near darkness to have some semblance of privacy.

I set the candle away from the water, propping it up with a number of stones.

"Sit here," I said, indicating a larger stone. "I'll help you remove your boots." He did, and I knelt at his feet to help him. "You may as well swim, to wash all the dirt off yourself. It will help you heal faster and make the wounds easier to treat."

When he stood, I unfastened his trews and pulled them down his legs so he could step out of them. And when I looked up at him and began to rise, I could see that he wasn't quite as weary as I had feared. "Seeing you on your knees before me is a stirring sight indeed," he said. "Swim with me."

"Warrior," I scolded him. "We need to attend to your injuries."

And there was more to his manner than warring fatigue and arousal. He seemed angry with me. Despite this discovery and before I made a point of getting to the bottom of it, I acknowledged a triumphant happiness at this: I was getting better at reading the finer details of his emotions. I was learning him. *I just want to learn you.* Admittedly, his terse movements, body language and the scowl on his face may not have been the most difficult of sentiments to decipher, but still, there was satisfaction in gauging the degree of his passions—and most of all, in knowing that maybe, just maybe, I could spend the rest of my days reading him and doing everything in my power to smooth his temper and cultivate his every happiness.

"I'll swim with you," I said, "if you tell me what you're thinking. What have I done to anger you?" I might have guessed that he would be angry at me for leaving Kinloch in the first place, for putting myself in danger, for putting us all in danger.

He was undressing me, and in his exhausted, bloodied, fractious state, his hands lost all their gentleness, peeling my clothing from my body in a rough demand. Wilkie pulled me into the water with him. The water was cold, yet not bitterly so, after the effects of recent unseasonably warm autumn days. Wilkie gasped as the water stung his abraded skin, and he dunked under the surface, staying submerged for several seconds. It was another thing I knew about him, and I could see it now: he was at ease in the water. He liked to swim.

When he reappeared, he looked somewhat refreshed, but still that hint of animosity lurked in his eyes.

I went to him and turned his back to me. Very, very carefully, I began to wash him with the specially made medicinal soap Ismay had created the recipe for; I had often helped her make the batches. I washed Wilkie's hair, letting the soapy water cleanse his wounds, and I gently scrubbed him free of dirt, sweat and blood. His poor, perfect body, scarred and cut, yet so beautifully made, with long, graceful bones and hard, sculpted muscles that flowed smoothly to the taut flatness of his stomach.

He was uncommonly quiet. At first I wondered if he was feeling a natural remorse for killing a man, even one as vile as Ogilvie. Maybe that was part of his agitation. This silence, though, felt more as though it was aimed at me.

"Tell me," I whispered.

His silence drew on, until I let the soap glide to his stomach, where I knew he was ticklish. He squirmed, and it was enough to open the floodgates of his ire. "*Never leave me,* I once said to you," he began, his voice low and laced with outrage. "And what was your response to that, Roses? What did you promise me?"

I remembered the conversation well, as I did every word he had ever spoken to me. "I said, 'I'll stay with you and soothe you, each day and each night.'"

"Yet what happens," he said coldly, "as soon as the first ripple of a doubt arises? You run! Straight into the hands of Ogilvie's henchmen!"

"You know why I had to leave. I was interfering with

your duty to your clan. I didn't want to put you in that position. Your brother gave you an order, and I didn't want to compromise your—"

"Grant me one favor, will you?" he interrupted. "In the future, let *me* worry about my duty and my clan. *And* my brother. If you hadn't deserted me so quickly, you would have learned—not minutes later—that there was an alternative to the situation that presented a better outcome for everyone involved."

I couldn't argue with that statement, except it did occur to me that there was one person involved who was most probably *not* at all pleased with the new outcome: Maisie Morrison. But I didn't mention her now. I also, fleetingly, wondered about Stella Morrison. How did *she* feel about her newly announced and sudden betrothal to Kade?

"And that's not all!" he said, enraged, and I suspected the whiskey's effects were making themselves known, as his words had a thrusting yet slurred edge to them, escalating as he spoke. "You neglect—after everything!—to mention to me that you bear a secret inked mark! Which just so *happens* to be the seal of King William's for his *mistress*. The very *same* mistress that happens to have born him his one and only *child*. The *same* child he has been searching for for over fifteen years. The *child* that is to be gifted with *the grandest estate in all of Scotland!*"

"I—"

"Did it slip your *mind?* Did you just happen to *forget* that you were the heir to vast royal wealth, which incidentally would have offered us a much less angst-ridden and less *life-threatening* route to our betrothal—which is something I *thought* you wanted?"

He was breathing heavily, his body hot to the touch in the cool water.

I felt a tear slide down to my jaw at his angry words and also my regret. Of course I wished that I had told him and shown him. I wished that I had trusted him.

"*Why,* Roses? Enlighten me, please. Because I know not what could have been going through your mind to hide all these secrets from me. And to walk out on *us* when I was still in the middle of negotiations."

It was true I knew very little about negotiations, of any kind. I'd never had need to negotiate much of anything, with anyone. I was told what to do, and I did it. That was my life. But now, I could begin to understand that families discussed things in this way. They argued and compromised. And, sometimes, they were able to come up with solutions, together. I didn't have much previous experience with any of these things, but I could see that now, with Wilkie, I would have need to learn to do better, as his wife.

If he would still have me.

I knew I had cleaned his wounds well. I turned him to me. "I have another memory of my early life, warrior." I wiped the hot tears from my cheeks.

His anger calmed somewhat at the sight of my tears, but he had not forgiven me, I could see it in his eyes. He waited for me to continue.

"It was just after I was adopted by my parents," I began, and my voice sounded shaky and mournful. "I was ill and my mother had consulted one of the old women of the clan… She was more of a seer than a healer. She was very old, very frail, with wrinkled skin and watery eyes. This old woman was called into our small house. She was searching my body for signs of illness. She came across the mark. She pulled her hands away as though stung by it, like it burned her fingertips. She made a strange noise. And then, she began… shrieking." More tears blurred my vision, but I didn't wipe them away. I knew more were coming. It was such a frightening, horrible memory and one that I had never told anyone. Until now. Just to speak of it upset me greatly. My voice was barely above a whisper, but I forced the words out. "She was screaming at me, and pointing. She was horrified. *A witch,* she called me. *'Tis a witch's mark,* she said. She said I would be beaten and flayed and burned at the stake if anyone was to learn of it. She said I *should* be burned. And my parents kept it hidden thereafter, bribing the old woman with wheat and barley, buying her silence. Some days we went hungry, just so we could keep her in rations. My parents made sure I had food, but there were days when they had to go without."

"Clearly this hag was mad," Wilkie said abruptly. His words had a strange effect on me. I felt relief, aye, and sadness, that my family had been wronged in this way. My parents' devotion to me had never wavered, not once, despite my brand. They had protected me and sacrificed much to keep me safe and alive. I missed them desperately in that moment, and I wished I could see them again, to show them the truth of it, to thank them and tell them I was sorry.

Wilkie's voice softened as I sobbed, completely undone. He held me closer, taking me in his arms and cradling my head against his chest. "You need not worry about the ravings of a senile old crow any longer, lass. 'Tis over now."

"I *was* going to tell you," I cried. "I hid it from you

because I was afraid you would be repulsed by me, like the old woman was. I wanted so much to be with you, and I knew that once you saw it you might burn me or cast me away—"

"I would *never* have burnt you, Roses," he said, raising my face to his, "and I would *not* have cast you away. You're my angel, lass. *That* is what you are. 'Tis what you always were and always will be. I love *you*. To utter madness. Have I not proven that to you, in every way that I know how? Say it to me. Say 'my warrior loves me to utter madness.'"

I sniffled. "My warrior loves me."

"Nay, Roses. My warrior loves me to *utter madness*." He paused, wiping my tears. "It pains me to think that you've carried this with you all these years of your life, along with all your other burdens. No longer, lass. You are free, to live your life as you were meant to. I'm here with you, always, to make sure that happens. You're not alone anymore. There are two of us now."

I beheld him, my warrior, and my heart felt as if it would break open with love for him.

"Before we return to Kinloch," he said, "you will promise me, right here and right now, that you will never, ever leave me again. Say it."

"I promise with my whole heart that I will never, ever leave you again."

"Are there any more secrets you'd like to share?" he asked insistently. "Because I demand to know about each and every one of them right this instant."

I was gently pulling him back to the edge of the river, mindful of his wounds and his treatment. We had drifted slightly downstream so would need to climb up a small bank to get back up onto the shore. "No more secrets, warrior. That was the only one. I swear it."

"Good. Because if you ever break this promise, I shall have to punish you."

"What will you do to me?"

"Oh, I'll think of something very—" He stopped as I was making a move to climb up the bank. I felt Wilkie's hands on my backside, which was, as I was positioned, partially exposed to him. He made a noise that landed somewhere between a sigh of surrender and an animal growl.

The ferocity of his pain and his anger lingered in him, and I was shocked at the way his hands were spreading me, revealing me to him. I felt his mouth on me. I felt the probing insistence of his tongue delving into my most intimate places, pushing into me, then pulling softly with the skill of his mouth. Then he rose over me. I felt his hands widening my stance and the hard pressure of him against my backside.

"Warrior, we should return—"

"Nay. Not yet."

There was a desperation to his touch, like the near-death experience had given rise to his baser vulnerabilities. Wilkie rubbed his shaft along my sensitive petals, dipping hotly into me, then removing his touch altogether. I tried to turn to him, but he held me in place, climbing onto me so his body was leaning heavily over mine, covering me. Again, slowly, he entered me, then withdrew, and the emptiness at the withdrawal was disconcerting, stealing pleasure and heat from my aching flesh. I had never thought of such a position, but I was crazed for more of his teasing, gliding promises. He touched me, using his fingers to open me to him, to moisten the delicate center of sensation.

"I'll have you this way," he whispered into my ear. "I have to have you. Now. Let me, lass."

Again the touch was withdrawn. He was testing me, gauging my acceptance. I made a small sound of frustration and tilted my hips back to him, offering myself in a wanton invitation for more. I was wild with relief when his touch returned, playing me, until I was rocking ever closer to receive him. I felt him position himself, deliciously stretching me as he slid farther. Then he buried himself in a driving, powerful thrust. I burst instantly from the pressure that filled me so exquisitely and so completely. He lifted my hips higher, and his hand stole to the exact place I needed it. The deep, forceful possession worked in time to the melting stroke of his fingers as he rode me gently, over and over. My bliss, which had begun at his very first drive, enveloped me in a profound haze of rapture. The pleasure was so acute I had to writhe against him, squirming against his big, relentless body, just to bear the excesses. He clamped his hands to my hips and thrust deeper into me than he'd ever been, then held. I could feel a shudder roll through him, then the lustrous beat of his own upheaval spooling richly into me. In his impassioned climax, his groans were pain-edged, almost as if he were stopping himself from crying. I, too, had fresh tears in my eyes from the intensity of this, and of us. My core rippled along with him, perfectly in time, as though my body sought to draw every drop of his essence into my very soul.

With his weight leaned heavily over me, Wilkie's hand coasted up my back, pushing aside the mass of my hair to kiss my skin. He kissed my mark, and the feeling of his lips on that secret, always-forbidden place, was stunning.

"How will I ever survive you, Roses?" he whispered close to my ear. "I just don't know how I will bear all the pleasure of you."

From a far-off distance, I heard our names being called. Wilkie's bath, to be sure, had taken longer than expected. I didn't respond at first; I was floating on the radiating effects of his loving.

But I was aware that he needed his treatment sooner rather than later. I helped him dress, and I dressed myself and collected the small candle that still burned. We returned up the path to the camp.

"He'd better be extremely clean," scolded Ismay.

She had already prepared the scene. A blanket was laid out close to the fire, and a number of bottles and jars were lined up near her bag. And Laird Mackenzie and Kade were on hand, as well as Fergus. This worried me. Would Wilkie be so pained that he'd need *three* men to hold him down? I hoped Fergus's appointment was merely as a guard, and not as one of Ismay's assistants.

"Roses, you sit there," Ismay instructed, pointing to a fur that had been placed some distance away from Wilkie's treatment area, as though she was wary that I might be more of a hindrance than a help to her. I was mildly irked by this, after all the times I'd helped her tend to others, albeit for more minor wounds than Wilkie's. I moved the blanket closer and sat.

First Ismay treated Wilkie's many smaller cuts, and she decided to stitch the small slice in his arm. Then she wrapped a bandage around it. Thankfully, Wilkie seemed swilled enough by the effects of the whiskey that he barely flinched during the stitching procedure, so I hoped his senses were suitably dulled. I thought he might even sleep, but his eyes remained half open and aimed straight in my direction.

Ismay nodded to Wilkie's brothers, who placed their hands on the back of Wilkie's shoulders and around his arms in a decisive grip.

"Just a little sting now," said Ismay to Wilkie. To his brothers, she whispered authoritatively, "Hold on tight."

And she began to meticulously drizzle the whiskey onto Wilkie's opened, raw flesh. Wilkie flinched violently, thrashing against his brothers' hold, grimacing and groaning with the agony of the burn. But Ismay continued, until she was satisfied that the wounds had been properly sterilized, taking little notice of her unruly patient's loud, furious response to her treatments. I'd never heard such curses in all my life.

And when she was finished, she asked Laird Mackenzie and Kade to continue holding Wilkie for a few minutes longer, as she smoothed the healing salve onto the wounds and bandaged them. She may have feared retribution.

By then, Wilkie's eyes were closed, and when his brothers released their hold, he lay still.

"Still alive, brother?" asked Kade wryly, yet with a note of unmistakable concern. I was learning Wilkie's brothers, too, I realized. I knew Kade well enough to recognize that he was wont to find humor even in the direst of situations. It was a quality I found intriguing. I couldn't help but think that Stella Morrison was in for a time of it with Kade Mackenzie. There were aspects to his fierce, direct countenance that were, occasionally, outrageously intimidating. But the more time

I spent around him, the more I could detect an underlying unruly playfulness to his character, which was both appealing and enigmatic; there were edges to this playfulness that suggested fun but also the distinct possibility of danger. Again I wondered what Stella's impressions of Kade were, and how she was reacting to the news of her impending nuptials.

"Aye," Wilkie muttered from the depths of a pillow, not sounding entirely convincing.

"I daresay he'll live," Ismay said. "And a good night's sleep will do him a world of good."

"Thank you, Ismay," I said. She smiled and packed away her medicines.

We settled into our sleeping furs for the night, close to the fire. Wilkie was next to me, his furs draped over us both. He lay on his side, facing me. The on-duty guards patrolled nearby as the others readied themselves for brief hours of sleep. Ismay lay close to Ritchie, I couldn't help but notice, and he was already snoring lightly, barely visible in the deep cocoon of his blankets. Laird Mackenzie stared into the fire while Kade sipped from a small silver flask. Fergus stood in the near distance, facing into the night.

In my life, I'd never had cause to consider preferences, in company, in family, in friends. My purpose had not allowed for me to dream. I considered my new fate, as the daughter of King William, if it was so, bound for a new life at Ossian Lochs as the wife of Wilkie, who would by rights become the new laird. It was a lot to grasp. I was more than a little intimidated by the thought of Ossian Lochs, and of joining its established clan as a newly entitled overseer, with only Wilkie by my side. It was true that Wilkie was all I needed. He was everything that was essential to my life. But if I were to look beyond that, beyond him, I could acknowledge that there could be more, too. Ritchie and Ronan would accompany us. And Fergus, the stoic, silent giant whose presence afforded me with a profound and newly valued sense of safety, might also come with us. And now Ismay, as well. I was sure she would join us; she had already voiced her intention to stay with me: my most trusted and only true friend in all the bleak days of my servitude, who had unfailingly offered me as much comfort as one can give in such circumstances.

I settled closer against my warrior, his strong arms holding me as tightly as they had in our very first fevered embrace. I looked up at the star-studded sky, listening to the low sounds of the darkness and all who were near. And as my heavy-lidded eyes watched first my own beloved, then one by one the people gathered around the softly crackling fire, I felt comforted by their company and their nearness. I was surprised to find the firelight blurring with my own tears as a dawning realization overcame me: these fellow travelers who surrounded me felt like, and were, *my family.*

CHAPTER TWENTY-ONE

WE WERE WELCOMED BACK to a relieved, excitable clan Mackenzie. My news, along with that of the king's imminent arrival and our impending marriage, had the clan fairly buzzing. And if I thought I'd been pampered and fussed over before, it was nothing compared to the insistent attention that now surrounded me. I was the chosen wife-to-be of the desirable, respected Wilkie Mackenzie. I was also the king's daughter, and the king himself would arrive at Kinloch the very next day, to view me for himself. So I must be readied to a suitable, highly presentable standard for the gathering tomorrow night, an event that would serve as not only a wedding and a king's welcome, but also of Wilkie's impending lairdship and the ensuing newly strengthened alliance and bond with the Stuart clan.

And I had returned from the Ogilvie battle in the disheveled, dusty, windblown state of a scantily clad and very weary traveler, so there was much work to be done.

The entire keep was being cleaned, spruced and decorated, and Wilkie's chambers, especially, seemed overrun with attendants whose sole purpose was to heal, cleanse and preen us into—at least for this occasion— the jewel of the Mackenzie crown.

The Munros would remain for the gathering.

The Morrisons had taken their leave during our absence and would return in a fortnight, when the wedding of Kade and Stella Morrison would take place here at Kinloch, yet another event that had the clan energized with speculation. And I couldn't help but overhear many of the circulating questions. Had Kade sacrificed himself so that Wilkie could marry me? It was understood that the two of them had only met for the first time just days ago, at the Mackenzie festivities. It was such a quick proposal, but after all, Stella was widely regarded as the most beautiful of the Morrison women. Had it been love at first sight, or was it merely Kade's split-second decision to take the lairdship on offer, one that had been all but refused by his brother?

I felt a nudge of remorse for Kade, and I hoped fervently that he hadn't stepped up only to release Wilkie from his duty. I suspected all eyes would be on Kade and his fiancée in the coming weeks and especially at the marriage, in an attempt to answer those very questions.

Wilkie had told me that, depending on the king's decision, we would remain at Kinloch until after Kade's wedding, to prepare our travel party and then make our way to Ossian Lochs.

I'd considered the possibility that the king would see me and inspect my inked mark, then declare that I was not the child he searched for, or that my tattoo was falsified, or that he had changed his mind about my inheritance. Truly, none of these scenarios filled me with dread. I had what mattered most to me: my warrior, who needed me as desperately and deeply as I needed him. If Ossian Lochs was not to be ours, I could have quite contentedly remained at Kinloch, at Wilkie's side, to live out our days. In fact it was an equally appealing outcome to me, so I couldn't quite summon nervousness, nor apprehension.

Effie took charge of Wilkie's injuries, muttering to him but mostly herself as she attended to his wounds as though miffed that he'd allowed such harm to come to his person, even after she'd taken such obvious care to heal his last batch of battle scars.

And Ismay attended to me, checking for bumps and bruises that may have gone unnoticed during the exhausting events of the past several days. She found me to be fit and without injury, aside from a few sore muscles from the long days of riding. Without discussing it, we both knew that she would accompany us to Ossian Lochs, if and when the time came, and I was profoundly glad of her company.

The fuse of Wilkie's temper had been shortened by his lingering pain, which had now given way to annoyance as the endless parade of attendants swarmed around us. We were treated, bathed—with the privacy screen barely dissuading our dedicated troops—fed, medicated and questioned, until finally Wilkie had had enough.

The intensity of past days, his own strung-out tiredness and our soon-to-be-wed status seemed to have heightened his protectiveness of me, and he refused to let me out of his sight. When Ailie tried to take me to the adjoining chambers, to try on my gown for the following evening, Wilkie snapped.

"I said Roses is not to leave my sight," he warned viciously, and there was a hard edge to him that caused us both to pause and consider him. He stood close to the fire, rebandaged and clad only in his undergarments.

His hair was still damp, and he held a goblet of ale in one hand, which he downed in one swig.

"Ailie," I said, giving her a light hug, celebrating her embrace very briefly, as we had several times throughout the afternoon, as sisters. "I think Wilkie needs his rest now. It might be best if you helped me with my dress in the morning."

Ailie nodded. "Aye. I think you're right, Roses. I'll see you tomorrow." She ushered the remainder of our helpers out and smiled as she pulled the door closed behind her.

I didn't go to Wilkie right away—I sensed he was feeling stormy and needed a moment to himself. I sat on the bed and began to brush the still-damp strands of my hair, to make it glossy. Sometimes Wilkie liked to brush my hair, in his gentler moments, but he was miles away from that particular state of mind now. He tipped the pitcher of ale to his goblet, to pour himself another drink, and cursed quietly when he discovered that the pitcher was empty.

"Would you like me to fetch you some more ale, warrior?"

"Nay," he said shortly. "I'll do it." Without looking at me, he put on his trews, leaving his shirt off, and grabbed the pitcher. He began walking toward the door. As he left he said, "Get into bed and wait for me."

The door closed forcefully.

I could hardly blame him for being tired and irritable or thirsty. I would do as he asked, and wait for him. And when he returned to me I would help him relax and ease away his tension with my kisses.

But it would take him some time to walk to the kitchens. While he was gone, I could take a quick peek at the dress Ailie had laid out for me in the adjoining chambers. She'd fashioned a wedding dress, she'd told me, out of crinkled white velvet. It was understated, she said, but one of her best pieces of work to date. It was this dress she'd hoped I would try on tonight, to see my reaction, and so she could adjust the fit if need be. My curiosity got the better of me, and I crawled out of bed and went to the door of the adjoining chambers, opening it cautiously to make sure no one occupied the room. It was clear.

I closed the door quietly behind me.

The dress had been laid over a chair, and when I held it up I could tell that it was, in fact, one of the finest I had yet seen. The soft material of the bodice had been inlaid with woven silk, and a delicate veil of lace rimmed the neckline.

I thought I had time. I would briefly try it on now— Wilkie would be many minutes away. Already I knew it would be the perfect choice for tomorrow night, an occasion like no other, when I would celebrate all that my life had become.

The feel of the dress's material was simply divine. And it matched the color of the end strands of my hair, which lay against it now. It fit me well, and I didn't think Ailie would need to make many adjustments.

But I mustn't linger. Wilkie might return any minute. And he would be alarmed to find me gone from his bed. He was already agitated from battle, injury and travel and also the effects of the ale he had already consumed. To find me gone would certainly upset him further and might even drive him to rash behavior. In fact, I decided my whim had been foolhardy, and I worried that Wilkie's recklessness, if he discovered me absent, would cause him pain or drive him further than his own safety.

Before I could undress, I heard his voice. He was searching for me. He burst with a violent rush of activity through the door, his muscles tensed and his sword raised. Such was the extent of his alarm that his sword was held only inches from my face.

His wildness held, his eyes crazed and feral as he searched the room for aggressors. And then his raging haze dissipated. He began to see me, and he beheld the dress I wore, taking some time with his observation, catching his breath as his chest rose and fell in rapid bursts, then slowly, more calmly.

He laid his sword down on the floor. And his rashness was suddenly and entirely gone. He picked me up in his strong arms and carried me to his bed, where he placed me with infinite care under his furs, lying next to me, on his stomach, so as not to pain his lashed back.

"I will spend my life forever searching for you, Roses," he said quietly, tracing one of my eyebrows with his fingertip. "You are my angel. My sun. And soon, my wife. You've been stolen from me, threatened and hurt. I die a thousand deaths each time I think of it."

"Hush now, warrior," I crooned to him, cushioning his head to the softness of my breasts, to calm him. "I'm here with you. I'll never leave you. I'm safe, with you, always." I stroked his hair and repeated gentle words, lulling him and quieting him. I cradled him against the beat of my heart all through the night. I dreamed of Wilkie's touch and woke to the succulent lapping waves of his beauty.

THE KING WAS DUE TO arrive in the early evening, to take part in the wedding reception. Our marriage ceremony was scheduled for the late afternoon. There was no more speculation about my identity: I had been accepted by the Mackenzie family and clan as Wilkie's betrothed, even without the assurance of the king that I was, in fact, his child. This gave me a sense not only of joy but of peace. I suspected it might have had something to do with Laird Mackenzie's remorse at having spurned me at first, as though he was making amends and wanted to prove his new loyalty. I suspected, too, that he was, at last, honoring his mother's memory by embracing Wilkie's choice. *Promise me this: always follow your heart.*

And the time had come.

The Mackenzie clan filled the quaint chapel, which was not large enough to accommodate the entire clan, so we were led through throngs of curious, welcoming faces. I was dressed in Ailie's white velveteen gown. My hair had been left down and decorated with a halo effect of tiny white roses, which also featured in my bouquet. Wilkie wore the full clan regalia of his kilt, complete with his sword. His gloriousness knew no bounds, and I could barely look at him, so overcome was I by his proud, masculine beauty.

The altar was attended by the Mackenzie minister. The Ogilvie minister was also in attendance, although he had been offered, I'd been told, an escort back to Ogilvie's even before we'd returned to Kinloch. Apparently, he'd decided to attend the wedding and perhaps even stay a little bit longer.

Next to the Mackenzie minister stood Laird Mackenzie, Kade, Ailie and Christie. Fergus, Ritchie and Ronan stood behind them, as guards and as newly named officers.

We knelt on a pair of red cushions that had been purposefully placed in front of the wooden altar, and the ceremony was underway.

The words spoken by the minister seemed far away and drifting. I was focused only on Wilkie's dazzling face and the warmth of his hand, which enveloped mine in a steady, devoted grasp. He was further bejeweled and illuminated by the colored light offered by a stained glass window set into the nearby wall. Red, orange and green hues colored his hair and the white of his shirt. His blue eyes, which had changed me and claimed me from the very first moment I gazed into them, were devout with love.

And he was gently pulling me to my feet as we were asked then to exchange our vows.

"Do you," began the minister, "W—"

"The king!" a man shouted from the open door of the chapel. "The king has arrived!"

All eyes turned to the rear of the chapel.

"Minister," said Wilkie. "We may ask the king to witness our vows, since he has arrived early."

"As you wish, Wilkie," said the minister.

After several minutes of fanfare and excitable murmuring throughout the chapel and out-of-doors, the king himself appeared in the door, like an apparition. Tall and robed, his dark silhouette was outlined by the sunlight.

Everyone stood.

The king, followed closely by four armed guards, walked toward us. His attention, as he drew closer, remained locked on my face, watching me with lively interest as he studied me.

He looked to be around fifty years old. His long hair was dark brown in color, as was his beard, which had streaks of gray laced through it. The first detail of him that reached out to me was his eyes. The shape of them, so similar to my own. It was the first time I had ever met someone related to me by blood, and I could not only see the resemblance, I could *feel* it as a connective, visceral link.

"My child," he said. His voice was deep and had a distinctive gravelly texture to it that sounded pleasing to my ears. The tone of it was comforting, and…fatherly. Not familiar but somehow still etched within me.

Without hesitation, yet gently, he wrapped his arms and the lavish garments he wore around me and gave me an honest, heartfelt hug. His embrace felt strangely restorative, and I felt myself sigh, drawing in the kingly scent of him and along with it an unfamiliar sense of well-being, of security and most of all, of resolution.

"Roses," he said.

"Father," I whispered, and only after I uttered the word, I hoped it wasn't inappropriate, that I should have called him "King William" or "Your Royal Highness" or some other greeting that befitted his unequaled status.

His wide smile more than reassured me.

After several moments, the king looked at Wilkie.

"You are Roses's husband?" the king asked.

"Aye. Almost. Wilkie Mackenzie," he said, bowing. "'Tis a great honor, Your Majesty."

"If you would allow it," said the king, "I would request to conduct the ceremony myself."

"I thank you, Your Royal Highness," Wilkie said. "We would be humbled, and honored."

Wilkie's hand was on my shoulder. "Would you like to see Roses's tattoo, Your Majesty?" Wilkie asked.

"Indeed I would," the king replied. "Although I do not need to see it to know that she is the child of Sophia, my cherished mistress, now gone to me. She was as blonde as you are, Roses, as refined and green-eyed. You look so very much like her," the king said, somewhat wistfully.

Wilkie loosened the ties of my dress and lowered the bodice just slightly at the back to reveal the mark. Unhurriedly, the king touched my tattoo, studying it closely. "Aye, 'tis the seal I made for Sophia. See the curl of the *S* and the design of three roses, her favorite flower. I can confirm that you, Roses, are the child lost to me for so many years. I am so very pleased to have found you."

"And I," I whispered, "am very pleased to be found."

Wilkie refastened my dress, and I turned to face the king.

"Your mother was the love of my life," he said to me. "Her beauty was astounding, her sweetness very nearly divine. Her fair hair and sea-green eyes were the envy of all who met her, my wife included." He paused, temporarily lost in his memories. "Sophia was killed by my wife's assassins, but not before Sophia succeeded in marking and hiding you. I have searched for you ever since." He addressed Laird Mackenzie and Wilkie. "So I must thank you, Mackenzies, for bringing her home. Your loyalty is highly admirable, as was your father's. I have heard much about your family's prowess on the battlefield. Wilkie, I have every faith that you will honor me well as the new laird of my Highlands crown. So, let's get this marriage underway."

There was a small cheer from the congregation. The minister handed the ceremonial book to the king with a deep bow, and the king began.

"Do you, Wilkie Mackenzie, take my daughter, Roses Stuart, to be your lawfully wedded wife?" He continued to recite the vows and asked for Wilkie's response.

The pressure of Wilkie's fingers on my own increased. "I, Wilkie Mackenzie, take thee, Roses Stuart, to have and to hold, from this day forward, in sickness and in health, to honor, to cherish, to love unconditionally, 'til death to us part."

"I, Roses Stuart, take thee, Wilkie Mackenzie, as my lawfully wedded husband..." I prayed for my knees to support me as I recited my own vows, my voice as steady and true as it might have ever been. "...'til death do us part."

Christie handed Wilkie a ring, and he said to me, "'Twas our mother's ring. Until I can get you something specially made, for us."

He slipped the ring onto my finger.

Kade stepped forward, drawing a knife from his belt. Wilkie was looking at me and offered his upturned palm to Kade, who sliced a small, neat line across Wilkie's palm. Then Kade reached out to me, requesting my hand. Although I wasn't expecting it, I didn't hesitate, offering him my raised hand. Kade drew an identical line across my own palm, then he placed Wilkie's hand in mine, palm to palm, so our blood could mingle. As it had before. The king wrapped a white linen strip around our wrists, binding us to each other.

"Wilkie Mackenzie," the king said, "I am pleased to welcome you to my family, clan Stuart. As husband to my daughter, I bestow you with the lairdship of Ossian Lochs, to oversee its resources and its army." The king turned to me, and he leaned to kiss my cheek. "Roses, daughter, child of my Sophia and heir to my Highlands throne, welcome back."

And then, I heard my father say the sweetest words I had ever heard spoken.

"By the grace of our Heavenly Father, I now pronounce you man and wife. You may kiss your bride, Wilkie Mackenzie."

And so he did.

EPILOGUE

OSSIAN LOCHS IS AS BEAUTIFUL as it is wild. Almost twice the size of Kinloch and with higher walls, it is a truly majestic estate. Much of it is windswept and craggy, but there are vast expanses of cultivated splendor, as well. I help oversee the gardens and the orchards, and have a team of highly capable landholders who carry out their duties with talent and experience.

And Wilkie has grown into his role as laird with grace and tenacity. His hotheaded nature has mellowed into one of determined and tireless leadership. He seems to have the energy of ten men, and his troops respect not only the skills he willingly teaches, but also the lengths he goes to as he guides and trains each and every one of them. There was some friction among the ranks at first, as there always is when a new leader enters the fray. But such is Wilkie's talent with the sword that any man who challenges him soon begs for mercy. Among his top-ranked officers are Fergus, Ritchie and Ronan, all formidable—and staunchly loyal—warriors in their own right. After a time, and with heartfelt respect, the warriors of the Stuart clan have pledged their allegiance to Wilkie's leadership, down to the last man. He rules as his brother does, and his father before him: with fairness and honor, with hard work, hard-won loyalties and genuine camaraderie.

Officially, we are Laird and Lady Stuart, but many of his higher-ranking men call him, as he allows, simply "Mackenzie."

Wilkie's scars map his body, and each day I tend to him and soothe him, and heal him with every remedy I know.

In the evenings, in the privacy of our own chambers, Wilkie continues to teach me to read and write. In these sessions, I see a different side to my warrior husband: a knowledgeable, patient nobleman who has traveled and studied and considered larger ideas than I have ever had need to contemplate. He seems to enjoy sharing this part of himself, and I, captivated, am a willing student, although I am easily distracted by the aspects of him I already adore, and the equally alluring newly discovered ones. Often, my learning is cut short to attend to more urgent endeavors.

The Stuart clan seems to enjoy the newfound stability of our presence. They grew weary of the skirmishes and upheaval that ruled their clan and their keep for many years, and they covet the new sense of peace and closure that pervades the mood at Ossian Lochs. As I do. Their questions, as mine, have been laid to rest.

Many of my clanspeople are related to me by blood, and I have reveled in these new, fascinating connections. This shared history bonds us as surely as memories do.

I have finally found a place that feels like home.

Our lives are not without menace, as Laird Campbell continues to threaten us with his continued bids for leadership, but our army is strong and well-allied. And my reappearance as King William's child, officially bestowed Ossian Lochs by the king himself, has dulled the rebellion beyond Campbell's own mind. Wilkie is ever watchful.

Ismay has just left me, and I am waiting for Wilkie in our private chambers. He has been acting cagey and excitable of late and says he has a surprise for me, which he will present tonight. I, too, have a surprise for him, but I'll let him go first.

He arrives, and his presence fills the room and my heart riotously and completely, as it always does. It is evening, just off dusk, and winter will soon give way to spring. For all his ferocity and newfound poise, Wilkie is playful tonight. He scoops me into his arms, and his kiss is full of exhilaration and devotion.

He sets me down, and I notice he is holding something in each of his hands. "'Tis time for your gifts," he says.

"What's the occasion? Why do you give me gifts?"

"'Tis my duty, as your faithful husband, to make all your dreams come true, every one," he says.

"My dreams have already come true. You are my dream, husband."

But he gets down onto one knee before me and gently grasps my left hand. He slides a ring onto my fourth finger and adjusts it. "Here is your first gift," he says. "One you should have received several months ago, in fact, but it took me some time to have it fashioned just so."

The ring is gold with a small sculpted rose at its center, and the rose has been encrusted with many tiny diamonds. I gasp at the elegance and the luxury of it. It catches shimmering light as I hold it up to admire. "So beautiful, warrior," I whisper.

"And now for your other gift."

"'Tis too much," I protest, but he holds up a piece of

cloth and turns me around. He places a blindfold over my eyes and gently ties it. I find myself smiling at his expectant, boyish behavior. He's brimming with an unknowable anticipation.

He picks me up easily, carrying me in his powerful embrace. I am being swept down the grand staircase of our manor and out-of-doors. I feel the cool air of the almost-spring evening. It will not be long now until the blossoms and the seeds begin to sprout, and I detect the scent of the earth beginning its renewal.

He continues to carry me, along a meandering path.

"Where do you take me, warrior?"

He sets me down and unties my blindfold.

We are in the gardens, in the midst of the pear orchard, where there's a small clearing. And in the clearing, now, is a small blond-wood cabin, lit from within so that cozy circles of welcoming soft light peek into the near-night. On one side of the cabin is an open lean-to, with shelves and dirt-filled pots. And there's a freshly dug well to one side of it.

I am speechless, and Wilkie is grinning at my stunned silence. He pulls me by the hand and leads me to the door of the cabin, which he opens, then closes behind us as he ushers us into the warmth. Inside there is a bed, laid with furs, a small stone hearth, where a fire has been laid and burns brightly, and nothing more.

"Here is our retreat," he says, "which we can retire to when we are in need of some peace and quiet. You can tend your seedlings by night, if you choose, and eat your pears under the light of the moon, when the mood strikes you."

I am nearly overcome with love for this warrior husband of mine, who understands the deepest corners of my soul and has cast his light into all my darknesses. I kiss him for a long time. I lightly stroke his hair and his face in a wordless plea for him to understand how very deeply he has captured my heart and all that I am.

I notice then my mother's glass-jeweled pin, placed in the center of the small mantel of the fireplace, catching yellow light. I am aghast at the sight of it. "Warrior. My pin."

"I had it retrieved for you."

He picks me up and carefully places me on the bed. He begins to unbutton the front of my dress—a new shell-buttoned light green creation of Ailie's, who visited not a fortnight ago with her new fiancé, Magnus Munro. My breasts are already fuller, and I wonder if Wilkie will guess my secret before I can tell him.

"I, too, have a surprise," I whisper to him, and he's suckling my nipples, playing them with his tongue.

"What surprise, lass?" he asks huskily.

"I had suspected it, and Ismay visited me today, and confirmed that it was true."

He's distracted and continues to pull with his mouth, sending warm channels of his passion deep into my body. He is fondling me and murmuring soft words. "I adore my wife. I worship you, my Roses. Your body is my haven. Your breasts are so very—" He stops, as my statement and his own discovery reveal a dawning realization. He looks into my eyes, and the blue of them is brilliant and fierce, questioning.

"Aye," I confirm. "A child. To be born at harvesttime."

He sits up, removing his touch, as though afraid he might break me. "Child?" he whispers.

I laugh at his intense awe and pull him back to me. "Aye, warrior. Our child."

And he is holding my face, looking into my eyes. "'Tis a miracle, lass."

"Not such a miracle." I smile. "Babies are born each day."

"Not *our* baby, Roses," he insists, charged and animated. I am reminded again of his size and his energy as his heat surrounds me and seeps into me, infusing my body with the profound and warming glow of true happiness. "'Tis the most miraculous thing on this earth," he says. "It will be the most cherished wee bairn who ever was born. With golden hair and green eyes."

"Or with black hair and blue eyes," I point out, still laughing lightly, relieved at his outrageous excitement; I had worried that he might be reticent, with our marriage barely four months past and our new home with so much work still to be done. But then again, I'd reflected, he certainly hadn't been reticent when it came to the act which might start a baby, not a once. "I had thought of a name," I tell him.

"What name? 'Tis a bit early to be thinking names, nay?"

"There's one that sprang to mind," I say, "fairly insistently, too, as soon as I knew for certain."

"What name is this?"

"Of course, if you don't agree, we can—"

"Tell me." Wilkie gets impatiently curious almost instantly when I keep any detail of my thoughts from him. I am teasing him, and he knows it, but still, he can't abide this small distance.

"I mean, if there's one that you prefer—"

"Roses," he says sternly.

I am, as I have been so many times before, rocked by his beauty and by my own completeness when he's near. My fingers smooth along the braid of his hair. "I thought…Mackenzie."

Wilkie's eyes glimmer at me. He appears to like this idea very much.

He kisses me and holds me until we are, again and always, as close as we can be.

Giving me everything he has to give.

* * * * *

At Castonbury Park, the line between those who live upstairs and those who work downstairs has never been so blurred....

From critically acclaimed authors

MARGUERITE KAYE
and ANN LETHBRIDGE

The Lady Who Broke the Rules

Anticipating her wedding vows and then breaking off the engagement has left Kate Montague's social status in tatters. She hides her shame behind a resolute facade, but one thing really grates…for a fallen woman, she knows shockingly little about passion.

Could Virgil Jackson be the man to teach her?

Lady of Shame

Lady Claire is notorious for the wild persona of her youth, but she must set it aside if she ever hopes to find a suitable match. Swapping rebellion for reserve, Claire returns to her imposing childhood home, Castonbury Park, seeking her family's help.

But when the dark gaze of head chef Monsieur Andre catches her eye, he seems as deliciously tempting as the food he prepares.

Available wherever books are sold!

New York Times bestselling author

KRISTAN HIGGINS

**asks: How far would you go
to get over a guy?**

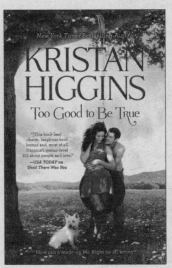

When Grace Emerson's ex-fiancé starts dating her younger sister, extreme measures are called for. To keep everyone from obsessing about her love life, Grace announces that she's seeing someone. Someone wonderful. Someone handsome. Someone completely made up. Who is this Mr. Right? Someone… exactly unlike her renegade neighbor Callahan O'Shea. Well, someone with his looks, maybe. His hot body. His knife-sharp sense of humor. His smarts and big heart.

Whoa. No. Callahan O'Shea is not her perfect man! Not with his unsavory past. So why does Mr. Wrong feel so…right?

Available wherever books are sold!

www.Harlequin.com

PHKH791

REQUEST YOUR
FREE BOOKS!

2 FREE NOVELS
FROM THE ROMANCE COLLECTION
PLUS 2 FREE GIFTS!